STAR WARS™

THE NEW JEDI ORDER

DARK JOURNEY

Also by Elaine Cunningham

Forgotten Realms: Songs and Swords
    ELFSHADOW
    ELFSONG
    SILVER SHADOWS
    THE DREAM SPHERES
    THORNHOLD

Forgotten Realms: Counselors and Kings
    THE MAGEHOUND
    FLOODGATE
    THE WIZARDWAR

Forgotten Realms
    EVERMEET: ISLAND OF THE ELVES

Forgotten Realms: Starlight and Shadows
    DAUGHTER OF THE DROW
    TANGLED WEBS

Spelljammer: The Cloakmaster's Cycle
    THE RADIANT DRAGON (book 4 of 6)

First Quest
    THE UNICORN HUNT

STAR WARS

THE NEW JEDI ORDER

DARK JOURNEY

ELAINE CUNNINGHAM

LUCAS BOOKS

ARROW

Published in the United Kingdom in 2002 by Arrow Books

1 3 5 7 9 10 8 6 4 2

First published in the United Kingdom in 2002 by Arrow Books

The Random House Group Limited
20 Vauxhall Bridge Road, London, SW1V 2SA

Random House Australia (Pty) Limited
20 Alfred Street, Milsons Point, Sydney,
New South Wales 2061, Australia

Random House New Zealand Limited
18 Poland Road, Glenfield
Auckland 10, New Zealand

Random House (Pty) Limited
Endulini, 5a Jubilee Road, Parktown 2193, South Africa

The Random House Group Limited Reg. No. 954009

www.randomhouse.co.uk

A CIP catalogue record for this book
is available from the British Library

Papers used by Random House
are natural, recyclable products made from wood grown in sustainable forests. The manufacturing processes conform to
the environmental regulations of the country of origin

ISBN 0 09 941032 X

Printed and bound in Germany by
Elsnerdruck, Berlin

For Erik Kulis, nephew and *Star Wars* fan, who stood up in a crowded theater and screamed, "NO!" at the conclusion of the battle between Obi-wan and Darth Maul.

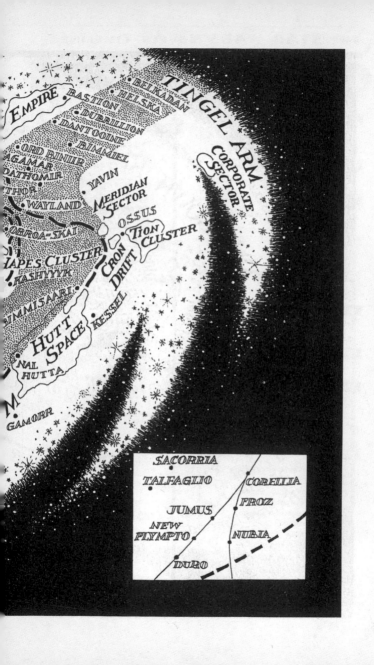

THE STAR WARS NOVELS TIMELINE

ACKNOWLEDGMENTS

Many thanks to Shelly Shapiro and Sue Rostoni for their guidance and patience throughout the writing process, and to Kathleen O'Shea David, who holds down the front line. I've appreciated the comments, suggestions, and attention to detail provided by LFL's keen-eyed guardians of continuity. Thanks to all the folks who batted around brainstorming e-mails, or simply shared information: Troy Denning, Greg Keyes, Mike Friedman, Matt Stover, Walter Jon Williams, and Aaron Allston. To Chris Perkins and Dave Gross over at *Star Wars Gamer* magazine, who gave me the opportunity to write a few more tales about Jaina and her friends. Thanks to the Star Ladies for their upbeat presence, and to Fred Espenchied, who makes a tremendous contribution to the online community. Thanks to Andrew Cunningham for all the discussions about black holes, dark matter, and *Star Wars* technology, and to Sean Cunningham, who shares my affection for Tenel Ka.

Finally, to R. A. Salvatore, who threw my name into the hat. Thanks again, Bob.

DRAMATIS PERSONAE

Han Solo; captain, *Millennium Falcon* (male human)
Harrar; priest (male Yuuzhan Vong)
Isolder; Hapan prince (male human)
Jagged Fel; commander, Chiss squadron (male human)
Jaina Solo; Jedi Knight (female human)
Khalee Lah; warrior (male Yuuzhan Vong)
Kyp Durron; Jedi Master (male human)
Leia Organa Solo; Republic ambassador (female human)
Lowbacca; Jedi Knight (male Wookiee)
Ta'a Chume; former Hapan queen (female human)
Tenel Ka; Jedi Knight (female human)
Teneniel Djo; Hapan queen (female human)
Trisdin Gheer; courtesan (male human)
Tsavong Lah; warmaster (male Yuuzhan Vong)
Zekk; Jedi Knight (male human)

ONE

A sunrise corona limned one edge of the planet Myrkr, setting its vast northern forests alight with a verdant glow. Viewed from space, the planet appeared as lush and green as Yuuzhan'tar, the long-lost homeworld of Yuuzhan Vong legend.

Two Yuuzhan Vong males stood at the viewport of a priestship, deep in contemplation of the scene before them. One was tall and gaunt, with a sloping forehead and sharp, aristocratic features scarred by many acts of devotion. These marks, and his cunningly wrapped head cloth, identified him as a priest of high rank. His companion was younger, broader, and so physically imposing that a first glance yielded no perceptible boundaries between armor and weapons and the warrior who wore them. He struck the eye in a single blow, leaving an indelible impression of a complex, living weapon. His countenance was somber, and there was an intensity about him that suggested movement even though he stood at respectful attention.

The priest swept a three-fingered hand toward the scene below. "Dawn: bright death of mortal night," he recited.

Harrar's words followed the well-worn path of proverb, but there was genuine reverence in his eyes as he gazed upon the distant world. The young warrior touched two fingers to his forehead in a pious gesture, but his attention

1

was absorbed less by the glowing vision of Myrkr than by the battle raging above it.

Silhouetted against the green world was a fist-sized lump of black yorik coral. This, an aging worldship housing hundreds of Yuuzhan Vong and their slaves and creature-servants, looked to be nothing more than lifeless rock. But as Harrar's priestship drew closer, he could make out signs of battle—tiny coral fliers buzzing and stinging like fire gnats, plasma bolts surging in a frantic, erratic pulse. If life was pain, then the worldship was very much alive.

"Our arrival is timely," the priest observed, glancing at the young warrior. "These young *Jeedai* seem determined to prove themselves a worthy sacrifice!"

"As you say, Eminence."

The words were polite, but distracted, as if the warrior gave scant attention. Harrar turned a measuring gaze upon his companion. Discord between the priest and warrior castes was growing more common, but he could discern nothing amiss in Khalee Lah.

The son of Warmaster Tsavong Lah stood tall among the Yuuzhan Vong. His skin's original gray hue was visible only in the faint strips and whorls separating numerous black scars and tattoos. A cloak of command flowed from hooks embedded in his shoulders. Other implants added spikes to his elbows and to the knuckles on his hands. A single short, thick horn thrust out from the center of his forehead—a difficult implant, and the mark of a truly worthy host.

Harrar knew himself honored when this promising warrior was assigned to his military escort, but he was also wary and more than a little intrigued. Like any true priest of Yun-Harla, goddess of trickery, Harrar relished games of deception and strategy. His old friend Tsavong Lah was a master of the multilayered agenda, and Harrar expected nothing less from the young commander.

Khalee turned to meet the priest's scrutiny. His gaze was respectful, but direct. "May I speak freely, Eminence?"

Harrar began to suspect Tsavong Lah's purpose in sending his son to a Trickster priest. Candor was a weakness—a potentially fatal one.

"In this matter, consider the warmaster's judgment," he advised, hiding words of caution in seeming assent.

The young male nodded solemnly. "Tsavong Lah entrusted you with the sacrifice of the twin *Jeedai*. The success of his latest implant is still in the hands of the gods, and you are his chosen intercessor. What the warmaster honors, I reverence." He concluded his words by dropping to one knee and lowering his head in a respectful bow.

This was hardly the message Harrar intended to send, but Khalee Lah seemed content with their exchange. He rose and directed his attention back to the worldship.

"In plain speech, then. It appears the battle is not going as well as anticipated. Perhaps not even as well as Nom Anor reported."

Harrar's scarred forehead creased in a scowl. He himself held a dubious opinion of the Yuuzhan Vong spy. But Nom Anor enjoyed the rank of executor and was not to be lightly criticized.

"Such words veer dangerously close to treason, my young friend."

"Truth is never treason," Khalee Lah stated.

The priest carefully weighed these words. To the priesthood of Yun-Harla and among certain other factions, this proverb was an ironic jest, but there was no mistaking the ringing sincerity in the younger male's tones.

Harrar schooled his face to match the warrior's earnest expression. "Explain."

Khalee Lah pointed to a small, dark shape hurtling away from the worldship at an oblique vector to the priestship's approach. "That is the *Ksstarr*, the frigate that brought Nom Anor to Myrkr."

The priest leaned closer to the viewport, but his eyes were not nearly as keen as Khalee Lah's enhanced implants. He tapped one hand against the portal. In response, a thin membrane nictitated from side to side, cleaning the transparent surface. The living tissue reshaped, exaggerating the convex curve to provide sharper focus and faint magnification.

"Yes," the priest murmured, noting the distinctive knobs and bumps on the underside of the approaching ship. "And if the battle against the *Jeedai* is all but won, as Nom Anor reported, why does he flee? I must speak to him at once!"

Khalee Lah turned toward the door and repeated Harrar's words as an order. The guards stationed there thumped their fists to opposite shoulders and strode off to tend their commander's bidding.

The swift click of chitinous boots announced a subordinate's approach. A female warrior garishly tattooed in green and yellow entered the room, a crenellated form cradled in her taloned hands. She bowed, presented the villip to Harrar, and placed it on a small stand.

The priest dismissed her with an absent wave and began to stroke the sentient globe. The outer layer peeled back, and the soft tissue within began to rearrange itself into a rough semblance of Nom Anor's scarred visage. One eye socket was empty and sunken, and the bruised eyelid seemed to sag into the blue crescent sack beneath. The venom-spitting plaeryin bol that had once distinguished Nom Anor's countenance was gone, and evidently he had not yet been permitted to replace it.

Harrar's eyes narrowed in satisfaction. Nom Anor had failed repeatedly, but never once had he accepted responsibility for his actions. In a manner most unworthy a Yuuzhan Vong, he had foisted blame upon others. Harrar had suffered a temporary demotion for his part in a failed espionage scheme; Nom Anor had merely received a reprimand, even though his agents played a significant role in the plot's failure. In Harrar's opinion, the blurred face testified that the gods' justice would, in time, be served.

The image of Nom Anor, imprecise though it was, nevertheless managed to convey a sense of impatience, perhaps even anxiety.

"Your Eminence," Nom Anor began.

"Your report," Harrar broke in curtly.

Nom Anor's one eye narrowed, and for a moment Harrar thought the executor would protest. As a field agent, Nom Anor was seldom required to answer to the priesthood. His silence stretched beyond the bounds of pride, however, and Harrar began to fear that Khalee Lah's suspicions had fallen short of grim truth.

"You have lost?"

"We have losses," Nom Anor corrected. "The voxyn queen and her spawn were destroyed. Two Jedi prisoners held on the worldship were freed. They escaped, as did several of the others."

Harrar looked to Khalee Lah. "You have sighted the infidels' escape ship?"

The warrior's eyes widened, and for a moment his scarred face held horrified enlightenment—a fleeting emotion that swiftly darkened to wrath.

"Ask who flies the *Ksstarr*: the executor or the infidels?"

This possibility had not occurred to Harrar. He quickly relayed the question through the attuned villip.

"Some of the Jedi managed to commandeer the frigate," Nom Anor admitted. "We are pursuing, and feel confident that we will add the capture of this ship to our other victories."

Capture. Harrar's gut tightened, for that single word confirmed the identity of the escaped Jedi.

"Capture!" Khalee Lah echoed derisively. "Better to reduce the defiled thing to coral dust! What Yuuzhan Vong pilot would wish to enjoin with an infidel-tainted ship?"

"Several Jedi fell to our warriors," Nom Anor continued, oblivious to both the priest's epiphany and the warrior's scorn. "The younger Solo brother was slain. The warmaster will be pleased to learn that Jacen Solo is alive, and our captive."

"Jacen Solo," Harrar repeated. "What of Jaina Solo, his twin?"

The silence held for so long that the villip began to invert back to its original form.

"We are in pursuit," Nom Anor said at last. "The Jedi will not be able to fly a ship such as the *Ksstarr* well or long."

"It is an outrage that they fly it at all!" Khalee Lah interjected.

Harrar sent him a stern glance and then turned back to the villip. "I assume that you will not take this Jacen Solo with you as you pursue his twin. It is said the *Jeedai* can communicate with each other over long distances, without either villips or mechanical abominations to aid them. If this is so, he will surely warn his female counterpart of your approach."

Khalee Lah sniffed scornfully. "What manner of hunter hangs bells around the necks of his bissop pack?"

This remark, impolitic though it was, surprised a smirk from Harrar. In his opinion, Nom Anor had become tainted by the infidels' decadence and weakness. The image of the executor plunging through muck and swamp water on the heels of a pack of fierce lizard-hounds was both incongruous and appealing.

The executor took time to consider Harrar's observation. "You have a military escort?"

"Twelve coralskippers accompany the priestship, yes. Do you wish us to break off in pursuit of Jaina Solo?"

The villip face-shape rolled downward and back in a semblance of a nod. "As you rightly observed, the risk of contact between these twin Jedi is considerable. I will take Jacen Solo directly to the warmaster."

"And so the glory goes to the executor, while his failure is thrust upon the priest," Khalee Lah said, snarling.

Harrar turned away from the villip. "You are learning," he observed softly. "But for the moment, let us disregard Nom Anor's ambitions. You were assigned to accompany me to Myrkr, no more. It is my task to oversee the sacrifice of the twin *Jeedai*. I must pursue. You are not obligated to accompany me."

The warrior didn't require time to consider. "This *Jeedai*, this Jaina Solo, flies upon a living vessel. That offends me. She escaped a worldship. That should not have been possible. She is a twin, which is rightly reserved as the province of the gods, or a portent of greatness. That is blasphemy. I would pursue her to the most wretched corner of this galaxy if it meant adhering myself to a pair of molting grutchins."

"Forcefully argued," Harrar said dryly. He turned back to the waiting executor. "We will retrieve Jaina Solo."

"You hesitate. Are you certain you can succeed?"

"It is the warmaster's command," Harrar said simply. He glanced at Khalee Lah and added with a touch of asperity, "And a holy crusade."

His sarcasm was lost on Khalee Lah. The warrior inclined his head in grave agreement, and his face shone with something Harrar had occasionally glimpsed, but never quite embraced.

A sudden chill shuddered down the priest's spine. Fervor such as Khalee Lah's had always struck Harrar as vaguely dangerous. The warrior's faith held a shaper's art, imbuing Harrar's facetious words with the sly irony the priest had always associated with his goddess.

And was it not said that Yun-Harla reserved her most cunning tricks for those who served her best?

TWO

Anakin is dead. Jacen is gone.

These thoughts resounded through Jaina Solo's benumbed senses, echoing through an inner silence as profound as that of the watchful stars.

These thoughts drowned out the sounds of battle, and the frantic, running commentary of the seven young Jedi who struggled to fly the stolen Yuuzhan Vong ship. Like her companions, Jaina was battered and filthy from days of captivity, and from a battle that had lasted too long and cost too much.

Only nine Jedi had fought their way out of the worldship and onto this smaller ship, bringing with them the body of their young leader. The survivors had taken the Yuuzhan Vong frigate analog quickly, with astonishing ease. Jaina had a dim recollection of searing anger and killing light, of her friend Zekk pushing her away from the pilot's seat and into the Yuuzhan Vong equivalent of a gunner's chair. She perched there now on the edge of the too-large seat, firing missiles of molten rock at the coralskippers pursuing the Jedi and their stolen ship.

Jaina watched with a strange sense of detachment as the alien ship released plasma at her command, as the death of coralskippers and their Yuuzhan Vong pilots was painted in brief, brilliant splashes against the dark canvas of space. All of this was a fever dream, nothing more, and Jaina was merely a character caught in her own nightmare.

Jacen is gone.

It didn't seem possible. It wasn't possible. Jacen was alive. He had to be. How could she be alive if Jacen was not? Her twin brother had been a part of her, and she of him, since before their birth. What they *were* could not be separated from what they were to each other.

Her thoughts tumbled like an X-wing in an out-of-control spiral. Jaina's pilot instincts kicked in, and she eased herself out of the spin.

Reaching out through the Force, she strained beyond the boundaries of her power and training as she sought her brother. Where Jacen had been was only blackness, as unfathomable as space. She went deep within, frantically seeking the place within her that had always been Jacen's. That, too, was veiled.

Jacen was gone. Jaina did not feel bereft, but sundered.

A burst of plasma flared toward the stolen ship. Jaina responded with one of her own. It streamed toward the incoming plasma bolt like a vengeful comet. The two missiles met like waves from opposing oceans, casting sprays of bright plasma into the darkness.

Zekk threw himself to one side, straining the umbilicals on the pilot's gloves in his attempt to pull the ship aside from the killing spray.

Fortunately for the Jedi, their Yuuzhan Vong pursuers were also forced to turn aside. This bought them a moment of relative peace—no immediate danger, no obvious target.

Jaina twisted in her seat until she could see the worldship where Anakin had fallen, where Jacen had been abandoned. It seemed odd, and somehow wrong, that such a terrible place could be reduced to a small lump of black coral.

"We'll be back, Jacen," she promised. "You hold on, and we'll come for you."

I'll come for you, she added silently. She would go after Jacen alone, if it came down to that, as Anakin had gone to Yavin 4 to rescue Tahiri.

Now Anakin was dead, and a battered and heart-broken Tahiri watched over his body. The small blond girl blazed in the Force like a nova—Jaina couldn't help but feel her anguish. The bond between Anakin and Tahiri was different from that shared by twins, but perhaps no less intense.

The realization hit her like a thud bug. Anakin and Tahiri. How strange—and yet it felt right and perfect.

Tears filled Jaina's eyes, refracting an incoming streak of molten gold into lethal rainbows. In the pilot's seat, Zekk muttered a curse and wrenched the frigate's nose up and hard to port. The alien ship rose in a sharp, gut-wrenching arc. Plasma scorched along the frigate's underside, sheering off the irregular coral nodules with a shrill, ululating screech.

Jaina jerked her left hand from its living glove and fisted away her tears through the cognition hood that covered her face. Meanwhile the fingers of her right hand slid and circled as she deftly brought her target into focus. She jammed her left hand back into the glove and squeezed it into a fist, releasing a burst of plasma at the attacking coralskipper—an instant before it launched a second plasma.

Jaina's missile struck the Yuuzhan Vong ship in that minuscule interval between shielding and attack. Shards of black coral exploded from its hull, and the snout heated to an ominous red as molten rock washed over it. Cracks fissured through the Yuuzhan Vong pilot's viewport.

Again Jaina fired, and again, timing the attacks with skill honed through two long years and too many missions. The coralskipper's projected gravity well swallowed the first missile; the second proved to be too much for the severely compromised hull. The ship broke apart, spilling its life out into the emptiness of space.

"I know that feeling," Jaina muttered.

A small, strong hand settled on her shoulder. She felt Tenel Ka's solid presence through the Force—there, but profoundly different. A moment passed before Jaina realized why: her friend's emotions, usually as straightforward and unambiguous as a drawn blaster, had been carefully shielded.

"We are doing the right thing for Jacen," Tenel Ka said stoutly. "Because they have only one twin, they will harm neither. We suspected as much, but now we have proof. They are not trying to destroy this ship."

"Couldn't prove it by me," Zekk muttered as he jinked sharply to avoid another plasma blast.

"Fact," the warrior woman said bluntly. "Zekk, for two years you've flown cargo ships—a true contribution, but poor training for this escape."

"Yeah? Here's another fact: I haven't gotten us killed yet."

"And here are several more," Tenel Ka retorted. "Jaina was in Rogue Squadron. She had access to New Republic intelligence on enemy ships. She has survived more dogfights than anyone here. If we are to survive, you must let her fly."

Zekk started to protest, but another barrage cut him off. He zigzagged wildly to avoid incoming fire and then put the ship into a tumbling evasive dive. The force threw Tenel Ka into the seat behind the pilot. She muttered something in her native language as she struggled into the restraining loops.

Jaina braced her feet against the irregular coral floor and steeled herself for the punishing buildup of g-force. She expected her cognition hood to bulge out like the jowls of a Dagobian swamp lizard, but it remained comfortably in place. She filed the data away for future use. In any New Republic ship, this maneuver would have been punishing; apparently, the internal gravity of a Yuuzhan Vong ship was far more complex and adaptable.

Even so, for several moments speech was impossible. Jaina quickly ran through the list of survivors as she considered Tenel Ka's words. Nine Jedi remained, just one more than half of their original strike force. Tahiri was only fifteen, and no pilot. She had been terribly wounded in body and spirit, and Tekli, the Chadra-Fan healer, was busy attending her. The reptilian Tesar, the sole survivor of the Barabel hatchmates, was working the shielding station in the stern. Lowbacca was needed everywhere, and since their escape he'd been dashing about patching the living ship's wounds. When his efforts fell short, he'd alternately cajoled and threatened the ship in Wookiee terms so vivid that Em Teedee, the lost translator droid, would have been hard-pressed to come up with genteel euphemisms.

That left Tenel Ka, Alema Rar, and Ganner Rhysode. Jaina quickly dismissed Tenel Ka. Yuuzhan Vong ships were not designed with one-armed pilots in mind. Forget Alema. The Twi'lek female was emotionally fragile—Jaina could feel her teetering on the edge of mindless, vengeful frenzy. Put Alema in the pilot's seat, and she'd likely plot a suicidal plunge directly at the worldship's dovin basal. Ganner was a powerful Jedi, an impressive-looking man whose role in this mission had been to serve as decoy for the real leader—Anakin. Ganner had his points, but he wasn't enough of a pilot to get them out of this.

Tenel Ka was right, Jaina concluded. Anakin had died saving the Jedi from the deadly voxyn. He'd left his last mission in Jacen's hands, not hers, but she was the one left to see it through. The Jedi—at least the Jedi on this ship—were now her responsibility.

A small voice nudged into Jaina's consciousness, barely audible over the screaming dive and the thrum and groan of the abused ship. In some dim corner of her mind huddled a small figure, weeping in anguish and indecision. Jaina slammed the door and silenced her broken heart.

"I need Ganner to take over for me," she said as soon as she could speak.

A look of concern crossed Tenel Ka's face, but she shrugged off her restraints and rose. In moments she returned with the older Jedi.

"Someone has to take my place as gunner," Jaina explained. She stood up without removing either the gloves or hood. "No time for a learning curve—better work with me until you get the feel of it. The seat's big enough for both of us."

After a brief hesitation, Ganner slipped into the chair. Jaina quickly settled into his lap.

He chuckled and linked his hands around her waist. "This could get to be a habit."

"Hold that thought," Jaina told him as she sighted down an incoming skip. "It'll keep your hands busy."

A surge of annoyance came from Zekk, but Jaina understood Ganner's flirtation for what it was. Ganner was tall, dark, and so absurdly handsome that he reminded Jaina of the old holovids of Prince Isolder. The scar across one cheek only served to heighten the overall effect. When Ganner turned on the charm, his pheromone count probably rivaled a Falleen's, but Jaina knew a shield when she saw one. Not long ago, Jacen had disguised his thoughtful nature with labored jokes. Perhaps it was best to leave Ganner's defenses safely intact.

"Put your hands in the gloves and rest your fingers on mine," she directed.

As Ganner wriggled his hands into the flexible gloves, Jaina reached out for him through the Force. She lacked

Jacen's empathy, but could convey images to Ganner using her own Force talent.

As she aimed and fired, she formed mental pictures of what she saw—the battle as viewed through the greatly expanded vision granted by the cognition hood, the blurry concentric circles that made up the targeting device. Through the Force she felt the grim intensity of Ganner's concentration, sensed a mind and will as focused as a laser. Soon his fingers began moving with hers in a precise duet. When she thought him ready, she slid her hands free, then tugged off the hood as she eased out of his lap. She pulled the hood down over Ganner's head.

The Jedi jolted as he made direct connection with the ship. He quickly collected himself and sent plasma hurtling to meet an incoming ball. The two missiles collided, sending plasma splashing into space like festival fireworks.

Ganner's crow of triumph was swallowed by the ship's groan and shudder. Several bits of plasma had splashed the frigate despite its shielding singularity and Zekk's attempts at evasion.

"Tenel Ka is right," Jaina said. "Let me have her, Zekk."

The pilot shook his hooded head and put the ship into a rising turn. "Forget it. You're in no condition for this."

She planted her fists on her hips. "Yeah? Everyone here could use a few days in a bacta tank, you included."

"That's not what I meant. No one could be expected to fly after losing . . . after what happened down there," he concluded lamely.

Silence hung between them, heavy with loss and pain and raw, too-vivid memories.

Then Jaina caught a glimpse of the memory that most disturbed Zekk—an image of a small, disheveled young woman in a tattered jumpsuit, hurling lightning at a Yuuzhan Vong warrior. A moment passed before Jaina recognized the furious, vengeful, bloodstained face as her own.

Suddenly she knew the truth of her old friend's concern. Zekk, who had trained at the Shadow Academy and experienced the dark side firsthand, was as wary of it as Jacen had been. In taking the pilot's chair, Zekk hadn't been considering her loss, her state of mind. He simply didn't trust her.

Jaina braced herself for the pain of this new betrayal, but none came. Perhaps losing Jacen had pushed her to some place beyond pain.

She brought to mind an image of the molten lightning that had come so instinctively to her call. She imbued it with so much power that the air nearly hummed with energy, and the metallic scent of a thunderstorm seemed to lurk on the edge of sensory perception. She projected this image to her old friend as forcefully as she could.

"Get out of the seat, Zekk," she said in cool, controlled tones. "I don't want to fry the controls."

He hesitated for only a moment, then he ripped off the hood and rose. His green eyes met hers, filled with such a turmoil of sorrow and concern that Jaina slammed shut the Force connection between them. She knew that expression—she'd seen it in her mother's eyes many times during the terrible months that followed Chewbacca's death, when her father had been lost in grief and guilt.

No time for this now.

Jaina slid into the pilot's seat and let herself join with the ship. Her fingers moved deftly over the organic console, confirming the sensory impulses that flowed to her through the hood. Yes, this was the hyperdrive analog. Here was the forward shield. The navigation center remained a mystery to her, but during their captivity Lowbacca had tinkered a bit with one of the worldship's neural centers. The young Wookiee had a history of taking on impossible challenges, and this task lay right along his plotted coordinates.

Suddenly the shriek of warning sensors seared through Jaina's mind. A chorus of wordless voices came at her from all over the ship.

The details of their situation engulfed her in a single swift flood. Several plasma bolts streamed toward them, converging on the underside of the ship—so far, the favored target. Coralskippers had moved into position aft and above, and others were closing in from below and on either side. Another ship came straight on, still at a distance but closing fast.

No matter what she did, they could not evade the disabling barrage.

THREE

Jaina held course, flying straight toward the incoming plasma bolts. At the last possible moment, she threw the vessel into a fast-rolling spiral. The plasma flurry skimmed along the whirling ship, not dealing much damage to any one part. When the scream of plasma grating against living coral ceased, she fought the ship out of the roll and kept heading straight toward the oncoming skip.

"Lowbacca, get up here," she shouted. "Clear me a lane, Ganner."

The Jedi gunner hurled plasma at the coralskipper directly in their path. As its dovin basal engulfed the missile in a miniature black hole, Ganner released another. His timing was perfect, and the skip dissolved in a brief, bright explosion.

Jaina quickly diverted the dovin basal to the front shield, and instinctively flinched away as a spray of coral debris clattered over the hull. She glanced back over her shoulder in Zekk's general direction.

"Zekk, you play dejarik much?"

"Play what?"

"That's what I thought," she muttered. While Zekk had concentrated on avoiding each immediate attack, the yammosk-coordinated fleet had been thinking several moves ahead, and had neatly maneuvered the stolen ship into a trap. She'd never been fond of dejarik or any of the other strategy games Chewbacca had insisted upon teaching her, but for the first time she saw the Wookiee's point.

Lowbacca padded up and howled a query.

"Get on navigation," Jaina said, jerking her head toward a rounded, brainlike console. "Hyperspace jump. Destination: anywhere but Myrkr. Can you input coordinates?"

The Wookiee settled down and regarded the biological "computer," pensively scratching at the place on one temple where a black streak ran through his ginger-colored fur.

"Now would be good," Ganner prompted.

Lowbacca growled a Wookiee insult and tugged the cognition hood down over his head. After a moment, he extended one of his retracted climbing claws and carefully sliced through the thin upper membrane. With astonishing delicacy, he began to touch neural clusters and rearrange slender, living fibers, grunting in satisfaction with each new insight.

Finally he turned to Jaina and woofed a question.

"Set course for Coruscant."

"Why Coruscant?" Alema Rar protested. Her head-tails, which were mottled with darkening bruises and practically quilted together with bacta patches, began to twitch in agitation. "We'll be shot down by Republic guards long before we reach the planet's atmosphere, unless the Peace Brigade gets to us first!"

"The Peace Brigaders are enemy collaborators. They have no reason to attack this ship," Ganner countered. "On the other hand, the Republic has no reason *not* to."

Tenel Ka shook her head sharply, sending her disheveled red-gold braids swinging. "Sometimes a live enemy is worth a hundred dead ones. A small ship like this offers no real threat. The patrol will escort us in, hoping to capture a live ship and curious to know the motives of the crew."

"That's my thinking," Jaina agreed. "Also, Rogue Squadron has a base on Coruscant, and there are people in the control tower who know all the pilots' quirks. If I can put this rock through some distinctive maneuvers, there's an outside chance that someone might recognize me. How's it coming, Lowbacca?"

The Wookiee made a couple of deft adjustments, then signaled readiness by bracing massive paws on either side of the console and uttering a resigned groan.

Jaina kicked the ship into hyperdrive. The force of the jump threw her back into the oversized seat and strained the umbilicals attaching her hood and gloves to the ship. Plasma bolts spread out into a golden sunrise haze; stars elongated into brilliant lines.

Then silence and darkness engulfed the Jedi, and a floating sensation replaced the intense pressure of sublight acceleration. Jaina pulled off the hood and collapsed back into her seat. As the adrenaline surge ebbed, Jaina felt the returning tide of grief.

She sternly willed it away and focused on her fellow survivors. The nervous twitching of Alema Rar's headtails slowed into the subtle, sinuous undulation common to Twi'lek females. Tenel Ka shook off her flight restraints and began to prowl about the ship—a sign of restlessness in most people, but the Dathomiri woman was most at ease when in motion. The Wookiee resumed his study of the navibrain. Ganner pulled off the cognition hood and rose, smoothing his black hair carefully back into place. He headed toward the back of the ship, most likely to check on Tahiri.

Jaina jerked her thoughts away from that path. She did not want to think about Tahiri, did not want to envision the girl's vigil, or—

She sternly banished the grim image these thoughts evoked. When Zekk approached the pilot's seat, she sent him a small, grateful smile. And why not? He was her oldest friend and a timely distraction—and he was a lot easier to deal with than most distractions that came her way these days.

Then his green eyes lit up in a manner that had Jaina rethinking her last observation.

"For a while, I thought we'd never see home again," Zekk ventured. He settled down in the place Ganner had vacated and sent Jaina a wink and a halfhearted grin. "Should have known better."

She nodded, accepting his tentative apology—and it was very tentative indeed. Her old friend tried to shield his emotions, but his doubts and concerns sang through.

"Let's get this over with now, so we aren't tempted to break up into discussion groups during the next crisis. You didn't want me to fly the ship because you don't trust me," she stated bluntly.

Zekk stared at her for a moment. Then he let out a long, low whistle and shook his head. "Same old Jaina— subtle as a thermal detonator."

"If you really believed that I haven't changed, we wouldn't be having this conversation."

"Then let's not. This isn't the time."

"You're right," she retorted. "We should have settled this days ago—all of us. Maybe then we wouldn't have come apart down there."

"What do you mean?" he said cautiously.

"Oh, come on. You were there. You heard Jacen obsessing over Anakin's motives and methods, trying to make him question himself at every step and turn. You saw what happens when Jedi stop focusing on *what* we're doing to quibble about *how* and *why*."

A small, humorless smile touched her face. "It's like

the old story about the millitile who could walk just fine until someone asked how he kept track of all those legs. Once he started thinking about it, he couldn't walk at all. Most likely he ended up as some hawk-bat's dinner."

"Jaina, you can't blame Jacen for what happened to Anakin!"

"I don't," she said quickly. Since this was Zekk, she added, "At least, not entirely."

"And you can't blame yourself for Jacen, either."

That, she wasn't ready to concede and didn't care to discuss.

"I was working my way toward a point," she told him. "Jacen was distracted by this nebulous vision of a Jedi ideal. And you were distracted by your fear of the two Dark Jedi we freed."

"For good reason. They took off and left us. They hurt Lowbacca and kidnapped Raynar. For all we know, they've killed him."

"They'll answer for all of that. Can I make my point?"

One corner of Zekk's lips quirked upward. "I was wondering when you'd get around to it."

The wry comment was so familiar, so *normal*. For a fleeting moment, Jaina remembered who they'd been just a few years ago—a fearless, confident survivor and a girl who ran toward adventure with heedless joy.

Two more casualties of the Yuuzhan Vong.

"It's like this," she said quietly. "For the last two years I've listened to Anakin and Jacen debate the role of the Jedi and our relationship to the Force. In the end, what did any of that amount to?"

Zekk leaned forward and rested one hand on her shoulder. She shook him off before he could speak empty words of consolation, or repeat cyclic arguments she'd heard too many times between Kyp Durron and her uncle Luke.

"Anakin started to figure it out," she went on. "I sensed it in him after Yavin Four. He learned something there the rest of us don't know, something that could have made all the difference, if only he'd had time to figure it all out. If there is such a thing as destiny, I think that was Anakin's. He has always been different. Special."

"Of course. He was your brother."

"He is—" She broke off abruptly, shook off the stab of grief, and made the necessary adjustment. "He was more than that."

Jaina took time to consider her next words. She wasn't introspective by nature; this had been in her mind since Anakin's exploits on Yavin 4, and she still couldn't get her hands around it.

"With Anakin's death I lost a brother, but the Jedi lost something I can't begin to define. My feelings tell me it's something important, something we lost a very long time ago."

For a long moment Zekk was silent. "Maybe so. But we have the Force, and each other."

Simple words, but with a layer of personal meaning offered like a gift, if only Jaina chose to take it.

"Each other," she echoed softly. "But for how long, Zekk? If the Jedi keep having 'successes' like this last mission, pretty soon there won't be any of us left."

He nodded, accepting her evasion as if he'd expected it. "At least we're going home."

She managed a faint smile, and privately marked yet another difference between her friend's perceptions and her own. Zekk had been born on Ennta and was brought to Coruscant when he was eight years old. He made his own way in the rough lower levels of the city-planet. Jaina's parents had kept living quarters in the city's prestigious towers for most of her life, but she had spent surprisingly little of her eighteen years amid Coruscant's artificial stars.

To Jaina, Coruscant wasn't home. It was merely the next logical move on the dejarik board.

FOUR

Within the confines of his XJX-wing, Kyp Durron stretched his lanky form as best he could. He settled back into the groove he'd worn into the seat over the course of two years and more battles than he would ever admit to fighting.

"How many *has* it been?" he wondered aloud.

A light on his console flashed, signaling a communication from Zero-One, the battered Q9 droid Kyp had recently bought cheap from the estate of a Mon Calamari philosopher.

IS THIS A REQUEST FOR DATA OR A RHETORICAL QUESTION?

Kyp smiled briefly and shoved a hand through his too-long dark hair. "Great. Now even droids are questioning my motives."

NOT AT ALL. IN GENERAL, THE DISCUSSION OF PHILOSOPHY IS READILY DISCERNIBLE FROM A CALL TO ACTION.

"I've noticed that," he said dryly.

TO AVOID FUTURE MISUNDERSTANDING, HOWEVER, PERHAPS YOU SHOULD GIVE DIRECT ORDERS IN SECOND PERSON IMPERATIVE; FOR EXAMPLE, "SET COORDINATES FOR THE ABREGADO SYSTEM," OR "DIVERT POWER TO THE REAR SHIELDS."

"How about 'Report to the maintenance bay for a personality graft?' " Kyp supplied helpfully.

A moment passed. IS THAT AN ORDER OR AN INSULT?

"Whatever works."

Kyp left Zero-One to ponder this and turned his attention to the task ahead. He took point position. On either side of his X-wing flew six pristine XJ fighters. These were Kyp's Dozen, the newest members of an evershifting fellowship of heroes or rogues or villains, depending upon whom you asked.

Kyp checked the navigation screen for their bearings. "Still playing philosopher, Zero-One?"

I FAIL TO COMPREHEND THE UNDERLYING SEMANTIC MEANING OF YOUR QUERY.

"It was what you might call 'a hint.' Stop gazing at your . . . central interface terminal and tend to astronavigation. We should be coming up on our hyperspace coordinates before long."

AS I AM WELL AWARE. IT IS POSSIBLE TO THINK AND ACT AT THE SAME TIME, the droid responded.

"Apparently you haven't attended any of the recent Jedi meetings," Kyp said.

YOU ARE THE ONLY JEDI WITH WHOM I INTERFACE. UNFORTUNATELY, I WAS NOT PROGRAMMED TO EXPERIENCE GRATITUDE.

Kyp grinned fleetingly. "Was that a non sequitur or an insult?"

WHATEVER WORKS.

"I take less abuse from the Vong," Kyp complained as he switched his comm to the designated open channel.

"Not long now, Dozen. Our primary mission is to protect the ship carrying the Jedi scientists. We're flying in groups of four. Each lieutenant will name command targets. I'll assess the situation once we emerge in Coruscant space and revise our strategy as needed."

"Hard to believe that Skywalker's Jedi are finally getting off their thumbs," observed Ian Rim, Kyp's latest lieutenant.

"You're forgetting about Anakin Solo," put in Veema, a plump and pretty woman who was edging into her fifth decade of life. Kyp liked her—at least, as much as he allowed himself to care personally about any of his pilots. Her sense of fun was legendary among certain circles, and her warm, inviting smile had probably started more tavern brawls than a bad-tempered Gamorrean. Anyone who crossed Veema, however, soon realized that she had dimples of duracrete and a talent for holding grudges that a Hutt might envy.

"Last I heard, Anakin went to the Yavin system, alone, against orders from Skywalker *and* Borsk Fey'lya," Veema continued. She let out a sound halfway between a sigh and a purr. "Young, handsome, reckless, and maybe a little stupid—definitely my kind of man! Care to introduce us, Kyp?"

"Why should I? I've nothing against the kid."

"He's not the only one taking action," observed Octa Ramis, the only other Jedi in Kyp's group. A somber woman whose solid frame spoke of her origin on a high-gravity world, Octa had been shifting to an increasingly militant position for some time. She was the first Jedi to join forces with Kyp—that is, if you didn't count Jaina Solo's temporary and Force-assisted cooperation at Sernpidal.

"I heard about a few hotheaded Jedi who take, shall we say, a very proactive approach to the Peace Brigade," Ian Rim said.

"What if they do?" Octa said, snarling. "Who cares what happens to those Sith-spawned cowards? Jedi for Jedi—I've no quarrel with that!"

"But others do," Kyp observed with a sigh. "I know

the three Ian's talking about. Maybe I should try to reel them in a bit."

He switched off the comm and addressed his astromech droid. "What would that make me, Zero-One—the voice of reason?"

I AM NOT PROGRAMMED TO APPRECIATE IRONY.

"Bring on the Vong," Kyp muttered as he switched back to his squadron.

"Talk to me, Dozen."

"For highest kill count, I've got two credits on Veema," Ian Rim offered. "No one can go through males of any species like she can!"

The woman's laughter tinkled, but Kyp heard the edge beneath the shimmering sound. "Better plan on using some of your winnings to buy me a drink."

"You're on. Anyone else want to get in on this?"

The chatter flowed over Kyp, fading into perceived static as he reached out with the Force, trusting his instincts and emotions to take him through the coming battle, as they had so many times before.

"You're pretty quiet, Kyp," a disembodied voice observed.

"Only on the outside."

He spoke without thinking. His comment was met with a moment's silence, then some uncertain laughter. None of the pilots had actually seen Kyp's darker side unleashed, but all of them had heard stories. No one dared speak of what he'd been, and what he'd done.

But it was always there.

"Five credits on Octa," Kyp said lightly. "And if you beat Veema's score by more than three, Octa, I'll throw in Zero-One as a bonus."

"I'll keep the margin down to two," Octa said somberly.

The Q9 unit let out an indignant bleep. This drew a burst of genuine laughter—partly because Octa's riposte broke the sudden tension, and partly because every pilot in the squadron recognized her humor as unintentional.

Most commanders Kyp knew wanted their pilots silent and focused as they approached battle. Kyp encouraged banter. It kept their minds occupied and allowed emotions to rise to the surface. He didn't know of any pilots—not live ones, anyway—who *thought* their way through a battle. The speed and ferocity of ship-to-ship combat was a matter of instinct, reflex, and luck. No one would ever mistake Han Solo for a philosopher, and he'd been flying longer and better than anyone Kyp knew.

When it came right down to it, what was there to think about? The Yuuzhan Vong had to be stopped: it was that simple. After today's fight was over, let the dithering old folks debate how the enemy had managed to move on Coruscant. He'd be off fighting the next battle.

Kyp glanced at the navigation panel and gave the order to go to lightspeed. Once the jump was complete, he settled down into the silence and darkness. With a discipline born partly of the Force, partly from long experience as a pilot, he willed himself to snatch a bit of sleep while he could.

He awakened abruptly as sensors announced the coming emergence from hyperspace. Stars flared into existence, and every light on his control panel came alive.

The Jedi glanced at the multitude of flashing icons on his display, each representing an enemy skip. "Trying to tell me something, Zero-One?"

EXPERIENTIAL DATA INDICATE THAT YOU DO NOT APPRECIATE SUBTLETY.

If anything, the droid had erred on the side of understatement. With a surge of dismay, Kyp realized he was leading his pilots into a maelstrom.

The skies over Coruscant strobed and burned. Ships of every size and description hurtled away from the doomed world. A vast Yuuzhan Vong fleet awaited them. A few escaped, aided more by the general chaos than any coordinated defense. There was no sign of the Jedi wing.

The Dozen swept in, holding their wedge-shaped formation. The only sign of their consternation was the silence coming from the open comm.

One of the Dozen, an early XJ prototype in pristine condition, dipped out of formation and started lagging behind like a distracted toddler.

Kyp frowned. "Five, acknowledge."

The ship swiftly moved back into place. "Five here."

The voice was ridiculously young—a boyish growl that had yet to achieve a genuine baritone. The pilot, Chem, was the son of a wealthy diplomat, a collector who'd filled a small warehouse with gleaming, never-flown ships. On his fourteenth birthday, Chem stole his mother's favorite ship and set out to track down Kyp's Dozen. He hadn't asked for admission—just followed the squadron around from one mission to another. After several standard months, and the loss and replacement of more pilots than Kyp cared to count, he'd taken Chem on as a regular. Since then, the kid had vaped seven Vong coralskippers and squandered his inheritance on such frivolous things as new XJs, concussion missiles, and fuel.

"Keep focused, Five. I'd hate to see you get a scratch on that showpiece of yours," Kyp admonished lightly.

"So would I, sir. Under those circumstances, I'd rather face the warmaster himself than the ship's rightful owner."

"Copy that," Ian Rim broke in. "I used to keep company with Chem's mother. You thought the Vong were mean and ugly?"

"She speaks well of you, too," Chem retorted without missing a beat. "Or at least of your flying skills. Says if you'd stuck to it, you could have been the best nerf herder on Corellia."

Kyp chuckled at the idea of the hotshot pilot sputtering along on a ponderous herding sled—an image that made *nerf herder* such a potent insult. The short exchange broke some of the tension he sensed in each of his pilots. All but one. A deep sense of unease remained in the youngest pilot.

He switched to a private channel. "Problems, Five?"

There was a moment of silence. "The lights are going out, sir. *Coruscant's* lights."

The Jedi nodded in understanding. Far below, the eternal, never-sleeping city-planet was fading into darkness, facing its first true night since time out of mind. Yuuzhan Vong drop ships, big as mountains, blotted out vast portions of cityscape as they settled down to the business of slaughter. Blastboat analogs spewed molten rock hot enough to melt the glittering towers into dark slag heaps. Enemy transports spat out coralskippers like obscenities. The rocklike ships whirled in a deadly dance, a meteor swarm choreographed by some unseen, malevolent power.

Then a squadron of coralskippers swept toward the Dozen and a burst of plasma blossomed against Kyp's forward shield.

"It's our job to hold back the night, Chem. Don't let yourself get distracted from that."

"Yes, sir!"

Kyp's sensors flared, alerting him to another fleet emerging from hyperspace. Kyp glanced at the Jedi wing and groaned. The "fleet" comprised perhaps a dozen X-wings, several battered E-wings, and a few ships that defied classification. All these ships protectively encircled a battered corvette.

"This Danni Quee travels in style. Impressed, Zero-One?" he asked, speaking too low for the comm to pick up.

NOT YET.

"Yeah, for once we're agreed."

Kyp switched back to the open channel. "Just like we practiced, Dozen. On my signal, break into fours. Lieutenants, call your targets. May the Force be with you all."

The Yuuzhan Vong fleet responded to the new threats with precisely choreographed, tactically sound maneuvers. Some of the coralskippers and a blastboat flew to meet the Jedi wing. Other units swooped down on evacuee ships like hunting hawk-bats, daring the fighters of both squadrons to pursue. Still others veered toward the Dozen.

"And guess what?" Kyp murmured. "There's enough of them to go around!"

The lead coralskippers began to vomit plasma. Kyp signaled the order to break, then tapped his controls. A modified thruster sent him in a sharp, vertical rise. The bolt streaked harmlessly past . . .

. . . and slammed into one of the ships behind him—a ship that shouldn't have been in that position.

Kyp didn't see the impact, couldn't hear the explosion or the rending apart of metal and ceramic. But he felt the flare of a young man's fear and disbelief, then the searing realization of what a moment's inattention could cost.

"Chem," he said through gritted teeth.

The Jedi let his guilt and grief flow, carrying a burst of Force power with it. His long fingers danced over the controls, sending a stuttering firestorm of lasers toward the oncoming Yuuzhan Vong.

To his surprise, the larger-than-average coralskipper setting a course for the Jedi corvette swallowed every bolt that came its way.

Kyp shook his head in astonishment. The stutter-trigger technique had been developed early in the war in response to the pattern of shielding singularities— miniature black holes, really—that the enemy's dovin basals generated. Somehow the Yuuzhan Vong, or at least this one, had found a way to counter this attack.

"You want to dance?" Kyp said grimly. "Fine with me. I'll lead."

He swept in, a laser firestorm leading the way. Several coralskippers circled in to support the larger ship. As the Jedi led them away, he carefully noted the shape and diameter of the big ship's protective shield. He jinked sharply, putting a passing military ship between himself and his attackers just long enough to drop a pair of concussion missiles. Quickly he darted away, drawing the Yuuzhan Vong with him and leaving the missiles floating like harmless flotsam.

Octa responded at once to this signal. She and the three pilots under her command unleashed a barrage of quick-stuttering laserfire at the big coralskipper.

Kyp reached out with the Force and eased the floating missiles toward the big skip. He reversed the flow of Force energy and brought the missiles to a stop just short of the dovin basal's reach.

While Octa kept the big skip busy, Kyp quickly took stock of the nearby battle. A large Corellian freighter, most likely carrying passengers fleeing the planet, managed to hurtle through the blockade just a few kilometers from the Jedi corvette. Immediately several coralskippers converged in attack. The refugees unwittingly led this new force directly toward Danni Quee's ship.

"Veema, get that freighter out of here," Kyp ordered.

A quartet of XJs darted off in tight formation to engage the enemy ships. Laserfire battled streams of plasma as Kyp's pilots provided a diversion for the fleeing refugee ship.

A thin bolt of plasma sheered through the wing of Veema's ship. The off-balance XJ tumbled wildly, hopelessly out of control, and crashed into the very ship it had been protecting. The XJ exploded—and took the freighter's port fusion engine out with it.

A huge fissure sizzled down the side of the battered freighter, brilliant from the explosion within. Kyp—his emotions open and raw from his own peculiar battle mode—felt the sharp surge of terror, and then the sudden sundering of every life on that ship.

With a great effort of will, Kyp snapped his attention back to the big coralskipper. The Yuuzhan Vong had apparently taken note of the protection given the old corvette. The big coralskipper moved inexorably toward Danni Quee's vessel. A stray laser beam struck one of the concussion missiles. It exploded: a white-fire blossom bursting from an eerie pink stem. The skip, however, had moved beyond the explosion's range.

But Kyp no longer needed this particular missile. He ordered Octa's squadron to regroup in a defensive position around the Jedi scientist's ship.

"As the Master says, size matters not," he murmured.

He released his hold on the second missile, not caring that it was swallowed by one of the coralskipper's stuttering singularities. Reaching deep into himself, he sought resources he had not used for many years.

Once before, Kyp had seized a ship and dragged it out of the fierce heart of a gas giant. Now he reached out with the Force and took hold of the dead freighter.

It shot forward with astonishing ease, moving steadily through the vacuum of space toward the shielded coralskipper.

Ian Rim's dark chuckle came through the comm. "Subtle as always, Kyp! Let's not let this one get away, Dozen!" he shouted.

The lieutenant spun off in a tight turn, his two surviving pilots following closely. They darted around the big coralskipper, cutting off its retreat, taking and returning fire from the other enemy skips. Their daring maneuvers soon exacted a price—Ian's ship got caught in a Yuuzhan Vong crossfire. The double blast of plasma proved too much for his shields, and the ship dissolved in a bright splatter of plasma and superheated metal.

The pilots Ian had commanded doggedly held the course he'd plotted. The XJs continued to harry the big skip, forcing it to keep up its stuttering shields as the dead freighter closed in. At the last moment, the surviving X-wings shot away toward safety.

The freighter never got close. One moment it was there; the next it simply disappeared into a void. What happened next was not exactly what Kyp had had in mind.

He'd hoped for a physical impact, or, barring that, that the freighter might overwhelm the dovin basal's capacity, leaving the big coralskipper vulnerable to attack. It had never occurred to him that the skip's multiple singularities might merge into one and fold in on the Yuuzhan Vong ship like a glove turning inside out. But suddenly, the freighter was gone. So was the coralskipper.

And so were the fleeing X-wings.

Death came to the pilots with a speed that neither fear nor thought could match. Neither of them saw its approach. None of their final emotions came through to Kyp—only a sudden, almost deafening blast of silence.

Grief and guilt rose in Kyp like a dark tide. He bore down, sternly crushing these emotions before they could alter his focus, his course. He would not do this. He would not give way to the uncertainty that had so crippled his fellow Jedi.

Yet he could not deny that once again, he had undertaken a massive use of Force power and, in doing so, had inadvertently caused the death of those close to him.

Kyp forced himself back into the battle. He quickly took stock of his situation. Only Octa remained, and two of her pilots. The four of them could still do some damage.

He hailed his surviving Dozen and named a vector reasonably free of battle. "We'll regroup in quartet formation under my command."

The ships responded at once, jinking a path through the Jedi ships.

Suddenly a surge of grief came from Octa Ramis, and then a brief, anguished epiphany, and, finally, fury. Kyp was not very surprised to note that her anger was directed not at the Yuuzhan Vong, but at him.

"Master Skywalker was right," she said with deadly calm. "You may consider this a desertion."

Her XJ peeled off and circled back to the Jedi wing. After a moment, the two surviving members of her squadron followed.

Kyp let her go.

Nine more of his pilots had died, adding their names to the lengthening roster of those who had died under his command since the war started. Though their deaths weighed heavily on Kyp, he accepted this as the fortunes of war. But never before had he crossed the lines he'd drawn long ago and brought about a comrade's death through the power of the Force. At this dark moment, it seemed to him that this single act negated all the good he had done, all his steadfast arguments, everything for which he stood.

A moment of indecision, no more, but the price was high. Coralskippers closed in on Octa's ships like a pack of voxyn.

Kyp streaked in, determined to take as many of them with him as he could.

Suddenly, inexplicably, the Yuuzhan Vong attack began to falter. Several of the coralskippers veered away in erratic, almost drunken flight. Octa Ramis took advantage of this seeming confusion to give pursuit. The other XJs followed.

Two skips hurtled toward the Jedi woman's ship. The enemy ships grazed each other, veered wildly apart, over-compensated. Back they came, slamming into a sidelong collision.

Shards of coral hammered the XJs with deadly shrapnel. Both of the ships spun away, out of control. Only Octa returned to the battered Jedi fleet.

"Objective secured," she said coldly.

Kyp could only nod. For months now, Danni Quee's team had been working on blocking a yammosk, a hideous, telepathic creature that coordinated many ships. Judging by the sudden confusion among the Yuuzhan Vong, they had succeeded.

But he, Kyp Durron, had failed.

Again.

A flood of emotion swept through him, and a dozen hard years suddenly fell away. For a moment Kyp knew the fresh anguish of his brother's death. The darkness of that terrible time flooded back, and the despair.

"Jaina," he murmured suddenly, for no reason that he could comprehend.

Kyp shook his head as if to clear it. Of course he was aware of pretty, pragmatic Jaina Solo—what Jedi wasn't?—but she didn't exactly fly in his orbit. There was nothing between them that could explain the fleeting connection; in fact, her reaction after the attack on the Sernpidal shipwomb suggested that Jaina wouldn't so much as spit at him if he were on fire.

At that moment a familiar ship soared into view, a disreputable antique that was nonetheless one of the biggest legends in the galaxy. Three coralskippers blundered after it, spewing lethal rock.

"Not the *Falcon*," Kyp vowed darkly, finding a measure of focus in this new threat. "Not a chance."

The Jedi dropped his remaining two missiles and used the Force to hurl them at the enemy ships. Once again he stopped them just short of the singularities. He busied the skips' dovin basals with a quick flurry of laserfire, then let the missiles hammer in. Two of the alien ships exploded. Coral shards melted as they hurtled through gouts of plasma thrown by a third ship.

The Jedi switched to hailing frequency. "*Millennium Falcon*, this is Kyp Durron. Could you use a wingmate?"

"You give a great audition, kid. Consider yourself hired."

Han Solo's disembodied voice lifted some of the burden from Kyp's shoulders.

His relief was short-lived. A Yuuzhan Vong blastboat made a ponderous turn and came in pursuit of the *Falcon*. The pilot noticed, too, and responded with an oath Kyp hadn't heard since his days as a slave in the Kessel spice mines.

"You install those vertical thrusters, like I told you?" Han demanded.

"Got 'em."

"Good. Use them."

Kyp punched the drive. His head seemed determined to burrow between his shoulders as the ship made a sudden leap. An enormous, ship-swallowing plasma comet scorched a path through the place he had just been—and directly toward his friend's ship.

But Han turned the *Falcon* abruptly up on her port side. The missile streaked past, taking out a pair of disoriented coralskippers before it cooled into tumbling rock.

The old ship leveled out and then whirled away, tracing an oddly teetering path as Han deftly evaded incoming fire. Then he abruptly flipped onto the starboard side. Another massive bolt shot by, missing the ship but heating the underside to a glowing red. The *Falcon* lev-

eled out suddenly. Two confused coralskippers collided
overhead.

"Hey, I *told* these people to use the flight restraints,"
Han protested, responding to someone whose voice was
beyond the reach of the comm. "Maybe if you'd issued a
royal edict?"

The contentious fondness in Han's voice identified
the recipient of his sarcasm. An odd, hollow sensation
settled in the pit of Kyp's stomach at the prospect of con-
fronting Leia Organa Solo.

He admired Han's wife greatly, but her presence often
left him keenly aware of the disparity between his
youthful choices and hers. Leia had become a member of
the Imperial Senate at sixteen, a hero of the Rebel Alliance two years later. At sixteen, Kyp had apprenticed
himself to a long-dead Sith Lord. He'd rounded out his
teen years by putting Master Skywalker in a near-death
trance, forcibly erasing the memory of an Omwati scientist, commandeering a superweapon, and destroying a
world and all its inhabitants. Thanks to Luke Skywalker's intervention, Kyp's crimes had been forgiven.
Kyp had no illusions that anyone would forget them,
least of all himself. Princess Leia did not remind him of
what he'd been, but rather, what he might have become.

On the other hand, Leia's presence on the *Falcon*
might explain why Jaina had come so forcefully to Kyp's
mind. Leia wasn't a fully trained Jedi, but Kyp suspected
her raw powers rivaled those of her brother. Perhaps
she'd heard something about her daughter and had inadvertently projected her response through the Force. Last
thing Kyp had heard, the Solo kids were involved in
some secret mission.

"From your last comment, I'd guess that Leia is flying
copilot," Kyp ventured.

"Looks that way," Han agreed. Kyp didn't need the
Force to hear the deep affection in the man's voice. But

there was also a deep weariness and a certain brittle quality—things that Kyp had never associated with Han.

"Is everything all right?"

Han's laugh sounded a trifle forced. "Leia's up to the job, if that's what you're asking. And we've got two Jedi Masters aboard for good measure—Luke's here, and Mara. What could go wrong?"

SOME CULTURES BELIEVE THAT RHETORICAL QUESTIONS HAVE A WAY OF TEMPTING FATE, Zero-One observed.

Kyp abruptly switched off the outside comm. "Who asked you?" he demanded.

RHETORICAL QUESTIONS ARE NOT DIRECTED AT ANYONE IN PARTICULAR. PERHAPS THAT IS WHY DESTINY CLAIMS THEM.

"Who did your philosophical programming—a cantina comic? *Destiny claims them!*" the Jedi scoffed. "Words to live by!"

EXPERIENTIAL DATA, KYP DURRON, SUGGEST THAT YOU DO PRECISELY THAT.

The sneer fell off Kyp's face. He switched off the communication screen linking him to the disturbing Q9 unit and blew out a long sigh.

Then he fell into place beside the *Falcon,* his eyes scanning the roiling skies for his next fight.

FIVE

Jaina slumped in the pilot's seat, too exhausted for sleep. She felt an approaching presence and turned to face Tekli, the young Chadra-Fan healer.

The furry little female looked perturbed—all four of the nostrils on her upturned snout flared, as if she were scenting the air for danger. Her large rounded ears were folded back into subdued half-moons, and her quick, almost furtive movements made her look more rodentlike than usual.

Jaina hauled herself upright. "How is Tahiri?"

"Sleeping." The healer sighed. "The broken bone in her arm is set, her wounds patched as best I can. But I do not envy her her dreams."

Dreams. Jaina grimaced at the thought. "Why take the chance? First opportunity, I'm going straight into a healing trance."

"That is probably wise."

Tekli stood quietly, her long-fingered hands tightly clasped. She looked as if she were trying to gather her thoughts, or perhaps her courage.

Jaina smoothed a hand wearily over her untidy brown hair. "This isn't a diplomatic dinner. How about we jettison the protocol and get to whatever's on your mind."

"You have set course for Coruscant."

"That's right."

"Is this wise? We are flying an enemy ship. We cannot

communicate with the city towers to relay our identities
and intentions."

Jaina folded her arms. "How many living Yuuzhan
Vong ships do you suppose the Republic has?"

The little Chadra-Fan blinked. "I don't know."

"Last I heard, two. By now they could both be dead
and useless. They don't seem to live long without regular
attention from the shapers—the Vong maintenance
techs. Chances are, the Republic will be so glad to get
their hands on a living ship and living pilot they'll give us
landing clearance."

"As they did to the supposed Yuuzhan Vong defector,
the priestess Elan?"

Jaina blew out a long sigh. "I see your point. How can
the Republic know that we're not faking surrender? For
all they know, we could be on a suicide mission to release
some biological weapon upon Coruscant."

"It has crossed my mind. No doubt it may occur to
others."

Jaina glanced at Lowbacca, who was still poking delicately about in the frigate's navibrain. "What about it,
Lowie? Any chance this thing can change hyperspace
destination without emerging to sublight speed?"

The Wookiee sent her an incredulous stare, then cast
his eyes upward and shook his head in disgust.

She shrugged this off. "So we emerge into Coruscant
space and keep out of the main lanes while we program
another hyperspace jump. There must be somewhere
that we can land this rock in one piece rather than as a
shower of gravel. Then we can make our way to a population center and send communications from there."

The Chadra-Fan's lopped-back ears perked up into
their usual, rounded shape. "Yes. Much better."

"Got a destination in mind?"

Lowbacca woofed a suggestion.

"Gallinore," Jaina mused. "That's in the Hapes Cluster,

but it's relatively close. If we are very careful, we could probably get in undetected."

Tenel Ka's head came up sharply. "I know Gallinore well. It could be done."

"But we'd be cutting right across Yuuzhan Vong territory," Ganner pointed out. "Chances are, we'd run right into heavy dovin basal mining."

"Good point," Jaina agreed. "This jump took us through enemy-held territory. The question is, how do the Yuuzhan Vong ships get through the minefield?"

Lowbacca pointed to the navibrain and went into a vigorous spate of growls and yelps.

The young pilot frowned. "What do you mean, the ship just went around them? How does that work?"

The Wookiee shrugged. Jaina's face was deeply troubled as she considered the possible implications of this. After a moment she shook off her introspection. "Anyone else have anything to add? Alema? Tesar? How about you, Zekk?"

"You're the pilot," Zekk responded. "But I see your point—we should come to a consensus before the need for action arises. Gallinore sounds good. How much longer in hyperspace, Lowie?"

The Wookiee held up a massive furred paw and began to count down from five. Jaina reached for the cognition hood and pulled it back over her head.

She was instantly flooded with images of light—not the expected, sudden appearance of blurry starlines, but a multiverse of frantically strobing, swirling lights.

The skies over Coruscant blazed with fleeing transport ships, darting E-wings and XJs, strangely undisciplined squadrons of coralskippers. Brief, brilliant explosions flared and faded, each coming on the heels of another in rapid cadence.

Lowbacca began to howl in protest.

"I *know* it's not your fault," Jaina yelled as she jinked

to avoid several pink streaks exploding from X-wing laser cannons. "You didn't get us lost. This *is* Coruscant."

"This *was* Coruscant," Zekk murmured, his voice hollow with shock and grief.

Ganner thrust him out of the way and dropped into the gunner's seat. "Line them up, Jaina, and I'll take them out."

A tiny blue comet flared toward them. The missile blinked out of existence meters from the ship. Immediately a secondary attack—a barrage of laserfire—hammered the coral hull. The frigate shuddered. Fine, black dust showered down over the Jedi.

"Those were Republic ships," Ganner said grimly. "I can't return fire on them!"

Instead, he sent a plasma bolt hurling toward a Yuuzhan Vong skip. Alema Rar lunged at him, seizing his arm with both hands and jerking his hand free of the targeting glove.

"We came dressed for the wrong party," she reminded him. "Keep that up, and *everyone* will be firing at us!"

Jaina opened her mind, reached out as far as the ship's considerable sensors could span. Information engulfed her. The data was staggering, the conclusion inescapable:

Coruscant was lost, and the fleeing New Republic ships were badly outnumbered by the invading force.

The Twi'lek was right: any attempt to help would only draw the ire of the Yuuzhan Vong and place the Jedi survivors squarely between the warring factions.

She glanced at Lowbacca, tilted her hooded head at an inquiring angle. For a moment, the Wookiee's face reflected her own conflicted thoughts. He offered a half-hearted comment about the enemy of an enemy being a friend.

Before Jaina could respond, a warning sizzled through the hood and into her mind. Her gaze darted toward a proton torpedo cutting a livid blue streak toward them.

"Something tells me," she replied as she dodged the Republic ship's missile, "that we won't be making many friends today."

Leia grimaced as a painfully familiar X-wing darted directly into the *Falcon*'s flight path.

"Are you sure Kyp Durron wasn't hooked up to that scrambled yammosk?" she said tartly.

"Watch," Han said in a smug tone. He delivered an open-handed whack to the control panel. A concussion missile exploded toward the Jedi pilot's ship. As if he'd expected this, Kyp whipped his X-wing into a hard, rolling turn. Han's missile put a solid hit on the skip pursuing Kyp.

A quick grin tugged at one corner of Han's mouth. "Taught him that one myself."

"Are you bragging or confessing?"

"Kyp's fighting on the same side we are," he reminded. "Not everyone agrees with his methods, but no one gives more than he does."

Leia closed her eyes as the ever-present grief swept over her in waves, followed swiftly by the stark fear that came from knowing she could lose two more children. "That's true enough. Kyp was more than willing to give your daughter to the cause."

Han fell silent for several moments, negotiating his way through a floating graveyard of newly dead ships with far more care than the effort warranted.

Too late, Leia realized how deeply her words had cut. Han had lost Chewbacca on Sernpidal. There was enough superstition in Han's makeup to view that planet's graveyard as a sort of interdiction field for Solo luck. To his way of thinking, Jaina's mission to Sernpidal had been a near miss, a tragedy just barely averted.

She glanced over at her husband. His bleak expression and haunted eyes recalled the terrible months after Chewbacca's death, and his struggle to accept the vulnerability of those he loved. When the realization of Anakin's death seared through her, she'd been too engulfed by her own agony to ease Han into that knowledge; in fact, from what she remembered, she'd thrown the terrible news at him like a brick of duracrete. Right now, he looked as if she'd hit him squarely between the eyes.

Remorse jolted through Leia. She was not the only one who had lost a son.

She touched Han's arm lightly. "Grief has a way of making people act selfish and stupid."

He sent her a quick, wary look. "Are we talking about me?"

"Not this time," she said, and sighed. "I'm sorry, Han. Jaina can take care of herself, and the Sernpidal mission probably ended up moving the war effort forward. That doesn't change the fact that Kyp lied to Jaina. Worse—he used the Force to sway her judgment. I just don't trust him."

"Luke does."

"Luke is . . ." She paused, considered. "Optimistic."

Han snorted. "Since when did you start pulling your punches?"

His wife responded with a wan smile and turned back to the navigational computer. Her fingers poised over the controls, uncertain. "Where do we go now?" she wondered aloud.

An out-of-control skip spun toward them. Bursts of fire erupted from the *Falcon*'s belly guns as Luke Skywalker reduced the vessel to rubble. A large chunk of coral slammed into the forward shields. The cabin lights blinked out, then flared uncertainly back.

"Anywhere but here," Han said. "Don't get me wrong: I'm glad to have Luke and Mara aboard. Your brother's not bad with weaponry, but he's not, well—"

"You?" Leia suggested.

Han managed a reasonable imitation of his old, cocky smirk. "I don't like to brag."

She began to input coordinates for a brief hyperspace jump. Her fingers faltered to a stop as a strange sensation crept over her—a presence perceived through the Force, yet one that felt more like a gathering storm cloud than a living being. Her brow furrowed as she tried to make sense of it.

The touch on her shoulder made her jump. "You're wound about three turns too tight," he observed.

Suddenly the answer came to her. She sat up, pulling away from Han. "Jaina!"

The color leeched from his face. "She's not . . ."

"No," Leia said hastily. "But she's still in danger—only now she's nearby. Circle around, head back toward the battle."

As Han pulled the *Falcon* around, Leia's brown eyes scanned the roiling skies. A Yuuzhan Vong frigate twisted through the confusion, several X-wings in close pursuit. Coralskippers converged on the frigate, surrounding it with a protective convoy. Several pairs of mismatched ships peeled away as the situation devolved into a chaotic dogfight.

Leia seized the obvious and logical explanation. Jaina had returned from her mission and gone straight to the nearest Rogue Squadron post. That would be like her. Communication being what it was, she might not have been able to get a message through.

Even as Leia's thoughts took shape, plasma spurted from a coralskipper and scored a direct hit on one of the X-wings. She felt a surge of fury in that nebulous Jaina-sense as the Republic pilot dissolved along with the ship, and then a colder, darker emotion took its place.

Her brows drew down in a worried scowl as she tracked the acrid scent of vengeance to her daughter's ship.

"There," she said, pointing toward the frigate and the

small fleet of beleaguered X-wings giving dogged pursuit. "Jaina's over there."

A grin broke over Han's face. He leaned toward the comm. "Kyp, you're about to join Rogue Squadron."

The only response from the Jedi's X-wing was an incredulous comment of a Q9 droid.

"Jaina's with those X-wings trying to take down that midsized rock, the one busy avoiding entanglement," Han explained. "What do you think: can a Yuuzhan Vong ship move that fast and maneuver that well, and still use its shields?"

"Let's find out."

Kyp veered off and circled wide, closing in on the frigate from above. Streams of red light poured from his X-wing and pelted the enemy ship. The dovin basal absorbed most of Kyp's shots in miniature gravity wells and dodged nearly all the rest through a series of deft, economical movements.

"Not bad," Han muttered, frowning as he stared at the midsized Yuuzhan Vong ship.

Suddenly the enemy frigate pulled away and described a tight, rising loop.

Leia clutched Han's arm. "It's coming right into your line of fire!"

"Yeah."

The laconic response earned Han an incredulous, sidelong glare. He shook off Leia's grip and reached for the intraship comm. "The big one's mine, Mara. You can pick off anything it brings our way."

"You're the captain," his sister-in-law replied.

Leia's face cleared suddenly as she understood the path his thoughts were taking. "Jaina? In that enemy ship?"

"One way to find out."

Han fired a missile at the frigate, waiting a hair's breadth longer than he had with Kyp. The Yuuzhan Vong ship rolled deftly aside as if the pilot had been expecting the attack. Han's missile struck one of the skips that trailed protectively in its wake. A shielding singularity swallowed the first assault, but Mara finished the job with a quick one–two attack.

"That's Jaina," Han said firmly. "Thousands of pilots can get from here to there in an X-wing, but how many could make a hunk of rock twirl like a Twi'lek dancing girl?"

"Han—"

"Two," he stated, answering his own question. "And I'm the other one."

Still dubious, Leia turned to the Force for confirmation. Again she reached out to Jaina. Again she perceived not the vivid, impetuous energy she'd always associated with her daughter, but a storm-cloud presence—cool, impending, pitiless.

Leia frowned. Anger led to the dark side. She had heard this so many times. Yet the emotions that rolled off her daughter were disturbingly familiar, and very like Leia's perception of her own father—not the spectral Anakin Skywalker who had begged her forgiveness, but his earlier, living incarnation as Darth Vader.

Never had Leia considered the possibility that Jaina, the most pragmatic and least complicated of her children, might slip into darkness. She reached for Jaina again, more insistently. Through the Force she sensed her daughter's rejected pain, her carefully shielded emotions—and her unacknowledged thirst for revenge. It occurred to Leia that ice could be as deadly as fire.

If this insight proved true, then she'd lost another of her children, this time to something more terrible than death.

"Decide," Han said tersely. "The Yuuzhan Vong could blame that frigate's maneuver on the scrambled yammosk, but sooner or later Jaina's gonna have to pick a side."

She quickly shook off her fears and switched the comm to hailing frequency. "This is Leia Organa Solo aboard the *Millennium Falcon*. The Yuuzhan Vong frigate nearby is under the command of my daughter, Lieutenant Jaina Solo. Her Yuuzhan Vong escort does not realize this. Hold your fire, and we'll see that the frigate escapes, and the coralskippers do not."

There was a moment's hesitation, then the pursuing X-wings pulled away.

The intercom crackled. "Leia, are you sure about this?" Mara asked. "I hate to admit it, but I don't feel Jaina out there."

She glanced at Han, who nodded. "We're sure."

The Yuuzhan Vong frigate, its way clear, shot off in rapid acceleration and disappeared into hyperspace. The *Falcon* followed, taking the short jump Leia had programmed.

Han's shoulders slumped. His hand found hers, claimed it. "We did the right thing, didn't we? I mean, letting a potential enemy go?"

The unwitting implication of his words nearly broke Leia's heart. She met her husband's eyes and read the rare moment of self-doubt written there.

"That was Jaina," she asserted, both answering and avoiding his question.

His gaze sharpened. "Then why do you look so worried?"

For a moment Leia was tempted to share her doubts, to see if they might dissipate if given voice. But if she was wrong, planting this seed in Han's mind would be selfish, even cruel. She would never accuse Han of favoritism, but Jaina had always been the child he understood best, the one who'd taken straight after him in talents and tastes, the kid who'd taken every opportunity to follow him around. Han would grieve terribly if Jaina were taken from them by this war, but he had lost others in battle and he could come to terms with it in time. This, though—this he could never comprehend.

"Well?" Han prompted. "What's wrong?"

Leia settled on a partial truth. "Jacen wasn't with Jaina. I can still sense him," she added hastily, "but he wasn't with her."

Han nodded, taking this in. "Then we'll have to trust them both to find their way back."

She blinked, startled again by the unintentional aptness of his comments. "You're right. They're grown now, and capable. But it isn't easy to let them go their own way."

"No, it isn't." He attempted a cocky grin and managed a decent if decidedly one-sided imitation. "Since when did any of us need things to be easy?"

Leia gratefully took his lead. Humor pushed back the numbing grief—if only for the time it took to smile.

"You've got a point, flyboy. If I needed proof of that, all I need to do is remember that we're still married."

He leaned forward, touched his forehead to hers. "Last time I checked."

His strength flowed into her, mixed with a sweetness that she'd feared they'd misplaced long ago. Leia lifted her face until their lips were a whisper apart.

"Check again."

SIX

A storm raged outside General Soontir Fel's viewport, the first of the winter monsoon season. Frozen rain swirled through roiling gray clouds and rattled against the transparisteel ports. Ice coated the duracrete landing pads and hung from the eaves of the Chiss barracks in neat rows, like ready weapons lining an armory shelf. Tall, blue-skinned pilots strode confidently over the slick walkways, aided by their spike-soled boots and their native athleticism.

Despite the steady hum of the room's heating unit, the cold seeped into Fel's joints. A phantom ache throbbed in his missing eye, despite the dark patch he sometimes wore. For the first time in his life he felt old and tired, especially when he considered the challenges ahead.

A hard winter was on its way, the general mused, one that could last for several Corellian years. The Chiss base, the latest of many that Fel had established over the years, was set in a particularly harsh environment of an inhospitable world. Most of his advisers had perceived no reason why anyone would choose to place a base here.

Fel only hoped that the Yuuzhan Vong would follow the same logic.

He turned away from the viewport to study the officer standing at stiff attention before his desk. The young man wore the formal black uniform of the Syndic

Mitth'raw'nuruodo's household phalanx, and the insignia of a colonel. His black hair was cut short, exposing the entire length of the scar that ran up from his right eyebrow well into his hairline. A thin streak of white hair followed the path of that scar, as if to emphasize the maturity that had come too soon, and at great price.

"We have had this discussion before, Colonel," Fel commented. "This phalanx is committed to the same goals you've espoused. We responded at Garqi. We fought at Ithor. The Imperial command recalled Admiral Pellaeon after that debacle, with what they considered to be good reason. Given the outcome of that engagement and the withdrawal of Imperial support, I saw little value in committing phalanx squadrons."

"I disagree." The young colonel bowed to emphasize that his words expressed opinion, but not disrespect. "I will concede that no one, not the New Republic nor the Imperial forces nor the Chiss, could counter the biological weapons that destroyed Ithor. The presence of this household's phalanx had no impact on this outcome. Ithor, however, was the only world utterly destroyed. The invaders have followed more conventional tactics in their subsequent conquests."

"And therein lies the problem. How successful were you and your Rogue Squadron allies in fending off any of these conquests through 'conventional tactics'?"

The young man's lips thinned. "My two squadrons were recalled shortly after Ithor, sir. We had neither the time nor the opportunity to make an appreciable difference. This is not an excuse, sir, but simple fact."

"Two squadrons," the general repeated. "Twenty-four clawcraft and a beacon ship. How much difference could this force have made at Ord Mantell? Or Duro? Hundreds, possibly thousands of worlds are under Yuuzhan Vong control."

"With respect, sir, I was commissioned in this household to serve and uphold the ideals of Grand Admiral Thrawn."

"Which did not, I might point out, include stupidity," the general observed coldly. "I expected better of you— a not uncommon dynamic between fathers and their sons."

Colonel Jagged Fel acknowledged the reprimand with a small bow and a faint, wry smile.

"You were trained by Chiss tacticians," Baron Fel continued. "Tell me: do we have the ships, weaponry, personnel, or for that matter the knowledge needed to take on these invaders?"

"We do not," Jag admitted. "Permission to speak freely?"

The baron lifted one hand in a gesture of assent.

"Chiss sages conclude that the Yuuzhan Vong must have spent generations traveling between galaxies. These invaders are not likely to consider the so-called Unknown Regions a daunting prospect."

"I agree," Baron Fel said. "The Chiss parliament does not, and neither do the Imperial leaders. The invasion path has swept steadily toward the Core Worlds, leading many to believe that the invaders will bypass both Chiss and Imperial territory entirely."

As Jag absorbed this, his pale green eyes narrowed and his jaw squared. "This phalanx has never been ruled by the thinking of tradition-bound Chiss senators, or by Imperial politicians whose first concern is personal power. Was a change-of-policy holocube issued during my recent absence?"

The general's eyebrows lifted. Jag inclined his head in a bow that held acknowledgment of his impropriety, but no apology.

"Chiss society pretends that Snydic Mitth'raw'nuruodo does not exist, but they know quite well that we are out here. They send their sons and daughters to this phalanx's academies and bases. They were more than willing to accept the protection and technology that Thrawn's conquests and alliances offered them, and they are willing to accept what we, successors to the grand admiral's goals, can do for them."

"But we could do more." Jag took a step forward, his expression intense, his formality forgotten. "You know what we have faced out here. The Yuuzhan Vong might have caught Borsk Fey'lya and his ilk unaware, but the Chiss have long expected something of this nature. In fact, we have turned aside foes that might have swept across the galaxy and left little for these new invaders to destroy!"

The baron's eyes narrowed, and his lips pursed as he considered his son's passionate words. "You speak of yourself as one of the Chiss. Do you see yourself in that light?"

Jag blinked, put off stride by this seeming non sequitur. "It is difficult to do otherwise," he said carefully. "I was raised among the Chiss, trained with them. Their rules and standards and expectations became my own."

"You met and exceeded these standards, and as a result you command your former Chiss peers," his father continued. "With rank comes responsibility. The course you propose shows little sense of responsibility for the pilots under your command."

Jag's face betrayed no opinion on this matter, but his bearing subtly reverted to a formal, military stance. "Sir, may I request that you list my failings plainly, so that I might address them."

"Do you know how to stop the Yuuzhan Vong?"

A hint of a frown touched his forehead. "No, sir."

"Then go find out. Report back. Once we've a better grasp of tactics and strategy, you'll have your squadrons back, and more besides."

Jag's eyes widened and flicked to his father's face. "Yes, sir!"

The baron grimaced and tapped a small metal cube on his desk. "You might not be quite so eager to hear this report. This holovid just came in from our agents in the Core. It contains, among other things, a recording of Leia Organa Solo's exhortation to the defenders of Coruscant. She urged them not to give up, as she has not, despite the recent death of one of her children."

This time Jag's gaze shifted fully to the general. "Which one?"

Fel lifted one eyebrow. "Excuse me?"

"Which of Ambassador Solo's children fell in battle?"

"Anakin, I believe. The younger son."

Jag nodded thoughtfully, and there was something very akin to relief on his face. "Was there any news of the other two?"

A speculative gleam crept into the baron's gaze. "You have met the Solo twins, I take it?"

"Jacen, no. Jaina Solo is a pilot with Rogue Squadron."

"Ah. I was wondering why such momentous news as Coruscant's fall went over your head with a meter to spare."

A faint color suffused Jag's face, and a faintly puzzled expression flickered in his eyes. Baron Fel suspected that his son was also somewhat unclear on that point. Well, he would learn soon enough.

Jag quickly veered away from his uncharacteristic tangent and back onto a more familiar vector. "Coruscant was not only attacked, but captured?"

"It would so appear. This leads us to your next assignment. In recent years, the New Republic has been characterized by increasing dissent. The loss of their central seat could polarize them for a very long time."

The baron fell silent. For a long moment, he studied his son. "You will be flying straight into a maelstrom."

Jag glanced pointedly toward the viewport, and the ice storm beyond. "This is what I was trained to do, no more."

"Then it's settled." Fel rose and handed a single holocube to his son. "This contains the most recent military updates, as well as the specs on the new ships you'll be flying. I'll leave the selection of pilots to you."

"Shawnkyr Nuruodo, my second in command, will accompany me." When the general began to protest, Jag's chin came up sharply. "You admonished me about responsibility, sir, and rightly so. I'm honored to scout for Syndic Mitth'raw'nuruodo, but I would rather not risk Chiss pilots needlessly. In all likelihood, we will need every one of them here."

"What about Shawnkyr?"

A fleeting smile curved Jag's lips. "Shawnkyr is a true member of a renegade phalanx, sir. She would not stay behind if I ordered her to."

"I see. A wise leader always tries to give orders that are likely to be followed. Why do you think I'm sending you?"

He extended his hand. They clasped hands briefly, then Jag stepped back and offered a crisp, formal bow.

Baron Fel watched his son stride to the door. When he was alone, he sank back into his chair, his shoulders slumped and his expression bleak and bereft.

There was no keeping Jag away from the growing conflict. Soontir Fel understood this, for he knew Jag well. He also knew from long experience what the young man was likely to face. The burden of sending his promising, twenty-year-old son into a seemingly impossible fight weighed heavily upon him.

Davin had been about Jag's age when he'd been sent to his final battle, and his sister Cherith even younger.

Soontir Fel rose and began to pace the room. He had never turned away from duty, and he would not now. But nothing he'd faced in his long career had been as difficult as this:

Sending his third child to serve, and most likely to die.

Jaina braced herself against the pilot's seat as the stolen Yuuzhan Vong ship accelerated toward lightspeed. The frantic, pulsing lights that marked Coruscant's last battle stretched out into fading lines, and then disappeared.

The calm and darkness of hyperspace welcomed them. Jaina ripped off the pilot's hood and scrubbed her head briskly with both hands. This did little to erase the images of Coruscant's death. Her heart still thudded in time to the chaotic pace of its destruction, and the cacophony of battle rang in her ears. She set it all aside as best she could and turned to Lowbacca.

"Good job. Where are we going?"

The Wookiee responded with a hollow moan and something that looked suspiciously like a shrug.

"You don't know?" Tenel Ka demanded, coming forward with quick strides. "How can you not know?"

Lowbacca huffed defensively, his gaze boring into Tenel Ka's gray-eyed challenge. Jaina placed a hand on the Wookiee's shoulder.

"Jumping to open space was the best thing to do under the circumstances. Lowbacca bought us time so we can all decide next steps. Together."

"I'll get the others," Tenel Ka said curtly.

She returned in moments with the other Jedi. Her one arm encircled Tahiri's waist in a manner that was half support, half sisterly embrace.

Tahiri was nearly clothed in bandages and bacta patches, but none of Tekli's ministrations had lessened the naked grief in her eyes, or the sorrow that radiated from her. The Chadra-Fan healer followed them like a small brown shadow, her large black eyes fixed upon her charge.

Jaina drew her personal shield closer around her and slid an objective gaze over the young Jedi. "You look better."

"Better than what?" Tahiri said.

Bitterness twisted the girl's tone, and wrath rose from her like steam. The scars on her forehead—marks resulting from her captivity on Yavin 4—had been augmented by a livid burn and a small but nasty cut. Apparently she'd refused treatment for these wounds.

Zekk and Ganner exchanged a quick, concerned glance, one that spoke of a familiar subject revisited. This realization sent a surge of irritation through Jaina. Tahiri would survive—*had* survived. She was not the only one who had lost Anakin. They'd all been diminished. Dwelling on their losses wouldn't solve the problems this moment presented.

"The ship's not doing well," Jaina said without preamble. "Judging from what I'm getting through the pilot's hood, and what Lowbacca has learned from poking around, I think we can fix it and feed it."

"Feed it?" Ganner broke in. "Should I be afraid to ask what it eats?"

"Only if you're a rock," Jaina shot back. "We have to put the ship down as soon as possible. The question is, where?"

"We've been gone only a few days, yet we return to find the Yuuzhan Vong on Coruscant itself," Alema Rar observed. "How can we know what worlds are occupied, and which are not?"

"This one suggestz we go to Barab One," Tesar said. The reptilian Jedi bared his fangs in what Jaina took to be a feral smile. "The Barabel homeworld is not in the invasion path. That is good. But if the Yuuzhan Vong come, that is better."

Jaina was beginning to develop an ear for the dark

humor that underlay Barabel speech, and she suspected there was a clincher line to come. "Let's hear it."

A sly expression crossed the scaly face. "On Nal Hutta, the Vong are invaderz. What doez one call them on Barab?"

"Prey?" she suggested.

Tesar flashed his fangs again and swatted her companionably on the shoulder.

Ganner rolled his eyes. "Now that we've gotten *that* out of our systems, how about a serious suggestion? Lowbacca named Gallinore. Since we've gotten this far without hitting any dovin basal mines, I add my vote to that."

"Makes sense," Zekk agreed. "As far as I know, the Yuuzhan Vong haven't targeted that system yet. But here's something else to think about. Hapes is closer than Gallinore. It's also more heavily populated, and most likely we could get back into active duty sooner if we didn't have to trek across a wilderness planet."

"True enough, but the inhabitants of wilderness planets are less likely to shoot Yuuzhan Vong ships out of the sky," Alema Rar pointed out.

Zekk acknowledged this with a nod. "I've been poking around the ship a bit, and I found something that looks like an escape pod. If we can figure out how to launch it, one of us could go ahead to prepare the way."

They all looked expectantly at Tenel Ka. "If this is the decision, I will go," she agreed, "but there are things about Hapes you should know. My father's homeworld has a history of anti-Jedi sentiment."

Ganner let out a brief, humorless laugh. "That's hardly an original notion these days. We should feel right at home."

"There is more," Tenel Ka began.

The others glanced at Jaina, then their eyes slipped hurriedly away.

She lifted her chin and met the issue head-on. "Centerpoint," she said, naming the superweapon that had accidentally destroyed hundreds of Hapan ships. "It was Anakin who enabled the weapon, a Solo relative who fired it. I'm sure more than a few Hapans will blame any and all Solos for this loss. So let's put the sabacc cards on the table, Tenel Ka. What kind of reception are Solos and Jedi likely to get?"

The warrior woman gave this question several moments' consideration. "An interesting one," she decided, speaking without the slightest inflection of humor.

Alema huffed and folded her arms. "Oh, good. I for one could use the excitement."

The others added their assent—minus the Twi'lek's sarcasm. Jaina held back to the last, using the time to consider other possibilities.

Her last visit to Hapes had been enlivened by the attempted assassination of the former queen mother, Tenel Ka's grandmother, an attack that had included Tenel Ka and the Solo twins. This event had not been a unique experience. During her eighteen years, Jaina could probably tally up more threats to her life than her mother had hairstyles. People tried to kill her—that's just the way it was. That didn't factor largely into Jaina's hesitation. Of greater concern was her fear that the Hapes Cluster might prove an unlikely staging ground for any attack against the Yuuzhan Vong.

She had no idea what form that attack might take. All she knew was that losing custody of Jacen Solo was going to be the very last thing a lot of Yuuzhan Vong ever did.

"Jaina?" Ganner prompted.

"I'm taking Tenel Ka's reservations seriously," she said, offering an explanation for her delayed response, "but I'm with Zekk. Dozens of worlds are so afraid of Yuuzhan Vong reprisals that they're not accepting refugees of any kind. Even if we were flying a Republic ship, we could get turned away more than once. We might be able to land on a sparsely populated world, but getting off it could be a problem. With Tenel Ka's connections, we'll be able to get the ships and supplies we need to get back in business."

"Sounds good," Ganner agreed. "Let's see what sense Lowbacca can make of this escape pod."

The Wookiee let out a tentative-sounding grumble.

Jaina whirled to face him. "You *heard* it? What does that mean?"

Lowbacca pantomimed pulling down the cognition hood. He went into a long explanation about the navibrain, and how it interpreted an object's gravity and used these data as the basis for its directional calculations. The escape pod, even when docked in the frigate, maintained a complex internal gravity, which the incredibly sensitive navibrain perceived.

A seed took root in Jaina's mind. "So you're saying this ship's navigation is based on its recognition of each planet, each asteroid, and everything else it encounters as a discrete entity, based on that entity's unique gravity?"

The Wookiee considered this, then woofed an affirmative.

"What about small gravitic fluctuations?" she demanded. "Like the kind a Yuuzhan Vong ship creates for propulsion?"

Lowbacca tipped his head to one side and sent her an inquiring stare.

"Before we launch Tenel Ka, I want to make sure we can track the escape pod," Jaina explained. "From what you're saying, it sounds to me like that's how it would be done."

Intrigued, he ambled off to test this theory. The other Jedi scattered to tend their duties, or to get much-needed rest. Jaina accepted Zekk's offer to take over for a while and made her way to one of the small coral alcoves that served as cabins.

As soon as she was alone, she allowed a small, triumphant smile to creep onto her face. If her suspicions proved correct, a Yuuzhan Vong ship could identify another ship by its unique gravitic signature. Jaina was confident that Lowbacca would find a way to isolate a ship's "signal." Her friend was stubborn, even for a Wookiee. Once he got an idea in his head, it couldn't be blasted out with a thermal detonator. And when he succeeded, Jaina would be one small step closer to finding her brother.

"We're coming for you," she promised as she stretched out on the hard, narrow bunk. "I'll find you, Jacen, I promise."

She paused for a moment, breathing carefully until she was able to control the entangled anger and grief and guilt that thoughts of her brothers evoked.

"And when I do, we've got a few things to settle," she added, imbuing her words with just enough snap and ire to catch Jacen's attention, wherever he was.

She listened for some response, some tiny sign that her twin heard. That he *was*.

Silence.

With a sigh, Jaina gave up the attempt. She began the preparation for the Jedi trance, a deep and healing state of reverie.

Her last conscious thought was gratitude that no dreams could follow her into the darkness.

SEVEN

Harrar stood at the viewport of his personal chamber, gazing into the richly starred blackness beyond. So many worlds lay beyond, offering not only conquest, but a much-needed haven as well.

He did not desire peace. Not really. Yet even as this thought formed, the priest lifted a three-fingered hand to trace a crack in the once smooth wall. His ship had once resembled a perfect, highly polished black gem. It was becoming shabby with age, as were most Yuuzhan Vong ships. Harrar suspected the priestship was nearing the end of its long life span.

The ship's condition, however, was nothing compared to the warmaster's dilemma. Tsavong Lah had sacrificed most of one arm to win the gods' blessing upon the conquest of Coruscant. The battle had been won, but the warmaster's implant still refused to heal. If the corruption progressed, Harrar's old friend—who was also his most powerful and reliable supporter—would be forced from his high place. The priest suspected that his destiny, no less than the warmaster's, depended upon the successful capture and sacrifice of the Jedi twins.

"Your Eminence."

The priest turned toward the sound, carefully hiding his surprise and his chagrin that he *could* be surprised. Despite his impressive bulk and the vonduun crab armor he wore even aboard ship, Khalee Lah walked as quietly as a shadow. Had he been any other warrior, Harrar would have suspected that he was deliberately trying to discomfit his clerical charge.

"I trust this intrusion is justified?" he said sharply.

Khalee Lah inclined his head. "We have located the stolen ship, Eminence. The *Ksstarr* was sighted near Coruscant, but it managed to escape during the confusion of battle. It emerged from darkspace again approximately midpoint between the worlds known as Kuat and Kashyyyk."

"And now?"

"We believe the *Jeedai* will head toward the Hapes Cluster. We have set course accordingly."

Harrar's lingering irritation deepened. "If the frigate is capable of darkspace travel, the *Jeedai* could choose from many destinations."

"That is true, Eminence, but Nom Anor's ship was damaged during its escape from the worldship. The *Ksstarr* is famished and wounded, and without proper care it will soon die. Surely even these infidels will sense it is nearing its limits."

"Your logic is thin," the priest noted.

Khalee Lah inclined his head in apology. "One of the *Jeedai*, a female, is a scion of Hapan royalty," he added. "This was learned during the breaking. Not from this *Jeedai*, but from another."

Harrar heard a note of grudging admiration in the warrior's voice. "This female did not succumb to breaking, I take it. Good. The additional gift of a worthy *Jeedai* may placate the gods for this delay in the twin sacrifice. What is this infidel called?"

"Tenel Ka. It is said that she fought well, though she has but one arm. Other infidels have replaced limbs with mechanical abominations. Not this one." His scarred lips shaped a predatory smile. "If fitted with a proper enhancement, she might prove a worthy opponent, or at least an interesting diversion."

"In that case, you may offer her yourself in a warrior's sacrifice," Harrar said. His sloped forehead furrowed as he considered this. "Many ships from Hapes died along with ours at the Battle of Fondor, destroyed by a killing light from some mechanical abomination. Given what is known of the infidels, it is widely believed that they tossed away what they deemed unimportant. Based upon this reasoning, the Hapes Cluster was considered unworthy of our notice. Yet if this *Jeedai* is typical of Hapan nobles, perhaps this merits new consideration."

The warrior sniffed. "The Hapes Cluster is not controlled by the Yuuzhan Vong, but it is vanquished nonetheless. Since Fondor, the infidels of the Hapes Cluster have huddled on their worlds and done nothing."

"And the *Jeedai* presence there?"

"None to speak of; in fact, there is much animosity against them. The Peace Brigade has found eager recruits among the Hapans. We have sent word ahead to several known agents."

Harrar studied the warrior carefully. Something was amiss. Khalee Lah had answered every question forthrightly, but he offered no more information than Harrar requested. "There is more," he observed. "You are not telling me all. A priest of Yun-Harla has ways of knowing such things."

This time the warrior's bow was deep and profound, and he touched two fingers to his horned forehead in a gesture of reverence. "I am a military commander, Eminence. Certain tactics depend upon secrecy for success. I can discuss these tactics only with my superiors."

The warrior's impolitic words sent a twinge of annoyance through Harrar. He banished it at once, for the warrior's candor, not to mention his keen piety, suggested a tactic likely to twist matters around to Harrar's benefit.

"You command my escort. Mine," the priest empha-sized. "You support the task given to me by no less an au-thority than Tsavong Lah. If the warmaster is not highly placed enough to suit you, consider this: what Yuuzhan Vong warrior is not subject to the gods? And who better to interpret the will of the gods than a high priest?"

Khalee Lah genuflected. "I am fairly rebuked. Com-mand me."

"You seem certain of the *Ksstarr*'s destination. Tell me why."

"We have heavily mined the areas under our control with dovin basals," he said slowly. "These have the ability to disrupt the flight of infidel vessels, sometimes even to pull them from darkspace flight."

"I know this," the priest said impatiently.

"These dovin basals also communicate with passing Yuuzhan Vong ships. The passage of every ship is re-corded, and the information passed to the yammosk in scouting ships. Potentially important information is passed to the commanders, perhaps up to the warmaster himself."

The priest's eyes widened. "So the military is moni-toring all Yuuzhan Vong ships."

"It was deemed prudent, Eminence. No disrespect was intended to the priestly caste or to our shapers."

Harrar kept his opinions on this matter to himself. "This policy makes our task considerably lighter. We will proceed to Hapes."

The scent in the chamber changed subtly, indicating an imminent emergence from darkspace. The priest and the warrior settled down in secured seats for the transition.

As the priestship shuddered and slowed, a host of still-unfamiliar planets and stars streaked into existence, then settled into fixed points of light. Khalee Lah nodded in satisfaction as he noticed several bright green pinpricks in the distance. The lights traced a half circle and began to move steadily toward the priestship.

"Peace Brigade," he said, his voice edged with disdain. "Years among the infidels, and this is the sort of alliance Nom Anor secures!"

"At least they are prompt, and capable enough to meet us at the indicated place. You should take care in suggesting that the executor's decisions might prove to be mistakes."

"There are those who believe they already have," the warrior said bluntly.

Harrar suppressed a sly smile. Once the ice broke, waters flowed freely. "You seem well informed of events near Myrkr."

"Naturally the military has informants on that worldship. The shapers on Yavin Four failed to meet their objectives, and we can ill afford additional failures. Much rested upon the success of the voxyn cloning."

This was important information, things that Harrar had not known, things that it might be dangerous to know.

"I see," he murmured.

"This precaution was deemed prudent," Khalee Lah went on. "Nom Anor has fallen short more than once. Members of his crew report to me, and I, in turn, inform the warmaster."

The priest decided to test the boundaries of the young warrior's candor—and his judgment. "Name these agents."

Khalee Lah did so, without question or hesitation.

"Did it never occur to you that your unguarded response might have purchased the death of these informants?" the priest said sternly.

"There is no one in this chamber but you and me," Khalee Lah said, his scarred brow furrowed in puzzlement.

"Two or twenty, it matters not. Tsavong Lah is in an extremely precarious position. His implants have not yet healed. There are powerful shapers and more than a few priests on the verge of declaring this to be a sign of the gods' disfavor. Information is like plasma; it can bind or it can burn. The fool who dispenses it too freely makes himself a weapon that anyone—warrior, shaper, priest, Shamed One, even infidel—can use at will."

The warrior's scarred face darkened with wrath. He rose slowly, ominously, to tower over the slender priest.

"Oh, sit down!" Harrar said irritably. "I was advising you to learn discretion, not admitting to treachery!"

Khalee Lah looked uncertain. "Your devotion to the warmaster?"

"Unchanged since our shared youth," he responded.

"You evoked the gods in order to extract military information!"

"I am a priest of Yun-Harla," Harrar said with exaggerated precision. "My words were shaped to suit a desired end. That is what we do. Put your mind at ease, and pray attempt to develop some subtlety."

The warrior inclined his head respectfully, then turned toward the viewport and things more closely aligned with his understanding. Together they watched the approach of the strange ship.

Harrar observed the infidel vessel with a mixture of fascination and revulsion. Although obviously mechanical, it was built to resemble a gigantic insect. Thin metallic wings angled up from a curved, segmented body. Two pairs of limbs coiled at either side of the body like reverse-articulated legs. The rounded cockpit resembled a head, and when viewed from the side, the glossy black viewport looked like an insect's huge multiple eyes.

"I underestimated these infidels. Who would have thought them capable of such blatant insult to the gods?" Khalee Lah muttered. He lifted his voice to the priest's guards. "Secure the infidel ship and bring all those aboard to me."

A green-and-yellow-tattooed female came at his call. Like Khalee Lah, she was sheathed in living armor. Hers was a mottled green, a good match for one of the verdant worlds so plentiful in this galaxy. One day Harrar hoped to claim such a world as his own, and the armor for his personal guard was shaped with scouting in mind. Now that he knew his travels were tracked and reported, however, he would have to exercise more discretion.

Harrar's attention snapped back to the two creatures who trailed the guard. His lip curled. These were two of the most disreputable excuses for human males Harrar had yet encountered.

Both were tall and might once have been considered well formed. One had grown too thin for health, and his prominent nose was framed by fever-bright black eyes. A persistent tic of one eye and a nervous twitching of that prodigious snout lent him a remarkable similarity to a hairless rodent. The other man had an abundance of bright reddish hair that rioted in a curly mass down to his shoulders and sprouted in an equally undisciplined fashion from his cheeks and chin. His lack of discipline knew no bounds: his massive arms had gone soft, and a slack roll of belly hung over his weapons belt.

Khalee Lah made no effort to hide his disdain. "Name yourselves."

Both men performed jerky, graceless bows. "Benwick Chell," the hairy one announced. "My copilot, Vonce."

"You are members of the Peace Brigade?"

"That's right."

"Why?"

The humans blinked in unison and exchanged wary glances. "Why?" the one called Benwick echoed.

"The question is simple enough," Khalee Lah said. "What do you hope to gain from this alliance?"

"Our lives," the man said bluntly.

Khalee Lah sniffed. "A paltry reward."

"That may be," the bearded man retorted, showing the first hint of spine since his arrival, "but it's hard for a dead man to spend reward credits."

"An interesting philosophy," Harrar broke in, "but a discussion best suited to other circumstances. We require more agents in this sector. Tell us what would prompt Hapans to join forces with the Yuuzhan Vong."

"There's not much to do. Most of it's already done. You have to know a bit of our history," the man began, warming to his subject as he spoke. "Hundreds of years ago, Hapes was settled by pirates."

Khalee Lah tapped at his ear, urging the tizowyrm embedded there to produce a translation he could understand.

"I have heard of pirates," Harrar broke in. "You waylay ships and steal their cargo."

"And sometimes their passengers," the man said meaningfully. "You might say the job you want done is preprogrammed into our computers."

"You are a fool," Khalee Lah said, snarling, "and your ship is a blasphemous bug. Our quarry, pathetic though it is, would splatter you with a single swat."

The human jerked his hairy red head toward the docking bay at the priestship's stern. "The wasp ship is a scouting vessel, no more. Once we find the frigate, we'll attack in force."

"And who would command this attack?"

Benwick's chin came up. "I would."

Khalee Lah threw up his hands and stalked away. The human pursued him. "Don't think I can't. I spent the last fifteen years in the Hapan navy, six of them as a squadron commander."

The warrior spun, bringing the man up short. "Why then do you not resist our invasion?"

"Tried that," he said shortly. "It didn't work."

Harrar was beginning to see the light. "You were at Fondor."

"My squadron was destroyed—thanks to the witch

queen and her meddling Jedi friend. So we returned to our ancestral profession."

"You deserted," Khalee Lah specified.

Harrar noted the storm brewing on the young warrior's face and instinctively took a step forward.

Not fast enough.

The warrior snapped his left arm up, elbow back and fist cocked by his ear, two fingers stiffened into a living weapon. He lashed out and drove his fingers into the big man's throat. The red-bearded man's head snapped back. He staggered several paces and then fell, clutching at his strangely blocked throat and gasping for air. Khalee advanced, and his eyes promised death.

A subtle nod from Harrar brought the female warrior darting forward. Khalee Lah thrust out one hand as if to brush her aside. She seized the big warrior's wrist and twisted, breaking both his concentration and his balance. Deftly she dropped to the floor and rolled, pulling the warrior down with her. She was back on her feet more quickly than Harrar would have believed possible.

Immediately she sank to her knees. Tipping back her head, she offered Khalee Lah her throat. The warrior fisted his hand as he rose, and the spikes on his knuckles formed a short, serrated knife.

"No," Harrar said firmly, stepping between the combatants. "This warrior will not be punished for following orders."

"I command the warriors!" Khalee Lah protested.

"And you, in turn, report to me," the priest pointed out. "Is it not my right to command you both?"

"You ordered her to attack me?"

"To stop you. The human was at Fondor. He may possess useful information."

Khalee Lah inclined his head, but his eyes still burned.

"Neeka Sot is not a true warrior, but a member of an assassin sect shaped from birth for quick attack and close fighting. She did not best you in battle. Had I not stopped you, you would have killed her easily. She is also my personal bodyguard," Harrar continued. "Surely you don't think that the military are the only ones who employ checks and safeguards?"

He left the dumbfounded warrior to work his way through this revelation and turned to the human called Vonce. The man's face had turned a sickly white, and he stared at his choking comrade with horrified fascination. The twitch in his eye had accelerated until that portion of his face resembled a small animal thrashing about in death throes.

"We will have the red-bearded man revived," Harrar assured him. "Tell me what you know of Jaina Solo."

A bit of color returned to Vonce's face, and the frantic twitching slowed to a rhythmic, involuntary wink. "We'd just finished a raid and were heading to Coruscant to unload our cargo. The lot of us got caught up in the retreat. We heard a broadcast sent by Leia Organa Solo, insisting that her daughter Jaina was piloting a Yuuzhan Vong frigate."

"That is consistent with what we know," Harrar agreed. "This Solo female is also *Jeedai*?"

The man scratched his big nose thoughtfully, then shrugged. "I've heard it told. Luke Skywalker is her twin brother, so I guess maybe that's true."

"Another twin," Khalee Lah said with a snarl as he came closer to listen. "So this new Solo female can speak with Jaina Solo through *Jeedai* sorcery?"

"I couldn't tell you about that, but I saw something else that might explain how the Solo kid got her message through. The frigate flew right into the flight path of the *Falcon* like it was daring Han Solo to fire at it."

"Is every third human in this galaxy named Solo?" Khalee Lah demanded.

Vonce responded with a fleeting grin. "Seems that way sometimes. Anyway, old Han fired and the frigate rolled away like it was expecting the shot, leaving the coralskipper right behind it in the fire path. Thing of beauty," he marveled, shaking his head. "Shame about the skip, o' course," he added hastily.

"And you believe this Han Solo recognized the maneuver?"

"Looks to me like they'd rehearsed it a time or two," Vonce agreed. "And right after that, the Solo woman got on the comm and warned everyone off the frigate. Right after *that*, we got a message through the villip choir describing the frigate and demanding that all those in the immediate area help the Yuuzhan Vong capture it. So I figure that Leia Solo was telling the truth."

"And what did you do then?"

"We fired a few shots at the frigate, at the underside like they told us. The ship dodged every vaping shot," he said wonderingly. "I've seen better pilots than the Solo girl, but not many."

Harrar glanced at Khalee Lah. As he expected, the warrior looked deeply disturbed by this testimony to the *Jeedai* twin's skills and cunning.

"You will be suitably rewarded," the priest told him.

He sent a meaningful look toward Neeka Sot. The warrior darted forward and leapt into the air. She landed on Vonce's shoulders, her armored thighs clamped tightly against his neck.

The weight of her bore him down to his knees. Neeka Sot rode him to the floor. Her left boot touched down lightly, and she pivoted hard to that side. Vonce's neck broke with an audible crackle as he fell. The warrior kept going, moving smoothly, not missing a step as she stalked toward the choking man.

By now Benwick's face was taking on a purple hue. Neeka Sot kicked his hands away from his throat and pressed her boot against the side of his neck. When she stepped back, the man dragged in air in a long, ragged gasp.

The female stooped and seized a handful of Benwick's curly red hair. She dragged him up onto his knees and held him upright by his hair.

Still holding her grip, Neeka Sot circled around to face the human. She jerked his head to one side, and then nodded to the priest.

Harrar took a tiny box from the folds of his head cloth. In it was a bright green creature. He tipped the box and spilled the small servant into the human's ear.

For several moments Benwick's shrieks of protest filled the chamber. Harrar held his patience with difficulty. Humans were ridiculously reticent to join with helpful creatures, regarding the sovereignty of their pitifully inadequate bodies as a higher good than greater strength and efficiency.

Benwick struggled and protested as if his opinions might actually make some difference. Finally the process was complete, and the human struggled to his feet.

He clutched his ear and glared at his comrade's body. "This is your idea of a reward?"

"We will be able to communicate with you more directly and efficiently," Harrar said. "With this advantage, you will be more likely to capture Jaina Solo than any of your fellow pirates. Now go. Neeka Sot would be most displeased if she thought that my gift was unappreciated."

The red-haired man sent a look of pure venom at the female warrior, but his bow to Harrar and Khalee Lah was acceptably respectful. He turned and strode down the corridor.

Neeka Sot bowed to Harrar and then dropped to one knee before Khalee Lah. Somewhat mollified by this show of respect, he gestured for her to rise and depart.

The priest turned to study the young warrior. "Your

convictions are as strong as the armor you wear, but not nearly as flexible. You are troubled when your notions are disrupted," he noted. "But mark well what we have learned here. Jaina Solo may prove a more formidable adversary than we expected."

"She is an infidel!"

"And we are not," the priest said pointedly. "Because of our devotion, we should understand how powerful and potent a trickster can be."

The warrior's gaze snapped to Harrar's face. "Surely you do not equate this human with Yun-Harla!"

"That would be blasphemy," the priest agreed. "I am merely reminding you that Yun-Harla teaches us that all is never quite as it seems. As befits a Trickster, the goddess sends her lessons when they are least expected, and in the most unlikely of circumstances."

As Harrar spoke, a shiver of premonition tingled through him. Fortunately the warrior seemed not to notice his unease.

"Unlikely indeed!" Khalee Lah agreed. "Nevertheless, only fools underestimate their enemies."

He bowed and strode from the chamber, leaving Harrar to contemplate the heresy he had just denied.

It was whispered that the *Jeedai* had more in common with the Yuuzhan Vong gods than the warrior caste wished to admit. Rumors spoke softly of a heresy that originated on Yavin 4, where some of the Shamed Ones looked to the *Jeedai* for deliverance.

Harrar wandered over to the viewport and gazed with unseeing eyes at the stars beyond, at the countless worlds awaiting shape and purity. He considered his words to Khalee Lah, and measured his own devotion to the goddess against the warrior's unwavering faith. And he wondered, as he often did, how one could worship without reservation a goddess who could never be trusted.

A lifetime of travel had spawned in him the longing for a homeworld. Perhaps a little heresy would bring another note of constancy to his life. And after all these many years as a priest, it might be a great relief to be able to believe in *something*.

EIGHT

The lights on the pilot console of the *Millennium Falcon* blinked sporadically, like the solar glowsign on a low-rent cantina after a few days of cloudy weather. Han Solo scowled at the controls, then balled his fist and slammed a much-dented section of the console. The sensors flickered back to life. He sent a sidelong glance and a smug little smile toward his copilot.

Leia shook her head, her brown eyes fixed on a small screen. "No good. The readouts from Artoo show we need more sophisticated repairs. And soon."

He leaned over and studied the technical data. "Yeah," he admitted after a few moments. "The problem is finding a quiet place."

"The Hapes Cluster," she suggested evenly, raising her eyes to her husband's face.

His eyes went cautious. "Last I heard, the Hapans weren't real fond of visitors."

"True enough. Not long ago, though, Teneniel Djo sent a message to the senate suggesting that she might open Hapes to refugees. I understand your hesitation," Leia said, referring to their unorthodox courtship and Han's residual distrust for his former rival, Isolder, now Teneniel Djo's husband. "But I made my choice, and so far, I haven't regretted it. Too much."

She didn't mention her last encounter with the former queen mother of Hapes, Prince Isolder's mother, Ta'a

Chume. She had made a point of mentioning her son's marital troubles, and her wish that Isolder had chosen Princess Leia as his wife rather than Teneniel Djo, a warrior woman from remote Dathomir. Leia knew how manipulative Ta'a Chume could be, and she certainly didn't want to add to a volatile situation. But at the moment, other considerations superseded these concerns.

"Tenel Ka was a member of the Jedi strike force," Leia reminded him. "That makes it possible, and perhaps likely, that Jaina will put the Yuuzhan Vong ship down on Hapes."

Han's eyes lit up. "Makes sense. She's a sensible kid, so you're probably right." The matter settled to his satisfaction, he began setting course for the Hapes Cluster.

"Should we get Luke and Mara's opinion?"

"When it's their ship we're flying, sure." He smiled briefly to take any possible sting from the words, then plotted their course and prepared for hyperspace.

When the jump was completed, he added, "Face it, they're not going to care where we put down. They'll only be onworld long enough for Mara to buy, beg, or steal a ship to take them wherever Lando took Ben."

"True enough," Leia agreed. She closed her eyes against the threat of sudden tears, and tried not to envy her brother and his wife their coming reunion with their son.

There would be no reunion with her baby, her Anakin. She wouldn't even have the grim comfort of seeing his body, of honoring the man he'd become with the solemn rites of a Jedi funeral.

Han reached over and placed one hand over hers. "I love you, you know. You're holding up great," he said quietly. "You're holding us both up."

She opened her eyes and turned toward her husband. "That's not true. You're the only reason I'm not curled up in a fetal position."

"That's not true, either. You're a fighter, always have been. You took one hell of a punch, but you got your feet back under you." He unconsciously rubbed his jaw as the metaphor triggered countless memories. "Hurts though, doesn't it?"

"Only when I breathe."

He lowered his head, nodded. The grief was always there, a wound open to every touch, every breeze. After a few moments, he suggested that they both try to get some rest.

"I couldn't possibly sleep," Leia said, but even as she spoke the words she realized how heavy her eyelids had become. The past day had spanned too many hours, held too many battles, brought too much grief. The weight of it all dragged Leia down into the copilot's seat and a troubled sleep.

She awoke suddenly as the old ship jolted and shook back into sublight speed. She glanced over at Han, and froze in midstretch.

He was hunkered down over the controls, his face grim as he struggled with the ship. Several large, dark objects loomed ahead.

Leia sat bolt upright. "Asteroid field?"

A burst of laserfire came from the belly guns as Luke and Mara responded to the threat. The bright lines streamed unerringly toward their targets—and then simply disappeared.

Leia caught her breath, let it out on a sigh. "I'll take that as a no."

"Dovin basal mines," Han said tersely. The *Falcon* finally slowed to maneuverable speed, and the scene beyond sharpened into focus. Dozens of large, rocklike objects, each shaped like the heart of some giant creature, floated in space—black holes against the bright backdrop of stars.

Han deftly maneuvered through the field of living asteroids. When they were clear, he glanced at the navigational controls. "Those things pulled us out of hyperspace. Must work like an interdiction field."

Leia was already at work finding their new coordinates and resetting the hyperspace jump. "How many times can the *Falcon* get yanked out like that before she falls apart?"

He shrugged. "Five or six."

"Which is it?" she demanded. "Five or six?"

He glanced at Leia, and his expression instantly turned sober. "You're serious."

She grimaced and reached for the controls. "I like to start with the worst-case scenario and work down."

They were pulled from hyperspace twice more before emerging in the Transitory Mists, an eerie cloud surrounding the Hapes system. "That wasn't so bad," Han observed as they left the Mists behind. "Didn't even slow us down much."

"It makes you wonder why they bother," Leia mused. "Unless . . ."

Han glanced at her sharply. "Unless those things have a way of recording what went by. The Vong could be tracking movement. Chances are, they know we're here."

"And them, as well," she replied, nodding to the scene stretched out before them.

The *Falcon* limped into a space lane nearly as busy as those surrounding Coruscant. Ships of all shapes and sizes streamed toward the ports of the royal city of Hapes, passing through a lane defined by two Hapan Battle Dragons. Several smaller ships buzzed here and there, cutting off the occasional vessel that tried to bypass the security point.

"Corellian freighter," Han noted, nodding toward a large cargo ship. "That one over there is a Republic diplomatic vessel. Chances are we'll see a lot of familiar faces on Hapes."

Leia just shook her head, both stunned and aghast at the scene before her. The time she'd spent shepherding refugees from one world to another had taught her some grim facts. The Yuuzhan Vong did not respect refugee sites; in fact, they targeted worlds that offered a haven to people displaced by war. Given Hapes's reclusive history, and the recent devastation of its fleet, this new course seemed not only strange, but suicidal. There was no way the decimated Hapan fleet could hold off even a minor Yuuzhan Vong attack.

"How long do you think it will take to complete repairs on the *Falcon*?" she asked.

"Hard to say. Why?"

She turned troubled eyes to his face. "Whether Teneniel Djo realizes it or not, she's made Hapes the next target for the Yuuzhan Vong."

"That base-born rycrit will be the last of the queen mothers, and the death of us all!" Ta'a Chume fumed as she paced the priceless mosaic covering the floor of her chamber.

A comely young man reclined on a settee, watching the tall, red-veiled woman with a mixture of concern and resignation.

To his way of thinking, Ta'a Chume was difficult to please and dangerous to cross, but she was also exceedingly powerful, and wealthy, and indulgent toward her favorites. No one could deny that the former queen mother was getting on in years, but she was still remarkably beautiful—straight and shapely, with elegant facial bones that defied the slackness and softening of age, and abundant red-gold hair only slightly silvered by time. All things considered, Trisdin was quite content with his lot.

"Teneniel Djo has ruled for nearly twenty years, despite her obvious limitations," he pointed out. "Surely that proves the strength and security of the royal house."

Ta'a Chume shot a venomous glare at her favorite. "You go among the common folk. What are they saying of Prince Isolder?"

His throat suddenly went dry. "He is greatly loved by his people—"

She cut him off with an impatient, imperious gesture. "Don't insult me with placating lies! My son committed a large Consortium fleet to the battle that destroyed it. Since the disaster at Fondor, there have been no fewer than seven attempts on his life. Some of them from members of the royal family!"

Most of them initiated by Alyssia, niece to Ta'a Chume and strikingly like her in appearance and temperament. Trisdin liked to think of the two women as morning and evening, and whenever possible, he divided his time accordingly.

"Where is the prince now?" he asked as casually as he could. "In safety, I would hope?"

Ta'a Chume stopped pacing and fixed a speculative look at the young man. "I persuaded him to go off-world."

"That must have been difficult. The prince is not one to run from trouble."

"To the contrary; he inevitably runs toward it! But even Isolder is capable of learning. Fondor proved that taking action before gathering adequate information can prove fatal. It was not difficult to convince him of the value of a fact-finding mission. He knows how vulnerable Hapes now is, and he wishes to learn as much about the invaders as possible. Thanks to Teneniel Djo, he'll soon have opportunity to test this knowledge!"

"I don't see why he allowed Teneniel Djo to open Hapes to refugees."

The woman's eyes flamed above her veil. "He has no right to gainsay her, and no power to do so. She is the queen mother."

"And as such, she should be honored . . . for as long as she can manage to hold the throne," Trisdin said, understanding his role. Ta'a Chume hated her daughter-in-law, but she was protective of the title and its power. She might wish to see the younger woman dead—she might even arrange it—but she would hear no slight upon the royal office.

Trisdin unfolded his long limbs and strolled over to Ta'a Chume. He stood behind her and began to massage her shoulders with practiced skill. "So many burdens," he crooned. "The Yuuzhan Vong, the debacle at Fondor, the issue of succession." Ta'a Chume went tense beneath his hands. "That has not yet been resolved?"

"No," she said shortly.

His arms came around her. "It's a pity your royal consort was only capable of fathering sons. What a queen any daughter of yours might make! Indeed, you are still young . . ."

Her mocking laughter cut him short. "Ambitious, aren't you? I've no desire to take another royal consort, and while you may flatter me all you wish, please keep your praise within the bounds of possibility!"

Trisdin shrugged this off. "It's a shame that Isolder's daughter favors her mother's culture."

"Culture!" Ta'a Chume echoed derisively. "You do the Dathomiri witch too much honor. Still, Tenel Ka is capable enough."

"But she has no sense of duty! She refuses to serve Hapes, as you have done—and continue to do."

Ta'a Chume resumed her pacing. "The issue of royal succession has become a point of contention between my son and his wife. Isolder grows ever more traditional, and he wants his daughter to reign, as is right and proper. Teneniel Djo insists that Tenel Ka remain free to choose her own path."

"At least Teneniel Djo was willing to bear another child."

"Willing? She insisted upon another child! And that has created another problem. My son is proud, and he knows full well the attitude of Dathomir's Witches toward males. Teneniel Djo and her ilk treat men as little more than slaves and breeding stock!"

It occurred to Trisdin to wonder how this differed substantially from the Hapan matriarchal view, but he quickly squelched an impulse he knew to be suicidal.

"No doubt Isolder's frustration led him to commit the Consortium to battle. I would not be surprised if the resulting failure left him more sensitive to perceived slights and insults than he otherwise would be. Perhaps the trouble between the prince and his queen will pass as his wounded pride heals."

"Unlikely," the former queen said darkly. "Isolder respects women of strength. What can he appreciate in a barbarian like Teneniel Djo? How can he willingly accept a subordinate role to someone so obviously unworthy?"

"Then the solution is to find him a worthy queen."

These words were treason, punishable by swift and certain death, but Ta'a Chume merely nodded.

"Therein lies the problem," she mused. "War is coming. There is no avoiding it now. We need a woman with ruthless intelligence, someone experienced in leadership."

"You alone fit that description."

She shook her head. "Once a queen mother has abdicated in favor of a successor, it is exceedingly difficult to take back power. The people need a warrior queen, and Teneniel Djo, for all her faults, fills that image."

"So does Princess Leia," he observed, suspecting where her thoughts might be headed.

"Leia has the breeding, the training, and the experience," Ta'a Chume agreed, "but she is more diplomat than warrior. And quite frankly, a new set of marital problems would inevitably arise. My son would swiftly come to resent her. She is simply too much woman for him."

And perhaps, Trisdin thought, *too much for Ta'a Chume as well!* The former queen's resentment of Teneniel Djo came in large part from the younger woman's refusal to be advised, much less controlled.

"You obviously would not wish to see a weak woman on the throne of Hapes," Trisdin observed. "But Isolder might be more content with a very young woman. No matter how competent she otherwise might be, he is more likely to feel himself in control of the situation. Naturally, a young queen would require advice from a wise and experienced mentor, and a woman of sense would not look to her husband for council."

Ta'a Chume stared at him for several moments. Her eyes crinkled, giving evidence to the smile spreading beneath her veil.

"I was not granted a daughter of my blood, but you're saying that perhaps I might yet train a successor, and mold a promising young woman into my own image."

"And keep Isolder happy and out of the way while you're doing it."

Laughter bubbled up from behind the crimson veil. "Trisdin, you are priceless! Now go and prepare yourself for the evening festivities."

He sauntered off, well pleased with himself. Ta'a Chume's smile held until the door shut behind her current favorite. Then she walked to the settee and sank down with a deep and troubled sigh.

There were more storms brewing across Hapes than Trisdin knew or could begin to imagine. Though not technically in power, Ta'a Chume had her resources, and forces loyal to her. One of these factions, a large and powerful group started by her mother before her, was anti-Jedi at heart and becoming more virulently so by the day. Matters were coming to the point that she had to re-ward them or risk losing their support. She could not risk such a loss—they were too powerful for her to allow them to take their strength elsewhere. This faction must either be placated or destroyed.

And although murderous attempts on the royal family were certainly nothing new, Ta'a Chume was growing burdened by the level of paranoia required to keep her-self and her household alive.

Teneniel Djo was doing nothing to help. This trouble-some Force had carried shockwaves from the Fondor debacle, causing Teneniel to lose her long-awaited, un-born second child. This was not yet known outside the palace; Ta'a Chume had kept it quiet under the guise of giving her daughter-in-law time to heal and grieve before making the announcement.

In truth, Ta'a Chume viewed such grief as a self-indulgent weakness, a luxury that Hapes could not af-ford. She had endured Teneniel Djo this long simply because the alternative—a coup by one of her nieces—was even less desirable. Alyssia was a venal little wretch, but she was also a practical woman. Her first act as queen mother would be to destroy Ta'a Chume and her descendants. Of this, Ta'a Chume was certain, for that was exactly the course she herself would take.

But Trisdin's suggestion offered new possibilities. With a curt nod, Ta'a Chume sealed the fate of her son, his wife, and all of Hapes.

Now all that remained was to find a promising young woman of whom Isolder might approve, and the lamen-table Teneniel Djo would go.

NINE

Jaina came awake suddenly, though no sound disturbed her trancelike state. She sat up, senses alert for whatever had roused her.

But the ship was quiet, eerily so. For someone accustomed to the hum and roar of engines, the silence of the Yuuzhan Vong frigate was disconcerting. Jaina wasn't sure exactly why she'd expected anything different; after all, what sound did gravity make when it bent? Would a black hole make a giant slurping noise whenever a dovin basal sucked up a proton torpedo?

She rubbed the nape of her neck with one hand and then stretched, drawing in a long breath. And realized why she'd awoken.

A faint, sharp odor filled the air, a scent she couldn't equate with any other she knew. Jaina pushed herself off the coral bench and hurried to the cockpit.

Starlines spun into view as the ship came out of its hyperspace flight. The odd scent must have been some sort of sensor.

The stars focused into sharp points, but faint lines remained—starlight refracted from some metallic, as-yet-unseen object.

In the pilot's seat, Zekk sat bolt upright, leaning toward the viewport. "Incoming!" he snapped.

Jaina spun toward the pilot's seat and leaned down to peer over Zekk's shoulder. A motley collection of ships—

some of them Hapan vessels, some more suited to pirates and smugglers—sped purposefully toward them.

Ganner slipped into the gunner's chair, his handsome face grim at the prospect of firing upon allies.

Zekk touched his hooded head to Jaina's. "You want to take this?"

"I'm going back to the escape pod. Unless Tenel Ka gets to Hapes, this could be the first party of many. Ganner, no matter what, you've got to protect her. That comes first."

"I know my job," he said.

Jaina gave his shoulder a brief squeeze to show that she understood his dilemma, then she hurried to the stern of the frigate. Tenel Ka was lowering herself into the black, seed-shaped escape pod, listening intently to Tahiri's swift-flowing advice. Tesar, Alema, and Tekli stood by.

The blond girl glanced up at Jaina's approach. She straightened and backed away.

"You're the closest thing we've got to an expert," Jaina reminded her. "This is no time to defer. Report?"

Tahiri grimaced and shrugged. "She's as ready as she'll ever be. I'd rather go myself, but it's her world."

"Tenel Ka?"

The warrior confirmed readiness with a somber nod.

"No lights," Jaina reminded, nodding toward the fluorescent, lichenlike life-forms gathered in small colonies inside the escape pod. "Head for the outskirts of the royal city. It's been two standard hours since sunset, so you've got at least a shot at secrecy. Get down as fast as you can, as close to the city as you can without drawing attention. We'll keep them busy and give you as much time as possible."

Tenel Ka looked to Tahiri. The young Jedi helped the one-armed woman pull the cognition hood over her head. Tahiri stepped back. The pod's opening irised shut, and the small vessel rose slightly from the floor.

The Jedi backed away. A door closed between them and the pod, and an exterior portal opened. The escape pod sped silently out into the dark vacuum.

Jaina headed for the cockpit, but came up short when Tahiri stepped into her path. The blond girl looked fragile but resolute.

"What can I do?"

"Go find Lowbacca," Jaina suggested. "He's still working on the tracking system. You know the Yuuzhan Vong language better than any of us. Maybe the ship will be more talkative if it's got a good listener."

Color drained from the young Jedi's face, but without hesitation she took off in search of the Wookiee.

Jaina understood Tahiri's fear, and respected the girl's refusal to pamper it. Anakin had told her a few things about Tahiri's rescue from Yavin 4. They'd stolen a ship, and the cognition hood had attempted to bypass Tahiri's true identity to pierce the "memories" the shapers had implanted.

Interesting, she mused.

The frigate shuddered and pitched as Hapan missiles bombarded it. Jaina staggered through the corridor, bouncing from one wall to the other as the ship rolled and jinked.

She struggled to the cockpit and ripped the pilot's hood from Zekk's head. "You said I was doing just fine," he said, showing a flash of wry humor.

"Obviously, I lied," she replied in kind as she tugged the controls over her own head.

He quickly yielded the seat, but continued to gaze anxiously at the viewport as Jaina settled in.

The ship's sensors flooded her with information, none of it good.

"Hyperdrive's out," she announced as she spun the ship

in an evasive maneuver. "Dovin basal is about played out. Looks like we get to choose between shielding and running."

"Run," Alema suggested.

Jaina did her best, dodging through an ever-shifting minefield of strobing lasers and proton torpedoes. Doggedly she led their attackers away from Hapes, away from Tenel Ka.

Alema let out a sigh of relief. "You're losing them! Good work."

Jaina surveyed the skies behind, using the sweeping peripheral vision granted by the hood. The distance between the Yuuzhan Vong ship and its attackers was steadily growing. But they kept firing, though they were well out of range. Jaina noticed the subtle shift in their vector, and traced their new path to a small black dot—a ship so small that it would be imperceptible had it not been backlit by killing lights.

"Hutt slime! They found Tenel Ka," Jaina said. She threw the ship into a tight turn and hurtled back into the fight.

"Looks like she's picked up a swarm of Hornet Interceptors," Ganner said. "Get me in closer. I can kill them from here, but not disable them."

A concussion missile sped toward the ship. Ganner sent a burst of plasma out to intercept it, and Jaina jinked sharply to avoid the resulting explosion.

"The Hapan pilots don't seem to share your concern," she shot back.

The older Jedi sent her an incredulous glance. "So what are you saying?"

Jaina hurtled past a pair of Hapan ships, which also changed course and continued pursuit. "If you want to talk, fine, but yield the chair to someone who wants to shoot!"

"Just line them up and hold steady," he said.

She brought the frigate around in a rising loop, then dived down between the two pursuing ships. A flurry of laserfire kept the dovin basal busy, but Jaina held a steady course to allow Ganner a clean shot.

Twice he fired, clipping the pursuing ships with plasma bolts. One of the Hornets exploded into shards of metal; another managed to evade the shot. But the flying debris ripped through the thin metal of the third ship's wings, sending it into an out-of-control spiral.

A surge of dismay came from Ganner, and his next shot went deliberately wide.

"We're under attack," Jaina reminded him.

"I might have hit that ship!"

"Sure, if it was the size of a battle cruiser! If you're not going to hit them, at least give them an argument."

The older Jedi turned away, his jaw clenched and his thoughts carefully shielded.

Meanwhile the Hapan ships continued to batter the Yuuzhan Vong vessel. Tesar did his best with the shields, but the shots were too many and too close. Again and again the ship shook as laserfire chipped at its hull. Worse, Jaina sensed that the overburdened dovin basal was nearing the limit of its strength. The escape pod soared off into the darkness, and none of the Hapan ships followed.

Now that Tenel Ka was safe, Jaina swung around and poured all the energy the ship could muster into an apparent retreat. The Hapan ships gave pursuit for several moments, then abandoned the effort.

"They're off to spread the word about us," Alema said somberly.

The Twi'lek pointed to the viewport. Beyond, tumbling slowly amid a drift of metallic debris, was one of the ships Ganner had accidentally destroyed. The Hornet was largely intact—only the rear segment of its insectoid body was missing.

"If we're going to salvage that ship for parts, we haven't much time."

"The comm system! Good thinking," Jaina agreed.

She turned back toward the battle scene. After a couple of experiments, Tesar managed to calibrate the dovin basal to use just enough gravity to pull in the damaged ship.

The ship was unpiloted—perhaps the pilot had had time to go EV. But the controls looked to be intact, and Lowbacca acted positively cheerful at the prospect of working with circuits and metal.

It didn't take him long to find what they needed. Bellowing triumphantly, he strode into the cockpit, lugging the disembodied comm unit and an attached power pack. He set the device on the floor, set hailing frequency, and handed the speaking unit to Jaina.

"This is Lieutenant Jaina Solo, a Rogue Squadron pilot, flying a commandeered enemy frigate. Come in."

She repeated her hail several times before an answering crackle came over the comm. "I never thought that static could sound so good," she murmured.

"This is Hesha Lovett, captain of the Hapan royal vessel," a female voice announced. "We've had reports of a Yuuzhan Vong ship. Yours, Lieutenant Solo?"

"I don't like to brag," Jaina said dryly. "We're seeking permission to land. The sooner we get out of this thing, the happier we'll be."

There was a moment's silence, then the comm crackled to life again. "By all means, Jaina. All of Tenel Ka's friends are welcome on Hapes, however they may choose to arrive."

Jaina jolted with surprise. The resonant, cultured voice with the crisply clipped accent was unmistakably that of Ta'a Chume, Tenel Ka's grandmother.

She quickly scoured her mental database for the proper way to address Hapan royalty. "Thank you,

Queen Mother. I wasn't sure we'd find a welcome. We were forced to fire upon Hapan ships."

"Hornet Interceptors," the woman said dismissively. "Pirates, most likely. The scouts who witnessed the battle were nearly as displeased by their presence as they were by yours. Is my granddaughter with you?"

Actually, Jaina was hoping that she'd been picked up by the Hapan scouts. "Well, not exactly. She went ahead in an escape pod to prepare the way for us. We didn't have any other way to communicate until we pulled in one of the Hornets and salvaged its comm."

"I will alert all patrols to watch for my granddaughter's arrival. By all means, land at the royal docks and come directly to the palace. I'll make sure the officials are expecting you, and that they do not try to channel you through the refugee camps."

"Refugees?"

"Yes," the former queen said, expressing a considerable amount of distaste with a single word. "You will be my guests, however, you and your friends. I will meet you at the palace."

It occurred to Jaina that the former queen mother seemed surprisingly, perhaps suspiciously, eager for their arrival.

Her first impulse was to ask why. A childhood spent under the tutelage of a fussy protocol droid, however, was not easily dismissed. Leia Organa Solo's daughter exchanged a few moments of proper small talk with Ta'a Chume, speaking as carefully and listening as intently as she'd observed her mother do over the years. But Ta'a Chume was no less skilled, and when the communication ended, Jaina had to admit it was a draw.

She slumped back in the pilot chair. "Ta'a Chume is up to something."

"How do you know?" Ganner asked.

She lifted one shoulder in a shrug. "She always is."

A joyful Wookiee bellow split the air. Lowbacca came whirling into the cockpit, spinning Tahiri in some sort of exuberant dance. He set her down and swept one paw toward the navibrain in a dramatic gesture.

"We did it," Tahiri said obligingly, but without spirit. "You found Tenel Ka?"

Lowbacca grinned and slipped into the navigator's chair. He yanked the hood down over his head, and his massive shoulders hunched in anticipation. Moments passed, and Jaina could sense his surge of anxiety through the Force.

Using the cognition hood, she switched her focus to navigation. The answers that came to her yielded a faint mental picture, a shadow of what Lowbacca must have been seeing.

"The escape pod is moving away from Hapes!" she said. "Either she's off course, or someone picked her up."

The Wookiee moaned an agreement, then began to set course for pursuit.

Tenel Ka felt the sudden jolt of contact, heard the scrape of grappling hooks finding purchase on the irregular coral hull. The moment of capture unleashed a flood of raw, recent memory. Pain and loss and fury—all the emotions engendered by her days in Yuuzhan Vong captivity—flooded the Jedi in a torrent.

She heard a mechanical whir and realized its meaning. Small drills busily bolted the ship to the grappling arms to ensure retrieval. No Yuuzhan Vong would sully their hands with such machines.

Reassured, she removed the cognition hood and smoothed her warrior's braids into place as best she could.

Now that the burden of flying the pod was lifted from her, Tenel Ka eased the shields she'd placed between herself and the tiny living ship. Fiercely independent, she used the Force only when necessary. To her way of thinking, maintaining some distance between herself and the Yuuzhan Vong or any of their creatures was absolutely essential.

Suddenly her unshielded mind flooded with a familiar mixture of warmth and humor, friendship and frustration.

"Jacen," she said wonderingly, recognizing the presence that meant more to her than any other.

For a moment Tenel Ka knew complete happiness, something she had deemed illusive since the day she'd realized that when Jacen looked upon her, he saw only an old friend. But happiness was a gift as fleeting as it was sweet. The light that was Jacen faltered, then blazed up into an agonizing white heat.

Tenel Ka, despite her stoic courage and superb conditioning, shrieked in rage and pain.

Her reserve shattered, and a lifetime of emotions carefully controlled and shielded erupted like a Dathomir volcano. Mindlessly she thrashed at the walls of her prison, pounding the coral with her one fist, determined to get out, to reach Jacen, to fight and die to free him.

Then the light was gone, and its absence was a blow more devastating than the first.

For a long moment Tenel Ka sat in the sudden darkness, stunned and silent. Her lips moved, shaping words of denial that she could not force past the unfamiliar lump in her throat.

The escape pod jolted heavily against the ship. Cutting tools hummed as they dug through the coral shell. Tenel Ka wearily regarded the discarded cognition hood. If she put it back on, she could open the hull with a thought. Her emotions were so raw that she could not bear the thought of joining with the ship.

A crack fissured through the pod, and a chunk of coral

tumbled into Tenel Ka's lap. She pushed it aside and un-clipped her lightsaber from her belt.

"Stand aside," she ordered, marveling at how cool and controlled her voice sounded.

A rich, glowing turquoise light leapt from Tenel Ka's lightsaber. She made short work of cutting through the hull and then rose quickly, her weapon held unthreaten-ingly low but ready, just in case.

At least a dozen people gathered around the pod, all of them human, all of them recognizably Hapan. Tenel Ka's long-ago ancestors had been pirates who vied with each other to find and capture the most beautiful mates pos-sible. What started as a peculiar measure of cultural status became a sort of selective breeding. In general, the people of Hapes were taller and more attractive than in-habitants of other worlds in the Hapes Cluster. All of her rescuers were tall and fair, though some looked decidedly the worse for wear.

They stood silent, perhaps from the surprise of finding a Jedi warrior instead of the expected Yuuzhan Vong. Tenel Ka's cool gray eyes swept over them.

Several of the crew wore crimson, which proclaimed them members of the royal guard. She noted several hard-knock civilians, too, all of them wearing worn or faded red clothing. Even those who sported the white uniform of the Consortium Navy had some bit of red about them, even if just an enameled pendant or a ban-danna. This ersatz statement of solidarity set off warning sensors in the back of her mind.

"What is this ship?" she demanded.

One of the men, a tall blond man who bore a faint re-semblance to her father, gave her a mocking bow. "Wel-come to the *Starsprite*, Princess. You're aboard a Beta Cruiser, formerly of the Hapan navy."

Tenel Ka's eyes narrowed as she took this in. The Beta Cruiser was a small battleship, far more maneuverable than the much-larger Hapes *Nova*-class cruisers. They'd been employed in large numbers at Fondor. Few had survived. Most likely the crew of this one was a diverse company of survivors: deserters from the Battle of Fondor as well as smugglers who saw their livelihood being swallowed by the Yuuzhan Vong invasion.

She wasn't surprised at his greeting. Not many Hapans would fail to recognize a one-armed Jedi with red-gold hair as their reluctant princess. Since they were pirates and deserters—not exactly men and women of honor—Tenel Ka assumed they planned to ransom her for the best deal they could get. But even as this thought formed, it was pushed aside by the animosity that radiated from them all.

Understanding flooded her in a quick, scalding rush. "You are Ni'Korish," she snarled, naming the faction inspired by her great-grandmother, a queen mother who hated the Jedi and had done her best to eradicate them. "I heard rumors of an attempted coup, an attack by cowards who lurk in shadows. That would be you?"

Her captor responded with a mocking bow.

"Tell me, how did the Ni'Korish fare? Is my mother yet alive?" she demanded.

"Regrettably, yes," the leader returned. "But she won't hold the throne for long."

Tenel Ka sent him a grim smile. "You do her an injustice if you think she will abdicate in exchange for my return, and you insult me if you suggest I would buy my freedom at that price."

He returned her smile, but his was even harder and held a reptilian leer. "We would never insult the queen mother or her Jedi daughter. The Yuuzhan Vong, however, are not so concerned with matters of honor and protocol."

His meaning was clear. Tenel Ka's lightsaber snapped up to guard position. "I will not be taken."

"Princess, you wound me!" he protested, placing one

hand over his heart. "We will return you to Hapes un-
harmed. Although we might be deserters, we are not traitors. All we require is your assistance in hunting down
Jacen and Jaina Solo. If you're a true princess of Hapes,
you'll gladly help us repay those who turned Centerpoint
upon the Hapan fleet."

A surge of wrath boiled through Tenel Ka, but she
kept her composure. "Do you know what befell a New
Republic ambassador who fell into Yuuzhan Vong hands?
He was slain, his bones decorated with gems and gold
and sent back to his friends. I would not deliver an
enemy to such a fate, and never a friend!"

His expression darkened, and he glanced at a knot of
uniformed men. "Then I'm afraid we'll have to make do
with you. If Jaina Solo thinks the same way you do, she
might be willing to trade herself for your freedom."

"She won't get the chance."

Before any of the Hapans could draw weapons, Tenel
Ka's turquoise blade leapt toward them like a proton
torpedo.

For a moment everyone in the cargo hold scuttled
back, intimidated by the wrath in the Jedi's gray eyes and
the blazing weapon in her hand.

Then the Ni'Korish leader pulled a vibroblade from
his belt, and others remembered that they, too, held
weapons.

They advanced, quickly encircling Tenel Ka.

TEN

The stolen Yuuzhan Vong ship careened through space at full power, following the barely perceptible signal emitted by the escape pod. Zekk sat at the helm. Tahiri wore the navigation hood, directing him according to information flowing to her from the navibrain. The small hands gripping the control were white-knuckled, but her voice remained steady and sure.

Jaina and Lowbacca huddled together away from the others. "You and Tahiri did great, but I've got another puzzle for you," Jaina said. "Danni Quee found a way to override the yammosk communications. That's the only explanation for the Yuuzhan Vong confusion over Coruscant. Any idea how she did it?"

The Wookiee went into a lengthy explanation, most of which went over Jaina's head with a meter to spare.

She put up a hand to halt the bewildering flow of information. "How do you *know* all this?"

Lowbacca hesitated, then woofed a response.

He had been recruited to work on the research team supervised by Danni Quee and Cilghal. That made sense to Jaina. The Force-sensitive scientist and the Mon Calamari healer had been spearheading one of many attempts to understand Yuuzhan Vong technology. Before coming to the Jedi academy, Lowbacca had had two passions: computer science and the study of Kashyyyk's complex plant life. It had been the latter that prompted him to go alone into the dangerous lower levels of his home-world's forests during his rite of passage to young adult-hood, and to pit himself against the deadly syren plant. The combination of computer skills and biological knowledge—not to mention his desire to take on the impossible—made him well suited to this study.

Lowbacca let loose a few sharp woofs.

"They had you taking apart captured ships? No wonder you knew how to mess with the worldship," Jaina mur-mured, remembering a prank he had played with a small neural center. "So you know how Danni Quee scrambled the yammosk."

The Wookiee shook his head and gave a mournful moan. He hadn't been there for Danni's breakthrough.

"Given your background, could you duplicate the results?"

Lowbacca considered, then woofed an affirmative.

"But can you go one step farther?"

The Wookiee listened with growing fascination as Jaina described her plan. His furry shoulders shook with laughter as he made his way toward the dovin basal.

Jaina watched, puzzled. Lowbacca returned in mo-ments, coming at a lope and carrying a familiar-looking object in his paws.

He handed a small globe to Jaina with a string of grumbled instructions. A slow, sly grin crept over her face as she understood what he'd found. She reached up and ruffled the fur on his head affectionately, and then went back to work.

"Is that what I think it is?" Ganner demanded, eyeing the villip with disgust.

She grinned at the older Jedi and turned to Zekk. "Let me have your seat."

He yielded the pilot's chair, and Jaina settled down, pulled on the hood, and began to stroke the oddly shaped globe.

"Are you sure that's a good idea?" Zekk ventured. "Can you talk and fly at the same time?"

Her only response was a derisive sniff.

"We don't know who will answer," he persisted.

"True, but chances are, that'll be something worth knowing. The more we can learn about this ship, the better our chances for survival."

The outer layer of the villip peeled back, and the tissue within began to reshape itself into the likeness of the Yuuzhan Vong who had been "attuned" to this villip. In moments Jaina held in her hands a horrific face, one marked by fringed lips and a tangle of scars.

She knew that face. Everyone in the galaxy with access to the HoloNet knew it. This was the warmaster Tsavong Lah. Not long ago, he'd sent a communication throughout the galaxy calling for the destruction of the Jedi, and demanding Jacen Solo. Jaina had seen that holovid replayed many times, but her blood boiled anew with each viewing.

"The sacrifice has been completed?" the warmaster demanded.

Jaina held the villip closer to her face and sent her brother's enemy a knife-edged smile. "Not yet."

The villip crinkled into an ominous frown. "You were to contact me when your duty was complete, Nom Anor, and not before. Pray you are not contacting me to report another failure."

She glanced at her friends, her brown eyes sparkling with something resembling her old spirit.

"Oh, this is too good," she marveled. "This is Nom Anor's ship! The villip must not be attuned to him, though, or you'd think Tsavong Lah would notice the difference."

Ganner threw up both hands. "I don't know, Jaina. You've definitely looked better."

"And you still look like a holovid hero. Where's the

justice in that?" she shot back good-naturedly. "Anyway, Lowbacca thinks this villip is a way for a ship's pilot, whoever that might be, to report to a fleet admiral. When you think about it, that makes sense. I don't have a complete handle on how villips work, but from what I hear they seem to allow one specific person to talk to one other specific person. But what happens if that villip connection is broken? They've got to have some way of communicating with a ship, not just a person. Lowbacca found this thing onboard, living in a hydroponic vat. Maybe the ship itself attunes the villip, and the pilot's connection with the ship allows communication."

"Who is this?" the warmaster demanded.

Jaina turned her attention back to the globe. "Let's put it this way: I'm contacting you to report another failure," she said, turning his earlier words back upon him.

Tsavong Lah's cruel eyes narrowed. "This is not Nom Anor. You are not even Yuuzhan Vong—the villip is translating." His face twisted with fury as the logical answer presented itself. "The *Jeedai!*"

"Got it in one," she mocked.

For a long moment, the image of Tsavong Lah merely glared at her. Then his frayed lips twisted in a sneer. "And this, I suppose, is where you offer yourself in your brother's place."

"Why bother? I know you won't let Jacen go."

"That is true enough, but are you so sure of your motivation?" he taunted her. "You are the lesser twin, the one who would fall in sacrifice. Perhaps it suits your purposes to keep your brother's sword far from your throat."

Jaina began to understand what this "sacrifice" entailed. "We would fight each other?"

"Of course! That is how it is done."

An image flashed into Jaina's mind from the time she and Jacen had been held captive at the Shadow Academy, forced into dark-side training. They'd been made to fight with lightsabers, long before they were ready for such weapons, and to fight for their lives against a foe cloaked in a hologram. They'd pitted her against Darth Vader—a symbol of her past, and a portent of her future. Jacen, however, faced the same apparent foe. Neither of them had realized until the hologram cloaking devices were shut off how near they'd come to killing each other.

Despite all she'd been through before and since, the horror of that moment still visited Jaina in dreams.

Her mind raced as she tried to improvise a plan. It occurred to her that it might be best to play into the war-master's perceptions.

"That's how it's always done," she agreed, letting the memory of the Shadow Academy imbue her words with dread. "Jacen and I are twins. This is our destiny."

"You understand this much, yet you run from destiny?"

She inclined her head in a bow. A look of surprise flickered over the villip-reflected face, indicating that her gesture of respect had somehow been translated.

"You are right, Warmaster. Nom Anor's ship is disabled. I can run no farther."

"What is your position?" he demanded. "Obviously you are wearing the pilot's hood. Ask the ship."

"A moment, please." She put the villip down carefully, then looked at Ganner and mouthed the words, *Get Lowbacca.*

The big Jedi nodded and sprinted off in search of the Wookiee. A few moments later a big, hairy fist thrust out into the central corridor and gave her a thumbs-up.

"Here goes," Jaina muttered, and turned back to the villip.

"I can't get an answer from the ship," she said, her tone defensive and edged with a bit of a whine. "Is there some way the ship could be traced through the yammosk that controls it?"

"Nom Anor is an independent agent. His ship answers to no yammosk. But sometimes a yammosk can pick up a stranded ship; the dovin basals are strongly inclined to link."

"This dovin basal is ailing," Jaina said eagerly. "Linking might keep it alive long enough for me to . . ."

She let her words trail off. A sneer crossed Tsavong Lah's reflected face as he read the meaning Jaina intended to portray. Obviously, he thought she was stalling for time, gaining needed repairs in hope of fleeing capture.

"I have sent agents to oversee the sacrifice. No doubt they are in close pursuit. You will be meeting them shortly."

Before Jaina could respond, the villip shifted back to its formless state.

"What now?" Ganner demanded.

Jaina's smile was thin and feral. "They'll come to us."

The warmaster set aside the offending villip and bellowed an order. A subordinate came at a near run, bearing a second, larger villip.

Tsavong Lah stroked the globe. No response. "Your other hand, Warmaster," the aide suggested.

He quickly did so, ignoring this latest reminder of how tenuous his new implant was. A villip, duly attuned, did not recognize the touch of his transplanted limb!

The globe shifted to reveal a face similar to his own in shape and expression. The reflected warrior was younger, his flesh taut and clear, but not less scarred. Elaborate black tattoos covered an angular gray face. A small horn protruded from a high, broad forehead.

"Warmaster," Khalee Lah proclaimed, inclining his head in respect.

"I have found the female," the warmaster said without

preamble. "She has offered to surrender—a ploy, of course, a pitiful attempt to buy time to escape. You will persuade the yammosk aboard the priestship to link with the frigate and accept this additional ship in its communication family."

"Of course, Warmaster."

"Inform Harrar that he may contact the *Jeedai* directly through the *Ksstarr*'s ship's villip."

An expression of surprise crossed the young warrior's face. "He possesses a commander's villip?"

"He holds it in trust," Tsavong Lah corrected. "When the *Jeedai* sacrifice is completed, he will pass it to you, along with the rank and honors that attend it. See to it that this day comes soon."

His son inclined his head in a deep bow. "I am honored, Warmaster, but I would do so regardless of reward. My personal advancement is a pale thing compared to the service due our gods."

The warmaster received this pious speech in silence. "Go, and do."

Again the young warrior bowed, and the villip quickly inverted. Tsavong Lah's lip curled as he regarded the villip. "Harrar seems to be failing," he said softly, "in more ways than one."

Jaina flew steadily toward Tenel Ka, following the directions Tahiri gave. She did not notice when the villip began to change. Zekk's soft, grim oath drew her attention back to the living communication sphere.

It depicted a thin, almost aesthetic-looking visage, not quite as garishly scarred as the warmaster's. An elaborately wound cloth swathed his head.

"Harrar, a priest of Yun-Harla, the Trickster goddess," the image said curtly. "It will be my honor to preside over your sacrifice."

"The honor is mine," Jaina said dryly. She went on,

"And thanks for the suggestion. I've been wondering what to call this rock. *Trickster* sounds just about right."

"That is not suitable. It is not possible. There is more to naming a ship than you could possibly know."

"It requires a special affinity, a deep attunement," Jaina said. "Is that one of the things I couldn't possibly know?"

Raw fury flooded the Yuuzhan Vong's face. "Whatever paltry tricks you may have in mind will serve no purpose. The attunement has been transferred. My ability to speak to you indicates that my ship's yammosk is making contact with your dovin basal. Any minor control you have over the *Ksstarr*—"

"The *Trickster*," Jaina corrected.

"—will be superseded," he finished, ignoring the interruption.

Tahiri let out a small gasp. To her credit, she did not remove the navigation hood.

"You are establishing contact?" Jaina repeated in feinted alarm.

"It is done."

Jaina turned the villip upside down, causing it to invert and break contact with the priest. She turned to her friends with a triumphant smile. The wave of shock and condemnation hit her like a physical blow.

"Before you say anything, let me explain. Lowbacca has been playing with the ship's sensors. We're receiving their signal, but blocking ours."

"You can't be sure of that!" Zekk protested.

"I'm sure," Tahiri broke in. "The Yuuzhan Vong ships manipulate gravity. That's how they move, shield, even navigate. I'm hooked up to this thing. I should know."

"Go on," Ganner urged.

"The sensors gather information from shifts in gravity fields. Every ship has a pattern, sort of like a signature."

"That's right," Jaina broke in. "Lowbacca used some

parts from the Hornet to rig up a mechanical disruption. The dovin basal doesn't know that the signals it's sending the yammosk are scrambled."

"It sounds feasible," Ganner said, doubt still suffusing his voice. "But if you're wrong, the Yuuzhan Vong might follow us to Hapes. We'd be endangering a world—a system—that is in no shape to defend itself."

"They know we're heading there," Jaina pointed out, "which makes a Yuuzhan Vong attack on Hapes all but a foregone conclusion. They'll have to make a stand eventually."

"They?" Ganner asked, eyeing her with speculation. "Not we?"

"I've got someplace else to be. The rest of you are welcome to come or stay, as you choose."

"You're going after Jacen," he stated.

She shrugged. "Was there ever any doubt?"

"What's your goal, Jaina?" Zekk said softly. "Obviously it's not survival. You don't really expect to rescue Jacen—not even you could be that . . . optimistic," he said, improvising in response to the lowering storm in her eyes. "The way I see it, that leaves vengeance."

"Which leads to the dark side," she said impatiently. "Spare me—I've heard all the arguments. Repeatedly. The way I see it, Jedi have a responsibility to act. Act! We don't have the luxury of philosophical debates. It was the schism between Jacen and Anakin, their endless dithering over 'what a Jedi should be,' that brought them both down."

"That's unfair," Tahiri whispered. "It's cruel."

"Is it? Let's look at the facts: Anakin is dead, Jacen was captured. If the surviving Jedi continue to dither, we will be destroyed and the Yuuzhan Vong will have won."

They stood in silence for a long moment as they considered her grim logic.

Alema was the first to speak. "We Twi'leks have a

saying: If you refuse to decide, the decision is made without you."

"Get the job done," Ganner agreed.

"Time to hunt!" the Barabel shouted from his position at the stern.

"You'll need a healer," Tekli said with a sigh of resignation.

Jaina turned to Zekk, a question in her eyes.

"I'll be remaining on Hapes, or going where I am most needed," he said softly, a world of regret in his eyes.

Who could need him more than Jacen? Jaina tamped down the surge of anger and accepted his decision with a curt nod. But she made no attempt to shield her emotions from him.

For a moment she felt Zekk waver, felt the strength of her vision override his deeply held beliefs.

Temptation welled, fierce and strong. She would free Jacen somehow, but it would be easier with the other young Jedi at her side. If she could sway Zekk, she could bring them all to her side.

Under her control.

It was a logical end to the path her thoughts had taken, yet Jaina quickly shied away from it. Swiftly, subtly, she pulled away from Zekk, hoping that he would not notice that she, not he, had caused him to question his hard-won values. The puzzlement that flickered through his Force-sense suggested that she'd succeeded—that he hadn't realized what she had nearly done.

She pulled off the pilot's hood and tossed it to Zekk. "I need some time alone," she said abruptly as she spun away from the other Jedi.

Her path took her toward the small chamber where they'd left Anakin's body. None of them followed her, but she felt their relief that she was taking steps to finally "deal with her grief."

And perhaps it was time. After the first terrible surge

of loss, Jaina had simply stored away her emotions. It was not so different, really, from the years she'd spent protecting herself from the constant bombardment of other people's emotions.

She hesitated at the threshold, staring at the quiet stranger laying on the Yuuzhan Vong bunk. He looked to be at rest, and his still form bore little resemblance to the image burned upon Jaina's mind. The grime of battle had been cleaned away, the terrible wounds bandaged and then covered with clean clothing—linen and leather scavenged from somewhere.

The features were Anakin's. The height, the form. But his ice-blue eyes had been closed, and the unruly brown hair neatly brushed. Jaina came closer, and without thinking she reached out and tousled it with the big-sisterly gesture she'd so often employed.

A soft step behind her announced Tekli's presence. "Better," the Chadra-Fan agreed. "That is how it always seemed to look."

Jaina turned to the little healer, her eyes dry and her heart cold. "Thank you for what you've done here. I didn't want our mother to see him as he was."

She turned and walked calmly away, acutely aware of the grief emanating from the Chadra-Fan. She accepted this with gratitude: it seemed right that *someone* should be able to grieve for Anakin.

Despite the wall she had built around her heart, Jaina sensed that Tekli was not grieving only for Anakin, but for her as well.

Harrar set aside the villip and glanced up at the young warrior, who was pacing the room like a thwarted thunderbolt seeking room to strike.

"The *Jeedai* has broken contact," Harrar said.

Khalee Lah touched two fingers to his forehead. "I have given my blood oath to bring her in, but I swear before you and all the gods that she will spend her last days in pain, and die without honor!"

The priest dismissed this vow with an impatient wave of one hand. "Did you mark her words? It seemed to me she implied that in naming the ship *Trickster*, she might in fact be employing the practice of naming ships for their pilots."

"Do you think her capable of such subtlety?" Khalee Lah scoffed.

"She is a twin. Surely that means something even where infidels are concerned, or the gods would not be so eager for this sacrifice."

"She is both *Jeedai* and twin," the warrior agreed, "but take care, Eminence, not to subscribe to the heresy that attributes too much power to these *Jeedai*. This female is not even a pale shadow of Yun-Harla."

"Of course not," the priest agreed. Still, a strange doubt lingered. "Attend me," he said, and strode off to consult with his yammosk keeper.

They made their way to the chamber that housed the monstrous battle leader. "You have made contact with the *Ksstarr*?" he demanded.

The keeper bowed. "We have, Eminence."

"I would confirm this."

"Of course!" The keeper moved aside, allowing Harrar to place one hand on the writhing, many-tentacled thing.

After a moment, Harrar lifted his gaze to the keeper's face. "The link is confirmed. Have you not found it peculiar that the *Ksstarr* has sent no return communication whatsoever?"

"It is ailing," the keeper ventured.

"It is silent!" Harrar snapped. He turned to Khalee Lah and then waited for the warrior to grasp the significance of this.

Horror crept over the scarred face. "It is not possible," he said, his voice dulled by shock. Despite his lesser stature

and the demands of protocol, he elbowed the priest out
of the way and placed his own hand against the neural
sensors.

"This is impossible," he repeated, despite the truth the
yammosk revealed. "Somehow Jaina Solo has blocked
the yammosk: information is flowing to her, but not back
to the priestship!"

Harrar drew him aside. "You advised me against equat-
ing this human with our great and devious Yun-Harla, and
rightly so. But perhaps you should consider the possibility
that she is somewhat more than you thought possible."

Khalee Lah stood for a moment, his bearing proud, his
scarred face conflicted. Then he inclined his head in a
chopping nod.

"Perhaps," he agreed.

ELEVEN

Jagged Fel eased his clawcraft into a long, spiraling descent over Ithor, searching the lifeless sphere for some remnant of the once verdant world he'd fought to save.

The dark, rocky planet bore a distressing resemblance to a Yuuzhan Vong ship. Dry riverbeds gouged the surface like the scars on the faces of their warriors. It was said that the invaders believed themselves created in the image of their gods. Apparently they were determined to pass along the favor.

Jag's comm crackled. "What do you hope to find here, Commander?" inquired a low-pitched female voice.

"A reminder," he said softly. "This is why we've come, Shawnkyr. This is why the enemy must be stopped."

He pulled his ship into close formation with his wingmate, close enough to see into the TIE fighter ball cockpit of the Chiss craft. Shawnkyr Nuruodo's pale blue face was composed, showing neither grief for Ithor nor condemnation of Jagged Fel's unorthodox views.

Jag wondered, briefly, what Shawnkyr really thought of their "scouting mission." A Chiss warrior did not strike first—this was not only tradition, but a matter of honor. Yet she had followed him to Ithor before and showed every indication of following him now regardless of the path he chose.

"Next coordinates?" she inquired, as if in response to his thoughts.

Jag consulted the navigational computer—a feature newly added to his clawcraft—and gave Shawnkyr the end points of a minor hyperspace route.

"That is in the Hapes Cluster," she observed.

"Yes. The queen of Hapes has opened the Interior Region world to refugees. If the Yuuzhan Vong follow their pattern, they will attack this system."

"House Nuruodo will wish to hear of this attack, if it occurs."

Jag heard the unspoken words. Shawnkyr was a member of the powerful House Nuruodo clan, which commanded the Chiss military. Shawnkyr's advice would carry considerable weight with the official Chiss military. This scouting mission would influence the path taken by the Chiss under General Fel's command, but it had potential for an even greater impact.

Until then, however, Jag and Shawnkyr were on their own. They could expect little from the desperate people they'd recently abandoned, and could offer them nothing but their own best efforts.

They fell silent as they prepared for the hyperspace jump. Their new clawcraft boasted navigational systems and hyperdrives far superior to their accustomed ships, as well as enhanced weapon systems. Jag had no intention of starting trouble, but he intended to walk away from any fight that found him—after winning it, of course.

The growing pressure of sublight acceleration pushed him back into his seat. He settled in as darkness enveloped the ship, intending to snatch a short rest during the hyperspace flight.

Sensors prodded him awake in what seemed like moments. Shawnkyr's ship emerged as a blur on his port side, like a nebular haze against the sharper starlines behind. The warning sensors on Jag's console awoke also, but as if from a nightmare: abruptly, screaming.

Jag's eyes focused on the slack, terror-stricken faces of two human pilots, clearly visible through the transparisteel dome of the freighter headed straight at him.

He threw his clawcraft into a sharp starboard turn, rising above the larger ship with only meters to spare. Shawnkyr peeled off in the opposite direction—a smoothly executed evasion honed by years of shared flight.

Jag flicked on the comm. "Regroup and pursue. Something must have prompted them to set these coordinates."

"Stupidity?" Shawnkyr suggested.

His lips twitched, even though he knew full well that his wingmate intended no humor. Shawnkyr held a typical Chiss disregard for "lesser races." He'd learned long ago not to take offense.

They sped off, tracing opposite sides of a wide circle, intending to meet in the center and fall into their accustomed side-by-side formation. Their regrouping point exploded into a flare of molten gold.

Four coralskippers, visible now in the wake of their shining missiles, advanced in diamond formation, focused upon the fleeing freighter. Again the Chiss vessels peeled away, this time coming back around to flank the attacking ships.

Jag veered sharply away from an incoming plasma bolt and then brought his clawcraft screaming up over the tight formation. He held position, and his fingers danced over the controls as he hurled a seemingly random barrage at the Yuuzhan Vong ships. But he observed carefully which laser bolts disappeared into blackness and which slipped past the enemy's organic shields.

The answering fire taught him even more. For several moments he evaded plasma bolts, and planned next steps.

"The enemy is compensating for damage," he informed Shawnkyr. "Wing ships have weapons and shields only on their outer sides. The aft ship has no weapons at

all—shields only—and the point vessel is pouring everything into attack."

"A suicide squadron," she concluded. "The freighter
is an important target."

"Or perhaps these coralskippers are damaged beyond
repair. The leaders figure they've got nothing to lose but
the pilots. Maybe the pilots made the decision to go out
fighting."

The Chiss female received this in silence, as she had all
of Jag's attempts to describe the Yuuzhan Vong's apparent
philosophy. There was nothing in Shawnkyr's culture that
could help her find logic in the notion of a "glorious
death."

"Point ship first," he said, coming around into firing
position.

Jag fired a concussion missile at the lead vessel.
Shawnkyr followed with a barrage of laserfire, exploding the missile just short of the alien's shielding, and right
in the path of the diamond-shaped wedge.

The lead skip pulled up sharply, but the leading edge
of the explosion caught it and sent it tumbling wildly. Jag
fired a second missile. The out-of-control ship exploded.
Shards of black coral streaked across the sudden bright-
ness, the opposite image of starlines against the blackness of space.

"Regroup right under the shield ship, and slightly
behind," Jag suggested. "Stay with it, and stay together."

"As ordered. But they won't hesitate to fire upon one
of their own."

"That's what I'm counting on. Get right in close, just
beyond its shielding range."

The two clawcraft dipped under the rear coralskipper
and sent a syncopated barrage of laserfire at the inner
sides of the damaged wing ships.

With astonishing agility, the coralskippers dipped
and crossed paths. They changed places and rose back

into formation, so that the viable weapons and shields pointed at the clawcraft. As Shawnkyr anticipated, the skips returned fire. The rear skip absorbed each of the plasma streams, swallowing one after another.

The trio of coralskippers moved in astonishing unity, dipping and twisting in an attempt to shake their Chiss shadow. But Jag and Shawnkyr held their positions, and each bolt of plasma disappeared into the guard ship's singularities.

"They may sacrifice this skip to take us out," Jag said. "The first time plasma hits your shield, get away, fast. Full power. If the rear guard skip isn't shielding, it could generate a gravity pull like a tractor beam."

The skips kept firing. Their coral hulls paled to translucency under the continued Chiss onslaught. Huge chunks of the skips ripped away and hurtled toward the stubborn clawcraft.

Jag yawed sharply to avoid a piece of the vessel nearest him. The body of a Yuuzhan Vong pilot shot from the wreckage of the other ship, aimed directly—and probably deliberately—at Shawnkyr's clawcraft.

A blue streak shot from Shawnkyr's vessel and reduced the once living projectile to a grim nebula. Jag tried to ignore the splatter on his cockpit viewer. He squinted up through it toward the underside of the sole remaining coralskipper. Its hull was also thinning. Heated coral paled to a ghostly translucence.

"Break!" he shouted as he leaned his ship sharply away.

Coral erupted into the sky, pushed along by a brief, bright explosion. Volcanoes were nothing new to him— one of the planets in Chiss territory had an extremely volatile geology. But seeing a living thing erupt in similar fashion made the Yuuzhan Vong seem at once more familiar and more unknowable. Jag doubted he'd ever be able to witness a volcanic eruption again without viewing it as the death throes of a mountain.

It didn't occur to him to share this thought with Shawnkyr. Long experience with the Chiss had taught him to keep fanciful notions to himself. Instead he switched his comm to hailing frequency.

"This is *Vanguard One*, a Chiss scouting vehicle. New Republic freighter, please identify yourself and tell us how we can further assist you."

There was a moment of silence, then the comm crackled. "This is the *Blind Mynock*. We have no valuables aboard, no passengers. There's no profit in boarding us."

Jag sent a sidelong glance at his wingmate. An expression of grim outrage had settled over the Chiss female's features. "We're not pirates," he said flatly. "If you require an escort, we will accompany you to Hapan space."

"We've no need of whelp-tending," the pilot blustered. "The *Mynock* has plenty of speed and firepower."

Jag's patience began to fray. "If you had weapons, you would have returned fire in the hope of protecting your nonexistent cargo and paying passengers. This sector has a history of piracy, so I understand your caution. On the other hand, it also has a demonstrated Yuuzhan Vong risk. If you'd rather take your chances with them, say so plainly and we'll respect your choice."

The comm crackled promptly. "They fried our navigational computer," a different voice said, "which is why we came so close to wearing your ship as a hull ornament. We'll have to input the jump coordinates manually. Problem is, we don't know them offhand. If you could see your way clear to giving us directions to Hapes, we'll be on our way."

Jag named the coordinates and watched as the freighter lumbered off, then lurched into sublight acceleration.

"Shall we follow them?" Shawnkyr asked.

"They don't seem eager for company," he observed. "But let's report to Hapes, see what information we can gather there. Maybe even pick up a few more pilots."

"A new squadron, Commander? You asked for a Chiss phalanx and were refused. Do you intend to build a substitute?"

"We could scout more efficiently with more eyes," Jag argued.

"True enough. And when this scouting squadron encounters the Yuuzhan Vong, it will be able to engage them more efficiently than could a pair of Chiss clawcraft."

"You make it sound as if we're on an offensive mission."

The female's clawcraft edged closer so that their wingtips were nearly touching. "Not at all, sir. Our mission is to scout out enemy activity, not to initiate battle through first-strike tactics. It is manifestly clear, however, that the Yuuzhan Vong have no such compunction. Once the first shot is fired—and it will be—we are obligated to defend ourselves."

Jag sent a startled glance at his wingmate.

"I know why we've come, sir," the Chiss said softly. "And so do you."

For once, Jag had nothing to add. "To Hapes, then," he said, and began to prepare for the jump.

TWELVE

The young Jedi gathered in the cockpit of the ship Jaina had named the *Trickster*, watching in silence as their stolen craft moved steadily toward a large Hapan ship. The vessel was moving steadily away from Hapes.

"Well, this ought to be interesting," Tahiri murmured.

Jaina silently agreed. "Are you sure they've got Tenel Ka?"

"She's been picked up, all right. The ship is mechanical, not organic. That's good news."

"But no guarantee of safety," Ganner added. "For all we know, they could be Peace Bri—"

He broke off abruptly, and the expression on his face suggested that someone had just hit him between the eyes with a hydrospanner.

Before Jaina could make sense of this, white-hot pain exploded through her senses. She ripped off the cognition hood, but the agony didn't lessen in the slightest. Dimly she realized that it came not from the ship, but from the other Jedi aboard. She felt them all, and all of them formed a single thought:

Jacen.

The surge ended abruptly, and the sensation disappeared.

For a moment Jaina sat frozen, stunned beyond speech. Jacen had appeared in the Force—but not to her.

Jaina could accept that her own grief and anger blocked

Jacen's ability to contact her. But as Jaina looked from one stunned face to another, she saw a different, darker truth. Her brother's death was written on Lowbacca's furred face and in Tekli's rodent-black eyes. It was in the sorrow that flowed from all of them.

Jaina was dimly aware of Zekk nudging her aside and taking over the pilot's chair. She slumped against the rough wall. Her whirling thoughts screamed denial, rejecting a truth she could neither sense nor accept.

Then a second storm hit her, a searing frenzy that was barely recognizable as Tenel Ka. Jaina felt the other woman's emotional storm, the rawness in her hand from beating against the walls of the escape pod.

But why could she feel nothing of her own?

Tenel Ka's grief turned to rage. Jaina experienced this, too, and with the same benumbed detachment. One part of her was startled by the depth and intensity of Tenel Ka's reaction. She'd been troubled by her father's response to Chewbacca's death, but Han's denial and detachment made more sense to Jaina than her friend's heartbroken frenzy.

Maybe her family wasn't a reliable measure of such things. The Skywalkers and Solos were no strangers to conflict, and they'd all stepped up at an early age. In matters of relationships, however, every one of them seemed a little vague on the coordinates. Her mother, conditioned through training and experience to hold the New Republic paramount, had nearly accepted Prince Isolder's offer of marriage. Leia had known that Han loved her, but somehow she'd misplaced the access codes to her own emotions. Had Jacen done the same thing? Had he loved Tenel Ka and never fully realized it?

Yeah, Jaina decided numbly. That sounded like Jacen— forever thinking about everything under a hundred distant suns rather than focusing on what was right in front of him.

As she herself was doing. With great effort, Jaina pushed herself away from the wall.

"Tenel Ka is still out there," she said in a cool, steady voice. "We need to focus on her."

For a moment every eye fixed upon Jaina. A symphony of emotions ranging from incredulity to anger to pity washed over her.

Ganner was the first to pull himself together. He threw himself in the gunner's chair. "You got it. Let's hunt them down."

Tesar hissed his approval and scuttled off to his station, his armored tail rasping against the rough coral floor. The rest of the Jedi set to work or strapped in for the pursuit.

As they neared the Hapan ship, they noted the small flight of Hornet Interceptors that followed it. These scattered and fled at the approach of the Yuuzhan Vong frigate.

"They've got the escape pod," Zekk confirmed. "Just pulled it through the hatch."

Ganner swore softly. "What I wouldn't give for a good ion cannon right about now. Something that would take out the controls, but not the ship."

"Force lightning," Jaina suggested.

"Oh, great," Tahiri muttered. "How Sith is that?"

"I'm serious." Jaina placed a hand on Zekk's shoulder. "We could do this. You graduated from the Shadow Academy. They must have taught you how."

He pulled the hood back and stared at her, as if he didn't trust his ears to decode this message without further data. As he studied her, horror dawned in his green eyes. Even Lowbacca looked at her strangely. A burst of laserfire erupted from the Hapan ship, cutting off any reply either Jedi might have made.

Jaina cast her eyes toward the cockpit ceiling. "All right, then, I've got another idea. Move over."

He quickly yielded the pilot's seat. Jaina tugged on the hood and coaxed the dovin basal to abandon shielding in favor of exerting a slow, steady pull. The ship jarred and shuddered as the Hapan ship's fire found its mark.

Alema Rar leaned over Jaina's shoulder and peered at the approaching ship. "You've got it in a lock, but with no escape pod or vac suits, how are we going to get to Tenel Ka?"

"She's coming to us," Jaina announced, her eyes fixed firmly on the Hapan ship. "Brace!"

The Twi'lek promptly dropped to the floor, her lekku twitching with apprehension. The cargo ship slowed as it neared the *Trickster*, but the impact was still enough to rock the frigate and send a shower of black coral dust cascading over the console. Alema rose to her feet, sneezing violently and repeatedly.

"After this war is over, I'm taking a vacation on Mon Calamari," she announced as she wiped her streaming eyes.

"Sounds nice," Zekk said absently, his concerned gaze still fixed on the young pilot.

"I'm going to find the largest coral reef on that world," Alema concluded grimly, "and then I'm going to blow it up."

"Hold that thought," Jaina suggested.

She mentally ordered the ship to breach the other vessel. On the wall just behind the cockpit, a viscous substance, similar in appearance to the Yuuzhan Vong's blorash jelly, seeped from the coral and outlined an oval portal. Foul steam began to rise as the solvent worked its way through the living hull.

The Wookiee padded over to observe. He leapt back as a neat two-meter chunk of coral tipped into the corridor. The smoldering edges were now as smooth as transparisteel. Yellow goo still seeped from the ship's walls and was swiftly eating through the ceramic and metal hull of the captured freighter. The melted substance hardened quickly, forming a solid, airtight bond between the two ships.

Once the steam subsided, Lowbacca poked experimentally at the portal. Roaring in satisfaction, he spun to one side and delivered a solid kick.

The "door" went in and fell hard, taking down two humans in red uniforms. Lowbacca strode over them, igniting his bronze lightsaber as he went. The other Jedi spilled through the portal, falling in on either side of the Wookiee.

A double *ping* sounded as blaster bolts greeted them. Tenel Ka's turquoise blade picked off both of them before her "rescuers" could respond.

Jaina pushed forward, stepping over the prone forms of three red-clad mercenaries as she took in the battle. At least six humans were sprawled on the floor, some of them moaning softly. One of these stirred and tried to push himself up onto his hands and knees. Lowbacca planted a furry foot on the man's rump with a force that sent him skidding facedown across the polished floor. His head struck a metal cabinet with a satisfying *thunk*.

Tenel Ka strode past the Wookiee without a glance, moving toward the last two men standing—tall, blond men in red uniforms and in fighting trim.

One of them tossed aside an empty blaster and pulled a stun baton from his weapons belt. The other fell into the ready stance of a Hapan kickboxer.

Jaina held out one hand to hold the others back. "Let her handle this. I've got a feeling she needs it. Sorry, Alema."

The Twi'lek woman shrugged and stood down.

Tenel Ka brought her lightsaber into high guard position, and then switched it off. She tossed the weapon to Tahiri without looking back. The young Jedi deftly caught it, and her lips moved as she murmured silent encouragement.

The kickboxer spun toward Tenel Ka, delivering two quick, feinting jabs and then snapping a high kick to her head. She leaned and slapped aside the kick with the metal band that encircled the end of her truncated arm. She turned her body in to the blow to add strength to the parry and to put herself into position for a side kick. This she delivered, hard, to her opponent's chest.

He staggered back, surprised by the unexpected power of the small woman's kick. Tenel Ka advanced, dropping to the floor suddenly and spinning into a low leg sweep. Her opponent leapt over the attack, an easy, agile move. The Jedi flipped onto her side and kicked again, higher, catching him on the inside of the knee just as he landed. He stumbled and went down.

Tenel Ka rolled away twice to gain some distance and then rose smoothly. Meanwhile her opponent got his feet under him and lunged up into a running charge.

She darted to meet him, throwing herself into a leaping spin and slamming her right foot directly into his face. Her left foot shot straight out and caught him just below the rib cage. She twisted as she fell and kept rolling away. The Hapan fighter reeled back and hit the wall, then slowly slid down.

Tenel Ka came up in a crouch, and her gaze snapped toward her final opponent. He advanced swiftly, stun baton leading.

The Jedi extended her hand. Tahiri threw the lightsaber back to its owner. It spun twice, end over end, and then slapped into Tenel Ka's waiting palm. A stream of turquoise light raced toward her attacker's throat and stopped a breath away, halting him in midstride.

Instinctively he struck out at the beam with his stun baton. The metal end sheared neatly off, and sparks exploded from the severed weapon. His blond hair leapt into spikes about his head and his eyes glazed. The weapon fell from his violently shaking hand, and he stumbled back into a benumbed retreat. Tenel Ka rose and matched him step for step, her lightsaber still at his throat.

Jaina felt a collective surge of dismay from the other Jedi. Impatiently she swept it aside and willed Tenel Ka to get on with it, get it over with.

Her thought must have carried to Tenel Ka. The warrior stopped abruptly, and her gray eyes sought Jaina's. Tenel Ka lifted her blade away from the man's throat and switched it off, still holding her old friend's gaze.

For a moment they were open to each other. Jaina felt the other woman's wrath, but also her determination. Tenel Ka saw these men as traitors to Hapes, and her duty, as a Jedi Knight and as the daughter of Hapes's queen, to see that they would be dealt with accordingly. Jaina had been sure that Tenel Ka simply needed to let off some steam; now she sensed how wrong she'd been.

She also sensed a question coming from Tenel Ka, a subtle seeking such as a Jedi might use to measure a stranger. And then, not even that. The warrior's formidable shields were back in place.

Jaina's own internal shields firmed, and she nodded in approval. "Good for you," she said, and her gaze took in both Tenel Ka and the Twi'lek. "Why waste energy on helpless coral reefs and Hapan pirates?"

The weird light in the Twi'lek's eyes flared. The look she sent Jaina was the sort that passed between kindred spirits, or perhaps conspirators.

"Save it for the Vong," Alema said in complete agreement.

THIRTEEN

Kyp Durron followed the *Millennium Falcon* in its hiccuping voyage through the dovin basal mines and into the confusion of Hapan space. After weaving through the chaotic traffic, he finally gained landing clearance. The worst behind him, he quickly set down his fighter next to Han's ship.

He swung out of his X-wing and gazed with dismay at the scene around him. The docking area outside of Hapes's royal city stretched as far as his eyes could see. Movable landing pads shifted to squeeze the ships together and make room for the scores of vessels still circling or hovering in the skies overhead. Refugees milled about, and their confusion was like a scent on the wind.

Then another, stronger wind swept through Kyp, a psychic blast of incredible power and pain. He staggered and caught hold of his battered ship as Jacen Solo's agony swept through his veins like molten rock.

His own astonishment mingled with the younger man's pain, for Kyp had no ties with Jacen Solo that would explain so powerful a connection. He didn't even like the young Jedi. In his view, Han's oldest son was a spoiled, self-absorbed brat who'd rather let the Yuuzhan Vong sweep across the galaxy like a plague of insects than sully his precious vision of the Jedi ideal.

Yet for some reason, Kyp was sharing what was

certainly a final agony. He couldn't imagine living through something like this firsthand. He wasn't sure he'd *want* to.

As the pain began to recede, a strong hand grasped his elbow. "Hey, kid—exactly how long have you been cooped up in that flying 'fresher?"

Kyp quickly pulled away from his old friend, shielding his thoughts and manufacturing a wry smile. "Too long, apparently. Give me a minute to get my land legs back, and I'll be fine."

Han nodded absently and glanced over at the *Millennium Falcon*. Luke Skywalker emerged from the ship on the heels of his redheaded wife. His arm encircled his twin sister's waist as they walked slowly down the ramp. Leia Organa Solo was pale but composed. Impatience crackled around Mara Jade Skywalker like sparks from a severed cable, only slightly muted by the sorrow that rose from them all.

Kyp bowed to the Jedi Master, but spoke to the Solos. "My sincere regrets over the loss of your son."

Leia's eyes drifted shut, and Han quickly moved to her side. "Thanks," he said, speaking quickly as if to spare his wife the necessity of words. "I won't deny it's tough. Doesn't seem right, outliving your youngest kid."

"Your youngest?" Kyp echoed in dismay. Jacen he could shrug off without much trouble, but not Anakin. Anakin Solo's star had been swiftly rising, making him the war's most visible and attractive Jedi hero. Anakin could have made a difference.

Too late, Kyp realized what his words revealed. Han's face turned gray, and he gripped Kyp's arm with bone-crushing force.

"You were talking about Jacen. What did you hear? What do you know?"

Leia placed a gentling hand on her husband's shoulder.

"Kyp might have felt what I did—a sudden surge of Jacen's presence, then a dimming."

Dimming wasn't the word Kyp would have chosen. He'd seen stars go nova with more subtlety. Concerned, he glanced toward Luke Skywalker. The Jedi Master's lips were compressed in a tight line. Grief and concern mingled in his eyes as he regarded his sister. His gaze shifted to Kyp's, drawn by the younger man's unspoken question. His slight, almost imperceptible nod confirmed that he, too, had felt Jacen Solo's death.

Mara stalked forward, her green eyes burning. Kyp didn't need the Force to read the warning written there: leave Leia her protective illusions, let her deal with this in her own time.

"Surely you have no problems shading the truth," Mara purred softly. "After all, you managed to deceive my apprentice. *My* apprentice," she emphasized.

Obviously Mara hadn't forgiven him for involving Jaina in his latest vendetta. Kyp had used his considerable Jedi powers to "nudge" Jaina into believing that an unfinished Yuuzhan Vong worldship was actually a superweapon. And yes, he'd asked the young pilot to become his apprentice, mostly as a means of putting her off stride and making her more receptive to his deception. Mostly.

"Warning me off?" he asked mildly.

She glanced toward Luke. "Only because he's been a good influence." Her eyes narrowed. "So far."

Mara spun away from him. "We need to find a ship," she said abruptly as she strode away. Luke followed, his eyes approving his wife's hard-won restraint.

Leia caught her brother's arm. "You'll send word if you have any news of the twins?"

"You'll know," he said softly. "You have a Jedi's instincts. You don't need anyone to tell you about your own children." His somber gaze sought Kyp's, and his usually mild eyes echoed Mara's warning.

Han's puzzled gaze shifted from face to face. He squared his shoulders and moved on to something he could understand. Draping an arm around Kyp's shoulders, he led him toward the *Falcon*. "C'mon, kid. Let's make ourselves useful."

"Flying?" Kyp said dubiously as he eyed the latest dings and creases on the venerable ship.

"Fixing," Han retorted. He opened a compartment in the *Falcon*'s hull and removed a laser torch. With a single flick he coaxed a small beam from it, as easily as any Jedi might awaken his lightsaber. "This plating here needs to be replaced."

The Jedi regarded the tool. "I'm not much of a mechanic," he hedged. He took it from Han and switched it off, hoping the older man would get the hint.

"Just cut off those rivets. How hard could that be?" Han's voice faded off as he disappeared into the hold.

Kyp shrugged and pulled out his lightsaber. He switched it on and removed the half-melted fasteners with a few deft flicks.

"I see you've found yet another appropriate use for your Jedi abilities," a caustic female voice observed.

He turned to face Leia. The older woman was still lovely, despite the weight of grief and worry in her eyes. Her brown hair was thick and glossy, and she wore it in a straight, simple style that made her look remarkably like her eighteen-year-old daughter.

Kyp produced his most disarming smile and enhanced it with the subtle nudge that had so disconcerted Jaina. He got the vivid impression of his effort striking an invisible wall and splattering like a mynock colliding with a Star Destroyer.

The Princess sniffed and spun on her heel. For no reason that Kyp could fathom, he fell into step with her.

Leia ignored him as she waded into the crowd of refugees, dispensing comfort. In a remarkably short time, the crowd had been herded through the initial registration and dispersed into small groups. Hapan landspeeders glided off toward the parklands beyond the city. The refugees who'd been injured during the escape from Coruscant lay on narrow white pallets. Medical droids rolled with quiet efficiency between the rows.

The collective suffering rolled over Kyp in waves. He fought back the memories—his home destroyed, his family dispersed, his childhood lost to slavery.

He noticed Leia watching him, her dark eyes narrowed in speculation. "There's a need here," she said. "One you understand better than most. Maybe you could make yourself useful for a change."

Kyp smiled faintly, but shook his head. "I don't think so. Not here, at least. Not this way."

Her eyebrows shot up. "For some people, doubt can be dangerous. On you, it's an improvement. So what *will* you do next?"

He considered the question, and the answer that came to him was not the one he'd expected. Kyp had assumed responsibility for fighting this war—and not just fighting, but fighting in a way that set the direction for his fellow Jedi. He'd even told Jaina that their generation needed to establish a new order, a new relationship with the Force. Perhaps on some level he'd been envisioning himself in this role. With Jedi certainty, Kyp realized that this task would fall to another.

Yet there was a place for him, an important one. "No change comes without conflict," he said slowly. "Perhaps my destiny is to be the irritant that forces the discussion, the blister that lets you know your boots don't fit."

To his surprise, Leia burst into laughter. She sobered quickly and fixed him with a challenging stare. "Not a bad analogy, but keep in mind the difference between a blister and a cancer. You're a young man, and already you've been given more chances than most people get in a lifetime. A lot of people wonder why you're still alive. The answer to that can be given in two words."

"Luke Skywalker," Kyp supplied without hesitation. "I understand how much I owe your brother."

"Really? You have a strange way of repaying your debts," Leia retorted. "You've done nothing to support him, and everything you can to spread dissension among the Jedi."

The whir of repulsor engines made further speech impossible. They watched as two strangely designed vehicles lowered skillfully onto the crowded docks— round cockpits reminiscent of the old TIE fighters, and four movable arms that at present were spread like the limbs of crouching beasts.

"Chiss vessels," Leia mused. Her face brightened as a familiar, dark-haired young man leapt from the cockpit.

"Jag Fel," Kyp observed flatly.

"Colonel Jag Fel," Leia added thoughtfully. Her face took on the inscrutable but pleasant expression that Han often referred to as her "diplomat face."

"You'll have to excuse me," she murmured, and then headed toward the young commander.

Kyp chose not to take the hint. He matched his pace to Leia's. Whatever came next, they would need pilots—and even if Kyp didn't like to admit it, pilots didn't come much better than the young man emerging from the Chiss clawcraft.

Colonel Jagged Fel's face lit with pleasure as he recognized Leia. A faint shadow entered his eyes when he noted Kyp at her side. That Kyp could understand. Their first meeting had been more cordial than a bar brawl, but that was the only positive thing Kyp could think to say about it.

The pilot drew himself up and greeted Leia with a crisp,

formal bow. He introduced his wingmate, a Chiss woman who stood nearly half a head taller than either Jag or Kyp.

"Is your presence here a portent of things to come?" Leia asked, a touch of hope in her voice.

Jag inclined his head in a bow of apology. "I regret to report that it is not. Shawnkyr and I are scouts for the Chiss, no more."

"Pretty impressive arsenal for a pair of scouts," Kyp observed, tapping one hand against the proton torpedo launcher.

"We don't seek trouble, but neither will we run from it," Jag said calmly.

Several uniformed Hapans strode toward them, flanking two men in bedraggled flight suits. One of them pointed to Jag. "That's him—him and the woman. They're the ones."

"Some of that trouble you didn't run from?" Kyp asked.

Jag's only response was a brief, cool stare. "Excuse me," he murmured to Leia, and then went over to speak with the officials. He returned in moments and sent a glance toward the Chiss. Immediately she swung back into her ship and began to power up the engines.

"We've been asked to undertake a short mission," Jag explained. "A Yuuzhan Vong frigate analog requires an escort to Hapes."

Kyp let out a burst of derisive laughter. "Who'd you have to kill to get that job?"

"The pilot is believed to be Lieutenant Jaina Solo," Jag continued, as smoothly as if the interruption had not occurred.

"I know," Leia said, a shadow of worry in her voice, "and I thank you for undertaking this. It won't be easy to get an enemy ship in unscathed."

Jaina, Kyp mused. *Coming here, and flying a Yuuzhan*

Vong ship. This has distinct possibilities. "Could you use another pilot?"

Jag regarded him for a long moment. "The Hapan officials do not seem entirely convinced that this is not some sort of ambush. They asked Shawnkyr and me to go because we have combat experience against the Yuuzhan Vong. It's entirely possible, however, that we were chosen for this task primarily because we are not Hapan, and are therefore considered expendable."

"Oh, if that's all," Kyp said dryly. "I've been expendable for years. And recently my status has been downgraded from undesirable to anathema."

Shawnkyr leaned over the edge of the cockpit, her red eyes taking Kyp's measure. She, too, had heard the tales about the rogue Jedi, but she did not look disapproving.

"You will fly under Colonel Fel's command?" she demanded.

"It's his mission," Kyp agreed. "What about it, Colonel?"

The young pilot accepted with a curt nod, then pulled himself up into his ship. Kyp sprinted toward his X-wing.

"What's this about, Kyp?" Leia called after him.

He stopped, turning to meet her questioning gaze. The suspicion he expected to see was there, but it was tempered with something softer—curiosity, if nothing more.

"The last time you agreed to take orders from someone, you twisted the situation and turned many of the best people I know into unwitting murderers. Including, I might add, my daughter. What are you after this time?"

Leia's words were harsh, but Kyp didn't consider them unfair. Like her brother, she was giving him a chance to make an accounting of himself.

It was better than he expected, and better than he deserved. His answering smile was slow and wistful, and almost entirely genuine.

"Maybe it's time I started repaying that debt I owe your family."

Leia watched as Kyp raced to his ship and lifted off, swinging into position on Jag Fel's port flank. She reminded herself that this engaging man was the same person who had destroyed Carida, who had fallen to the dark side and nearly killed her brother Luke, who had tricked Jaina into using her name and reputation to bring the Rogue Squadron into his latest vendetta.

"Bring her back, Kyp," she said softly, "and you'll make a good-sized dent in that debt. But if you hurt her again, or anyone of mine, you'd be safer turning yourself over to the Yuuzhan Vong."

FOURTEEN

Zekk lowered himself into the pilot's seat of the captured Hapan ship and then reached over to help his copilot with her restraints. Like Zekk, Tenel Ka was swathed in an evac suit, a helmet near at hand. She waved off his assistance and buckled herself in deftly, completing the task more quickly with her one hand than Zekk could with two.

The look she sent him was faintly challenging, and the energy she projected through the Force had an edge to it. Zekk understood that this had very little to do with her missing limb. Tenel Ka hadn't become any more competitive since her injury, but then, Zekk hadn't noticed that she'd become any *less* competitive, either.

He pretended to scowl. "How is that fair?" he said in mock complaint. "You've had more experience with Hapan vessels."

"Results, not excuses," she advised, but a ghost of a smile touched her lips as she turned to the console and began to power up the engines.

Jaina thrust her head into the cockpit, and the grin on her face was that of the girl Zekk had known long ago. "Turn up that music and let's get ready to dance."

The Jedi pilot smiled faintly, understanding exactly what she meant. The hum and whine of the Hapan ship's engines was surprisingly welcome after the eerie silence of the dovin basal.

Her smile dimmed as she studied Zekk. "You sure you want to do this?"

Zekk didn't see much of a choice. The two ships were still connected, firmly melded together by the strange substance the *Trickster*'s coral hull had secreted. They were as open to each other as two enjoining rooms. Zekk could hear Lowbacca's deceptively fearsome howl as the Wookiee herded captive pirates through the portal to the Yuuzhan Vong ship.

And that, he noted grimly, was the problem—that two-meter oval doorway between the two ships. Tahiri claimed the Yuuzhan Vong ship could heal itself, but there was nothing to be done about the breach in the Hapan vessel. Cutting the ship loose would leave nearly a fifth of it open to the vacuum of space. They could abandon it, of course, but that would mean losing a salvageable cargo ship and, more important, the fourteen short-range fighters stored in the hold.

At the moment, none of this seemed terribly important to Zekk.

"It should be an adventure," he said, trying to keep his tone light. "I've never flown in tandem before."

Jaina came up behind the pilot's seat and leaned down, resting her chin on his shoulder and sliding her arms around his neck in the sort of casual, friendly embrace they'd exchanged many times over the years. "It's not the stupidest thing we've ever done."

"Who could argue with that?"

She chuckled and rose. The quick click of her boots faded as she passed through to the Yuuzhan Vong ship.

Zekk glanced at Tenel Ka. The warrior studied him with cool, gray eyes that saw far too much. He grimaced and looked away.

"It is difficult to live among Jedi," she said, acknowledging his chagrin. "I was not able to grieve Jacen in private."

"And I can't worry about Jaina without everyone knowing about it."

"Worry?" Tenel Ka repeated the pale word, rejected it. "You are afraid for her. You are afraid *of* her."

"Shouldn't I be?" he said softly.

"She's not Jaina as I knew her at the academy, but who has not been changed by this war?"

He couldn't dispute this. "Still, I don't like it."

"Neither does she," Tenel Ka said evenly. "Jaina would have emerged as a leader in time, regardless of circumstances. The battle at Myrkr forced her down this path before she had time to consider where it might end. Leadership involves finding a compromise, a balance. Nowhere is this more important than within the leader herself. She must be able to take action and to focus all her decisions toward a desired end, while remaining grounded in principle."

He considered the warrior woman. "You've thought about this."

"At length," she agreed. "Jaina is dealing with her loss by taking charge. This is a good response, one that returns to her a measure of control. But in detaching herself from her pain, she is also losing an important balance within herself." Her face turned grim. "I have seen what a leader who lacks this balance can become. We must watch her carefully."

Zekk looked away. "You'll have to do the watching. I'm moving on."

"You would abandon a friend?" she demanded.

"As you abandoned Jacen?" he snapped back.

Nothing in Tenel Ka's face acknowledged the hit. "I know you didn't mean that," she said calmly. "But I also know that if Jacen were in danger of sliding into the dark side, I would want to do whatever I could to pull him back."

This was the first time any of them had put their concern for Jaina into words. For a moment they were silent, sobered by the grim possibility.

"And what if she can't be pulled back?" Zekk asked. "I've taken that path, and I know what a Dark Jedi can do. If it comes to that, someone will have to stop her."

"By any means necessary," she agreed, once again giving voice to their shared fears.

"And I couldn't do that. No matter what, I just couldn't do it."

"I see." Tenel Ka turned her gaze straight ahead. "Then you are right to go."

Jaina slid on the cognition hood and urged the drifting *Trickster* into motion.

The ship balked, confused by circumstances it did not understand, and by the metallic bulk attached to it. Jaina gritted her teeth and reconsidered the wisdom of this attempted salvage. They might be able to fly and land in this formation, but if challenged, they wouldn't be able to put up much of a fight.

A trio of starships appeared in the distance, so suddenly that Jaina had the uncanny feeling that she'd conjured them with her unspoken fears. Faint lines of light slid out of hyperspace and slowed into focused, rapidly approaching dots.

She snatched up the comm Lowbacca had rigged up and opened the frequency to hail. "This is Lieutenant Jaina Solo of Rogue Squadron, aboard the Yuuzhan Vong frigate *Trickster*. The ship is under New Republic control. There are no Yuuzhan Vong aboard. Repeat, this is not an enemy ship. Hold your fire."

"Relax, *Trickster*. We're here to see you safely down," announced a familiar voice—the last voice Jaina expected or wanted to hear.

"Kyp Durron," she said coldly. "You might as well turn

around right now. I wouldn't follow you out of an ocean if
I were drowning."

"Hear me out before you open fire. Your parents are
on Hapes, in the refugee center. I told the princess I'd
bring you back. Now, you *could* send me back to Leia
empty-handed, but we all know what path a vindictive
spirit might take you down."

She absorbed his dark humor in silence as she considered his words, and the likely consequences of his presence. Her parents had enough to deal with without the
added grief that always seemed to follow Kyp Durron
like fumes from a faulty exhaust.

"Don't use my family in another of your tricks—if
they're really on Hapes at all."

"This is Colonel Jag Fel, Lieutenant Solo," another
voice broke in. "I have seen your mother on Hapes, and
the request for an escort came directly to me from landing
control. Kyp Durron is speaking the truth, and flying
under my command."

A strange, unsettled feeling coiled in the pit of Jaina's
stomach, and a little rush of gladness entered her heart
like a spring breeze. She did her best to ignore both.

"Under your command? Don't believe it," she said
bluntly. "If Kyp can twist a Jedi's thoughts, he can make
you think anything he wants."

"Thank you for your concern, but I hope I'm not quite
so weak-minded as that."

"So do I," she retorted, a little stung by the glacial tone
that had entered Jag's voice. His response didn't exactly
come as a surprise, though. Pilots were renowned for
their pride, and she'd just stomped on the edges of his.
Still, if Jag was determined to fly with Kyp, someone
ought to tell him he'd set course on a dangerous vector.

"Suit yourself. But while you're watching my back,
keep an eye on your own."

She firmly clicked off the comm and concentrated on

flying the ship. The *Trickster* rebelled against its mechanical hitchhiker, and Jaina waged a silent but fierce argument with the ship in an effort to keep it from shedding the pirate vessel. Finally the sentient frigate yielded to a compromise.

"Lowbacca, Ganner, can you put that panel back in place?"

"You're not thinking about abandoning them?" Alema Rar demanded.

"The ship wants to," she replied, "but it'll settle for a chance to heal itself. It's a good precaution."

Lowbacca waved Ganner aside, then wrapped his long arms around the coral oval and heaved. He set it down in front of the portal with a resounding thud and then shouldered it into place. Immediately a dark goo began to seep from the surrounding wall, filling in the crack and binding the portal back into the wall.

Jaina clicked on the comm. "Zekk, if you can lock down the breached chamber, do it. Just in case."

"Already done."

She turned her attention to the task of flying the ship— and keeping a mental connection open to her fellow pilot. Talking was useless, for there were no words to equate one technology with the other. The two pilots communicated through feelings, impressions, adjusting their speed and direction to match each other precisely. Jaina had jokingly described their shared flight as a dance, and that's precisely what it felt like—a dance between enormous, mismatched partners.

All went well until they entered Hapes's atmosphere. The *Trickster* shuddered as the dovin basal adjusted for the planet's gravity. A loud, groaning creak announced that the heat and turbulence of reentry was straining the seal between the ships. The messages coming to Jaina through the cognition hood were garbled, as if the ship were confused.

Suddenly Jaina was none too happy about their chances. She tossed a look over her shoulder. Tahiri was right behind her, a place she seemed to be taking with increasing frequency. "Tahiri, you've flown in these things before. How did you land?"

"We crashed, mostly," the girl admitted.

The ship shook and pitched as it neared the ground. "It's panicking," Jaina realized. "It thinks the attached ship is pulling it down."

"Let me try," Tahiri offered, prodding Lowbacca out of the navigation chair. She pulled on the hood. After a moment she shook her head. "No good. It's not listening anymore."

"You hear that, Zekk?" she called through the comm.

"Cut us loose," he said tersely.

Jaina relayed her intention to the ship and then wrenched the frigate to one side. The seal released at once, and the *Trickster* soared away from the pirate ship.

Her heart crawled into her throat as she watched the damaged ship spiral slowly toward the ground. It was scant meters from crashing before Zekk finally managed to pull out of the spin. He brought the ship into a rising turn, then slowed to a hover as the repulsor engines came on. The cargo ship lowered onto the landing dock, coming to rest heavily but safely.

To Jaina's relief, the *Trickster* calmed and followed its erstwhile partner down to the dock. As soon as the Yuuzhan Vong frigate set down, she suggested that it rest and then yanked off the hood.

The other Jedi had left the ship by the time she finished shutting down. When she reached the open hatch, she noted them standing together in a tight knot. Several Hapan military officials supervised the removal of the fighter ships from the cargo hold of the captured vessel; others led the pirates away.

Jaina hurried down the ramp, and her eyes sought out

Zekk. "You didn't have a choice," he said before she could speak. "There were two people on my ship, twenty on yours. I would have done the same thing."

Jaina nodded her thanks. Before she could say anything, Tahiri caught the arm of a passing docking official. "How can we get a repulsorsled? We have a casualty aboard. We need to take him to his parents in the refugee camp."

The woman pulled away and swept a hand toward the grassy area beyond the dock. Rows of wounded lay on white pallets. Sheets had been pulled up over many of them. "I'm sorry, but yours is hardly a unique situation."

Jaina's eyes narrowed. She came to stand at Tahiri's side, faced down the official and moved her hand in a slight subtle gesture. "You will find Han and Leia Solo in the refugee camp and inform them that their daughter has arrived."

The official's eyes widened, only partly due to the subtle Jedi compulsion. "This casualty you spoke of. That wouldn't be Anakin Solo, would it?"

This set Jaina back on her heels. "You've heard?"

"Who hasn't!" she said, her tones rounded with near reverence. "The HoloNet—or what's left of it—has been playing Princess Leia's exhortation to the people of Coruscant almost nonstop since the battle. Of course I'll send word!"

The woman hurried off. Tahiri shifted her weight from one foot to the other, and glanced back toward the Yuuzhan Vong ship. Impatience and repugnance came off her in waves, and an almost frantic desire to get away. Still, Jaina couldn't see wandering around the refugee camp with this particular cargo in tow.

"Maybe we should wait for my parents here," Jaina suggested.

Green fire flared in Tahiri's eyes. "How can you think

about leaving Anakin in there one nanosecond longer than we have to!"

Jaina was about to point out that Anakin was past caring about such things. Yet it was hard to forget the grim compulsion that had driven her to recover her brother's body from the worldship, at great risk to herself and the other Jedi.

She tamped down her impatience. "Be practical. We can't exactly cruise around Hapes with a repulsorsled. My parents will want a funeral—well, my mother will, anyway—and she'll make sure everything is handled in a dignified, proper fashion."

The official hurried back, followed by a repulsorsled and two somber-faced assistants. "They look sort of dignified," Tahiri ventured.

"All right," she conceded. "They can get him off the ship." She told them where to find her brother's body. In short order they emerged from the ship, flanking a white-draped sled. Tahiri's eyes filled.

Jaina abruptly turned and put several quick paces between herself and the young Jedi. She folded her arms and leaned against the *Trickster*, staring out over the bustling docks.

Before long she noted a two-person landspeeder skimming toward them. Almost before it stopped, Leia flung herself from it and hurried to her daughter, her eyes bright with relief.

She stopped abruptly when her gaze fell on the sled, and the color drained from her face.

"We brought Anakin with us," Jaina said. "Jacen we couldn't get to. I'm sorry."

Leia took a long, steadying breath and tilted her chin into its familiar, imperious angle. From the corner of her eye, Jaina noticed Tahiri mirroring the older woman's gesture, as if the outer form might serve as a vessel to hold something of Leia's strength.

She stepped forward and embraced her daughter. "Don't worry about Jacen," she said softly. "He might seem fragile at times, but he's a survivor."

Jaina stiffened, startled by her mother's comment. Leia was as sensitive to the Force as any trained Jedi, and in Jaina's opinion, the epitome of grace under pressure. How could she block this?

Her eyes sought out her father's face. Han looked from her to Leia, his eyes wary. He must have read the truth in Jaina's eyes, because suddenly the color seeped from his face, leaving it gray and haggard and . . . old.

And suddenly Jaina had one more reason to hate the Yuuzhan Vong.

Her gaze slid away from the shattered face of the man who was both her father and her childhood hero. She eased out of her mother's embrace, keeping her hands on Leia's shoulders. "Mom, Jacen is gone. We all felt it." One way or another, she added silently.

The older woman shook her head. "He's still alive," she stated, quietly but with implacable conviction.

For a moment Jaina was at a complete loss for words. She stepped aside so that Leia could confront at least one of the grim realities before her.

For a long moment the woman stood, gazing at the still, white-draped form of her youngest child. Her eyes welling with unshed tears, she reached out a shaking hand to fold down the drape covering Anakin's face. One droplet traced a wet path down her cheek and she brushed it away, blinking hard. Han, his own eyes glistening, came to her side and took her hand. But when she looked up at Jaina, blinking back tears, Leia's voice was steady.

"Was it hard?"

Jaina glanced at the bier. "Let's just say he didn't make it easy for them."

"He wouldn't," Leia said with a faint, sad smile. "But I

was asking about you. I was among the Yuuzhan Vong briefly, so I have some idea of what you might have faced—what Jacen might still be facing. But I survived, and so did you. And so will Jacen. We have to believe that."

Leia gazed at her fallen son for a long moment. Softly, she stroked his cheek, then bent to kiss his forehead. At last, she turned and began to walk ahead. Her husband and daughter exchanged a helpless glance and then fell into place on either side.

"About Jacen," Han ventured, his voice shaking a little. "I don't want to believe it, either, but . . . There's got to be a way to make sure. Maybe Luke could—"

"No," Leia said firmly. "He couldn't. Jacen is alive. I know it. I just can't explain why I know it, or how."

"We all felt Jacen's presence," Jaina said. She added carefully, "It seemed like . . . a farewell."

"I felt that, too. But there's a difference between closing down and winking out. I felt Anakin's death. Not Jacen's."

"Neither did I, and I'm his twin." She took a deep breath. "Mom, I think you need to consider the possibility that you might be in denial. A mother's intuition is a powerful thing, but so are the instincts of half a dozen fully trained Jedi."

"Don't start in on your mother," Han cautioned. "Not again, and *especially* not now."

Jaina sent him an incredulous stare.

"Don't look at me like I just kicked an Ewok," Han said. "I've heard about some of the comments you've made, about her not working at being a Jedi, not being there as a mother." He stabbed a finger in her direction. "No more."

For several moments, father and daughter faced each other wearing identical expressions of outrage. Then Jaina bobbed her head in a curt nod.

"All right, maybe I've said some things in the past

couple of years that I'm not proud of. But would *you* want to be judged on the three or four worst comments you've made since this war started?"

Han's silence was more eloquent than words.

"Don't judge me for a few stupid remarks," she repeated softly. She and Leia locked stares. "Somehow, I doubt that Mom does."

Her mother smiled faintly. "I was younger than you when I joined the Senate. Almost immediately I started using my position to cover my work with the Rebellion. Bail Organa tried to dissuade me. I called him a coward."

"Well, there you go," Jaina said, as if that settled everything.

Han's gaze shifted from his wife to his daughter. Never had the resemblance between them been stronger than at this moment. He shook his head in bemusement. "And here I thought I was outnumbered by the Vong," he muttered.

Jaina enfolded him in a quick, hard hug. "Take care of Mom," she whispered.

Han held her off at arm's length and glanced toward the group of solemn young Jedi gathering around Anakin's bier. "You're not staying?"

"I've said my good-byes." Jaina pulled free, exchanged another look with her mother, then strode off without a backward glance.

It was pure instinct that sent Han after her. Leia stopped him abruptly, one hand on his chest.

"She's your daughter," Leia reminded him. "She has to deal with loss in her own way and in her own time."

Han considered this. The expression on his face was that of a man who gazed into a mirror and disliked what he saw. He grimaced and passed one hand over his face.

"She's my daughter," he admitted, "and I'm an idiot."

His eyes held apology for all he'd done and said in the

months following Chewbacca's death. Leia manufactured a shaky smile. "Don't be too hard on yourself."

"Yeah, well." He fell silent, and his gaze shifted slowly, reluctantly toward the draped sled.

"I hope Anakin saw things the same way Jaina does," he said at last. "I'd hate to think he judged me—or worse yet, himself—by the stupidest three or four things I've said since this war started."

"He knows," she said. "And he doesn't."

He looked at her, his expression wistful. "You sound so sure. You're sure about Jacen, too, aren't you?"

"Yes."

Han considered this, nodded. "That's good enough for me."

Leia's heart overflowed. She went into Han's arms—the last sure haven in the galaxy—and turned her face into his chest to hide the tears she could no longer contain.

FIFTEEN

Jaina's pace quickened as she left the docks at a dead run, as if she could outpace the memory of her father's face when he'd realized that both his sons were gone. Before she knew it, she was churning along, weaving mindlessly through the turmoil of ships, overworked officials, and confused refugees. She paused only long enough to duck into one of the public refreshers most docking areas provided as a convenience to pilots—and then only long enough to sonic off the worst of the grime.

Feeling somewhat calmer, she set a direct course for the palace. Its labyrinthine marble halls were the best place she could think of to lose herself for a while.

Ta'a Chume's efficiency confronted her at every turn. Palace guards ushered her through; servants offered refreshment and then quietly withdrew when she waved them away.

Moving on autopilot, she found her way into a courtyard garden and down shaded paths that seemed designed with solitude and secrecy in mind. She slumped down on the moss-covered rocks artfully piled beside a carved bench and finally allowed herself to feel.

What she felt, mostly, was numb.

Since leaving Myrkr, her path had seemed clear. The first order of business was to survive, to finish the task Anakin had passed to Jacen, to bring the other young Jedi to a place of safety. And after that, to rescue Jacen.

Jaina hadn't allowed herself to think of anything else, to feel anything that might distract her from these goals. Her headlong progress had been stopped short, and she felt as dazed as if she'd flown a landspeeder into a tree.

She felt the approach of a powerful presence, and glanced up as a tall, graceful woman emerged from the shadows of a fruit arbor and glided purposefully down the path toward her. The woman wore a softly draping gown, and her russet hair gleamed above the scarlet veil covering the lower half of her face. Feeling resigned but not at all surprised, Jaina rose and dipped into a bow.

Ta'a Chume waved away the formalities. The former queen mother settled down on the bench and motioned for Jaina to join her. She removed her veil, revealing a still-elegant face distinguished by fine, sharp bones. "It is good to see you alive and well, Jaina. I heard about your brothers."

Jaina took the offered place beside Ta'a Chume and braced herself for yet another round of meaningless condolences.

This response seemed to amuse the former queen. "I take it you've had your fill of platitudes and exhortations?"

"You might say that."

"Then let's get to the heart of the matter. Your brothers are dead, and those responsible still live. The only reasonable question is, what are you going to do about it?"

There was something refreshing about plain speech, and even an odd sort of comfort. "That's the question, all right."

The older woman patted her shoulder. "You will find your way to an answer soon, of that I am certain. And tonight will be an excellent time to start. There will be a diplomatic dinner at the palace, and you would do well to attend. Now, then," she said briskly, "I suggest that we find you a suitable gown and gems." Her eyes slid quickly over Jaina's stringy brown hair. "And perhaps a hair stylist."

Jaina shrugged this off. "I'm a pilot. Appearances aren't important to what I do."

"That's quite apparent," Ta'a Chume murmured. But her eyes slid over the young woman, taking stock, measuring potential. A speculative gleam entered her eyes. "Tell me, do you wish to avenge your brothers?"

Jaina attempted to plot a direct path between these two topics but quickly gave up the effort. "I wouldn't have put it quite that way, but yes, I suppose I do."

As she said the words, Jaina realized the truth of them. All her life she'd heard that anger and revenge were paths to the dark side. At this moment, that hardly seemed to matter—in fact, such concerns struck her as petty and self-indulgent. The galaxy was fighting for survival, and the Jedi weren't doing much better on that score than anyone else.

She realized that Ta'a Chume had been speaking for several moments and focused her attention back to the former queen.

"In order to achieve this, you will need to win support from the Hapan military," Ta'a Chume concluded. "Beauty is a tool to be used, just like intelligence or talent or power or even this Force of yours. Don't disdain it."

"It's more important on Hapes than in most places. More common, too." Jaina shrugged. "No matter what I do, I'd fall short of your world's standards."

"Nonsense, on all counts. I suspect that you possess many resources you have not yet considered."

Jaina regarded the older woman. The former queen was a powerful presence in the Force, yet she possessed formidable shields. Jaina could get no sense of what she was thinking, but she took what she knew of Ta'a Chume and made some assumptions.

"You want something from me," she said bluntly. "Forgive me, but I'm running short on time and illusions."

Ta'a Chume smiled, not at all offended. "All I ask is that you keep your mind open to all possibilities. These are strange times, and you may find yourself in a position to accomplish things you never dreamed possible. Now, about that gown."

She rose and headed for the palace. After a moment, Jaina followed. Ta'a Chume had access to ships, fuel, and ammunition—all the things Jaina would need to take the fight to the Yuuzhan Vong—and apparently the former queen was willing to trade.

Jaina had no idea what currency Ta'a Chume had in mind, but that didn't particularly worry her. She almost looked forward to matching wits with someone who'd made an art form of deception and intrigue. Like lightsaber practice, it might serve to sharpen her wits and skills in preparation for a real battle.

And unlike Ta'a Chume, Jaina had the Force with her. Light or dark—it didn't matter. Those distinctions seemed artificial to her, half-understood concepts whose time was done. As Kyp Durron had said, this was their time, their war. The younger Jedi needed to decide what to do and how to do it, and then live with the results.

For the first time a tinge of unease darkened Jaina's thoughts. "Hurling black lightning is one thing," she muttered, "but quoting Kyp Durron puts me lower than I ever expected to get."

The comm unit in Kyp Durron's X-wing crackled. "Vanguard Three, acknowledge."

The calm, emotionless tone of Jag Fel's voice set the Jedi's teeth on edge, but he clicked the channel open. "Sir," he said in ironic imitation of the Chiss woman's stern military manner.

If Jag picked up on Kyp's tone, he didn't let on. "The

squadron is preparing to make the jump to Gallinore. By all reports, this world is rich in unusual plant and animal life, just the sort of planet likely to draw the Yuuzhan Vong's interest."

As far as Kyp could tell, the invaders were not particularly discriminating. Ithor had been a forested paradise, and they'd burned it to ash and rock. Duro, on the other hand, was a foul slag heap. That planet they chose to rebuild.

It occurred to him to wonder how the Yuuzhan Vong might transform Coruscant. He decided he didn't want to know.

"Setting coordinates," he said, reaching for the controls that would relay this request to Zero-One.

"Belay that," Jag told him. "The others will go ahead with Shawnkyr. We two will stay behind to practice maneuvers."

An amused beep came from the astromech droid, but Kyp was too astounded to respond. *Practice maneuvers?* Exactly who and what did this kid think he was, and more important, to whom should Kyp send his body?

"Vanguard Three?" the commander prompted.

"Acknowledged," Kyp said through gritted teeth.

He watched the other four ships disappear into the blackness of hyperspace. Six ships total, half the number he himself had commanded, and all of them reduced to skulking around the Hapes Cluster watching for signs of an invasion that, in Kyp's opinion, was a foregone conclusion.

"You think our efforts here are wasted," Jag observed.

"Let's just say that I'm accustomed to a more proactive approach. Hello," he said abruptly, glancing down at flashing sensors. "What have we got, Zero-One?"

SEVEN SMALL CRAFT. ALL ARE ARMING WEAPONS.

"Looks like today was worth waking up for after all.

Let's strike up an acquaintance." Without bothering to defer to his "commander," Kyp accelerated and swept toward the small fleet.

As he neared, he made out the distinctive wasp shape of the ships, the single dark viewport that from the side resembled an insect's eye. The triangular wings were folded down close to the crescent hull for sublight flight, lowered from the upright V they assumed in atmosphere. In either flying condition, these ships could be deadly foes.

"Hornet Interceptors," Jag observed. "Quite likely the same fighters that scattered when we approached Lieutenant Solo's captured pirate ship."

A sardonic smile tugged at one corner of Kyp's mouth, and his irritation changed to interest. Of course they were the same ships—the Hornets weren't equipped with hyperdrives, and their base ship was sitting on the Hapan docks with a two-meter hole burned into its hull.

It would appear that the starched and polished Chiss commander had brought him out on a hunting expedition. This had possibilities.

A bolt of greenish light streaked toward Kyp. He dodged the missile and returned fire.

The agile Hornet rolled aside and came back with a second attack. Two more ships circled around behind Kyp as he and his first opponent dipped and spun in a deadly dance. He grimaced as a laser bolt exploded against his shields.

Even with the Force guiding him, Kyp was hardpressed to match several faster, more agile ships. "Zero-One, get a lock on the forward ship's maneuvering jet."

Icons flashed onto the targeting screen and zoomed into tight focus. When the droid beeped a confirmation, Kyp fired.

A blue laser bolt leapt toward the Hornet, skimming past the hull and slipping just under the deflector-shield projector. A brief spark announced the hit, and the Hornet listed heavily to one side.

Kyp spun away and came back at the damaged ship from above. He fired several laser streams at the ship's insectoid head. The first few shots took out the Hornet's shields. With half its maneuvering capability gone, the ship presented an easy target, and the pilot knew it.

The cockpit broke away as the pilot evacuated. The Hornet tumbled slowly away, as dead as the decapitated insect it resembled. Kyp pulled his X-wing into a sharp, rising circle, coming completely around and firing as he swooped down toward the remaining Hornets.

His attack sheared through one of the folded wings, and another ship went into a spiral. Kyp juked sharply to avoid return fire from one of the two surviving Interceptors.

With one hand he kept a steady barrage of laserfire pummeling the nearest ship, focusing on the Hornet's starboard power generator. He sighted down the riveted joints where two curved segments met in the center of the ship. Still working the laser cannon, he launched a proton torpedo and then reached out with the Force.

The Hornet rolled sharply to port to evade—just as Kyp nudged the torpedo's flight slightly aside. The missile stuck the ship dead center and shattered the segment's joinery. Centrifugal force and the evasive turn did the rest, and the rear half of the ship ripped away. From above, it appeared that a pair of gigantic, invisible hands had seized the ship and twisted it into two parts.

Kyp turned his attention to his fourth and final opponent. To his surprise, Jag Fel was already on it. The younger man's clawcraft led the ship in a dizzying chase, openly taunting it to employ its turbocharged cannons. Several times the Hornet spat green fire. Each time Jag deftly evaded.

The Chiss ship spun away from the Hornet and began

to climb, positioning for a diving attack. Kyp realized the strategy and came in from the opposite side. The two ships dived toward the Hornet, showering the midsection with laserfire.

Red heat began to pulse through the rear fuselage. The two scouts veered aside as the ship exploded from within.

Smart move, Kyp congratulated silently. Turbocharged laser cannons were as much a liability to the Hornets as they were an advantage—even a few shots could render the big guns unstable. Still, Jag Fel's approach to the problem was as crazy as any airborne stunt Kyp had ever pulled.

But the young commander seemed unimpressed with his own daring. He was already on the comm, scanning for any ship close enough to pick up the evacuated pilots.

Once Jag had ensured retrieval of the surviving pirates, the two scouts fell into the side-by-side formation the Chiss-taught commander seemed to favor.

"So," Kyp said conversationally, "is that your idea of practicing maneuvers?"

For several moments the only response to his rhetorical question was the faint crackle of an open comm. "You approached the Hornets without waiting for my command. Is this common practice?"

"For me? Absolutely."

"I was referring to the New Republic in general. Gathering information is a vital function, but to whom should I report? I'm accustomed to clear chain of command, and the efficiency that results. While I understand that the fall of Coruscant dealt an enormous blow to the New Republic, the survivors seem fractured and contentious."

"No argument here," Kyp said, "but for the record, I haven't been using the term *New Republic* for years. A government is like a fighter ship: after the first couple of decades it picks up a few dings and loses its shiny new look."

"Point noted. Given my upbringing, I frequently have to remind myself not to refer to you as the Rebel Alliance," Jag said with a touch of wry amusement. "I don't wish to offend, but it's a mystery to me that you managed to defeat the Empire."

"We have our moments," he said in a dry tone. "The Republic's utter lack of direction is actually a clever ploy to confuse our enemies."

"And that works?"

"Not that I've noticed, no."

Jag lapsed into thoughtful silence. "I appreciate your candor, and your willingness to hear me out. Would you be offended by a personal question?"

"That seems unlikely. Go ahead."

"Why is Jaina Solo so angry at you?"

An irrational flicker of irritation shimmered through the Jedi Master. "Oh, that. It's a long story with a number of sordid chapters. Why not ask her yourself?"

"Two reasons. First, I don't wish to intrude upon personal matters. Second, I suspect that you *did* resent that question," observed Jag, "and I suspect that sending me to Jaina is your way of ensuring that I'm suitably punished for my presumption."

This canny observation annoyed Kyp, and then amused him. "Depends what you consider personal. She helped me bring the Republic into a strike on a Yuuzhan Vong shipyard. The Vong were building new worldships there. I wanted her to believe they were superweapons. Once convinced, she was very convincing."

"Ah."

"Ah?" he repeated. "That's it? You're not going to lecture me on the evils of aggression?"

Jag considered this for a moment. "I was raised and trained among the Chiss. To them, first-strike tactics are unthinkable, dishonorable. We are defenders, not aggressors. But in this conflict, can we really argue that carefully considered aggression is different from holding back until the enemy strikes first? We know from the onset that battle is inevitable."

Another convincing voice, Kyp mused. It was difficult to miss the spark of interest between Jag Fel and Jaina. The two of them, with a little guidance and a nudge or two in the right direction, could become a very potent force. He briefly pondered the possibilities of this, and the logistics.

"Your father's a baron, right?"

"He is. Why do you ask?"

"Diplomatic vessels have been coming in from all over the cluster. Word has it there's a state dinner at the palace this evening. If you want to talk to Jaina, that title might get you invited."

"The palace?" Jag echoed incredulously. "She is not with her parents?"

"Not from what I hear."

A long, astonished sigh hissed through the comm. "That, I do not understand. I also lost two siblings in battle. At such times, family provides much-needed support."

"She has friends in the palace. Jedi," Kyp specified. He let that remark lie where it fell.

"I see."

Jag's cool tone suggested that enough had been said on this subject. Kyp considered and discarded several next-step remarks, searching for the words most likely to move the young pilot in the desired direction. "Do you believe in destiny?"

"If you mean the faithful development of inborn abilities and adherence to the duty at hand, then yes, I do."

"Close enough. Have you considered the possibility that the people in this galaxy simply don't know what to do about the Yuuzhan Vong, and never will? That perhaps the answer will come from an outsider's perspective?"

"I hadn't thought in quite those terms, no."

Kyp considered the wreckage of the Hornet Interceptors and the skill and conviction of the young commander from the Unknown Regions. "Well, maybe you should."

SIXTEEN

Tenel Ka made her way across the ridge of the palace armory's steeply sloped roof, running lightly and in perfect balance. The sprawling inner courtyard lay below her, and from this vantage she commanded a clear view of the west gate. Several guards were stationed on either side of the portal, which was used only by members of the royal family. Her father was due to return shortly, and a strong premonition prompted Tenel Ka to set her own watch.

She sped up as she approached the end of the roof and hurled herself into the air. Soaring over the three-meter divide without benefit of her Jedi powers, she landed in a crouch on the lower, flatter roof of the palace kitchens.

As she sprinted toward the western edge of the roof, she scanned the gardens and pens below. Guards walked the parameters of the palace walls, vigilant against threats to the royal family, but from time to time they seemed to forget how many royals had fallen to members of their own household. Other than the garden maze, the kitchen wing offered the best potential ambush sites. It was also conveniently situated right next to the west bailey.

The brazen keening of dugglehorns cleaved the air, announcing Prince Isolder's approach. Tenel Ka crouched and crept cautiously to the edge of the roof.

Several cooks stood at a long wooden table, transforming a small mountain of game birds into the main course for the evening feast. The steady thump of the cleaver set a counterpoint to the chatter of the young boys who plucked the feathers. Beyond this scene of domestic slaughter lay the herb garden. Two men in loose Hapan tunics picked bitter herbs for salad. Both wore hoods to protect their skin from the bright afternoon sun. More servants went about other tasks—picking berries for pastries, lugging foaming pails of cream from the milk house, scything down clusters of nuts.

Tenel Ka's cool gray eyes darted over gardens and outbuildings, looking for anything that seemed out of place. All appeared to be as it should be. She watched as one of the older men climbed the stairs to the blizcot, a large birdhouse that enticed the plump little bliz to enter and nest. Their tiny, pink-shelled eggs were a Hapan delicacy and would certainly be included on the evening menu. The old man climbed slowly, hauling himself along the railing with one hand and clutching an egg basket with the other.

A very large egg basket.

The Jedi warrior ripped a flat stone tile from the roof and rose to her feet. Three things happened in rapid succession:

The west gate opened to admit Isolder. The "old man" whipped a blaster from the oversized basket and pointed it at the prince. Tenel Ka hurled the tile with all her strength, sending it spinning toward the assassin.

Her aim held true, and the tile struck the arm holding the weapon with a force that spun the assassin around and sent him tumbling down the stairs. The shot went wild, pinging down into the orchards, sending golden fruit plummeting and launching birds into startled, squawking flight.

The palace guards were upon the assassin before he'd reached the bottom. Ubris, an impressive female warrior who'd been with the prince since before Tenel Ka was born, hauled the assailant to his feet and jerked off the hood.

A hush fell over the courtyard. The assassin was a young woman, and her face was familiar to them all.

Tenel Ka climbed down a trellis and stalked toward the defiant woman. She stopped a few paces away and gazed into a face very like her own.

"Greetings, cousin," she said coolly. "Aunt Chelik must be desperate for the throne if she is willing to sacrifice her own daughter to get it." Without waiting for a response, she turned to the guard and nodded. Ubris hauled the traitor away.

Tenel Ka took a long breath, for she understood the sentence awaiting her blood kin. An attack against a member of the royal family was punishable by death, but recently this law had proved an insufficient deterrent. At this rate, the prison yards would soon rival the palace kitchens for legal carnage!

She turned away and went to greet her father. The prince stood inside the west bailey, listening to his bodyguard's description of the near escape. He was a tall man with a fighter's disciplined physique. Pale gold hair was pulled severely back into a single thick braid, framing a face that was exceptionally handsome even by Hapan standards. From a few paces away, he didn't look much older than Ganner Rhysode. Only the fine lines around his eyes and the weariness in them suggested the weight of his years.

The gaze he turned upon Tenel Ka was both proud and somber. "Princess, they tell me that I owe you my life. Clear thinking, quick action—essential qualities for a ruler."

Tenel Ka suppressed a sigh and turned up her cheek for her father's kiss. "Welcome home. You had a profitable trip?"

"Walk with me, and I'll tell you about it." He smiled down at her. "But please—not on the rooftops."

They left the kitchen area for the protected inner gardens. Even there, Tenel Ka kept alert, scanning the arbors and alcoves for signs of movement, comparing the length and shape of shadows to the objects that cast them.

"You know of course that your mother has opened Hapes to refugees," Prince Isolder began.

Tenel Ka's face clouded with dismay at her father's formal, distant tone. Things between her parents had been strained for quite some time.

"The people displaced by war need a haven," she observed.

"I don't disagree. But the queen mother's decision ensures that we will face the invaders. I've spent much of the last year finding and studying what information we have been able to amass. The more we understand these Yuuzhan Vong, the better our chances of survival."

It was on the tip of the Jedi woman's tongue to say that she knew far more about the invaders than she wished to.

"You were among them for a time," he went on. "Tell me what you learned."

One grim picture after another flashed into Tenel Ka's mind: scenes from the terrible days of captivity in the Yuuzhan Vong worldship, the battle that followed, the agony of leaving behind the young man she had loved since girlhood. What could she tell her father of this?

"They are devoted to their religion," she said at last.

He nodded. "I have read the debriefing given Elan, the traitor priestess. The Yuuzhan Vong venerate two gods in particular: Yun-Harla, the Trickster goddess, and Yun-Yammka, the Slayer. Battle and deceit—these are the enemy's passions."

"We spoke to two of the Yuuzhan Vong through their

villips," Tenel Ka related. "One of them made mention of this Yun-Harla. Jaina named the stolen ship *Trickster* in an attempt to annoy and distract them. She succeeded."

"From what I know of the Yuuzhan Vong, they would see that as blasphemy," Isolder agreed.

She leaned forward, her gray eyes intense. "Of what significance are twins?"

Isolder thought this over. "Judging from the information available, twin births seem to be uncommon among the Yuuzhan Vong. I can recall three mentions. Each was thought to be a portent of some great event. In each, one twin killed the other as a prelude to some great destiny."

Tenel Ka nodded thoughtfully. "And if one twin dies in some other fashion?"

"I don't know. It seems likely that the survivor will still be viewed as an important person. Why do you ask?"

"Jacen Solo is dead," she said bluntly, "and the Yuuzhan Vong know he has a twin sister."

Isolder sent her a sympathetic look. "I see."

"With respect, I don't think you do. I fear for Jaina's safety, yes, but the Yuuzhan Vong can do far worse than kill. Tahiri, Anakin Solo's friend, was captured on Yavin Four and turned over to the shapers. They scarred her body and implanted memories in her mind in an attempt to make her over into something more like them."

"Jaina is not under their power."

"Not directly, no. But if the Yuuzhan Vong perceive her to be the central figure in some important event, they may create a situation that will force her into that role. It is a form of shaping."

Isolder gave her shoulder a comforting pat. "She is a strong-willed and resourceful young woman."

"Fact," Tenel Ka agreed, "but the path she is taking concerns me. In claiming affinity to their Trickster goddess, she has thrown down a challenge they cannot refuse. And in taking on this role, she has already begun to assimilate the Yuuzhan Vong's expectations. I do not like to contemplate what Jaina's 'great destiny' might be, as defined by these invaders and her response to them."

"Is this so different from what we all must do? No one is born free of the burden of expectations."

She cut him off with a swiftly upraised hand. "If you're trying to nudge me onto the throne of Hapes, you might as well save your time and mine."

Her father was silent for several moments. "You have seen your mother since your return?"

"Of course!"

"Then you have seen the truth: if you do not take the throne, someone else will have to."

Tenel Ka began to pace, trying to think of some rebuttal. But the specter of Queen Mother Chelik was all too credible. The woman was niece to Ta'a Chume and a legitimate heir. She would swiftly repudiate her daughter's attempt on Isolder's life, and no one would be able to prove her involvement. But Tenel Ka would know, of course, and so would her ailing mother.

No wonder Hapes had a history of distrust for those with Jedi powers! The ruling queen mothers survived by their ability to dissemble and manipulate. They did not appreciate those who could see through their plots and perceive the venal natures doubly hidden beneath scarlet veils and beautiful faces.

Tenel Ka had few illusions about her family. Chelik was not the worst of Ta'a Chume's possible successors. Alyssia, younger sister to Chelik, was even more devious. Alyssia was too canny to make an open attack on Prince Isolder. More likely, she had slyly manipulated Chelik's daughter into acting on her mother's behalf. The girl would be executed for this crime, and the loss of an heir weakened Chelik's bid for the throne.

Such was the royal family, its court, even Hapan culture. Tenel Ka could not conceive of a life defined by these values. Would she, like Jaina, reshape herself to the expectations of her foes?

"Will you at least consider the possibility?" Isolder pressed.

Tenel Ka ran her hand over her red-gold hair, plaited as always into the braids of a Dathomiri fighter. "I'm not a ruler, but a warrior."

"Who better to lead in time of war? Surely your grandmother has also urged you along this path."

"I haven't seen much of her," she said. It hadn't escaped her notice that since their arrival, Ta'a Chume had taken more interest in Jaina than in her own royal heir. There was no jealousy in this observation, but a great deal of concern. Jaina was no fool, but she couldn't possibly know the truth of the old woman.

A terrible thought occurred to her. Perhaps the real threat to the Hapan throne came not from the branches of the family tree, but from the root. Ni'Korish, the queen mother before Ta'a Chume, was remembered for her virulent hatred of the Jedi. But perhaps Ta'a Chume understood the potential of a dark Jedi ally, and sought to coax Jaina down this path for her own purposes. With Darth Vader's granddaughter beside her, Ta'a Chume could easily scythe through the various plots and reclaim her throne. A woman who could order the death of her eldest son's betrothed, and perhaps even the man himself, was capable of anything.

"You look worried," the prince observed. "Is all well with Ta'a Chume?"

"She is as she ever was."

"I see," Isolder said slowly. "Then I would say that there is ample cause for worry."

Tenel Ka gave a grim nod. For the first time, father and daughter were in complete accord.

* * *

The banquet hall in the royal palace glittered with candlelight, a charming anachronism that the Hapan diplomats seemed to take in stride. There was much about this world that reminded Jaina of her mother's stories of Alderaan—the tradition, the formality, the emphasis on beauty and art and culture, the sense of being transported into a vital and vibrant re-creation of past times.

Musicians played softly in alcoves upon instruments Jaina had only seen in books. Fresh flowers filled the room with a heady scent, and servants moved with quiet efficiency to remove plates and refill glasses.

The use of human servants disconcerted Jaina, but there was not a droid to be found anywhere in the palace. Nor did the food have the flat, homogeneous flavor that came from a synth unit. Since this was a diplomatic dinner and Jag Fel was the son of an Imperial baron, he had been invited. He sat across from Jaina, re-splendent in a formal black uniform. All things considered, she might have enjoyed the experience . . . had she been in a better state of mind, not to mention a more comfortable gown.

She tugged at the laces cinching her waist and looked up to see Jag Fel observing her. "I'd be happier in a flight suit," she said ruefully.

"No doubt, but you look lovely all the same."

It was a polite phrase, an expected response. Jaina had received similar compliments at a hundred diplomatic affairs. But none had ever set her cheeks flaming—a response that none of her Jedi training seemed able to mitigate.

She deliberately turned to watch the first dance. Prince Isolder led his daughter through the elaborate steps. Tenel Ka danced as she fought—with singular grace and fierce, absolute concentration.

"I wonder what might happen to a man who stepped on her toes," Jag mused.

Jaina shot a startled look at him and noted the faint, wry lift to one corner of his lips. "Their heads are mounted on the trophy room wall," she said with mock seriousness.

A slow smile spread across his face, and Jaina's heart nearly leapt out of her low-necked gown. She glanced at the floor. Other dancers were joining in. On impulse, she nodded toward the growing crowd and said, "They've created a diversion. We could probably sneak out and look around for those trophies."

Jag rose and executed a formal bow. "May I have the honor of shared evasive maneuvers?"

Chuckling, she took his offered hand. They merged into the swirling crowd, working their way toward the doors.

They emerged into the hall, hand in hand, grinning like mischievous children. This was a new side to the somber young pilot, one that intrigued Jaina. Judging from the expression on Jag's face and the sense of wonder coming to her through the Force, this playful moment was something new to him, as well.

One of the paneled doors opened, and a slender, red-clad figure stepped from the banquet chamber into the hall. "Jaina. I'd hoped to have the opportunity to speak with you."

The lighthearted moment vanished. Jag greeted the former queen with a crisp, proper bow and excused himself. He nodded to Jaina and then disappeared back into the swirling crowd. Ta'a Chume led the way to a small receiving room across the hall. Neither woman spoke until they were settled down.

"Enjoying yourself?" Ta'a Chume inquired.

"I think I was about to."

The queen's eyes took on a speculative gleam, but she

did not comment on the turn of phrase. "Teneniel Djo should have led the dancing, but she did not attend. Do you know why?"

Jaina shook her head.

"Her health did not permit. She was expecting a second child, an heir to the throne of Hapes, or at the very least a son who might find a suitable wife. Then came the attack upon Fondor and the destruction of the Hapan fleet. Teneniel Djo is not precisely a Jedi, but she is what I believe you call Force-sensitive."

"That's right," Jaina confirmed.

"She felt the destruction of the fleet, the deaths of our pilots. The shock was more than she could bear. The child was born too soon, and born dead. Teneniel Djo has never fully recovered."

The disdain in Ta'a Chume's voice put Jaina on the defensive. "It's possible to feel actual pain through the Force, and to experience strong emotions. One of the things a Jedi learns to do is guard against constant bombardment. Teneniel Djo's sensitivity was stronger than her shields. That doesn't make her weak."

"Be that as it may, I am not interested in philosophy, but governance. My son's wife is not able to attend a diplomatic dinner, much less lead the entire Consortium into war. Isolder is no fool, nor does he shirk his duty. It's time for him to divorce Teneniel Djo and find a new wife, someone capable of ruling during a time of war."

Jaina regarded the older woman warily. "I'm not sure why you're telling me this."

"You're in a position to understand such complexities. Your mother was a ruler—a queen of sorts—for many years. Tell me, what came first in your family?"

"She walked a better balance than most people could have," Jaina said shortly. "My father doesn't complain. Much."

"A very pragmatic response," Ta'a Chume approved.

"I see you don't subscribe to the myths surrounding marriage. It's not at all what the poets try to make of it, but rather a pragmatic, mutually beneficial alliance, one that is entered into when expedient, and abandoned when it is of no further value."

Jaina began to get a lock on Ta'a Chume's target. "You're considering my mother for Teneniel Djo's job, and you want me to act as intermediary. With all respect, Your Majesty, you might as well jettison that idea with the rest of the trash."

The queen's eyebrows shot up. "Are you always so direct?"

Jaina shrugged. "It saves time. Who knows how long we might have circled around that point, otherwise?"

"Perhaps so. Then let's speak of more pleasant things. Baron Fel's son seems a promising young man."

"He's an excellent pilot."

"So are you. But if you are to be an effective leader, you'll have to know enough of men to be able to take their full measure." She paused for a sour smile. "Don't expect too much."

Jaina rose. "I'll keep that in mind."

The queen watched her leave, then her gaze shifted to a painted screen. "What do you think?"

A young man in festive garb strolled into the room. "I think I've missed something," Trisdin observed. "If I didn't know better, I'd think you're nudging your protégée toward this would-be nobleman with bad fashion sense."

Ta'a Chume sent an arch glance toward her favorite. "Colonel Fel's formal manner lends itself well to court life and conventions, and his military record is most impressive. He is earnest and handsome and idealistic—very much as Prince Isolder was at that age."

The woman smiled like a hunting manka cat. "Jaina

Solo has little understanding of her own personal power and appeal. She must discover it before she can use it."

"Ah!" he said slowly. "An unseasoned girl is not likely to take on as daunting a task as a married prince, especially not a man who courted her mother, and who is father to one of her friends."

"Jaina is not worldly enough for my purposes just yet. Perhaps this Jag Fel can help." Ta'a Chume aimed a cool smile at her favorite. "Feel free to contribute your own efforts to the cause."

Trisdin's blue eyes narrowed at the casual, offhanded manner in which she offered his services. "It would be my pleasure," he agreed, not without malice.

The glance Ta'a Chume sent him showed understanding but no offense. "Charm the girl," she instructed. "Offer her a sympathetic ear when her handsome young pilot meets his unfortunate but inevitable end."

She walked away, leaving Trisdin staring after her. He intended to do all that Ta'a Chume asked—he really had little choice in the matter—but he could not help but wonder what his own "inevitable end" might be.

And knowing Ta'a Chume as he did, Trisdin suspected that Prince Isolder would be the next to offer consolation.

SEVENTEEN

Jaina eased open one of the ballroom doors and peered in. Her eyes swept the glittering assembly, looking for a tall, straight figure clad in somber black. The room was a swirling sea of bright colors and glittering jewels.

There was no sense of Jag's presence, either. Like some of the people she knew—Wedge Antilles, Talon Karrde, and her father—Jag projected a strong presence through the Force, an energy very different from that of a Jedi but powerful in its own way.

And now that she thought of it, here was yet another gap in the conventional Jedi view of the Force. It couldn't perceive or affect the Yuuzhan Vong, or account for people like Han and Jag. Maybe "light" and "dark" were not opposites after all, but simply two aspects of a Force far more varied and complex than any of them believed possible. She stretched out with her senses, trying to catch some glimpse of these larger horizons.

Suddenly a powerful presence flooded her awareness, and these thoughts vanished like the blade of a switched-off lightsaber. Jaina whirled to face Kyp Durron.

For a long moment she simply stared at the Jedi Master, disconcerted and slightly disoriented by the rush of his power over her senses. At the moment of his arrival she had been without shields, without boundaries. Jaina felt as if she'd awoken from a deep trance to find herself gazing directly into a sun.

He reached around her and firmly shut the door, leaving them standing alone in the corridor.

Jaina's shields swiftly returned, and the details of this unexpected meeting began to take focus.

Kyp was somberly dressed in sand-colored Jedi robes, and his silver-shot mane had been tamed into dignified curls. Carefully controlled anger rolled off him in waves, and the expression in his blazing green eyes left little doubt concerning its target.

Jaina's chin came up in an unconscious imitation of her mother's regal poise. "Kyp. I suppose you left dozens of mind-controlled servants and guards behind you, stumbling around the palace in confusion. That's your style, isn't it? Not to mention the only way to explain your presence here."

"Getting out will be easier. You'll be with me."

"I don't think so," she said coolly.

"Think again. I'm here to take you to your brother's funeral."

That was the last thing Jaina had expected. Kyp's blunt pronouncement tore a veil from her heart, and for a moment the terror and fury and agony of Anakin's death filled her senses.

Jaina hurled away these emotions and replaced them with an anger that matched Kyp's. She planted her fists on her hips and stared him down. "You're going to 'take me'? You and what Sith Lord?"

He stabbed a finger at her in a gesture that reminded her a little too much of her father in a parental snit. "Don't challenge me, Jaina."

"Give me one good reason."

His eyes raked over her, and the expression in them dispelled any fatherly comparisons. "You couldn't channel the Force wearing that dress. There isn't enough room in there for it to squeeze through."

Jaina's cheeks flamed, but no suitable retort came to

mind. Worse, she had to admit that his words touched on the truth. She'd left her lightsaber in her room—the clinging scarlet gown wasn't designed for such practicalities.

A disturbing truth came to Jaina: if she had her lightsaber at this moment, she would use it. Kyp lifted one eyebrow, as if he sensed her unspoken challenge.

This was uncharted territory for Jaina, and she was not at all sure of her course. But one thing was abundantly clear—she could hardly avoid the funeral now that Kyp had brought it so forcefully to her attention.

"I'll change," she said stiffly.

Kyp shrugged a leather strap off his shoulder and tossed her a canvas bag. He jerked his head toward the side room where Jaina and Ta'a Chume had spoken. "In there."

Teeth gritted, eyes blazing, Jaina marched into the room. The door shut behind her, and she whirled to find Kyp standing there, arms folded.

"Oh, you'll definitely want to rethink this last decision," she told him.

He nodded toward the painted screen. Muttering, Jaina strode over and put the barrier between her and the Jedi Master. In the bag was a pair of low, soft boots that she recognized as her mother's, Jedi robes identical to those Kyp wore, and a lightsaber. Jaina switched it on and considered the blade's distinctive blue-violet hue.

"You went into my room."

"That's not a capital offense. Turn off the lightsaber before the temptation to dispense justice overwhelms you," he said dryly.

She thumbed it off and turned her attention to the complex fastenings of her borrowed gown. Finally she stripped it off and tossed it over the screen. The loose Jedi robes were a relief—or would have been, under different circumstances.

Finally she came out, grim-faced but resolute. "Let's get this over with."

Kyp led the way to a side door, past a surprising number of guards and servants who appeared every bit as disoriented as Jaina had expected.

Jaina's indignation surged high, then ebbed just as quickly. She couldn't exactly fault the rogue Jedi for doing what every other Jedi did without guilt or debate. Uncle Luke routinely used mind control to sway people in small, day-to-day matters, as had his first Master, Obi-Wan Kenobi. No one seemed to question whether it was appropriate for a Jedi to use the Force to overpower other minds. In this regard, Kyp was no different from any of the more conservative Jedi. He just happened to be unusually good at this particular trick.

They passed through the grounds and to the out-building housing royal transport of various kinds. Kyp settled down on a landspeeder. His long fingers moved deftly over the controls, and the vehicle hummed to life.

Jaina sat down behind him. The landspeeder rose and skimmed quietly through the streets. They left the royal city behind, passed through the docks and circled the edge of the vast refugee camp. Kyp headed for the dense shadows of the public forest, and then eased the land-speeder through narrow paths that wound up a steadily climbing slope.

As they sped up the mountain, the trees began to thin and then gave way to scrub. Twin moons rose, casting their pale light on the strange rocky formations crowning the mountain. Gathered there, their somber faces clearly visible in the light of a hundred torches, were her family and friends.

Kyp pulled up the landspeeder a respectful distance away. Jaina quickly scrambled off and strode toward the gathering. It was bad enough to arrive with Kyp, worse to come dressed alike. She would not complete the illusion of dutiful little apprentice by walking respectfully at his side.

Jaina's gaze swept the small crowd, starting with her parents and then skimming over a surprisingly large group. All the survivors of the mission to Myrkr were there. Tenel Ka stood off to one side, still in the elaborate gown she'd worn earlier that evening. Jag Fel was with her, and Jaina noticed several others whose festive garb stood in stark contrast to the somber gathering. Their presence eased Jaina's discomfort over her mode of arrival—obviously Kyp had brought word to others at the palace as well.

Then her unwilling gaze shifted to the center of the circle, and all other considerations dissipated.

They had brought Anakin here, and placed him on a high, flat stone. A ring of torches surrounded him, a bright border separating him from those who bore witness to his passage.

The shadows stirred, and Tahiri stepped into the circle of light. "Anakin saved my life," she said simply. "The Yuuzhan Vong locked my body in a cage and tried to do the same thing with my mind. Anakin came to Yavin Four, alone, and brought me out."

She fell silent as she gazed into the torchlight. A yearning expression crossed her scarred face, as if the impulse to follow Anakin one more time was too strong to ignore. Leia stepped forward and rested a hand on the girl's shoulder. Jaina couldn't see her mother's face clearly, but something in it seemed to pull Tahiri back. The girl's shoulders rose and fell in a profound sigh, and she yielded her place to another.

"Anakin Solo saved my life," a soft, tentative voice repeated. A young refugee boy stepped into the firelight, and Jaina's heart simply shattered.

He was a near-exact image of her brother at that age—

tousled light brown hair, ice-blue eyes, even the dent in the center of his chin.

"I never met Anakin," the boy said. "People tell me I look like him. I don't know why the lady on Coruscant wanted me to look like this. She promised that my mother and sisters would be safe if I let them change my face. I don't know why," he repeated. "All I know is that looking like Anakin saved me. Maybe it saved my family, too."

"Viqi Shesh," Kyp murmured, naming the devious senator Jaina had distrusted for quite some time. "Han told me about it."

Jaina silently added another name to the list of scores as yet unsettled. Her eyes widened as her father stepped into the firelight.

"Anakin saved my life," he said softly. "Mine, and a shipload of people I would have let burn into starfood. He made the hard decision at Sernpidal, the right decision. I hope he knows that."

Jaina's jaw dropped as Kyp Durron moved into the light. "I knew Anakin mostly through reputation, but I suspect that someday I will be able to stand before a solemn assembly and tell how this young Jedi changed— even saved—my life. The deeds of heroes send ripples spreading through the Force. Anakin's life continues to flow outward, touching and guiding those who have yet to hear his name. Most of us here use the Force—this young man embodied it."

Others came forward, but Jaina didn't hear their words. She'd always known that Anakin was different, special. It seemed odd that Kyp Durron would be the one to find the words that eluded her.

At last the voices fell silent, the torches burned low. The rising moons converged, then began to sink along their separate paths toward the jagged forest horizon. Luke picked up one of the torches and moved forward.

This was the moment Jaina had dreaded most. Anakin was gone, and she understood that what was left was little more than an empty shell. But she had fought so viciously to win him away from the Yuuzhan Vong, and for what? To stand by and watch him destroyed now? It didn't seem right. Nothing about Anakin's death did.

Luke Skywalker approached the stone bier and lowered the torch. The flame spread, limning Anakin's body in golden light.

The fire dissipated into thousands of dancing motes. These rose slowly into the sky, shimmering against the darkness like newborn stars. As they slipped away into the night, it seemed to Jaina that the stars shone a little brighter.

Tears filled her eyes as she gazed at the empty bier. A glimmer of insight flickered on the far edges of her perception—a glimpse, perhaps, of what Anakin might have known, might have become. Jaina blinked away the tears and slammed shields around her emotions.

Zekk came toward them. Jaina tensed. If just one person put his arms around her, she would shatter like overheated glass.

Kyp eased forward, subtly placing himself in the young Jedi's path. Zekk's gaze slid from her to the Jedi Master, and his dark brows drew together in a frown.

"We're returning to Eclipse tomorrow morning with Master Skywalker."

She folded her arms and nodded acknowledgement. "So this is good-bye."

"You're not coming?"

"Not for a while."

He simply stood there, awaiting some word of explanation. Inspiration struck, and Jaina seized it at once. "Kyp asked me to be his apprentice." She swept both arms out wide, inviting inspection of her borrowed robes. "I'm thinking about maybe taking it for a test flight."

Zekk regarded her silently. "Then you're right—this is good-bye."

He turned abruptly and strode away.

Jaina dropped her arms to her sides and managed a wry smile. "Well, that was rude."

"Get used to it," Kyp said softly. "Once word of this little evasion of yours gets around—and that should take about fifteen nanoseconds—you'll find that rogue Jedi live in a world of temperature extremes. Things are either very hot or very cold."

The incredulous stares leveled in her direction put her back up. "Evasion? Are you so sure I wasn't serious?"

"No, I'm not," he countered, "but then, neither are you. When you make up your mind, let me know. In the meanwhile, good luck with your friends," he said, nodding toward the several young Jedi storming toward them. "When they're finished with you, help yourself to the landspeeder. I won't be returning to the city."

Then he, too, slipped away into the night, leaving Jaina alone to face the approaching firestorm.

The next morning Tenel Ka started her day with a twenty-kilometer run followed by an hour of weapons training under the critical eye of her father's swordmaster. The old man watched intently as she went through her routines.

Finally he nodded. "The sword and javelin are as good as ever. The feet, better. You will have to avoid battles that require you to use spear or staff."

Tenel Ka accepted this advice with a nod, even as she noted that it was of limited practical value. In many ways, Hapes was an archaic culture. The physical disciplines she had learned with traditional masters had kept her in good trim, but they were of little use in fighting the sort of battles that lay before her.

Still clad in a lightweight leather garment fashioned from Dathomir lizard skin, Tenel Ka made her way to her mother's room, as she did each morning. Teneniel Djo often seemed cheered by this reminder of her homeworld.

As Tenel Ka entered her mother's chamber, anticipation skittered over her like insects. She could never know just what she would find.

As usual, her mother sat at the window, staring out into the palace gardens. Her rich red-brown hair had faded to a dull and indeterminate shade, and she was far too thin. She looked disturbingly like a winter-starved bird, too dazed by cold and wind to take flight. But she looked up as Tenel Ka entered, and her brown eyes turned wistful at the sight of her daughter's lizard-skin garments.

"That was a bright green once," she observed. "It is faded, and wearing thin. When did you last have new leathers made? A year, almost two," she mused, answering her own question. "The Yuuzhan Vong have held Dathomir for at least that long."

Tenel Ka pulled a chair up close to her mother's. She seemed unusually alert this morning; indeed, her eyes studied her daughter's face with concern.

"You are troubled. The Yuuzhan Vong?"

"Nothing these days is entirely unrelated to the invaders."

"They will come, of course," Teneniel Djo said matter-of-factly. "You must prepare."

She suppressed a sigh. "Mother—"

The queen reached over and patted her knee, cutting short the familiar protest. "I know your heart. You have never wanted to rule, and I would not wish it upon you. I chose a man, not a crown. Soon I will have neither. Isolder will find my successor."

"You are getting stronger," Tenel Ka said stoutly.

The queen smiled faintly. "I do not expect to die anytime soon. But neither can I rule."

She turned to the window and pointed out past the branches of a tzimernut tree. "There, in the mists. Hidden shipyards prepare, rebuilding the fleet lost at Fondor."

Tenel Ka stared at her mother, uncertain how to respond. The queen slid a large emerald ring from her finger and passed it to her daughter. "That is not a gem, but a holocube. The information is contained within. Safeguard it, and see that my successor receives it when the need arises."

Tenel Ka hesitated, then slipped it onto her finger. "I seldom wear such things. Perhaps I should, so that this one is not so obvious."

Teneniel Djo's faded eyebrows rose, and she smiled approvingly. "A good thought."

Her smile faded, and her energy seemed to dissipate with it. A film settled over her eyes and she suddenly looked smaller, older, and infinitely weary.

Tenel Ka kissed her mother's cheek and let herself out of the room. One more disturbing interview awaited her.

She made her way to the royal family's docking bay, a vast structure near the palace. The Yuuzhan Vong frigate had been moved into the city for fear of sabotage, and a number of guards encircled the parameters.

More guards than usual, Tenel Ka noted. Several among them wore the distinctive red uniform of the palace guard. They snapped to attention as she passed, giving her the salute reserved for the royal family.

"Up here," an imperious voice announced.

Tenel Ka glanced up at the walkway that surrounded the huge room. Her grandmother and father stood together. Not quite together, she amended. The distance between them, and the set of her father's shoulders, suggested yet another disagreement in process.

Apparently the morning promised not one unpleasant interview, but two. Tenel Ka sprinted up the stairs, resigned to having this done and over with so she could turn her attention to Jaina.

She nodded to her father and kissed the cheek that Ta'a Chume presented. "You have seen Jaina this morning?"

The former queen scowled and nodded to the alien ship.

Before she could speak, the howl of an irritated Wookiee rent the air. The guards below parted to allow Lowbacca to enter. Other than Tenel Ka, he was the only member of the Jedi strike force who had elected to remain on Hapes, and other than Jaina, the only civilian granted access to this secured site.

Tenel Ka watched Lowbacca with deep concern. The Wookiee's friendship with Jaina, combined with the volatile temper and loyal nature of his species, painted his perceptions in broad and simplistic strokes. He seemed unaware of the changes occurring in his friend, and quite willing to go along with whatever Jaina had in mind.

The Wookiee lumbered toward the frigate with a large crate of rocks in his arms. He dropped it with a heavy thud and began to feed the rocks, one at a time, into an opening that appeared in the ship's hull. Finally he bent over to pick up the empty crate. The ship spat out a pale gray stone, hitting Lowbacca squarely on the rump. The Wookiee jolted upright and spun toward the ship, shaking his fist and howling in outrage.

Jaina popped her head through the hatch. Her face was smudged, and her medium length brown hair looked as if it had been styled in a wind tunnel.

"Hey, it wasn't me! Can I help it if this thing is a fussy eater?"

This remark coaxed a wistful sigh from Tenel Ka. It was so like Jaina as she had been two years ago.

"You seem troubled," Isolder observed.

"Nostalgic, perhaps," she admitted. "It is good to see Jaina tinkering with a ship, even one such as this."

"I'm sorry you think so," the former queen said tartly. "She has better things to do with her time. That young woman is a born leader. She should be pursuing her destiny, not acting the part of a mechanic!"

"Perhaps she is doing exactly that. An understanding of the enemy ships could make an enormous difference," Isolder said. "She is taking an admirably singleminded approach to solving the puzzle it presents."

Tenel Ka shook her head. "She's not solving a puzzle. She's creating one."

A speculative gleam lit Ta'a Chume's eyes. "An interesting notion. Can you expand on that?"

The Jedi shrugged. "At this point, it's just a feeling. Jaina is extremely difficult to read through the Force."

The older woman nodded approvingly. "The ability to hide thoughts and shield emotions is invaluable, as your mother's illness illustrates so poignantly. But surely something else prompted your observation, some specific event."

Tenel Ka sent a cool glance at her grandmother, acknowledging the comment about her mother but not rising to the bait. "Jaina and Lowbacca managed to block the frigate's tracking mechanism. At the time, this aided our escape. I suspect she is seeking another way to exploit this."

Isolder nodded. "Such knowledge could prove extremely valuable."

"Fact. But because of who Jaina is—a Jedi, and Jacen Solo's twin—she can't afford impulsive actions and shouldn't take unnecessary risks. She's plotting something, and I cannot follow the path her mind is taking."

"Perhaps I should speak to her parents," the prince mused.

"And what makes you think they'll have more influence on their daughter than you do on your own?" Ta'a Chume snapped, sending a fulminating look at Tenel Ka. "If you must meddle, speak with Jaina directly. Perhaps she will be wise enough to take advice."

The prince's lips thinned at this criticism. Before he could respond, a light step on the walkway stairs drew their attention.

Jag Fel climbed the stairs. He stopped when he noticed the Hapan royals and dipped into a low bow. "Your pardon. I came seeking Tenel Ka. The captain of the guard sent me here."

Ta'a Chume's gaze took in his black flight suit, the helmet under his arm. She looked to her granddaughter. "I suppose you've made arrangements to fly off somewhere. You seldom see fit to grace Hapes with your presence for more than a few days."

"I was hoping, Your Majesty, that Tenel Ka might be able to help me find Jaina. I'm recruiting pilots to help scout this sector."

Ta'a Chume pointed to the frigate. Braying yelps of Wookiee laughter wafted from the open vessel, followed by a female voice raised in a string of imaginative curses.

"It's well that you've had combat experience," she said in a dry tone. She raised one hand in a peremptory hail to catch the nearest guard's attention, then pointed first to Jag and then to the Yuuzhan Vong ship. He snapped a salute, his fist touching his temple.

"Good luck," she told Jag. She made a little gesture of dismissal, and the young pilot bowed again and left promptly, as was proper. But he clattered down the stairs to the docking bay with an alacrity that had little to do with protocol.

The former queen watched his quick departure with a speculative little smile. "He hasn't a chance of recruiting Jaina for this or anything else," she pronounced. "Mark me, any interest there will be fleeting at best. Jaina won't waste much time on a mere pilot."

"Her mother didn't think as you do," Isolder pointed out.

Ta'a Chume turned a patronizing smile on her son. "Jaina is not her mother, though I'm not surprised you can't tell one pretty face from another."

He blinked in astonishment as the old woman's meaning came clear. "I have never considered her in that light!"

"Just as well," the queen said tartly. "While I would not shed tears if you decided to seek a new queen, I would prefer that you look elsewhere. Jaina Solo's breeding, training, and temperament would serve her well, but she is a young woman and would require much guidance. Unless you plan to rule Hapes yourself, you would do well to seek a more seasoned consort."

Isolder turned his gaze away. "No man can rule Hapes," he said in a flat tone.

"My point precisely! The problem is that someone must." She arched an eyebrow. "Perhaps it is time for me to resume the throne."

"Never," the prince said. "That, I will not allow."

"That, you cannot control!" she retorted. "If your daughter will not rule, your wife must. If Teneniel Djo cannot, then find a wife who can. Because if you do not, then a member of my family will fill the void and will no doubt kill the three of us in the process! Choose, and then act, or the choice will be taken from you!"

She spun and stormed off. Isolder watched her for a moment, then turned and stalked off in the opposite direction.

Left alone, an enlightened Tenel Ka stared down at the alien ship and the determined young woman who had become the fulcrum of yet another plot.

She realized now why Ta'a Chume had not been nudging her toward the throne of Hapes. She had found another young woman who suited her purposes even better.

The guards parted to allow Jag access to the ship. He walked up to the ramp, a simple incline similar in design to that of most frigate-class ships. But there all similarity ended. The alien vessel looked more like an asteroid than like any ship he'd ever seen. He placed a tentative hand on the hull. The surface was as rough and irregular as the coral reefs in the oceans on Rhigar 3, the near-tropical blue moon that circled the Syndic Mitth'raw'nuruodo training academy.

Jag couldn't imagine how the Yuuzhan Vong had coaxed a colony of tiny creatures into forming a space-going vessel. It was said that these ships were alive, almost sentient. He cautiously tapped on the hull.

The response was immediate and vehement. Jaina Solo burst into view, her pretty face dark with frustration. She stopped short when she saw him, and stood framed in the open portal, her hands braced against the sides.

For a moment all Jag could do was stare. She was liberally daubed with pale green gel, and several wisps of hair stood up in shining spikes.

"I've come at a bad time," he said at last.

"That depends," she retorted. "If you're interested in having a shower, you're in luck. There's one on this ship and I just figured out how to start it."

"Ah," he observed.

Her brown eyes raked over him. "On second thought, the last thing you need is more spit and polish. And when I say 'spit,' you have no idea how literally I'm speaking."

A long-buried emotion stirred, one so unfamiliar that it took him a moment to find a name for it. Chiss, as a rule, did not get angry, and Jag had learned to model his reactions accordingly. "And what is it, precisely, that I do need?"

His cool tone had a paradoxical effect on the young woman. Jaina's eyes flamed. "You tell me. You're the one who's barging in here and interrupting my work."

"I came to offer you a ship, and a place in the Vanguard Squadron."

"Thanks," she said flatly, "but I've got a ship. It just needs a few adjustments."

His eyes skimmed over her, taking in her disheveled appearance. Humor stirred, and his irritation receded. "And how is that going?" he inquired politely.

Her chin came up. "Great. No problems."

Fierce brown eyes dared him to contradict her. To his surprise, Jag wished he could linger and do precisely that. The prospect of fighting with Jaina Solo was surprisingly intriguing. His squadron, however, would soon be expecting him.

"I should leave you to your work."

"Fine. Good. You do that."

She looked as eager for him to leave as Jag was to linger. That stung. He inclined his head in a curt farewell, left at a crisp pace, and didn't look back.

Only one thing kept Jaina from scraping a handful of goo off herself and hurling it at the retreating pilot: her dignity had suffered enough for one day.

She shrugged and turned back to the ship. Lowbacca stood just inside the door, a broad grin on his ginger-furred face.

"I don't see what's so amusing," she told him coldly.

He had the nerve to chuckle.

On impulse, she reached high and fisted both hands in the long fur on the Wookiee's head. Dragging his head down to her level, she planted a kiss on his forehead and then plastered herself against him in a quick, hard hug.

She backed away, considerably cleaner than she'd been only a moment before.

Lowbacca looked at her with puzzlement. A large gob of gel dripped from his chin and landed on the duracrete floor with an audible *splat*. He looked down at his goo-matted fur and yelped in outrage.

"Now that," Jaina told him, "is funny."

The planet known as Hapes had rotated twice since Harrar's priestship emerged from darkspace. During that time, the priest's commander and crew had worked without rest or pause to track the stolen ship.

When finally Khalee Lah came to the priest's chambers, Harrar suspected, quite correctly, that he had come to admit defeat.

"We have lost scouting ships," the warrior concluded, "and a number of the traitor-slaves."

"It surprises me that the Hapan infidels can still mount much of a defense," Harrar mused. "They were sacrificed at Fondor, yet they still fight and fight well. Our first duty is to retrieve Jaina Solo, but it appears that the Hapes Cluster might yet provide other worthy sacrifices."

"It seems unlikely," the warrior said in a dismissive tone. "The fighters are survivors from Coruscant. These might provide a few gifts for the gods, but not these Hapan cowards."

"We received reports that several ships were destroyed by a species known as the Chiss, a reclusive people who live on the edges of this galaxy."

"There are countless races in this galaxy," Khalee Lah said. "These ships are too few to make the Chiss a serious threat."

A surge of irritation coursed through the priest. Pride was a fine thing, but a wise leader was never blinded to the possibility of failure. Not for the first time, he wondered if perhaps Khalee Lah's presence aboard Harrar's priestship had more to do with penance than honor. "Perhaps these few are scouts?" he suggested.

The warrior considered this. "It is possible."

"If a few fight so well, what of a full-scale assault? It may be advantageous to learn more of these Chiss and why they've come."

Khalee Lah frowned. "Our first task is retrieving the Jedi twin. The Warmaster depends upon our success."

"And we will accomplish this task," Harrar said with as much patience as he could muster. "The Warmaster also relies upon priests of Yun-Harla to gather information that will be useful to the Yuuzhan Vong. Alert your warriors to make every effort to capture one of these Chiss."

Khalee Lah still looked doubtful, so the priest added, "Soon the Jedi twin will be ours. You will move on to new challenges, new glories. If these Chiss prove to be worthy adversaries, who better to lead the assault against their home worlds than Khalee Lah?"

"On that, we are in accord." The warrior smiled, and the fringes on his scarred lips seemed to separate into short, narrow fangs.

Harrar noted the birth of new ambition in Khalee Lah's eyes and was satisfied. If the young warrior looked upon every infidel as an opportunity for glory and advancement, he was less likely to dismiss them as "unworthy opponents." They had made that mistake with Jaina Solo before. Harrar suspected that she might be canny enough to exploit this.

Perhaps, he mused, this ersatz trickster was exactly what she claimed to be—a being subtle and powerful enough to warrant comparison with Yun-Harla. The thought both dismayed and intrigued him.

"You look troubled, Eminence," Khalee Lah observed.

"Thoughtful," Harrar corrected. He smiled faintly, obscuring his heresy beneath a masquer of cynical amusement. "War is often replete with irony. I wonder what the commander of these far-traveling infidels might think if he knew that his every attack was not a deterrent to the Yuuzhan Vong, but an invitation!"

EIGHTEEN

Early the next morning Prince Isolder followed a guard into the refugee camp, trying to ignore the sharp-eyed warriors following closely behind him. Bodyguards were a necessity for someone in his position, and he could think of few times when he had been truly alone on his homeworld. But as he walked between rows of simple tents, he was keenly aware of how much these people had lost, and how grating the pomp of Hapan royalty must be to them.

His guide stopped before a tent no different from the others. "You may leave me here," Isolder announced. His blue-eyed gaze swept over his escort, including his bodyguards in this instruction. They bowed and retreated.

He tapped on the support post and received a noncommittal grunt in response. Sweeping aside the opening flap, he ducked into the first of two rooms.

Han and Leia Solo sat at a small folding table. They were both holding steaming mugs, and they looked up at him with weary but keenly measuring eyes.

Isolder was struck by the similarity between the two, something that went beyond any explanation of common experiences and their recent shared losses.

Han Solo fit the image of aging pirate down to the last centimeter. Stories gathered during years of adventuring were written in his collection of lines and scars. Two days' worth of stubble roughened his face. He'd gotten a little thicker, a little grayer, a little tougher—nothing surprising there.

The change in Leia, however, was startling. Her short hair had begun to grow out and she wore a fitted flight suit. She was thinner than Isolder remembered, and her face looked pale and small without cosmetic enhancement. Despite her casual appearance, or perhaps because of it, she looked far younger than her years. But gone were the artful coils of brown hair, the softly draping gowns, the regal posture—everything that had caught his eye twenty years ago. She could have been any other tired warrior preparing to face another day's battle.

Then her face changed. Her chin came up, her lips curved in a welcoming smile, and the grief and weariness in her eyes receded behind a well-practiced mask. Princess and diplomat, she rose and circled the table to greet him, both hands outstretched.

"Prince Isolder," she said warmly. "Thank you for accepting us here. The people of the Hapes Cluster have already given so much."

He took her hands and raised them to his lips. "Fondor was my mistake, Princess. You tried to warn me about sending the fleet. Let's have no misunderstanding on this matter, or any other."

"Sounds like you've got things on your mind," Han observed as he hauled himself out of his chair.

"Stay, please," the prince told him. "What I have to say concerns you both."

Han shrugged and dragged a crate over to the table while Leia found another mug. They settled down and took sips of the thick, potent beverage.

"How was your journey?" Leia asked.

"Informative, and also disturbing. I learned several things that might be of importance to your family. Among the Yuuzhan Vong, twin births are considered a portent. One twin battles the other, and the winner goes on to an important role in a pivotal event."

Han nudged Leia. "Don't worry, sweetheart. You can take Luke. You'll just have to fight dirty."

She sent her husband a subtly quelling glance. He held up both hands in mock defense, and his teasing grin brought a spark of mingled amusement and exasperation to her eyes. Isolder thought he much preferred that response to the calm, practiced warmth she turned upon him.

"Please excuse the digression," she murmured.

"Of course. Tsavong Lah has stated, publicly and unequivocally, his intentions for your son Jacen. It is likely that this ire will now shift to Jacen's twin sister."

The warmth faded from Leia's eyes. "Jacen is still alive," she stated firmly.

Isolder sent a puzzled glance at Han. "You've probably been told otherwise," Han said. "So have we. But Leia says no, and I'm putting my credits on her."

She shot him a quick, grateful look and then turned back to Isolder. "Your point is understood, nonetheless. The Yuuzhan Vong seem obsessed with the notion of sacrifice. If twins have so much power in their eyes, they'd probably see a twin sacrifice as an especially potent offering to their gods."

"There is more," the prince said. "I have spoken with Tenel Ka, and observed Jaina at work on the Yuuzhan Vong ship. She has named this ship the *Trickster*, referring both to Yun-Harla, the Trickster goddess, and to herself. She did this to mock a Yuuzhan Vong priest in pursuit of her and the other young Jedi. Immediately thereafter, she confounded their ability to track the stolen ship. It seems possible that she is laying down a challenge, perhaps even goading them on by taking on the role played by their Trickster goddess."

Han's eyebrows rose, and a lopsided grin spread over his weathered face. "A goddess, huh?"

Leia sent him an incredulous stare, leaving no doubt that she didn't share his skewed pride in their daughter's methods.

He quickly squelched his smile. "You can't say the kid lacks ambition."

With a sigh, Leia pushed back from the table. "I'll talk to my daughter. Jaina has always been impulsive."

"Not to mention stubborn," Han pointed out.

"I'm not going to argue with her. I'm going to encourage her to put her plans—whatever they are—on the table. Then we'll discuss them, with the intention of focusing and refining her logic."

Han turned a wry look toward Isolder. "Not going to argue," he repeated. "Do me a favor—make sure this 'discussion' takes place in an open space, with no flammable materials around."

"You're not coming?" Leia asked.

"I've got some work to do on the *Falcon*. You two go ahead."

He spoke easily, with none of the competitive tone that had characterized his previous dealings with Isolder. The prince was not surprised. The look that passed between the two suggested a tie no former suitor could threaten, much less sever. Han gave his wife a quick kiss and then poured himself another cup of sludge.

But as Isolder moved the flap aside for Leia to pass, he heard Han's softly spoken advice: "Watch your back, sweetheart."

The prince understood that Han was not referring to the dangers implied by a former suitor. And knowing Ta'a Chume as he did, he found himself in complete agreement.

* * *

Leia Organa Solo understood that even during difficult times, certain protocols were inviolate. She could
not go anywhere in the palace complex without paying
her respects to the reigning queen mother.

She gave her name at the gate and was quickly led to
Teneniel Djo's domain. The uniformed guards took her
to a sleeping chamber rather than an audience room. For
a moment, Leia didn't recognize the woman who rose
haltingly from a chair to greet her.

When Teneniel Djo first came to Hapes as a young
woman, she'd been something of an oddity: a forthright
warrior among scheming patricians, a moderately attractive woman in a land whose people were renowned
for beauty. Her short, compact build set her apart from
the lithe Hapans, as did her ability to sense and use the
Force. Leia sensed at once that this ability had weakened
to almost nothing.

Teneniel Djo's reddish brown hair was dull and thinning, and her skin had faded to an unhealthy sallow hue.
She was far too thin. Her eyes were deeply shadowed and
so devoid of expression that she might have been mistaken for a blind woman. The constant intrigue of the
Hapan court must have been a slow poison to the Dathomiri warrior. Leia suspected that the defeat at Fondor
and the loss of her unborn child had been merely the final
blows.

They exchanged a careful embrace. Teneniel Djo
pushed Leia off to arm's length and regarded her with
dull resignation. "You have been chosen?"

Leia hesitated, unsure how to answer, or what to ask.
"I came to Hapes with the refugees," she said, considering this path as safe as any. "Han and I plan to leave
shortly."

None of this information seemed to register in the
queen's eyes. "Tenel Ka has the ring."

"Of course," Leia agreed.

The small woman turned away and resumed her sightless study of the garden. Leia tried several times to engage Teneniel Djo in conversation, but nothing pierced the strange fog that surrounded her.

Finally she abandoned the effort and walked quietly from the room. She shut the door behind her and nodded to the two guards who stood watch. They returned her salute, but Leia noticed the irritated expression in one man's eyes. She tracked his gaze over her shoulder.

A young man sauntered toward them, wearing the bright red color of the royal house and an expression of extreme self-satisfaction. He swept into an extravagant bow.

"An honor, Princess Leia. Ta'a Chume wishes to speak with you."

From the way he said this, Leia wasn't sure whether the honor was being expressed or conferred. "And you are?"

"Trisdin Gheer, companion to Ta'a Chume."

A mottled flush rose in the faces of the guards. Leia felt both anger and embarrassment coming from them and understood that she had just been insulted. Apparently sending a courtesan to fetch her was offensive in the extreme.

This left Leia with two choices: ignore the insult and appear ignorant of Hapan custom, or acknowledge it and appear ungracious. Ta'a Chume, it would seem, was in rare form today.

"Ambassador Gheer," she repeated pleasantly but pointedly. "I must apologize—your name is unfamiliar to me. I haven't seen it on the diplomatic rolls, or heard you speak in the senate. Perhaps you're new to Ta'a Chume's service?"

His smirk faded. "I joined her household recently."

"Well, I'm certain we'll see more of you in the near future. Ta'a Chume's diplomatic envoys always seem to move on quickly." She smiled. "Shall we?"

The guards' silent mirth followed them down the hall. Trisdin set a brisk pace and made no further attempt at conversation. He delivered her to a small audience room and then flounced off.

Ta'a Chume rose to greet Leia, offering no comment on Trisdin. "It was good of you to visit Teneniel Djo. A sad thing, is it not?"

"These are difficult times," Leia pointed out.

"But there are others who bear greater burdens with grace, you yourself among them." The older woman inclined her head. "Our condolences for the loss of your sons."

"Anakin is gone," Leia said, her thoughts touching briefly on the solemn funeral rites she had attended the night before, and the cleansing awe of feeling her son return to the Force. "Jacen is only missing."

"Of course," Ta'a Chume said smoothly and without conviction. "You must find great consolation in your daughter. I wish Teneniel Djo had been able to convey a similar sense of duty to her own daughter, but that is perhaps the least of our queen's failures. But enough of Hapan woes. I assume you'd like to see Jaina." She began to walk down the corridor. Leia fell into step.

"Have you any idea of Jaina's future plans?" Ta'a Chume asked.

Warning sensors hummed in the back of Leia's mind. "In times such as these, how far ahead can any of us plan?" she responded. "Our best efforts need to focus on survival. Jaina is a fighter pilot, an exceptional one. That requires her complete attention right now."

"She is a squadron leader, I assume?"

"No. She's in Rogue Squadron, and feels lucky to be there. Most of the commanders are legends."

"No doubt she's creating her own. Wars build legends, even if they accomplish little else."

"Why this sudden interest in my daughter?"

The queen mother spread her hands. "I lost my oldest son, and as you know, Isolder is deeply involved in this conflict. It is far more difficult for us to see our children fight than it would be to go into danger ourselves."

It stuck Leia as odd that Ta'a Chume was speaking to her as if they were contemporaries. Before this, she had always endeavored to impress upon Leia her relative youth and inferior status.

"Jaina is no longer a child," Leia observed. "Neither is Isolder."

Ta'a Chume's eyes crinkled in amusement. "You placed those comments in proper order. Isolder has many fine qualities, but the path to wisdom is longer for men. No woman finds an equal in a man her own age."

"An interesting view."

"One you apparently share. Han Solo is several years older than you, I believe."

"He has a running start on that path to wisdom," Leia responded dryly.

They emerged from the main palace building into bright sunshine. Ta'a Chume nodded toward an enclosed landspeeder, a larger-than-usual vehicle piloted by a well-armed driver.

"Jaina is no doubt working at the royal docking area. It is not far to walk, but I would prefer that you take this precaution." Her eyes clouded. "There was an attempt on Prince Isolder just yesterday, within the palace grounds."

Leia thanked the queen for her concern and climbed into the armored vehicle. It rose into the air and glided off toward the docks—far too slowly for Leia's peace of mind. Although refugee camps could be uncertain and even dangerous, she hoped to persuade her daughter to leave the palace and return to camp with her.

She found Jaina inside the rocklike vessel, poking experimentally at a small, crenulated sphere.

"A familiar sight," Leia commented with a smile. "You tinkering with a ship."

Jaina pushed away the little globe. "Nothing works the way it should," she complained. "No wires, no circuits, no cables. What's on your mind?"

Leia placed her fingers on her temples to pantomime dizziness. "That was a rather abrupt change of topic."

"Mom," Jaina said wearily. "Just spill it."

"All right. Prince Isolder came to see me." She related his concerns in a few terse words.

"The Yuuzhan Vong are trying to round up all the Jedi," Jaina reminded her. "My situation hasn't gotten much worse than it was. Frankly, I'm more worried about you."

"Me?" Leia looked startled, then her face cleared. "I see. You must have heard about my initial reaction to Anakin's death. I felt him go, and something in me shattered. Without your father, I might not have found my way back. He has been a rock."

"Like you were for him after Chewbacca died. It sounds like the two of you are even."

Leia smiled faintly. "Depends who's counting. Let's get back to you."

"Not exactly the usual graceful segue, Mom."

"You want blunt?" Leia demanded. "Then how about this: I can't feel you through the Force. I can sense when you're nearby, but not much more."

Jaina blew out a sigh. "Don't take it personally. I'm shielding. A lot of things have happened recently that I wouldn't share with anyone I liked, and half the people I despise."

"That's a lot to carry alone," she said, gentle invitation in her tone.

The young woman shrugged.

Leia started to put a hand on her daughter's shoulder, then thought better of it. "So. Tell me about this ship."

Jaina looked relieved at the change of topic. "We're just starting to figure out the Yuuzhan Vong technology. I've been gathering all the information I can get about the blocking device Danni Quee used over Coruscant."

"As I understand it, the block is a transmitter of sorts that effectively scrambles the signals sent by their yammosk."

"That's right. The yammosk communicates mind-to-mind. It's hard to block that. The scrambler is a device that makes it difficult for the yammosk to think. A small but extremely powerful comm unit is affixed to a projectile weapon and embedded into the hull of the ship containing the yammosk. I hear Danni's team prepared scores of these to make sure that one of them got through the shielding singularities and managed to adhere. The comm units were designed to receive an extremely high-frequency signal, one that would set up a vibration throughout the ship and prove impossible for the yammosk to ignore."

"And that's how you blocked the tracking capability of this ship?"

"No, there's an important difference," Jaina said. "The Yuuzhan Vong ships communicate mind-to-mind with their pilots, who in turn communicate with their commanders through villips. It's the yammosk that coordinates everything. Although the yammosk communicates through mental projection, much of the incoming information comes in other forms. The yammosk tracks individual ships by their gravitic signatures."

"Go on," Leia urged.

"Gravitic signatures," Jaina repeated. "The Yuuzhan Vong space technology is based on their manipulation of gravity. Small gravitic fluctuations provide motive force. The ships not only move through the use of gravity, but shield and even navigate. It's incredibly sophisticated, how a ship gathers information about its surroundings.

And each Yuuzhan Vong ship can be identified by other ships through subtle variations in its pattern of gravitic fluctuations. I call that the gravitic signature. Since these ships are living things, I suspect that their signatures are like fingerprints, with no two alike. I haven't had a chance to test that yet, but I will."

"That sounds like a dangerous project."

"Sure, but think how useful that information would be! Right now we can block their yammosk signals—at least, we can until the shapers figure out how to get around the high-frequency distraction. But consider how much more we could do if we could not only block their signals, but send them misinformation?"

"Enter the Trickster," Leia murmured.

Jaina's eyes turned feral. "You've got it."

She regarded her daughter thoughtfully. "How do you propose to do this?"

"I'm still working on that," Jaina admitted. Her gaze strayed to Lowbacca, who was hunched over what appeared to be an enormous villip.

"Then I'll leave you to it."

She caught her mother's hand as she turned to go. "Thanks, Mom."

"For what?"

"You didn't bring up Kyp Durron."

Leia's smile took on a sardonic edge. "I never thought you were serious about becoming his apprentice. When your father mentioned in Kyp's hearing that you weren't planning to attend Anakin's funeral, he took after you with all the subtlety of an avenging Gamorrean. I'd assumed the apprentice comment was meant as a jab at him, prompted by his heavy-handedness."

"Something like that," she said absently. "Is Dad upset that I almost didn't go to Anakin's funeral?"

"Since I nearly had to use a stun baton on him to get

him to attend Chewbacca's memorial, I think he understands. Just make sure that you do." She started to add something to that, then changed her mind. "I'd hoped to bring you back to the camp, but I can see that's not going to happen. You've got work to do here. Be careful."

Jaina promised she would, and held on to her impatient sigh until the brisk click of Leia's footsteps faded away. She picked up the villip and resumed her attempts to attune it.

A tapping at the open portal distracted her. Muttering imprecations, she stomped toward the door. She was momentarily nonplused to learn that her visitor was Jag.

"I came for an apology," he said without preamble.

Jaina folded her arms. "Fine, but make it quick. I'm busy."

"Actually, I came prepared to listen."

Her eyebrows leapt up. "Then I hope your schedule is wide open, because you're likely to be standing there for a very long time. I didn't do anything wrong."

"You deliberately tried to provoke an argument."

"Yeah? So?"

He stared at her for a moment, shoved a hand through his short black hair. "How did an Alderaanian princess end up with such a daughter?"

Jaina's temper flared. "Do you want the short answer, or do you need someone to explain the details to you with charts and diagrams?"

Spots of color appeared high on his cheeks. "That's not what I meant, as I'm sure you know."

His discomfiture was oddly satisfying. If this had been a fencing match, Jaina would have awarded herself a point. Scenting victory, she reached out with the Force and considered the emotions she perceived in the young man's powerful presence. He was angry, more than a little embarrassed, and not entirely certain about his purpose in coming here.

Uncertainty, she decided. Of all the emotions she sensed coming from Jag Fel, that one would bother him the most. So she envisioned a thick fog, then sent it toward Jag like a psychic shove. His brow furrowed, and he glanced around in puzzlement.

"Why are you here, Jag?" she asked, just to twist the knife a bit.

He composed himself quickly. "Tenel Ka told me that you will be training with Kyp Durron. Since Kyp flies under my command, may I assume that you'll be joining the Vanguard Squadron?"

"Tenel Ka was misinformed. So are you, if you think that Kyp does anything for anyone unless it suits him."

He studied her for a long moment. "Assuming you're right, I get the impression that Kyp is not the only one playing some sort of game."

"And winning," she added smugly.

"Since that perception gives you such apparent satisfaction, I hope the rules of engagement can be modified for solitaire." He executed a deep and extremely formal bow and strode off.

To her surprise, Jaina realized she was grinning like a well-fed Hutt. Baiting the Chiss commander was the first truly enjoyable thing she had experienced in a long time. Watching his retreat was satisfying, for more reasons than one. Jag Fel was one of those people who looked good from every angle.

She felt Lowbacca's presence approaching. He came up beside her and grumbled a question.

"I don't have anything against Jag Fel," she commented. "He can be a lot of fun, whether he means to be or not."

Lowbacca made a derisive comment about her idea of fun.

Her bright mood tarnished as she perceived the likely

source of Lowbacca's concern. "Stow it," she snapped. "I am in no mood for more dark-side dithering."

She spun away into the ship. The Wookiee's furred forehead pulled down in puzzlement as he considered his friend's outburst. After a moment he shrugged. His uncle Chewbacca had often warned him that humans tended to make everything more difficult than it had to be.

From what he'd observed pass between Jaina Solo and the black-haired pilot, Lowbacca was inclined to agree.

NINETEEN

"I don't believe we finally got this Sith-spawned monstrosity to sit up and say hello," Jaina murmured, gazing in fascination at the villip she'd finally managed to attune.

Her image stared back at her, twisted a bit and looking as she might appear if viewed through a dense fog and after several shots of Corellian brandy. The lips moved in sync with hers, and the voice, sounding deeper and smoky and somehow menacing, spoke in precise duet with her own. Jaina looked up at Lowbacca and grinned. The Yuuzhan Vong creature twisted the gesture into something distinctly sinister.

Jaina blinked, impressed by the transformation. "Wow. Let's hope the Yuuzhan Vong see me that way," she said to Lowbacca, nodding to her villip.

The Wookiee glanced from the reflection to the original and tipped his head quizzically to one side. He shrugged, not seeing much of a difference.

Jaina didn't take offense, since Wookiee perceptions of individual humans were usually expressed in terms of scent. She smoothed a hand over her villip. When it inverted back into a formless blob, she pushed back from the table and stretched.

"We'll get back to this tomorrow. I've got some arrangements to make before we can take the next steps."

Lowbacca tipped his head to one side again and grumbled a question.

"I'll tell you all about it in the morning," she said as she rose. "Why don't you get some sleep, pack your gear. If all goes well, we'll be leaving early. On a completely artificial ship," she added, knowing what the Wookiee's next question was likely to be. "Complete with metal and ceramics and computers and all those other lovely abominations."

The Wookiee whuffed contentedly and picked up the inverted villip. Jaina patted his shoulder affectionately, then hurried from the docking bay to her room in the palace. She could hardly approach the former queen of Hapes seeking a favor wearing a patched mechanic's jumpsuit. Ta'a Chume had made a point of commenting on Jaina's appearance, and the way Jaina saw it, showing that she took the older woman's advice to heart might lubricate the negotiations.

Later, scrubbed and brushed and cinched into a borrowed Hapan gown, Jaina set out to find Ta'a Chume. Gaining audience was far easier than she'd anticipated—the first palace servants she ran into took her directly to the former queen's residence.

As Jaina followed the servants through gleaming marble halls, she considered the probable significance of their response. Ta'a Chume might not be the reigning queen, but surely there were many demands on her time. The servants would not take Jaina directly to their mistress unless they'd been instructed to do so.

Yes, Ta'a Chume was definitely up to something.

A little smile of anticipation touched Jaina's face, and a feeling not unlike the surge she experienced when powering up her X-wing for a mission.

That analogy didn't fade when she entered Ta'a Chume's chamber. Jaina knew a command post when she saw one, despite the silks and glitter and art that decorated this one.

The older woman reclined gracefully on a settee, surrounded by perhaps a dozen people. Some wore the uniforms of the royal guard; others scribbled notes onto small datapads. Servants moved quietly about the room, bringing what was needed before they were asked. One of them slipped the cape from Jaina's shoulders and indicated with a nod that she should approach.

Jaina tilted her chin up and moved into the room. Ta'a Chume noticed her and glanced at a dignified servant.

Apparently that was some sort of signal well known to the retainers, for all bowed deeply and left the room at once. All but one—an extremely handsome, fair-haired young man Jaina remembered seeing at the palace dinner two nights past, never far from the former queen's elbow. He sent her a long, slow smile and strode over to a side table for a bottle of wine and three goblets.

Ta'a Chume removed her scarlet veil and smiled up at Jaina. "You look lovely, my dear, as I knew you would. Not many young people are willing to take advice. And you came at an excellent time, as I was about to pause for refreshment. You will join me, of course?"

Jaina took the indicated seat and accepted a glass of what appeared to be liquid gold. Small, shining flecks swirled through the effervescent wine. She took a tentative sip.

"Not like that," the young man objected with a smile. "Let me show you." He sat down beside Jaina and enfolded her hand and the goblet she held with both of his. "You swirl it around, like so," he said, moving their enjoined hands in a slow circle. "The art is to awaken it gently and coax warmth into it. Only then is the sweetness revealed."

Jaina stared at his too-close, too-handsome face for a

startled moment. Her first impulse was to burst out laughing—she'd seen more subtle and convincing performances from Mos Eisley street performers. A glance at Ta'a Chume convinced her that this wouldn't be wise. The older woman was watching with a faint smile and sharp, measuring eyes.

So Jaina guided the cup down to the table and tugged her hand free. "Thanks, but I never developed a taste for this sort of thing."

A quick, wry lift to Ta'a Chume's lips suggested that the vaguely dismissive comment had hit the right note. "You were introduced to Trisdin?"

"Not him specifically," Jaina said. She gave the young man a sweet and blatantly insincere smile. "But I certainly feel as if we've met before."

Ta'a Chume chuckled. "I suspect he has much the same feeling. Thank you, Trisdin. That will be all for now."

The courtier rose, his handsome face blandly smiling and showing no sign of insult taken or even perceived. But as he left, Jaina caught a whiff of dark emotion—not quite rage, but a deep frustration.

She dug a bit deeper, and sensed a native cunning that went far beyond anything his vapid persona suggested. For the first time, she felt a flicker of interest in the young man, and with speculative eyes she watched him glide from the room.

"Trisdin is decorative enough, but he does not warrant your interest," Ta'a Chume said in mildly accusing tones. "A moment ago, you made that admirably clear."

Jaina's gaze snapped back to the queen's face. "Do you have him watched?"

"Naturally. Why do you ask?"

"There's more to him than he wants anyone to see." She shook her head. "I can't sense anything more specific than that."

"Interesting," Ta'a Chume observed. She put her own

goblet beside Jaina's. "Now, what have you come to discuss?"

"It's about the pirates who were brought to Hapes for trial," she began. "I'm wondering if it might be possible for me to question one or two of them. Privately."

The queen lifted one auburn brow. "To what purpose?"

"That would take a bit of explaining," Jaina hedged.

"As it happens, my afternoon is free."

She nodded and dived in. "Months ago, when Jacen and my uncle Luke were traveling together, they came across a Yuuzhan Vong encampment worked by slaves from many species. The Vong had implanted these slaves with a small coral-like creature, some sort of mind-control device that ate away at their personalities. Jacen got himself captured and implanted. Fortunately Uncle Luke cut the creature out before it could do any real damage, other than leave a little scar right here." Jaina paused and touched her face just below the cheekbone.

"I have heard of these implants. Go on."

"On Yavin Four, the slaves had less invasive implants. Maybe the Yuuzhan Vong found that mindless slaves were not as efficient as those who retain some vestige of their personalities. On Garqi, the slaves were forced to fight. As far as I can tell, all these implants are variations on a theme."

Ta'a Chume nodded thoughtfully. "And if the Yuuzhan Vong can modify these creatures to various purposes, why not you?"

"That's my thinking," Jaina agreed. "If the captured pirates have been given implants—and I'm betting they have—I'd like to have the implants removed and altered."

"An excellent notion, as far as it goes. You've no doubt considered the obvious problem: If these creatures form a mental link between the slaves and their Yuuzhan

Vong masters, won't the Yuuzhan Vong be able to perceive any changes?"

"Hard to tell. The Yuuzhan Vong can impose mentally transmitted orders on their slaves, but they don't seem able to pick up what the slaves are thinking. If they could, Anakin wouldn't have been able to infiltrate their base on Yavin Four.

"On the other hand," she continued, "there are variations among these implants, and it's hard to know what they can and can't do. I'll just have to make sure that there's no information to transmit."

"You feel confident that you can accomplish this?"

Jaina gave the queen a slow, cool smile. Then she picked up her glass and glanced at the door. She reached out with the Force, sending a powerful compulsion to the presence she sensed lurking there.

Trisdin entered almost immediately, making it apparent that he'd been listening at the door. Ta'a Chume's eyes turned glacial.

The courtier came over to sit beside Jaina and cupped her hand and the glass in it with both of his.

"Not like that," he advised her, smiling warmly. "Let me show you how. You swirl it around, like so. You must awaken it gently and coax warmth into it. Only then—"

"Is the sweetness revealed," Ta'a Chume broke in coldly. "Thank you, Trisdin. Once was rather more than enough. Leave the door slightly ajar behind you as you leave. I want to hear the sound of your fading footsteps. Rapidly fading," she added pointedly.

He sent the queen a puzzled look and rose to do as he was bid. For a moment the two women listened to the courtier's departure. Ta'a Chume turned to Jaina, eyeing her with open respect—and a good deal of speculation. "Your point is well made."

"Too well," Jaina said dryly. "I tried to strip from his memory everything he'd heard me tell you, but apparently I rewound him a bit too far. As you observed, that wine glass trick wasn't worth repeating."

"Even so, this is most impressive," Ta'a Chume mused. "What such skills would be worth to a queen!"

An image of Ta'a Chume as a Jedi flashed into Jaina's mind. She banished it as quickly as possible. "I need to know what those Vong communication devices can do. I promise you, the pirates will remember nothing of the process."

"Why should it matter, if they are in prison?"

"It wouldn't—*if* they were imprisoned."

"I see." Ta'a Chume smiled faintly, approvingly. "As a means of creating spies or saboteurs, this has promise."

"I'm not trying to change the pirates' allegiance. What I want is a viewport into the Yuuzhan Vong technology. We don't understand much about them, and our lack of knowledge is the best weapon they have. The Republic scientists have been working on finding answers, and they've been making some progress. These implants could be another key to unlock the puzzle of communication."

The queen considered this. "But you lack the expertise," she concluded, once again getting to the heart of the matter.

Jaina grimaced and nodded. "I can fly just about anything that works and fix just about anything that doesn't—as long as we're talking about conventional vehicles. The Vong technology makes no sense to me. I was wondering if someone on Gallinore could be persuaded to help me."

"Gallinore," Ta'a Chume mused. "Yes, that might work."

"I've read that many of Gallinore's unique creatures were bioengineered," Jaina continued. "It seems to me that the Gallinore scientists might be closer in procedure and purpose to the Yuuzhan Vong shapers than most of the New Republic scientists."

"I agree," Ta'a Chume said. "And they have the further benefit of not being New Republic scientists. What they discover, you can share with the Republic, in your own time, and after your own purposes have been met—or not at all."

Jaina held the queen's gaze for a long moment, letting the silence confirm this observation.

The older woman smiled. "I will provide the ships and supplies you will need for the trip, as well as certain letters of introduction. Will Colonel Fel be accompanying you?"

Jaina shook her head before she had time to consider it. It just didn't feel right, involving Jag in this.

"Tenel Ka will go, of course. She is an excellent guide."

The Jedi grimaced. "I doubt she'd approve of either the mission or my methods."

"She doesn't need to know. But I can see the difficulty you might face if forced to carry out your plans in secrecy and without assistance. Is there someone else whom you can trust, someone more pragmatic than my granddaughter?"

An image flashed instantly into Jaina's mind—a lean face surrounded by waves of silver-shot black hair, and green eyes that laughed and compelled and deceived.

"I know someone," she said shortly. "I'm just not sure that I can trust him."

Three men slumped in the prison cell, awaiting Hapan justice in glum silence. They were still wearing the red garments they'd had on the day they brought that she-rancor princess aboard their ship. An assortment of bruises and bumps gave painful testament to the Jedi woman's unexpectedly strong resistance.

Soft footfalls echoed down the corridor. The men sat up and exchanged wary glances. It was time to put their whispered plans into action. Escaping was risky and uncertain, but the alternative was a fast trial and a slow execution. They were unlikely to get a better chance.

Their leader rose and moved into position beside the door with a swagger that belied his churning stomach. Not long ago, Crimpler been a promising Lorellian kick-boxer—never yet defeated, with a growing reputation for sizing up his opponents. Then came word of the Yuuzhan Vong invasion, and he'd been drafted into the Hapan navy and sent into a match that, in his opinion, couldn't be won. The Fondor disaster had merely confirmed what he already knew.

So he'd deserted and turned to pirating, where his knack for finding and exploiting vulnerability could be put to profitable use. He'd underestimated Tenel Ka, and that still grated. For the first time, he truly understood the anti-Jedi sentiments of the Ni'Korish fanatics among them. The way Crimpler saw it, if you couldn't read your opponent, you couldn't win the fight. And that, in his opinion, was why the Yuuzhan Vong were taking over the galaxy.

The man who entered the cell was dressed in the colors of the palace guard, but not the uniform. Crimpler sized him up in one quick glance—tall and strongly built, but no real threat. Muscles built through enhancements and prissy exercise routines were easy to spot, and usually worse than useless. At a distance, he might be taken for a guard, and he was probably counting on that. An assassin, probably. It wouldn't be the first time the royal family had decided to forgo the trial and move straight to the execution.

Crimpler snapped a high kick, aiming for the man's nose. To his surprise, the man managed to fling up a forearm and block the attack.

He pushed into the cell and stepped away from the open door, holding up both hands in a placating gesture.

"Not the face," he insisted. "You'll have to make it look real, unfortunately, but leave the face alone."

Obligingly, Crimpler delivered a side kick that caught the guard just under the ribs and folded him in half. The man went to his knees, wheezing, and held up a hand to indicate that the effort would suffice.

The pirate didn't see things that way. He seized a handful of glossy blond hair and jerked the man's head back. "What is this about? What are you setting us up for?"

His victim's lips worked soundlessly for a moment as he struggled to gather breath. "You're to escape," he managed at last. "Take the transport docked by the guards' post outside the prison. Access and launch codes." He patted a small pocket on his tunic.

Crimpler yanked on the man's hair. "Why?"

"You're Ni'Korish," the man said simply, as if that explained all.

And in a way, it did. With war on the horizon and an ailing queen mother on the throne, Hapes was a hive of political intrigue. The anti-Jedi movement was as good a rallying point as any for an ambitious woman on her path to power, and Hapes had no shortage of such women. Crimpler wondered, briefly, which one of them owned this particular pawn.

His curiosity was short-lived, and so was the guard. Crimpler tossed the man's body aside and patted it down. The promised codes were there, and several knives and a small stun baton had been tucked into his boots and sleeves.

Crimpler quickly passed out the weapons and then squinted at the barred transparisteel window placed high on the wall of their cell.

"This one was an idiot, but someone's planning is right on the money," he mused. "It's nearly time for the evening meal. Most of the guards should be doing rounds. Let's go."

He stepped over the body and sent a glance up and down the hall. The three men hurried down the quiet corridor. As they came to a turn, the laughter of a pair of approaching guards gave sudden warning. They flattened themselves against a wall and waited for the moment to strike.

Crimpler leapt out to meet the guards, both feet snapping out high and slamming into the men's throats. He kicked off, bending his body back and landing lightly on his hands. A quick push changed his momentum into a graceful back flip. He landed on his feet, bounced once, and then charged forward.

But the guards were down, silenced by the first attack and finished by the other pirates, who put to good use the knives the Ni'Korish traitor had thoughtfully left them.

The two pirates quickly stripped off the guards' uniforms and donned them. Crimpler walked between them, playing the role of prisoner as they hurried to the guard house.

Six guards sat around a sabacc table. With a quick kick, Crimpler upended the table and pinned down three of them. The rest of the battle went nearly as quickly. Stepping over bodies, the pirates made their way out to the landing.

"Three ships," one of the men muttered. "Seems to me this is a bit too neat and tidy."

The same thing had occurred to Crimpler, but there was no turning back. "Save it for your memoirs. Go!"

The men scrambled to the ships. Crimpler hoisted himself into a battered E-wing and began to power up. But his movements felt oddly slowed, as if he were moving through water, or caught in the throes of a nightmare.

With growing dread, he watched the other pirates take

off, unopposed. His own fingers had stopped as if they'd been stuck to the controls with the Yuuzhan Vong's blo-rash jelly.

The E-wing hatch opened, and Crimpler stared into the face of a lean, green-eyed man.

"This the one you wanted?" the man asked someone beyond Crimpler's limited field of vision.

Small fingers probed his neck, and found the tiny lump where the Yuuzhan Vong had placed the bit of coral—the thing that marked him like a prize bantha and identi-fied him as a trusted collaborator.

"He'll do."

The voice was young and female, and Crimpler caught a glimpse of a pretty face with large brandy-brown eyes peering out from under a fringe of shiny brown hair. There was nothing in that face, those eyes, to explain the shiver of dread that passed through Crimpler's im-mobile body.

Then the pain came, and darkness began to squeeze at his mind like a huge and pitiless fist.

His reaction, oddly enough, was one of relief. At least this time, his instincts had not betrayed him! The girl was trouble, that was plain enough. Crimpler could still size up an opponent with the best of them. He savored that thought, and took it into the darkness with him.

Ta'a Chume dropped the report into a carafe of deep purple wine and watched as the delicate flimsiplast dis-solved into a sodden mess. It was unlikely that anyone could decipher the message, which was written as if from an admirer, styled into a highly formalized poem filled with high-flown language and elaborate code.

To the former queen, the message was unmistakable. Jaina had been right about Trisdin. A closer examination into Trisdin's affairs revealed him to be a spy of Alyssia, one of Ta'a Chume's nieces. A well-placed rumor convinced him that the pirates who'd attacked Tenel Ka were in fact assassins capable of doing away with the current queen mother and her Jedi heir, if only they could escape custody to try again. According to the dissolving message, Trisdin's body had been found in the pirates' empty cell.

And so Trisdin had died as the traitor he truly was. The best way to handle men, in Ta'a Chume's observation, was to allow them to follow their natural inclinations.

Manipulating him into "liberating" the pirates was a most convenient way of disposing of the young man—while advancing the purposes of Ta'a Chume's new protégée.

With Jaina safely away from Hapes, it was time to act. Ta'a Chume reached for a thin sheet of flimsy and began an equally cryptic response. It was time to send another ambassador to solve another problem—a problem Ta'a Chume had faced before, and one of her few and bitterly regretted failures.

Twenty years ago, Han Solo had refused to relinquish his princess to the Hapan royal family. This time, Ta'a Chume intended to ensure that he made a very different choice.

TWENTY

Jag Fel's borrowed landspeeder skimmed along the streets of the Hapan city. Another time, he might have found the ornate buildings and their tropical gardens interesting, but today he was too deep in thought to care overmuch about his surroundings.

For most of his twenty years, Jag had devoted himself to learning military tactics, first from his family and then at the Chiss military academy. He'd devoted nearly as much time to developing logic and problem-solving skills as he'd spent learning to fly. But when it came to Jaina Solo, all this hard-won expertise abandoned him.

Jaina Solo was an excellent pilot, but her skills were no match for his own. In simulated flight, he'd shot her out of the sky nearly every time. For that matter, he could name several Chiss who'd flown under his command who matched her skill, and a few who were even better. Jaina was a Jedi, which was interesting but basically irrelevant.

He'd gone looking for Jaina again this morning, hoping to mend the incomprehensible quarrel between them, only to learn that she'd just left for another world in the far-flung Hapes Cluster. And she'd taken one of Jag's best pilots with her, without any request, formal or otherwise.

It bothered him that she hadn't requested a leave of

absence for Kyp Durron. Even a Rogue Squadron pilot should have had more regard for protocol than that!

But she had not, and now she and Kyp were gone.

And Jag was on his way to the refugee camp, which made less sense to him than anything Jaina had done.

But if Jag was honest with himself—which he invariably was, even though he often found it a highly uncomfortable habit—he had to admit that his real purpose was a desire to meet the infamous Han Solo.

Princess Leia had disdained suitable personal and political alliances in favor of a rogue—a disgraced Imperial officer who'd found his niche as a smuggler. If any logic had guided her choice, Jag intended to find it. And if there was none, perhaps the alliance that had created Jaina Solo would serve as enlightenment—or perhaps as deterrent.

Almost before he realized it, Jag had left the city behind. The vast landing docks were crowded with ships and bustling with refugees, most of whom seemed determined to get offworld. Tempers were high, and the white uniform of the Hapan militia was much in evidence.

Beyond the landing docks lay vast open areas—parklands and lakes and deep forests that provided hunting and recreation for the citizens of the royal city. This had been given over to the refugees. As Jag approached, he struggled to see something of the land's reputed beauty.

The sheer sprawl of the refugee camp staggered him. Rows of tents stretched across what had once been a parklike vista and disappeared into a distant forest. Jag showed his credentials to the perimeter guard and made his way down seemingly endless rows of tents.

A refugee camp was an incredibly noisy, pungent place. The displaced people of Coruscant crowded closely together, and thousands of voices mingled in a loud and discordant symphony. The narrow aisles teemed with beings of many species. Most brushed past Jag with averted eyes, encircled by the intense, artificial privacy that over-crowded conditions tended to foster.

The only unifying factor that Jag could perceive was the foreboding that hung over the encampment, as palpable as morning mist. No doubt all the residents knew the pattern of Yuuzhan Vong aggression. The presence of refugees was a potent lure to the invaders. He had the feeling that a familiar red button had been pushed, and everyone awaited the coming detonation.

Jag counted off the tents until he came to the one that had been assigned to the Solo family. While he was still several paces away, he heard muffled thuds and grunts coming from the enclosure. The sudden flare of a cooking fire in the small space between this tent and the next sent several silhouettes leaping onto the durasilk—an unmistakable tableau depicting an uneven battle.

Jag drew his one-handed charrik from his weapons belt and kicked into a run. He tore open the flap and charged in, leading with the small Chiss blaster.

A fist flashed up over his guard and into his face. Jag's head snapped back, and he staggered back a couple of paces as he shook off the blow.

It took Jag only a second or two to regroup, but by then his assailant had already turned his attention to another foe, a tall man in Hapan uniform. The brawler delivered a punch that spun the Hapan around and sent him crashing facedown onto a folding table.

A familiar, lopsided leer lifted the corner of the man's split lip, and he hurled himself at a burly warrior who was crouched in guard position. The two of them went down with a crash, taking a makeshift shelf and several pieces of battered crockery down with them.

This, then, was Han Solo, and Jaina's father.

Feeling strangely enlightened, Jag took quick stock of

the battlefield. Han Solo and the man he'd just taken down had struggled to their feet. They lurched about the tent, sometimes grappling for a disabling hold, then the next moment hauling back a fist to deliver a short-arm jab.

The uniformed Hapan was pushing himself away from the shattered table and onto his hands and knees. He lifted one hand to his belt and fumbled for his blaster.

Jag fired a short stun bolt that sent the man pitching forward, then swung his weapon toward the next assailant—a burly Hapan woman who'd snatched up a chair and hoisted it aloft with both hands. This she brought down, hard, in the general direction of the two struggling men.

Jag quickly fired a stun charge, but this only served to send the woman hurtling forward, adding momentum to her already impressive swing. The three combatants went down in a tangle of limbs.

Striding forward, Jag hoisted the uniformed man—the only person still moving—and tossed him off the aging Rebel hero. The Hapan dived for the tent wall and scuttled under the durasilk. Jag briefly considered pursuit, then knelt beside the too-still man.

Han Solo had fallen heavily, facedown, into the broken crockery. There was a large lump on his temple where the chair had struck him. Jag eased him over, and winced at the sight of the deep gash that rose from one cheekbone in a sharp angle, and then up deep into the hairline. The graying hair was dark and wet with blood.

Jag rose quickly and strode out of the tent. He seized the arm of a passing Bothan, a male wearing some sort of military uniform.

Feline eyes narrowed in menace, and the Bothan jerked his furry arm free of Jag's grip.

"Summon the guard, and get a medical droid at once," Jag snapped out. "Han Solo requires medical attention."

As Jag expected, the Bothan's eyes widened. "At once," he agreed. "I'll alert others to search for Leia Solo."

He hurried off and Jag ducked back into the tent. The short-term stun charge had already worn off, and the assailants had disappeared. He looked around for something to stanch Han Solo's cut, and noticed for the first time the shining pile heaped against one wall of the tent.

Jag got a fleeting impression of small sculptures, ropes of azure pearls, ornate metal caskets heaped with gems. This, however, was a puzzle for another time. He kicked aside a painted vase and snatched up what appeared to be a small linen shirt. This he wadded up, preparing to press it against the wound.

"Wait," a female voice demanded.

An older, grimmer version of Jaina pushed past him and dropped to her knees beside Han Solo. Her fingers gently slid into the matted hair and inquired about for a moment. She grimaced and drew out a sharp fragment.

"Good. It wasn't in very deep," she murmured, and held out one hand. Jag placed the wadded shirt in it. She gently held it in place with one hand. The other she splayed over her husband's chest. Her eyes drifted shut, and an intense listening expression fell over her face. A medical droid rolled into the tent and gently nudged Leia aside. Jag extended a hand, which she accepted with instinctive grace. She rose and watched as the medical droid tended the wounded man.

"There's a thin crack in the skull," the droid announced.

"*Han's* skull. How is that possible?" she marveled in a distracted tone.

She took a long, steadying breath. By the time she turned to Jag, she was the calmly controlled diplomat he had first glimpsed at the diplomatic reception over Ithor.

"I hear that you stopped the fight and called for assistance. Thank you. I'd appreciate anything you can tell me about the attack."

He described the scene he'd stumbled into, gave a brief description of the assailants, and then drew Leia's attention to the pile of treasures in the corner of the tent. She caught her breath in a quick, startled gasp.

"I take it this was not an attempt at theft," he concluded.

"Those things aren't mine," Leia said in a tightly controlled voice, "and they never will be."

"I'm not sure I understand," Jag ventured.

Leia glanced up at him. "The giving of a dowry is a Hapan custom. Twenty years ago, Prince Isolder sent ambassadors to Coruscant and presented me with a pile somewhat larger than this." She paused for a brief, humorless smile. "Obviously, I've depreciated over time."

"More likely Hapes's resources have been sorely strained by the war."

This time the woman's smile held genuine amusement. "When this war is over, Colonel Fel, you would do very well in the diplomatic service. For the moment, though, a few questions more. You said that some of the assailants wore uniforms. What kind?"

"Hapan royal guards, I believe. The uniforms were of one piece, like a flight suit. Quite fitted, deep red."

"Not even Ta'a Chume would be bold enough to send uniformed assassins," Leia mused. "They must have come to speak to me, and found Han instead. He would not be amused by their offer."

The droid spun to face them. "The patient is stabilized. He can be moved for treatment. Proper medical transport awaits just outside the camp. Permission to arrange interim transport."

Leia nodded her thanks and the droid rolled out. She knelt beside her husband, and a flicker of indecision touched her face.

"You are apprehensive about sending him to a Hapan medical facility," Jag surmised. "Forgive me, but I'm not unfamiliar with General Solo's early reputation. No doubt I'm not alone in this knowledge. Is it possible that this attack was an assassination attempt carried out in plain sight?"

She considered this, and then nodded. "That's an astute observation. It wouldn't be the first time Han was provoked into a fight. Once the first punch is thrown, how does one prove whether any resulting death was an accident or an assassination?"

"That was my thinking, yes. I understand the tactics, but not the motivation."

"The former queen mother does not approve of the reigning queen, and she has made it plain more than once that she considers me a possible replacement. It's entirely likely that she views Han as an 'inconvenience,' a problem that needed to be resolved."

Jag shook his head in astonishment. "Surely even a former queen is constrained by laws."

"Of course, but Ta'a Chume is devious and vengeful. I can't evoke Hapan law without risking repercussions against the refugees, and she knows I understand her well enough to realize this." She blew out a sigh. "This is a delicate situation. Maybe Jaina would have a better read on things. She's been living in the palace."

"Unfortunately, she left Hapes very early this morning for Gallinore. I came to bring you word," he added hastily, seeing the faint touch of sadness, or perhaps regret, that touched the woman's eyes. Though this was as close to a lie as he ever intended to come, he hoped that Leia would assume her daughter had sent him to bring word of her departure.

Leia didn't offer comment one way or another. "In that case, perhaps I should take Han offworld. The refugees are scattering, most of the Jedi have left, and there is little more for me to do here. Will you be in contact with Jaina?"

"Of course."

The words came out before he considered their implication. Something flickered in Leia's eyes—speculation, and then, to his surprise, a moment of profound relief.

The medical transport had arrived, and Jag tucked away the questions he could not ask and helped the droids shift the wounded man onto a repulsorsled.

As they left the tent, Leia turned to him. "You've done so much already, but may I ask you for one more thing? Go to the docking bays and ask for the *Millennium Falcon*. You'll find a young Jedi named Zekk working on it. He looks a bit like a young Kyp Durron—dark hair and green eyes, similar height . . ." She trailed off and she studied Jag appraisingly.

For a moment Jag thought she might comment on the fact that this description could just as well have been applied to him. In his opinion, there were far too many dark-haired, green-eyed men in Jaina Solo's orbit.

"Would you tell him to get the *Falcon* ready to fly? Tell him to round up any of the other Jedi who haven't yet found transport."

Jag promised to do as she asked, then walked with her beside the sled to the gate of the camp. As they prepared to part, he asked, "What shall I tell Jaina?"

"Tell her about her father. She should know about that. Tell her we've gone to join her uncle Luke. She'll know where." Leia hesitated, and again that far-seeing expression fell over her face. "Tell her—and this is important—that I trust her to find her way back."

Jag frowned, uncertain that he'd decoded these

seemingly contradictory instructions. "I'm not sure that I understand."

"Neither will she," Leia said as she moved off. "At least, not for a while."

TWENTY-ONE

The Hapan light freighter glided smoothly into the darkness of hyperspace, and the four Jedi settled down for the trip to Gallinore. Although this fact-finding mission was taken at Jaina's instigation, Kyp Durron had the pilot's seat.

This puzzled him, for in his observation, it wasn't in Jaina's nature to defer. She seemed content enough with the copilot's chair, and had spent much of the trip so far tossing cheerful comments back over her shoulder to Lowbacca and Tenel Ka. Try though he might, Kyp couldn't get past the shields just under Jaina's bright facade—a fact that intrigued him greatly. Few Jedi were his match for sheer force of will, yet this eighteen-year-old girl managed to keep him out.

Since the Force was of little assistance in breaking through Jaina's shields, Kyp turned to other methods. "You cleared this trip with Colonel Fel, I assume."

For the first time, he felt a ripple in Jaina's composure. "I don't need his permission."

"Maybe not, but technically speaking, I do."

"Why?" she retorted. "Since when have you answered to anyone but yourself?"

He sent her a sidelong glance. "Don't hold back, Jaina. One of these days you've got to learn to speak your mind."

Her response was a derisive sniff. "Jag Fel is an independent scout loosely affiliated with the Chiss. He needs pilots, and you agreed to fly with him. That's all. Why should you answer to him? You're a Jedi Master and the leader of an independent squadron."

"All of whom are dead," he said flatly.

Jaina fell silent. After a few moments, she said, "You really know how to stop someone in midrant."

"It's a learned skill," he responded. "When you irritate enough people over a sufficient period of time, you become the recipient of many a rant. Every now and then, it comes in handy to be able to shut them off."

"Is this one of the skills you wanted to teach me?"

Kyp turned in his seat to face the young Jedi. She regarded him steadily, her brown eyes unreadable. "Are you considering my offer? Would you really become my apprentice?"

"Maybe. Is the job still open? Or was it ever?"

He glanced back into the small passenger cabin. Lowbacca was busily tinkering with a small mechanical device, and Tenel Ka seemed deeply engrossed in the information on a large data card. Whatever she was reading made her face appear even more somber than usual. Their other "passenger" was in no condition to listen in, even if he hadn't been hidden away in the hold like so much baggage.

"When I made the offer, it was mostly to throw you off stride," he admitted. "You'd heard all the stories about me, and you've heard several of my debates with Master Skywalker. You were predisposed to be suspicious of me. It's much harder to dismiss someone when you're considering him, even on a subconscious level, as a possible mentor."

She nodded, not offended by his blunt words. "That's what I thought. I still don't appreciate being manipulated like that, but I'll admit it was a good strategy. When you told me that the unfinished Vong worldship was a superweapon, I sifted your claim through the same filters I'd use for the words of any other Jedi Master. Without that, I might have seen past the smoke to your real purpose."

For some reason, the admiration in her voice put Kyp on guard. "And knowing this, you could trust me as your Master?"

In response, she glanced toward the hold, where their unwilling passenger was hidden. "I trusted you last night."

"Yes," he said dryly. "We still need to have a talk about that little venture."

"We will," she responded. "Right now, though, it's better if you keep a bit of distance from this. My family name and my connection to Rogue Squadron helped you pull off that attack on the Vong shipyards of Sernpidal. No offense, but your name and reputation would not have, shall we say, quite the same impact on my current project."

This pronouncement surprised a rueful chuckle from Kyp, but it also stung enough to prompt a return shot. "Then why didn't you take a file from my data banks? Jag Fel's sterling reputation might have added some gloss to this mysterious enterprise."

The slightly mocking light in Jaina's eyes died, but her smile remained in place. "Maybe he'd prefer not to sully that reputation through association with a scruffy 'Rebel' mechanic," she said lightly.

Kyp felt the undercurrent of truth beneath her words, and his own perception of Jaina shifted significantly.

He'd always viewed the oldest Solo child as a Jedi princess—not precisely spoiled, and certainly no stranger to hard work and personal trauma, but the fortunate recipient of a loving family, enormous talent, good training, and a comfortable life. Despite all this, Jaina assumed

Baron Fel's son perceived her to be a faintly disreputable character. The strange thing was, she was probably right.

Even stranger, as far as Kyp was concerned, was his dawning suspicion that Jag Fel was not far wrong. Though Kyp hadn't considered this before, there might be a good explanation for his inability to pierce Jaina's mental shields. The dark side was extremely difficult to perceive—as he had reason to know. He and Jaina, despite the differences in their heritages and early lives, might be more alike than he would have thought possible. Most Jedi were willing to risk their lives. He and Jaina were prepared to risk far more.

Jaina leaned toward him and waved one hand in front of his eyes. "Copilot, hailing Kyp Durron. Come in, Rogue Jedi."

He snapped his attention back to the moment and gave her what he hoped was a reassuring smile. "I wouldn't concern myself with Colonel Fel's opinion. He's an excellent pilot, and he's doing what he can to fight this war. But as I've been saying to anyone who'll listen and dozens who won't, the Jedi need to do more."

"I agree. One thing I learned long ago is that you can't fix a ship without getting your hands dirty," Jaina said softly.

For a moment they regarded each other, in complete accord.

A small voice in the back of Kyp's mind warned him that this was Han Solo's daughter, reminded him of the enormous debt he owed his old friend, and what he owed to Luke Skywalker. What he had in mind for Jaina would be regarded as yet another betrayal, and there would be no forgiveness for him this time.

Kyp understood full well the dangers of the path he was walking, and he knew that Jaina's capitulation ought to bother him. But if truth be told, he welcomed her slide from conventional Jedi thought.

Anakin Solo was dead, and gone with him was Kyp's best hope for a new and more inclusive understanding of the Force. Perhaps Jaina would be the one to have the larger vision. He'd seen the way she automatically took charge, the way other young Jedi followed her confident lead. Maybe she had both the power and the credibility to stir the Jedi out of their complacency.

And if not, at least there would be two Jedi who had the satisfaction of knowing they'd given everything they had, used every resource at their disposal, without stopping to count the personal cost.

In Kyp's opinion, no true guardian could do any less.

Gallinore, famous for its rainbow gems, was a verdant world with stunningly diverse plant and animal life. The rainbow gems, living creatures that took thousands of years to mature, were only one of the many marvels to be found in the fields and forests. And many of these living things had been created or altered in the labs of the planet's sole city.

While Tenel Ka went to deal with the city officials and Kyp kept watch over the "baggage," Jaina and Lowbacca headed to the sprawling research district.

Ta'a Chume's letter of introduction earned them full cooperation and unquestioned access to the facility. Within moments, Lowbacca was seated before a terminal, his furry digits flying as he sifted through computerized records of the Gallinore research, looking for anything that might provide a link between a technology that he and Jaina could understand and the secrets of the *Trickster*, their stolen Yuuzhan Vong ship.

Jaina turned to the technician who hovered at the Wookiee's shoulder. "I need to speak with Sinsor Khal. Can you show me where I might find him?"

A peculiar expression crossed the young woman's face, but she pulled out a comlink and relayed Jaina's request.

In moments an armed escort arrived and guided her through a maze of pristine white halls. They left her before a large door, nodded toward a palm reader mounted beside the door, and left at a much faster pace than that which had brought them.

Jaina shrugged, then placed her hand against the device. The door irised open. It snapped shut behind her with a clang like that of a prison door.

She stepped into a large room, one crowded with so much equipment, all of it in such disarray, that for a moment Jaina suspected she was viewing the result of a head-on collision between two large ships.

Jaina crept through the room, surveying it as she might a battlefield. When she knew all she needed, she slipped out the way she came, retraced her steps through the corridors, and made her way back to their ship.

She quickly described the situation to Kyp. He listened intently, his expression inscrutable. His eyes flickered, once, when she concluded her proposal by noting, "You asked me to be your apprentice. Here's where it starts."

"So this is your price," he observed. "You have a high opinion of your value."

Jaina spread both hands. "I'm the last of the Solos. That's got to be worth something. Do you want me or not?"

For a long moment the two Jedi locked stares. "You know we could never speak of this," Kyp said.

"Who would I tell?" she retorted. "Uncle Luke?"

He lowered his head in a slow nod, holding her gaze. "All right, then. Let's get this done."

Two hours later, Jaina stood behind Lowbacca, much as she had when they last parted. The Wookiee shook his head as if to clear it, then began to study the terminal as if he were just getting acquainted with the system. The time he'd spent carefully erasing all evidence of Jaina's passing was forgotten.

She turned to the technician who stood behind them. "I need to speak with Sinsor Khal. Can you show me where I might find him?"

The woman responded to this request with the same bemused expression that had characterized her first reaction. Thanks to Kyp, she had no recollection of any previous conversation.

She gave orders through a comlink, and several armed guards came to escort Jaina to the scientist's lair. They set a slower pace than they had the first time, however. Jaina suspected they'd be puzzled by the bruises they'd discover come morning.

Again they left her before the door. For the third time that day, Jaina let herself into the scientist's lair.

A tall, sandy-bearded man in a red lab coat strode forward to meet her, beaming in welcome. "Lieutenant Solo! The subject is ready. Come along. We'll get started at once."

She followed Sinsor Khal through a seemingly random maze of tables and computer consoles to a gleaming expanse of metal, a large table surrounded by a narrow ditch that led into a drain. The captured pirate had already been strapped to the table, facedown.

Jaina fiercely willed herself not to think about the transfer, or what it had cost. As Kyp had observed, this was something of which they could never speak.

"I can't tell you how delighted I am to finally get my hands on this new biotechnology. Let's see what we have here."

He moved quickly to the pirate and picked up a small laser tool. With a deft flick, he removed the coral device and dropped it into a small vial.

"We'll run tests on the creature itself, and also on the

subject. Blood tests, tissue samples, brain waves—you'll have it all in short order."

The scientist started work at once, apparently having forgotten her presence. Jaina stood by, watching without protest as Sinsor gathered samples and downloaded the information to his central computer.

"Interesting," he mused, staring at the screen. "Most interesting."

Jaina came up behind him. The computer showed several columns of numbers and a moving image that resembled a swarm of Dagobian frog tadpoles within an ovoid enclosure.

"This is a single cell, taken from the adrenal gland. See these small, mobile black dots? They are genetically related to the coral creature."

"It spawns?"

"In a manner of speaking. Coral reefs are communities of living organisms. The Yuuzhan Vong have refined these communities, organizing them into something that functions as a single creature. Apparently the coral can reproduce, sending microscopic offspring through the bloodstream and into every cell."

"But how does the implant communicate with these offspring?"

The scientist tapped the screen. The image disappeared, and a stream of symbols flowed. "This is the genetic sequence of the spawn found in the bloodstream. I'll compare it to spawn taken from other parts of the subject's body. If my assumptions prove correct, these creatures will be subtly different, depending upon their chosen location—blood, neurons, spleen, and so forth. Yet they are all part of the same organism, even when scattered. And I suspect that as they spread, they incorporate their host into what might be termed a compound organism. Any impulse sent to the central coral unit is communicated throughout the host subject. At this point, where one organism ends and the other picks up is largely a matter of philosophy."

Jaina nodded slowly as she took this in. "If you wanted to alter one of these implants, how would you go about it?"

"We'll examine the genetic code of these spawn, and then determine which elements occur naturally, and which appear to be implanted. These new additions or changes provide the most fertile soil for adaptation."

Jaina grimaced. "And how many years will that take?"

Sinsor looked mildly offended. "You might be surprised how obvious these little splices can be to the trained eye. Our computers are advanced, and much faster than anything the Republic's so-called scientists have in their arsenal."

"You think you can alter one of these creatures?"

"I'm confident of it. Come back in the morning, and we should be ready to play around with the next generation."

Jaina nodded and wove through the crowded workroom to the door. The palm reader on this side did not immediately open the door, but relayed her request to the central control. A metallic voice assured her that her escort would arrive shortly, and she settled down to wait.

It was obvious that Sinsor Khal was under confinement. After having watched him in action, Jaina guessed that his disregard for his subjects' well-being had gotten him in trouble more than once. On the other hand, this semi-imprisonment also provided a perfect forum for unsanctioned experimentation.

She wondered what the next morning would bring. No doubt there would be some way to impress her will upon the altered creature—and upon any future recipients.

That raised an interesting question: the Yuuzhan

Vong's creatures were not affected by the Force, yet some of them—the lambent crystal in Anakin's lightsaber, for example—communicated by some sort of mind-to-mind ability, sometimes with individuals who were Force-sensitive. That defied logic, and negated everything Jaina knew about the nature of the Force.

Jaina sensed that she was near to a new understanding—she could feel it, like a shadow perceived only at the corner of her peripheral vision.

She closed her eyes and allowed impressions to come to her. The teeming life of Gallinore swept over her like a silent surf. The bright green music of the forest filled her senses, and answers she could not quite decipher mingled with the rasp of insects and the music of birdsong.

A smile slowly crept over her face. If the answers to her questions were out in the wilds of Gallinore, Jaina knew just the person who was likely to find them.

The path was a narrow, rocky ledge that clung tightly to the steep slope. Tenel Ka moved confidently up the trail, her muscled limbs coiling and stretching with a grace and joy that reminded Jaina of a bird in flight. Tenel Ka had put aside her Jedi robes for the short, lizard-skin costume she preferred, and her red-gold hair had been tightly plaited into a single thick braid. Her arms swung lightly as she strode along, and from the back her missing forearm was not at all apparent.

The way broadened into a small, flat landing that overlooked a deeply forested valley and the mountains beyond. The Dathomiri woman halted and waited for the other Jedi to catch up. Jaina hauled herself up the last few steps and flopped down onto a large rock.

"Great view," she told Tenel Ka. "I really needed this."

Her friend nodded. "As did we all. We spend far too much time in sedentary pursuits. It is difficult to maintain the conditioning level we reached as students."

Lowbacca struggled up in time to hear this comment, and he yowled a testy disclaimer.

"You can get back to the computer in the morning," Jaina told him.

Tenel Ka's searching gaze settled on a nearby mountain, and her eyes lit up. She pointed across the divide toward a rocky slope. "If you look carefully, you can see the opening of a cave. See the colored lights flashing?"

Jaina shielded her eyes with one hand and squinted. "What is that?"

"We call them firedrakes. They are very large flying insects that can emit colored light, as well as heat and sparks of energy. At night, the patterns can be quite impressive and beautiful. It's nearly sunset. They'll emerge from their hiding places soon."

Lowbacca glanced at the setting sun and grumbled.

"I don't see why we can't stay," Jaina argued. "Sure, the path is steep, but it's the same going down as it was on the way up."

"I've walked this path many times. It is not difficult to follow, and the sight is worth seeing," Tenel Ka said. "When I was a child, there was some attempt to bring the firedrakes to Hapes, but they do not adapt to other worlds than this."

Her smile took on a sharp edge. "My grandmother will not brook defiance, not even from nature itself. I remember seeing festival lights, artificial displays that duplicated by mechanical and chemical means the lights of the firedrakes. It was not the same."

"We'll stay," Jaina said, glancing at the Wookiee. Lowbacca grumbled agreement and the three of them settled down to watch.

Night fell swiftly over the mountain, and the firedrakes began to emerge from their caves. Soon a swarm of them gathered, wheeling about in swift, graceful flight. Their multicolored lights traced ribbons against the deepening shadows.

The Jedi watched the display in fascination. A certain wistful contentment crept over Tenel Ka's face.

"We should return before full dark," she said reluctantly as she rose to her feet.

They began the trek down the path, glancing from time to time toward the valley and the firedrakes' continued flight. The creatures had spread out, and their lights came in short, rapid blinks.

"They are hunting," Tenel Ka explained. "The short flashes seem to be a signal to summon the others."

Jaina turned to watch. She stumbled over a loose stone, and would have fallen had not Lowbacca seized her arm. He admonished her with a sharp woof.

"I was watching," she retorted. "But not with the Force, so I guess you've got a point . . ."

Her voice trailed off as she reached out with her senses. Danger was sweeping in.

She reached for her lightsaber and spun back toward the mountain peak. Several enormous creatures glided toward them on silent wings. Jaina got the impression of a dark wind and a stabbing flash of verdant lightning.

Her lightsaber streamed up to meet the attack. She spun to add force to the parry, and the violet blade sheered through the descending bolt.

This changed the momentum of the creature's attack, and the enormous insect rolled in the air and crashed into the path, tumbling down toward Tenel Ka. The warrior leapt over it, igniting her turquoise lightsaber before touching down.

Instinctively Jaina ducked and slashed out high. An enormous gossamer wing enfolded her like a veil, and the creature that had just lost it slammed into the mountain wall. It bounced off, rolled across the narrow path, and then crashed down the incline. Showers of colored light erupted from it like sparks from a severed wire.

Jaina threw off the wing and dropped into guard position. She reached out with her senses, for there was nothing to see but a tube of faintly strobing light—the "lightning bolt" she'd perceived in the initial attack was nothing but a firedrake's severed proboscis. The creatures resembled the bloodsucking insects she'd seen in the swamplands of a dozen worlds, but at a size she'd never imagined possible.

Tenel Ka switched off her lightsaber. "Darkness," she advised. "The lights may draw others."

The Wookiee padded up and growled at Tenel Ka. "I have never heard of such behavior. They hunt in packs, and are said to be clever."

"They'd have to be, to plan a distraction," Jaina said. She glanced out over the valley. The rapid flashing of hunting insects still lit the sky.

Tenel Ka gazed out at the flashing lights. "I never would have thought them capable of ambush."

Enlightenment came to Jaina in a quick, bright flood, and a plan began to take shape in her mind. Tenel Ka sent her a questioning look.

"I was just thinking about battle tactics," Jaina said by way of explanation. "Underestimating the enemy is a common mistake. Jedi don't expect to be outwitted by bugs."

"Fact," Tenel Ka agreed ruefully.

And neither do the Yuuzhan Vong expect to be outwitted by "infidels," Jaina added silently. She would give the Yuuzhan Vong precisely what they expected to see, and then, like the hunting firedrakes, she would come at them from the darkness.

TWENTY-TWO

Leia had seen sunsets on a hundred worlds, strolled through the incomparable art galleries of Alderaan, marveled at the treasure rooms of countless palaces and museums. Seldom, however, had she seen any sight to rival the image of Han and his infant nephew, faces a few centimeters apart, regarding each other with identical expressions of dubious curiosity.

Ben Skywalker, who sat enthroned on his mother's lap, formed an opinion first. The baby crowed with delighted laughter and flailed his tiny fists. A random swing caught Han on the nose and sent him reeling back, clutching his already bruised face.

"They grow fast," he managed.

Luke cleared his throat and Mara hid a smirk behind one hand. Her brother-in-law sent her a mock glare. "Kid takes after his mother."

"I was aware of that risk," Luke said lightly. "We could happily talk about Ben all night, but perhaps you should fill us in on the Hapan situation. You might start by explaining why you look like someone who went several bad rounds with a Wampa."

"That's probably close to the truth—or as close as I'm likely to come," Han said, rubbing at his bruised jaw.

"He doesn't remember many of the particulars," Leia put in.

In a few words, she described the events that had precipitated their departure from Hapes. "Judging from the dowry gifts, it seems likely that Ta'a Chume is returning to the notion of finding an 'appropriate' wife for Isolder. Han, obviously, would be a deterrent. Jag Fel, the young man who stopped the fight, wonders if perhaps they goaded Han into fighting in lieu of a conventional assassination attempt."

"That would work," Luke agreed. "I don't need the Force to tell me who threw the first punch."

Han pantomimed a look of wounded innocence and touched the fingers of one hand to his chest. The expression wavered, and his eyes took on the unfocused look of someone in deep thought.

"Han?" Leia asked.

"Just thinking about what Luke said." He glanced at his bruised knuckles. "I remember throwing the first punch, and maybe one or two after that. A few bits and pieces are coming back. There's something else, too, something important. I can't quite grab hold of it."

"It'll come," Leia said firmly. "Don't rush it. You've got several days of recovery time ahead, and the inactivity will be bad enough without you making yourself— and those around you—crazy."

"Yeah." Han rubbed his jaw again, let out a frustrated sigh. "I hate not remembering what I did. I always remember, even after a long night in a bad tavern."

Mara turned to her husband. "How about it, Skywalker? Will you still fight for me after we've been married for twenty-odd years?" She lifted one red-gold brow.

Luke met her gaze, and her teasing challenge. "What do you mean by 'still'? You do your own fighting. If I forget that, I'm not very likely to survive until our twentieth anniversary."

The Jedi warrior shifted the squirming baby to her shoulder and smiled contentedly. "It's such a comfort to be understood."

Jaina returned from Hapes two days later, armed with Sinsor Khal's discoveries and several data cards of related information. She and Lowbacca hurried back to the *Trickster*, eager to get back to work on the Yuuzhan Vong ship.

She and Lowbacca dragged the escape pod into a small enclosure and set to work. Jaina took one of several altered implants she'd brought back in flasks of a mineral-rich, rapid-growth medium Sinsor had devised. The coral creatures were still much smaller than the one they'd reimplanted in the pirate, but Jaina thought they might serve.

She took a tiny welding tool from one of her pockets and sheared off a slice of the pod's miniature dovin basal. She fitted an implant into an irregularity of the rocklike structure and then pressed the small piece back into place.

"It should be able to heal itself," Jaina said. "And if I'm right, this should alter the gravitic signature."

Lowbacca let out a string of yelps and growls.

"I know they can't trace us right now, and yes, I want to keep things that way. But the only thing better than no information is misinformation," Jaina replied. "We want them to be able to track down and destroy one of their ships—just not this particular one."

Lowbacca was silent for a long moment, then he whuffed sharply.

"Of course it will work," she said stoutly. "The next step is finding a delivery method to implant other Vong ships. For that we'll need ships and pilots willing to go head-to-head with our galaxy's uninvited guests."

The Wookiee's eyes widened in enlightenment.

"That's right," she agreed. "That's why we need Kyp Durron."

Kyp settled down on the duracrete bench and regarded his prisoner. The Hapan pirate floated in a bacta tank, and would likely be there for quite some time. When he was healed of everything but his lost memory, Kyp would turn him loose.

That knowledge bothered him less than it ordinarily would. Freedom to pillage the skies seemed a small recompense for what the man had endured.

Kyp silently listed the laws he and Jaina had broken, and the lines they'd crossed. Helping prisoners escape from the Hapan officials, holding one of them and transporting him to another world, submitting him for scientific testing. He didn't even want to think about the transfer of the pirate from their ship to the scientist's lab. But he couldn't ignore this particular disaster, or the conclusion it left with him.

Jaina was in trouble.

As he'd expected, she had proven to be a talented student. She'd very quickly followed Kyp's lead, and had wiped inconvenient knowledge from the minds and memories of Gallinore scientists—including Lowbacca, a Jedi and probably her closest friend.

Kyp could have lived with that. He could not have stood by and watched while this man was "tested" into a near-death state. But Jaina had.

His apprentice had adopted his argument that the end result was more important than the path that led to it. She had pushed this philosophy to its far edges, forcing Kyp to consider whether there might, after all, be boundaries.

Kyp supposed there was a certain cosmic justice to this.

"So what next?" he muttered. Kyp wanted to defeat the Yuuzhan Vong. So did Jaina. Any energy he put into curtailing her efforts diminished the energy both of them could direct against the invaders. But how far could he let her go?

And more important, if and when the time came to stop her, would he be able to?

Jaina smoothed the skirt of her gown and settled down in the chair Ta'a Chume offered. The tight Hapan garments still pinched, but she was growing accustomed to them. "I heard about Trisdin."

"And you've come to offer condolences?" the former queen said archly as she reached for her wine goblet.

"Actually, I came to get an eyeful of his successor," Jaina responded in kind.

Ta'a Chume sputtered on the sip she'd just taken, and set the goblet aside. "You were right about him. His loyalties were uncertain. A rumor reached him that the imprisoned pirates could serve his interests, and those of the woman he wanted to see on my throne."

Jaina quickly got a lock on the queen's target. "So you didn't send him there to free them."

"Not directly, no."

"And if he hadn't been killed by the prisoners, he would have been caught and tried for treason."

"According to Hapan law." Ta'a Chume lifted an inquiring brow. "You don't approve?"

"Actually, I do. No matter what happened, it doesn't reflect back on you. I assume his ties to this aspiring queen can be traced."

"Naturally. Her name, by the way, is Alyssia. This latest scandal might be enough to neutralize her. If not, I may require your assistance."

Jaina nodded, accepting this. She set down the goblet

of gold wine she'd been sipping. "Tell me about Sinsor Khal."

"He was once a respected Hapan scientist with precisely the expertise you required. Unfortunately, this expertise was achieved at the cost of horrendous—and highly illegal—experimentation. But I suspect you've already come to this conclusion."

Jaina nodded. "Are there others like him?"

The woman regarded her for a long moment. "How many do you need?" She sniffed at Jaina's incredulous laugh. "Progress of any sort is not easily won. There are bound to be failures along the way, and if society deems these mistakes criminal today, tomorrow it will embrace the achievements that spring from their work. Men and women with intellectual curiosity should be funded and encouraged, away from the judgmental eyes of those who possess more righteousness than foresight."

"So you shut them up, hid them away," Jaina clarified.

Ta'a Chume waved this aside. "Most of them hardly notice. A well-funded lab and the freedom to work is a dream to these scientists, not a punishment. The Yuuzhan Vong are a reality, my dear, and they must be dealt with. What do you propose?"

Jaina quickly described the next phase of her plan. The former queen listened carefully and made several suggestions.

"This is excellent," she said when at last Jaina had finished. "Your brothers will be avenged, and the defense of Hapes greatly strengthened. I'll see that you have everything you need." She extended a slender, jeweled hand.

Jaina took the offered hand without hesitation, but not without a certain doubt. For days now, she had been living in the palace, accepting the older woman's advice and hospitality. Today, however, a new line had been crossed. Kyp Durron might consider her his apprentice, but in truth, Jaina wondered if her real education was taking place at the hands of Hapes's former queen.

She rose abruptly. "I'd better get to it."

"Of course," Ta'a Chume agreed.

Jaina spun and walked out of the queen's residence, inexplicably eager to put some distance between her and Ta'a Chume. She rounded a corner quickly, and had to pull up short to keep from plowing into Tenel Ka.

The Dathomiri warrior's one hand flashed out to catch and steady Jaina. "I often leave my grandmother's presence at such a pace."

Jaina smiled before she realized that Tenel Ka seldom resorted to humor.

"You have visited Ta'a Chume frequently," the Jedi observed.

"She invited me to stay at the palace," Jaina said, and shrugged. "I can't exactly ignore her."

"Fact. But the time you spend with her exceeds the demands of propriety."

"I haven't been keeping a log. Is this a problem for you?"

Tenel Ka ignored the truculent challenge. "You are a Jedi. You should be able to sense that nothing good can come from my grandmother's hand."

"She's concerned about Hapes," Jaina retorted. "Someone should be."

"I don't know anyone who is not. If the battle comes to Hapes, we will fight."

"And lose! The Yuuzhan Vong can't be fought with traditional Jedi methods. Their warriors and their living weapons are beyond the Force. To deal with them, we have to understand them. We have to beat them at their own game."

Tenel Ka's face furrowed into a concerned frown.

"Be careful, my friend. There is danger in making too diligent an attempt to understand the enemy. It's impossible to study something for long without being changed by it."

Jaina sniffed. "If I start feeling the urge to tattoo my face, I'll be sure to let you know."

"This is not what I mean," she said quickly. "My concern is for things of far more—"

"That was a joke," Jaina broke in impatiently. "And as for changes, my feeling is that by the time this war is over, none of us will be the same, even the Jedi. Maybe especially the Jedi."

Tenel Ka was silent for a long moment. Her direct gray-eyed gaze softened, as if misted over by future possibilities. When she regained her focus, she looked troubled.

"You might be right," she agreed softly.

The priestship glided through the sky like a malevolent gem, its many polished sides gleaming in the reflected starlight. In the control room deep in the heart of the ship, the priest Harrar stood by the yammosk pool, his fierce gaze shifting from the many-tentacled creature to the tattooed warrior at his side.

"You have not been able to reestablish contact?" he demanded of Khalee Lah.

The warrior inclined his scarred head. "No, Eminence," he admitted. "The shaper continues to study the problem."

Harrar began to pace. "The warmaster depends upon the Jedi sacrifice. *Demands* it!"

"Several of the Peace Brigade collaborators have reported. They have recovered two of the humans taken by the *Jeedai* we seek."

Harrar's scarred brows met in a sudden scowl.

"What motive might she have in sending them back?" he mused.

"They claim to have escaped."

"And the priestess Elan claimed to be a defector. This *Jeedai* was able to block the yammosk—a most unexpected development. What more might she have done?"

The warrior snorted derisively. "Forgive my presumption, Eminence, but it seems to me you give this infidel far too much credit."

The clatter of boots announced the humans' approach. Khalee dismissed the escort with an absent wave and rounded on the pirates.

"Tell us," he demanded.

The pirates gave a meandering and self-serving version of a story Harrar had already heard. He cut them off when he could bear no more. "So after your warriors were bested by a one-armed female, you surrendered your ship and submitted to captivity."

"But we escaped, and we returned," one of the men dared to say. "That's got to mean something."

"I'm sure it does," Harrar agreed. "What, precisely, remains to be seen."

He nodded to Khalee Lah. The warrior spun forward, his hands moving in a blur. Several quick, precise jabs sent the men staggering back, clutching at their throats and gasping like beached fish. Harrar took a small coral shard from his sleeve and cut the slaves' implants free. He examined them carefully.

"They seem unchanged. Release these men."

Khalee Lah drove one of his fists into each man's stomach. They fell to their knees, dragging in ragged gulps of air.

"Sacrifice them," Harrar instructed, "and then set course for the Hapes Cluster."

The warrior bowed deeply. "Your Eminence, we lack the forces for an effective attack on a planet of that size."

"We need not attack the planet," the priest said grimly. "Just the *Jeedai*. And unless I am very mistaken, she will come to us."

TWENTY-THREE

Jag Fel made his way to the *Trickster*'s docking bay on the first day after Jaina's return. She glanced up from her work and scowled.

"Yes, I took one of your pilots. But Kyp is back and in reasonable working order. If you have any complaints, take them up with *him*." She jerked a thumb in Lowbacca's direction. The Wookiee obligingly rose, folded his massive arms, and fixed Jag with a challenging stare.

The pilot's gaze flicked over the Wookiee and then returned to Jaina. "I came with a message from your mother."

He quickly told the story of the attack on Han, and Leia's decision to leave Hapes.

"Where did they go?"

"She said they would rejoin Luke Skywalker, and that you would know the location."

"Makes sense," Jaina said absently. "How badly was my father hurt?"

He described the injuries and repeated the medical droid's assurances.

"My mother must have been surprised," Jaina murmured. "She always said Dad's skull was thicker than a Star Destroyer's hull."

Jag's lips twitched. "She intimated something along that line."

Jaina shook her head and blew out a long sigh. "Knowing my father, this might have started with some sort of misunderstanding. I'll talk to Ta'a Chume about it."

"Perhaps you should reconsider that," Jag said carefully.

Jaina's ire returned. She propped her fists on her hips. "Oh? And why's that?"

"I don't trust the former queen mother. Frankly, I'm rather surprised that you do."

A sharp clatter drew their eyes to the walkway overhead. Tenel Ka stood there, her face inscrutable. After a tense and silent moment, she turned and strode out without a word.

Jag scowled. "That was unforgivably tactless of me."

"I wouldn't worry about it. People who eavesdrop deserve whatever they hear," Jaina observed.

"Perhaps, but I should speak to her."

He nodded to Jaina and hurried after the Hapan princess. "Your Highness, a word," he called after her.

She stopped and turned toward him. "My name is Tenel Ka," she reminded him.

"Of course. I wanted to apologize for the insult to your family. It was not my intention to gossip or offend."

The Jedi stared at him for a moment, and then turned away. "Walk with me," she called back. Jag matched his pace to her stride. "You followed me from the docking bay, which is precisely what I hoped you would do. I observed you and Jaina together at the diplomatic dinner. It seems likely that she would assign more value to your opinion than to mine."

His smile held considerable irony. "I haven't noticed that. Perhaps Jaina Solo's regard is one of those mysteries that only Jedi can perceive."

"Of late Jaina has been . . . difficult," Tenel Ka admitted. She related her recent argument with Jaina, and her concerns about Ta'a Chume's influence on her.

In lean words, she told Jag the stories that continued to circulate about Ta'a Chume: she was probably behind the death of her first son's betrothed, and possibly behind the subsequent death of her son.

"My grandmother might be an old woman," she concluded, "but do not take Ta'a Chume lightly. There is always more than what you see. What concerns me is that there is probably much more to her current plans than even Jaina realizes."

"I see," he said slowly. "The attack on Han Solo puzzled me. Though I know Prince Isolder once courted Leia, I don't see why Ta'a Chume would go to such extremes on her son's behalf."

Tenel Ka stood for a moment as if in indecision. Then she bobbed her head in a curt nod and motioned for Jag to continue to follow her.

They took a landspeeder to the palace and then made their way to the opulent chambers of the queen mother. "This is my mother's favorite room," Tenel Ka said, and pushed open a massive door.

For a moment Jag assumed the room was empty. There was no sound, no sense of any living presence.

"There," the Jedi said softly, indicating a chair nearly hidden in a curtained alcove. A small, still figure slumped there, eyes staring straight ahead.

Tenel Ka led the way into the room and stooped over the chair. "We have a visitor, Mother," she said softly.

The woman's brown eyes flicked up to Jag and then returned to the window. She took no further notice of them, though Tenel Ka spoke about the plight of the refugees, the Consortium's worries about a Yuuzhan Vong attack, and the attempts to rebuild the fleet. None of these concerns pierced the deep torpor surrounding Hapes's reigning queen.

At last Tenel Ka fell silent. She leaned forward and touched her forehead to her mother's, as if doing so could lend the older woman some of her determination, her clarity of thought. She quickly kissed her mother's cheek and rose, striding out without glancing back at Jag.

He followed her to the door. When it closed behind them, she leaned against it and allowed her pain-filled eyes to drift closed.

"This," she said grimly, "is the woman who will command the defense of Hapes. Do you understand why my grandmother wishes to replace her?"

"Princess Leia will never accept such a role."

Tenel Ka's eyes flew open. "Is that what you think is happening?"

"What other interpretation is there?"

"I know my grandmother. She will never fully relinquish the throne. Perhaps she envisions ruling a second time, through someone younger and more tractable than either my mother or Princess Leia."

Her meaning slowly came to Jag. To Tenel Ka's surprise and his own, he broke out laughing. "Up to a certain point, logic suggests you're describing Jaina Solo. But only up to a point! *Tractable* is not a word that comes readily to mind when her name is mentioned."

"Fact," the Jedi agreed. "Still, it is something to consider."

Jag tried to envision Jaina as a ruling monarch and swiftly abandoned the attempt. "Let's assume that she agreed to this. How would she go about gaining the throne?"

"Since no daughters were born to Ta'a Chume, Prince Isolder is the legal heir to the throne. His wife rules."

After a moment, it occurred to Jag that he was gaping like a Mon Calamari. He shut his mouth so abruptly that his teeth clicked. "Prince Isolder would agree to this?"

"He may not have a choice," Tenel Ka said grimly. "If she decides that this is a good path to power, she will find a way to take it."

"Ta'a Chume has that much power?"

The Jedi regarded him somberly. "I was not speaking of my grandmother."

Jaina faced down the stubborn Wookiee. "I don't see what else we can do."

Lowbacca glanced at the ready ship and grumbled an argument.

"Hapes doesn't have the sort of people we need. This is experimental technology, and it's vital that we get it right. There are no better techs anywhere than on Kashyyyk," she said, naming the Wookiee homeworld.

Lowbacca harrumphed and folded his arms. Jaina's patience began to fray. "All right, let me put it this way. Your family owes my father a life debt. He doesn't seem willing to claim it himself, so I'm doing so in his name."

Lowbacca growled in puzzlement. The choice Jaina put before him was an awkward one, and she knew it. Her friend was caught between honoring a life debt and bringing some of his people into the path of a Yuuzhan Vong attack. Knowing the warrior culture of the Wookiee, Jaina was confident about the outcome.

With another heartfelt groan, Lowbacca hoisted himself into the waiting Hapan ship, and set off to bring some of his clan's best technicians into grave danger.

Kyp's X-wing drifted quietly in space, controls darkened and only enough power flowing to supply the life-support systems. Even Zero-One, his astromech droid and would-be conscience, remained switched off.

He watched as two small Hapan ships darted past, headed toward the coordinates of a short hyperspace jump. Kyp waited until they had disappeared, then powered up and urged his ship to follow.

His X-wing emerged into a vicious firestorm. Several Yuuzhan Vong coralskippers surrounded the Hapan ships. Plasma bolts tore at the blackness like bloody claws.

"Two ships," Kyp muttered. "Only two, against this!"

He jinked hard to port to avoid an incoming bolt, then wheeled around in a tight circle and closed in on one of the skips. Two of the enemy ships veered off into wild, erratic flight.

"Looks like there's a little too much confusion on that implant, Jaina," Kyp said as he switched on the comm to Zero-One. "Lock down target."

ACKNOWLEDGED.

Bright blue icons leapt onto his control screen and narrowed down into tight focus. A warning sensor hummed, and the single light flashed for a one–two–three countdown. Kyp hit the button at two.

A proton torpedo dropped into the sky and hurtled toward one of the confused skips. Blue light flared past a stream of plasma, turning the golden bolt into an eerie green. Kyp threw his ship into a side roll, spinning it away from the enemy barrage.

His weapon struck dead center, and the coralskipper exploded into shards of dark coral. Kyp veered away from the blooming cluster of shrapnel and chose his next target. In moments another bright explosion blossomed against the sky.

His comm unit crackled. "Vanguard Three, is that you?"

Kyp recognized the voice of one of Jag Fel's best Hapan recruits. "Seth! What in the blue blazes are you doing out here?"

"You don't know?"

At that moment, Kyp *did* know. These weren't scouts, sent up in pairs by Colonel Fel. These two men were sacrifices.

"Fall back. I'll cover you."

"Cover us, but try not to blow up every skip. I sure don't want to do this again."

A quick, syncopated cluster of plasma bolts erupted from two of the skips, converging on the Hapan fighter. The small vessel disappeared in a burst of white fire.

Kyp muttered an oath and swung away to protect the final ship. Despite Seth's request, he took out three more of the Yuuzhan Vong skips before following the battered Hapan fighter back to its base.

In the docking bay, Kyp swung out of the X-wing and sent a furious mental summons for his "apprentice."

"You don't have to shout," a calm female voice announced.

Jaina strode into the docking bay. Bypassing Kyp, she went up to the surviving pilot. "Did you get any?"

The man glanced at Kyp. "One. Maybe."

She nodded and turned away. Kyp seized her arm, and the two Jedi locked angry stares. "They're gathering data," she said at last. "Important data."

"How many pilots have you sent up? How many returned?"

"Most likely a higher percentage than those from your command," she shot back.

"People die in war. I accept that, and so do the pilots who fly with me. But I never deliberately threw their lives away. How good is your tracking data?"

"Getting better."

"So you had a good idea of how many skips were patrolling that sector. And you sent up two men."

"We don't have enough of the implants yet, or the delivery weapons, to justify sending up more," Jaina argued. "You would have made the same decision."

"Which brings us to the next issue. These pilots apparently think I ordered this mission."

Jaina merely shrugged. "You used my name and influence when it suited you. I'm here to learn from the master."

A tall, slender woman moved toward them, and a nod from her brought guards hurrying to disperse the small crowd of pilots and mechanics that had gathered on the perimeter.

"Difficult times call for hard decisions, young man," Ta'a Chume said sternly. "Selecting a leader is a difficult thing, and should never be done lightly. Once done, however, a constant second-guessing of a leader is worse than having none at all."

Kyp blinked and then turned to Jaina. "Who is this?"

"The former queen of Hapes," she said curtly. "Ta'a Chume, this is Kyp Durron, Jedi Master. He's training me."

For some reason the woman found this amusing. "If you have anything worthwhile to impart, I suggest you stop whining and get to it."

Ta'a Chume turned to Jaina. "I will be offworld for a day or so. We will speak again upon my return."

She glided off, and Kyp drew Jaina aside. "You said you were here to learn. Listen carefully, and see if you can wrap your mind around this: from now on, anything you do will be cleared through me. You will not assume that my actions, past or present, justify yours."

"Oh, please," Jaina scoffed. "Next thing I know you'll be telling me, 'Do as I say, and not as I do.' "

"That's the general idea."

Her sneer faded. "You're serious."

"As a thermal detonator. Start filling me in."

Jaina nodded. "A quick recap. A yammosk communicates with smaller ships through some sort of telepathy. The daughter ships move, shield, and navigate through gravitic fluctuations. These are both created and received by the dovin basal. Each of these creatures has a genetic imprint, a distinct and unique voice that's formed by its gravitic signals. When the dovin basal picks up information, they know what ship originated it. You with me so far?"

Kyp nodded. "Go on."

"Danni Quee discovered how to jam a yammosk signal: we took that one step farther." She described the process Lowbacca had used to isolate and define the pattern of the captured ship's signature.

"The pattern is very subtle. Right now we can disrupt it, using the coral implants."

"Yes, I just saw that demonstrated," Kyp noted.

"We've learned a lot from the skips we've managed to mess up. What we're doing now is trying to get the skip so confused that it loses contact with the yammosk altogether."

"I'd say you're there."

"Next step, then. All skips seem to fly and shield in pretty much the same way. It's the navigation that depends upon unique information. Lowbacca has been working on a small mechanical device, a repulsor, that could mimic the *Trickster's* gravitic code. This would overlay another ship's 'voice,' letting us create decoys that will lure the Vong into traps. The Yuuzhan Vong are looking for the *Trickster*. We're going to make sure they find and destroy her—not once, but several times."

He stared at her for a moment, then let out a long, slow whistle. "It's good. I'm in."

Her answering smile reminded him of a predatory tusk-cat. "Lead on, Master Durron."

TWENTY-FOUR

Isolder walked down a row of Wookiees, all intent upon the jumble of small metal parts on the tables before them. The furred technicians hardly seemed to notice his passing.

He turned to his mother. "What is it, precisely, that you wanted me to see?"

The former queen picked up a small device and handed it to him.

His eyes narrowed as he noticed a strange mark etched into the metal. "I have seen this before, on the dossier of a Yuuzhan Vong spy, a priestess Elan. This is the symbol for Yun-Harla, the Yuuzhan Vong Trickster goddess!"

"Who, it would seem, has been reincarnated here on Hapes," Ta'a Chume said. She swept one hand wide in a gesture that encompassed the vast workroom. "This is Jaina Solo's doing."

Isolder regarded the object in his hand. "What is this?"

"It's a miniature repulsor, and its effect on a ship is hardly noticeable by most measures. But it alters the unique gravity patterns of a Yuuzhan Vong ship just enough to change how other ships perceive it."

"I'm not sure I understand the importance of this."

Ta'a Chume hissed out a sigh. "Your daughter and her Jedi friends stole a Yuuzhan Vong ship. The enemy is rather keen to get it back, not to mention the young

Jedi—and in particular Jaina Solo. They are no doubt looking for the ship, and in time they will come to Hapes. This will confound them, at least for a time. It's a temporary measure."

"But it has promise," Isolder mused. "In conjunction with the Hapan fleet, we might be able to set up an ambush."

The queen smiled faintly. "An excellent suggestion. That's precisely what is needed—experience, mature guidance. Jaina has a natural flair for leadership and strategy, but she lacks the authority to move her plans ahead. As do you," she added. "I've been doing what I can to support her efforts, but my role is also limited. The queen mother is the only one with full authority to authorize such an attack."

Isolder frowned. "Teneniel Djo is unlikely to do this."

"Then replace her. You wanted Leia once, or thought you did. Her daughter would make twice the queen."

"Jaina? She is of an age with my own daughter!" he protested.

"A bit younger, actually. But she has a military background, combat experience, and the sense to listen to suggestions. She has been raised by a diplomat, knows how to act in public, and is highly presentable. You could do worse."

The prince started to object. He shut his mouth abruptly and glanced at the object in his hand.

Not long ago, he had taken the fate of the Hapes Consortium into his hands. His error of judgment had cost hundreds of ships, thousands of lives. Ta'a Chume was offering him another chance to aid his homeworld, a chance to redeem his mistake—a regency of sorts, overseeing the reign of a capable but inexperienced queen. He doubted any such opportunity would come again.

"I will consider it," he said at last.

* * *

Lowbacca was not in the tech hall. Jaina asked around and received only furry shrugs and cold stares from the Wookiee techs. Finally she headed off to the *Trickster*'s docking bay.

Her friend was there, but not in the ship. He was perched on the rail of the upper walkway. That provided Jaina with a clue to his state of mind. During their days at the academy, Lowbacca often went off alone to meditate in the treetops of Yavin 4's jungles. Here, in Hapes's royal city, this was as close to the canopies of his home-world as he was likely to find.

Jaina quietly climbed the stairs and leaned onto the rail beside him. "How many did you lose?"

Lowbacca let out a terse yap, a number high enough to make Jaina wince. "If I'd known the Wookiee ships were going to meet with that much resistance, I would have sent an escort."

Her friend looked at her for the first time, and there was no mistaking the rebuke there.

"I know where Harrar's priestship is, and the little fleet connected to his yammosk," Jaina snapped. "I don't know the location of every Sith-spawned hunk of rock in this galaxy! Yet."

Lowbacca's dark eyes searched her face, and he conceded this with a nod. Still, he looked troubled.

"What we're doing is worthwhile. Important. I'm sorry that some of your friends died, but we've got to move forward. The Yuuzhan Vong shapers are fast. They'll figure out what we know and then they'll do something else. Our window is very small."

She leaned toward him. "Are you with me?"

He climbed off the rail.

Anger, like a powerful wind, swept into the docking bay. Jaina sighed. "That would be Kyp."

The Jedi Master stormed into the building and up the

stairs. The guards who moved to stop him flew aside, untouched by any visible hand or weapon.

The Wookiee stepped forward, and Kyp aimed a psychic blast that sent the two-and-a-half-meter, ginger-furred Jedi staggering back.

He seized Jaina with the same dark energy and spun her to face him. "You've been holding out on me again. You've been sending up pilots, Hapan pilots, in ships that give off the *Trickster*'s signal. That's first cousin to a suicide mission!"

"We need more time," Jaina retorted. "We're close to finding a way to lure the Vong into a trap. In the meanwhile, this little diversion is keeping them busy. They're finding my ship all over this quadrant."

Kyp shoved a hand through his hair. "There's a line between dedication and fanaticism. I think you passed it a few kilometers back."

"That's rich, coming from you!" she scoffed. "The Vong are off chasing ghost ships, rather than focusing their energy on attacking Hapes. Fighter pilots know the risks, and they know they're saving thousands of noncombatants."

"Results are not enough," he countered. "Not for you."

She sent him a look of pure disbelief. "I heard what you didn't say," she marveled. "You said, 'Not for you.' What you thought was, *Not for Darth Vader's granddaughter.*"

"You're my responsibility now," Kyp persisted.

Jaina laughed. "I wish Uncle Luke could hear this! *Paralysis and inactivity, not the dark side, will overcome the Jedi.* Haven't you said that a hundred times?"

He blew out a long sigh. "When is another pilot due to go out?"

"She's powering up now," Jaina admitted.

The older Jedi spun toward the door. Jaina pulled her lightsaber.

Kyp stopped dead at the click and hum unique to the traditional Jedi weapon. He slowly turned to face her, hands raised in a placating gesture. "I don't want to fight you."

Her violet blade rose toward his throat. "You'd change your mind if the stakes were high enough."

"Don't be ridiculous. You wouldn't kill me even if you could!"

"The idea isn't without a certain appeal, but it's not what I had in mind. If I win, you fly the rest of this battle under my command. If you win, I'm yours. No more holding out, no more games. I'll keep the channels open, act like a real apprentice."

He considered her for a long moment. "Done."

His lightsaber leapt from his belt, flipped in midair, and slapped down into his hand. The glowing blade hissed toward her. Jaina vaulted above the flamboyant attack and flipped over Kyp's head. He rolled aside to avoid a possible slashing counter and came up in a crouch.

Jaina backed down the stairs, her weapon at high guard. He advanced, then darted forward with a quick feinting lunge.

She anticipated his move and leaned away from it, then quickly changed directions and lunged for him, sweeping her arm up into a rising parry that threw his lightsaber out wide. Her wrist twisted deftly to disengage the shining blades, and then she leapt straight up.

Kyp somersaulted down the stairs, turned, and came up with his lightsaber held high and ready. The younger Jedi dropped to the floor beside him and delivered two quick, testing jabs. He parried both. They drew apart and circled, taking each other's measure, exchanging blows that became less tentative with each strike.

Jaina's confident smile began to falter. "I'm not going to let you stop this next flight."

She whirled away from Kyp's high, slashing attack and caught his weapon in an overhead parry. A quick twist brought her around to face him. He disengaged and stepped back. "Who said I wanted to stop the mission? I want to fly it."

Jaina blinked. "You do?"

"If the mission is that important, I'll go myself."

"Forget it. The Jedi are too few and too valuable to risk."

"I know," he agreed, "and that's precisely why I need to go."

She stepped back, still in guard position, and eyed him warily.

"Let's just say I'm taking my responsibilities seriously. I don't want my apprentice to make some of the same mistakes I made."

Jaina's lightsaber flashed forward, forcing him to parry. "What apprentice? You haven't beaten me yet."

"I will," he said with a cocky smile. "And we both know it. We also know how difficult expectations can be. You've got to live up to your famous parents, which in some ways is even more difficult than living down a monumental failure."

"You can't compare our situations."

"We both lost brothers."

"And maybe hitting the Yuuzhan Vong hard will give some meaning to my brothers' deaths."

"I tried to avenge my brother," Kyp reminded her, "and I ended up killing him. Your mother thinks Jacen's still alive. What if she's right?"

Jaina lowered her lightsaber, and her face was a study of stunned fury. The older Jedi shifted his weight to the balls of his feet, gaining balance in preparation for the coming attack.

But Jaina switched off her weapon. "You want the mission? Take it. But you'd better survive it. We're not finished here. Not by a long shot."

She stormed out of the docking bay, leaving Kyp staring thoughtfully after her.

Jag Fel came into the docking bay in time to catch part of the battle, and some of the conversation. He began to understand Tenel Ka's concern for Jaina, and on impulse he sprinted over, catching her by the back exit.

He skidded to a stop and suddenly realized that he had no idea what to say. Jaina eyed him warily.

"I came to thank you for your help," he said.

"What are you talking about?"

By now he'd fallen into more of a rhythm. "Word has it that you've been recruiting Hapan pilots, getting them back into the skies. I don't have enough scouts to cover this area. Every set of eyes helps. And when the time comes to fight, there will be more pilots prepared and aware."

Some of the ice around Jaina's heart seemed to melt just a bit. For some reason, Jag's comment took some of the sting out of her recent encounter with Kyp. "We all do what we can."

"You and your family have given more than most," he observed. "Forgive me, but I heard what Kyp Durron said to you. I know how difficult these times can be. I, too, lost two siblings in battle."

Jaina bristled. "So what are you saying? That my loss is no greater than anyone else's? Anakin and Jacen no more important than any other casualty?"

Too late, Jag realized that this was not the sort of truth that a grieving person could absorb. "That's not what I intended to portray."

Her ire faded quickly. "Forget it." She blew her bangs away from her eyes, a small gesture that seemed incredibly weary. "So why did you come? You're not usually one for small talk."

And that, Jag noted, was the dilemma. He couldn't exactly blurt out, "Don't marry Prince Isolder."

"You have a natural gift for leadership," he continued. "People will follow you, whether you want them to or not. Rank is not important to someone like you."

Jaina's face went very still. "This is all very interesting, but where is it going?"

"I just wanted to express an opinion," he said, feeling incredibly awkward. "The rank you were born with suits you very well. Anything more would be redundant."

"I see," she said in a flat tone. "Coming from the son of Baron Fel—a jumped-up Corellian dirt farmer—that's worth about as much as Ithorian currency."

Jag began to feel his own temper rise. "Why must you take offense at every turn?"

"Why must you answer questions that no one bothered to ask?" she returned heatedly.

To Jag's astonishment, she turned and fled. He watched her go, wondering what meaning she might have heard in his words that he had never intended to place there.

Jaina slowed to a walk as soon as she left the docking bay behind, but her heart held pace, hammering in her ears.

What was Jag Fel's problem? Sure, maybe she'd flirted with him a little at the diplomatic dinner, but had she ever given him reason to warn her off?

Keep to her rank. Yeah, right. Keep out of *his*, most likely!

For some reason the notion of a Baroness Jaina must have crawled up his exhaust and nested, and, honorable and forthright guy that he was, he just had to let her know that this wasn't in the sabacc cards. Well, thanks for the clarification, but who asked?

Jaina took a long, steadying breath and tried to banish Jag Fel from her thoughts. He was a distraction, and that was the last thing she needed right now. She'd been surprised by Jag's visit, but she wasn't even sure if she cared enough to be angry about it.

But she kicked at a parked repulsorsled, just in case she was.

TWENTY-FIVE

Harrar's priestship and its military escort approached the Hapes Cluster, following the reports of sightings of their stolen frigate.

"There," Khalee Lah said, stabbing at the living map with a taloned finger.

Tiny, luminous creatures moved slowly across the screen, marking the place where the yammosk had discerned the signature of the stolen ship. There was a definite pattern. The thief was venturing farther out of Hapan space each time. The next foray would take her directly into the priestship's path.

The warrior glanced at Harrar, his split lips stretched in a leer of anticipation. "The warmaster will have his *Jeedai* sacrifice. We hunt," he snapped at the crew. "Summon every ship within communication range that has engaged this would-be Trickster. She has hidden long enough in the shadow of Yun-Harla. Soon those who whisper words of heresy will see this infidel for the pitiful creature she is!"

As the crew hurried to do Khalee Lah's bidding, Harrar settled down in an observation seat and prepared to watch the battle. A now familiar prickle edged down his spine as he prepared to confront the *Jeedai*.

Khalee Lah took the command chair. His long, knobby finger caressed the nodes as he gathered information. "The *Ksstarr* is approaching."

The priest glanced toward his commander. "Alone?"

"With an escort." The warrior's sneer was visible beneath the hood. "One small ship."

A strange wave of disappointment swept through Harrar. He had expected better from Jaina Solo. "Capture them both."

When Kyp emerged from hyperspace, his controls immediately began to flash warnings. The programmed hyperspace jump had brought him directly between two flanks of Yuuzhan Vong ships. Immediately all the lights began to converge on his location. Soon they'd be in visual range, and they would know that he wasn't flying the stolen Yuuzhan Vong frigate. More, they'd know that there *was* no *Trickster*—except for the one who'd sent an X-wing up to project the stolen ship's unique signal.

"Planned this a bit tight, didn't you, Jaina?" he murmured. A sharp jolt hit Kyp's fighter, and sensors flared out a low-shield warning signal. One of the ships was using its dovin basal to strip off his shields.

Kyp boosted up the inertial compensator, expanding the protection this system gave to ship and pilot several meters and moving it out beyond the ship's normal shields—a trick invented by Gavin Darklighter early in the war. Even as he did, he realized that this was no solution. Gavin had not been flying alone.

Two coralskippers closed in, and again Kyp felt the tug and pull of the gravity beams. He dialed down the inertial compensator. Too much stress, and it could pull the ship apart from the inside.

A second X-wing exploded out of the darkness of space. A blue flash burst from it, and the big ship dissolved in a bright flare. The coralskippers released their hold on Kyp's fighter and circled around to deal with this new threat. His comm crackled.

"Get out of there, Kyp," Jaina warned.

"And leave you alone? I don't think so."

"Turn off the gravitic transmitter—lower left console, yellow dial. Find a ship about the *Trickster*'s size. Strafe it. I'll be right behind you."

A faint smile curved Kyp's lips. He glanced at the screen and selected a target, then relayed its coordinates to Jaina.

The two X-wings swept toward the frigate analog. Kyp leaned on the splinter-shot trigger. Hundreds of underpowered bolts sprayed the coral ship. A small black hole swallowed most of them, but many of the small lasers found a mark.

So, too, did some of the small concussion missiles Jaina fired.

"The seed's been planted," Jaina said. "Let's go."

Kyp turned his X-wing into a rolling turn and then shot off toward the mists. The stars stretched into lines, echoing the smile that spread over his face.

The seed had been planted, all right.

Khalee Lah removed the cognition hood and nodded to his secondary pilot. He turned to Harrar and brought himself up at sharp, military attention.

"Eminence. The *Ksstarr* has been secured."

The priest rose and followed the warrior to the large bay that filled the entire lower level of the priestship. Warriors ringed the captured ship.

"Open it," the commander ordered.

Before anyone could respond, the hatch irised open and a small ramp lowered. The heavy tread of a warrior in vonduun crab armor thudded down the ramp.

"What is the meaning of this?" he thundered. His ire faded into slack astonishment as he found himself face-to-face with Khalee Lah.

He did not seem to notice that the commander was

equally astonished. The warrior pilot fell to one knee, fists thumping his shoulders. "Command me. My life is yours."

Harrar moved forward. "You will report to the coral-skipper bay. A ship will be given you. This one requires the attention of the shapers."

The pilot rose, saluted again, and strode away. Harrar dismissed the warriors with a single curt gesture.

The priest turned to Khalee Lah, suppressing an unholy impulse to gloat. "This is not the *Ksstarr*," he said with what he thought to be admirable restraint. "Perhaps none of the ships we encountered was."

"One of them will be," the warrior snarled. He snapped his gaze up to Harrar's. "We need more ships. Jaina Solo will be found, and she will be sacrificed. This I swear, by the goddess she blasphemes!"

Jaina adjusted the cognition hood and picked up the standard comm device Lowbacca had installed in the *Trickster*.

"Get ready," she warned the pilots flying with her. "I'm sensing a small fleet coming out of hyperspace. They should be within firing range soon."

"Too vapin' soon," another pilot retorted.

A faint, nervous chuckle wafted through the open comm, dying quickly as the Yuuzhan Vong fleet streaked out of the blackness of hyperspace.

Coralskippers veered swiftly away from larger corvette and frigate analogs, scattering into well-disciplined ranks. Behind them were three oddly shaped vessels that defied classification. Starlight gleamed off the polished black facets of a large, gemlike ship.

Jaina's eyes narrowed. She remembered that ship from Myrkr. It had arrived just as she and the other Jedi escaped. This would be the priestship. Well, it was in for a few surprises.

"Just like in practice," Kyp's voice put in.

A metallic beep and whir came over the comm. "More advice from Zero-One?" one of the pilots guessed.

"You might say that. He observed that we can proceed as we did in practice—at least, until the inevitable variables occur."

"I can live with that," the pilot shot back. "One droid's variable is another person's luck."

Jaina smiled faintly. In Rogue Squadron, prebattle chatter was strictly discouraged. Kyp maintained that it kept the pilots loose and ready to react. At any rate, it kept them from dwelling too darkly on the battle ahead.

"Why do you call your astromech droid Zero-One?" a low-pitched female voice asked.

The smile fell off Jaina's face as she recognized Shawnkyr, the Chiss female who flew with Jag. The Chiss woman had maintained her distance, flying every mission and keeping to herself. But her strange red eyes seemed to follow Jaina, echoing and even magnifying Jag Fel's dubious opinion of the "scruffy Rebel pilot."

"It's a bad joke based in old technology," Kyp explained. "The droid belonged to a Mon Calamari philosopher who was some sort of expert in ancient cultures and technology. Apparently there was a computer system based on binary code, and the Mon Cal was fond of saying, 'Simplicity can be achieved; life is all just zeros and ones.' "

"Binary code. That explains a few things about your droid," Jaina quipped, and was rewarded with a rude, metallic buzz.

A flare of plasma scorched the sky, falling short of the Hapan fleet.

"First phase is yours, Colonel Fel," she said.

Jag acknowledged with a double click. The two Chiss clawcraft vectored sharply away, and ten Hapan fighters followed them. They broke up into tight formations of four, each of which singled out a coralskipper for attack. They sent out a coordinated barrage of laserfire—as well as other, smaller projectiles that slipped between the dovin basal's shielding bursts and embedded deep in the rough coral hull.

"Your turn, Kyp," she prodded.

The rogue Jedi took three X-wings and peeled away, leaving Jaina's frigate alone and apparently unprotected. Lowbacca moaned anxiously.

They watched as the coralskippers advanced, battling their way through Jag's disciplined squadron.

"Most of them should have the repulsors by now. Get ready," she said slowly, "and . . . *now!*"

The Wookiee broadcast a signal to the repulsor devices, and suddenly two-thirds of the attacking coralskippers whirled away, responding to the gravitic messages informing them that the *Trickster* was now behind them.

"Here's where it gets interesting," Jaina murmured.

She ordered the frigate to advance at maximum speed. As they soared into the midst of the Yuuzhan Vong fleet, Lowbacca prepared to activate the small repulsor units attached to the skips.

Streaks of disabling plasma flared toward Jaina—all of them aimed at the underside of her ship. By now she understood the *Trickster* well enough to follow this strategy. Nom Anor's ship was heavily armored, with an extremely thick lower hull. Attacks to this section activated the dovin basal, allowing other ships to generate gravitic tractor beams to pull Jaina in.

But Jaina didn't allow them to distract her dovin basal. She wove the frigate through the battle, twisting and dipping in the wildest and most reckless flight of her life, daring the enemy to follow and fire upon her.

In the confusion that followed, the Yuuzhan Vong ships relied upon their sensors—which in turn directed their fire to whatever ship was currently broadcasting the

Trickster's signal. Not every ship was as well armored as Jaina's. Two coralskippers went up in bright, brief flames.

Suddenly Lowbacca howled in alarm.

"A glitch?" Jaina yelled back. "No glitches! You can't broadcast the signal to more than one ship at one time!"

Even as she spoke, the Wookiee's mistake led to a happy accident—the three Yuuzhan Vong skips receiving the signal converged on one another. A simultaneous eruption of plasma exploded from all three ships, followed by a secondary explosion that reduced them to a massive spray of coral shards.

"Glitches can be good," Jaina conceded.

As the battle devolved from one level of chaos to another, Harrar's growing superstition moved toward terrified belief.

The *Jeedai* twin was performing seemingly impossible feats of movement, strategy, and destruction. With one ship, she evaded their best pilots, destroying some of their swiftest skips. She was nowhere, and everywhere.

All around him, the crew members begin to murmur the name *Yun-Harla* in a mixture of awe and dread. The priest could not bring himself to chastise them for this heresy.

Khalee Lah strode into the control room, his scarred face grim. "How do you wish to proceed, Eminence?"

The priest considered only for a moment. This decision might end his career, but it was the only reasonable option.

"Order the retreat."

The survivors returned to the Hapan dock, spilling out of their ships with cheers and hoots of laughter, falling into back-thumping embraces. Jaina smiled faintly as she strode down the *Trickster*'s ramp. The task she had in mind was far from finished, but they'd made a good start.

She was lifted off her feet and spun around in an exuberant circle. Kyp set her down, beaming.

Jaina felt Jag Fel's approach. Her exuberance dimmed as she turned to face the young colonel.

"That was astonishing. If you ever feel in need of a title, you should consider 'commander.' I'd be happy to consider you in that light."

"Gee, a girl can't hear that too often," Jaina said dryly.

A flicker of puzzlement entered Jag's eyes. Before he could ask, a tall, blue-skinned female strode over.

"No Chiss would fly under this woman's command," the Chiss said sternly. "I am surprised, Colonel Fel, to hear you use words such as *commander* with such imprecision."

In Jaina's current mood of dark exhilaration, it was easy to shrug off the Chiss's comments. It wouldn't be the first time the Chiss female—not to mention her human commander—had revealed a deeply inbred arrogance. So she didn't think much of it when Shawnkyr pulled Jag aside to give him a private earful.

Later that night, the pilots were celebrated as heroes in the vast city square. Jag Fel did not attend the ceremony. Jaina smiled and danced, but all the while she wondered what the Chiss pilot had said—and why she cared about any of it.

Far away, in the Skywalker quarters on the hidden Jedi base, Luke settled his sleeping son carefully into his cot. He stood for a long moment, gazing into the tiny face.

A nameless dread seized him, a fear for this child that went beyond any concern he'd ever had over his own life. Luke searched his feeling through the Force, and found that his Jedi instincts on this matter were almost neutral.

Ben was in no immediate danger, and the aura of the future did not hang over Luke's sudden fear. The surge was something different, something that any parent, and perhaps every parent, might experience.

Han and Leia entered the room. Luke's sister came up beside him and wrapped her arm around his shoulders. "Parenting is the most terrifying thing I can imagine, even under the best of circumstances," she said softly. "When you bring a child into dangerous times, it's even worse."

Luke felt the grief and guilt lurking beneath her calm tones. No response came to him—what words could mend the loss of two children? So he merely returned her embrace, trusting his brother-in-law to find a way to lighten the moment.

Han cleared his throat and manufactured a wry grin. "I don't know what you're worried about, Luke. Anything that wants to get near Ben has to go through Mara."

"Me?" Mara retorted in kind. "I can just imagine how you'd react if someone intruded on Jaina's space."

Han's face suddenly went blank. His wife pushed away from Luke and rushed over. "What is it? What's wrong?"

"I remember starting that fight," he said slowly, "and I remember why. Ta'a Chume's ambassadors made an offer of marriage on Isolder's behalf—not for you, Leia, but for Jaina."

Leia's eyes flew into rounded moons. "Well, that would certainly explain the mess you made of your knuckles! What did they offer?"

"A trade. We don't try to talk Jaina out of marrying Isolder, they *don't* hand over the refugees."

"That's ridiculous," Mara put in. "Jaina would never agree to a trade."

Now that the first jolt of surprise had passed, Leia wasn't so sure. "I almost did."

"What about Teneniel Djo?" Han demanded.

The three Jedi exchanged a concerned look. Mara fielded the question. "Unless her left hook is a lot better than yours, I'd say she's in trouble."

TWENTY-SIX

After the ceremony, Ta'a Chume called Jaina aside for a private meeting.

"You've done extremely well, but the Yuuzhan Vong will be back. It's time that you knew my mind. I want Teneniel Djo off the throne, and Isolder to marry a queen capable of ruling during war."

Jaina shrugged. "Unless you want me to help Teneniel Djo pack, I have no idea why you're telling me this."

The old queen sent her an arch, sidelong look. "I've often thought of how frustrating it must have been to always labor in the shadow of a famous mother."

"A torpedo is launched, but no target is in sight," Jaina observed.

"The target is very obvious. This is a common concern for young women in your position."

"It's the sort of thing that crosses your mind, sure, but war has a way of making adolescent angst seem petty."

"But pettiness does not end with adolescence," Ta'a Chume went on. "No doubt you've noticed Tenel Ka's recent hostility toward you."

"We've had our differences. There's a lot of that going around among the Jedi."

"When did my granddaughter become concerned with philosophy? No, Tenel Ka is prompted by a fear of being displaced by someone more worthy."

Jaina massaged her temples with both hands, feeling a

bit dazed by this surreal conversation. "Someone like my mother, I suppose. Is that what you're preparing me for? If so, I don't follow the logic. Instead of Princess Leia's daughter, I'd be Queen Leia's heir. Not exactly coming out of the shadows, if that's what you're concerned about."

The queen smiled like a sabacc player about to place a winning hand on the table. "You misunderstand, my dear. In these brutal times, Hapes needs a warrior queen—not Teneniel, not Tenel Ka, not Princess Leia. A queen who seeks to understand the enemy, and attack boldly."

Her meaning hit Jaina like a Yuuzhan Vong thud bug. Unaccountably, she began to giggle. "I can just picture my father's reaction to this idea. We're talking about Han Solo here—I'm surprised your ambassadors didn't have to kill him in self-defense!"

"This is quite serious," Ta'a Chume insisted.

With difficulty, Jaina composed her expression. "I can see that. I didn't mean to offend—really, even the suggestion is an enormous honor. But I'm just not interested."

"Why not?"

"Why not?" she echoed. "For starters, I'm too young."

"Nonsense. You're eighteen, about the age your mother was when she set her heart on an older man."

"Speaking of my father, how many days did your ambassadors spend in a bacta tank?" she said pointedly.

"I'm sure he'll come around to the idea. He is a reasonable man."

"He's never been accused of *that* before," Jaina retorted. "But that's neither here nor there. I don't know about Hapan customs, but no one tells me who to marry. Not my parents, not my friends."

"And not me," Ta'a Chume concluded with a faint smile. "At least consider it."

Jaina promised she would and went to look for Jag Fel, intending to question him about the fight he'd interrupted.

Her initial certainty had faded. She hoped that her father had just been acting predictably, but her danger senses prickled. What if he did not "respond reasonably"? What if Teneniel Djo did not step aside? How far would Ta'a Chume go to get her way?

Since landing on Hapes, Jaina had been convinced that Ta'a Chume had a plan in mind for her. She didn't want to believe this of Ta'a Chume, despite all she knew and sensed of the older woman.

She couldn't find Jag anywhere, though she eventually tracked his ship to an extremely inconspicuous corner of the city docks. Nor could she find anyone who had seen him recently.

She considered, briefly, reaching out with the Force to find him. Jacen had gone into deep meditation to find Corran Horn after the attack on Yavin 4, but this had never been her strong suit, and even those Jedi gifted with perception had difficulty finding specific people—unless, of course, they had some deep connection.

She decided instead to seek answers in a Jedi trance, and made her way to the quiet of her palace room.

As she sank deep into thought and out into the current of the Force, an image began to emerge as if from a dark mist. Jaina saw a small, slim girl in a brown flight suit. The girl's shoulders were hunched in tense anticipation, and she clasped an unfamiliar lightsaber in both hands.

Jaina's heart jolted as she recognized herself, and understood the context of this vision. And then she was swept deeper, leaving the detachment of the spectator behind as she entered fully into the Force-inspired memory.

A tall, black-clad figure strode toward her, his red lightsaber ready for attack.

The image of Darth Vader did not inspire the fear her

infamous grandfather had earned, but a very different sort of terror.

Once again she relived the moment of horrified realization that she'd fought Jacen, cloaked in a holographic disguise.

"Jacen?" she whispered.

The specter advanced. She rose to her feet, reluctantly, and switched on the blade the Shadow Academy Masters had given her. The battle swept over her on dark wings, fierce and fast and desperate. Jaina threw all her skill into parrying the blows and landing none. The nascent skill Jacen had possessed from an early age made this a difficult task.

In this vision, however, she was not a trained Jedi Knight, but a young girl torn from her home by a group of Dark Jedi, forced to fight untrained. Jaina fought not as she now was, but as she had been. In the end, she struck without intending to.

The Dark Lord staggered and went down, his gloved hands grasping at the smoking line Jaina's lightsaber had seared across his throat.

She dropped her weapon and hurried to her opponent, tugging at his helm, praying that she would see Darth Vader's face beneath, or even her own.

The holographic disguise faded away, and Jaina's heart simply shattered. A lanky boy sprawled on the ground, his brown hair tousled and his sightless eyes looking faintly puzzled.

Jaina pushed herself to her feet and stumbled back. She hadn't killed her brother. She had not.

Her own disguise did not fade away, so she wrenched off the helmet. The visor opened of its own accord. Startled, she dropped the helmet and watched it roll slowly toward Jacen. It stopped, and Kyp Durron's face gazed out at her. His lips moved, but she could not hear his words.

Jaina awakened from the vision with a start, breathing as hard as if she'd just run a twenty-kilometer sprint with Tenel Ka. Slowly she became aware of an urgent voice, and turned dazedly to face it. She recoiled at the sight of Kyp Durron's concerned face.

"You brought me out of the trance," she repeated. "Why?"

He rocked back on his heels and placed a hand on her shoulder. "Maybe I have some sense of what you were going through."

She shook him off, but she couldn't dismiss the vision or its obvious symbolism. And there was something compelling in Kyp's watchful green eyes that, for once, had nothing to do with the Force.

"I never had the problems that Jacen and Anakin had with the Force," she said slowly. "They debated its true nature, and struggled to understand what it means to be a Jedi. I just did what needed to be done. Up to now, that has always been enough. Now I'm being forced to question, and to choose."

She told Kyp about Ta'a Chume's offer. "I'm not considering it, but it made me think. The queen mother operates behind a line I'm not willing to cross."

"Which begs the question of what your parameters are."

"Exactly. And I realized that I've unwittingly crossed a number of lines without paying attention."

"I've crossed a few myself," Kyp agreed. "It's hard not to—the vapin' things keep moving."

She smiled faintly. "This is a decision point: I can back out now, or I can move forward and push this offensive as far as it will take me."

Kyp studied her. "You're going to continue, whatever it costs you."

"I don't see any other way," she said with a helpless shrug. The way she saw it, a Jedi would willingly sacrifice her life in service against evil. Faced with the

Yuuzhan Vong threat, how could she turn away from this darker, greater sacrifice?

"Did you find the answers you sought?" Kip asked.

Jaina started to say no, but a brief, vivid vision enveloped her—an image of a tiny Jag imprisoned in the tangle of an X-wing's circuitry. The mental picture faded as quickly as it came, leaving Jaina with two startling realizations: first, the outer edges of the "maze" actually followed the pattern of the lower levels of the palace. But even more startling, Jaina realized that she could feel Jag's presence through the Force.

That should have been impossible, given her particular talents. She couldn't even connect to her own twin brother. She'd had to feel Jacen's death through the collective pain of several Jedi. Whereas Tenel Ka—

Realization slammed into her. She could sense Jag Fel's presence for the same reason that Tenel Ka had been so open to Jacen. The connection had grown unobserved. Or perhaps it had always been there.

Kyp took Jaina by both shoulders. "What now?" he demanded, giving her a little shake.

Without responding, she pulled away and raced off in the direction her vision had indicated.

TWENTY-SEVEN

Jaina and Kyp found Jag exactly where Jaina had envisioned him—in a small room hidden deep in a labyrinthine maze.

Kyp felt her bright anticipation, the excitement that came with her sudden realization. Without realizing it, she was expecting Jag to experience a similar moment of epiphany.

That dream shattered the moment Jag Fel looked up at his rescuers. He glanced at Jaina, and a shuttered, disinterested expression fell over his face. Kyp felt the young woman's surge of pain, and her conviction that Jag Fel might admire her courage and talent, but he regarded her as a scruffy and undisciplined rogue.

The "Jedi princess" quickly swallowed her shock and reached into her pocket for a small multitool. With a few deft flicks she picked the complicated locks—a skill she had no doubt learned from her "scoundrel" father.

The sound of footsteps echoed through the halls. Kyp and Jaina glanced at each other, then looked to the ceiling. A tangle of pipes crossed it, some five meters overhead. They both leapt, catching hold of the pipes and waiting.

Jag had the presence of mind to push the door shut. One of the locks clicked, and he settled down.

His guards took several moments to figure out the

locks. When they entered, grumbling, the two Jedi
dropped from their perch.

Jaina stepped over a downed guard and into the
corridor. "How did you get yourself down here?" she
demanded.

Jag sent her a quick glance. "After the battle,
Shawnkyr took me aside and warned me that in implying
that I'd honor you as a commander, I was putting my pilots in the service of Hapes' future queen. That I was
taking sides in a coming coup."

Jaina looked dismayed. "Your Chiss friend must have
overheard some of Ta'a Chume's people talking about it."

"That's right. Congratulations, Lieutenant. Or would
'Your Majesty' be more appropriate?"

"These days she prefers 'Trickster,'" Kyp offered.
"What's a queen, next to a Yuuzhan Vong goddess?"

Jaina shot a quick glare in Kyp's direction. "Don't help
me. This queen business is ridiculous. It wasn't my idea."

"The queen's retainers were of the impression that you
were another Ta'a Chume, an ambitious woman who
would gladly seize this opportunity. They also spoke of
eliminating obstacles, a job they were hired to do."

Jaina stopped and seized his arm. "Does this have anything to do with my father?"

"That was my assumption, too. I sought out Han's 'assailants'; ambassadors who went to negotiate a marriage
alliance between Prince Isolder and Jaina. I feel certain
that Han was not attacked so much as subdued."

"I know all this," Jaina interrupted, "but I don't
understand why you were detained."

His lips firmed into a grim line. "I was stopped on my
way to find and warn Tenel Ka. You're of legal age and
don't require your parents' permission. If you wish to
marry Isolder, no one can stop you. Logically speaking,

what would this obstacle be but Queen Mother Teneniel Djo?"

Harrar watched as Khalee Lah paced the command center of the priestship. "Our fears have come to pass: the warriors under this command are beginning to voice questions and doubts. This is a more insidious danger than defeat in battle."

"Some even question your fitness to command," one of the guards observed. "Yun-Harla mocks us through her new chosen one . . ."

The warrior whirled toward the challenger, his face twisted in fury. "Challenge accepted," he grated out.

The priest began to intervene, then decided against it. Khalee Lah required an outlet for his fervor. Better to send a warrior into battle than a zealot.

"You and you," Khalee Lah said, pointing to two of the largest warriors. "The challenge will be three against one. We will see who has the favor of the gods!"

Mere moments later, Khalee Lah stood over the bodies of his challengers. He glanced up at the clanking footfall of the priest's bodyguard.

The female strode in, dutifully ignoring the bodies of the slain warriors. "We recovered some debris from one of the ruined ships, Eminence. I thought you would wish to see this."

Harrar claimed the small metal device with an expression of extreme distaste. "This is Yun-Harla's mark! What blasphemy is this?"

"It was found affixed to a hull fragment—one of the ships sacrificed in the battle against the *Trickster*."

"One of the ships we accidentally destroyed," Khalee Lah corrected testily, "and perhaps this abomination will show us why."

He took the device from the priest and twisted it as if he would crack the metal in half. Suddenly he went flying upward, slamming into the ceiling of the chamber as if he'd been thrown there by unseen hands.

"Brilliant," Harrar murmured as he gazed at the furious, floating warrior. "The device defies gravity, as do our dovin basals. When affixed to a ship, it might override the ship's gravitic voice. Any ship so marked might appear to our sensors to be a different ship, even the stolen frigate. Since you are considerably lighter than a ship, the effect was far more drastic and pronounced."

The warrior managed to switch off the device. He fell to the floor, rolled twice, and came up on his feet. Gathering his composure, he showed the device to the surviving guards.

"Look on this, and understand your heresy. Go tell the others that this *Jeedai* is nothing but an infidel, one who will die as easily as any other. Go!"

The guards went, and Khalee Lah hurled the device to the floor. "In my anger, I have touched a blasphemous device. I am unclean, and will lay that crime at the female's feet as well!"

He whirled toward Harrar. "Alert the warmaster, Eminence, and request that all ships in this sector converge. We will find this *Jeedai* if we have to leave all the worlds of Hapes in smoking ashes!"

"Teneniel Djo," Jaina repeated, staring at Jag Fel's grim face. Though she was stunned by his conclusion, she could not refute it.

They raced through the halls and into the royal apartments. Guards moved to stop them; Force lightning caught them and threw them aside.

They found Tenel Ka in her mother's room, sitting beside the window. She held her mother's hand in both of hers. Jaina knew at a glance that they all had been too late.

"Poison," Tenel Ka murmured. "They did not even give her the dignity of a final battle."

Jaina placed a hand on her friend's shoulder. "We'll find whoever did this."

The Jedi lifted burning eyes to Jaina's face. "I will not have my mother's life dishonored by your vengeance."

She fell back a step. "Is that what you think this is about? Do you think I'm dishonoring Anakin? Jacen?"

An alarm sounded, rising in pitch and volume as it sang out the invasion alert. Tenel Ka gently released her mother's hand and stood. She held out one hand, fingers spread to display the large emerald ring. Then she abruptly clenched her fist, and a hologram leapt into the air between them.

A nebulous swirl of darkness and mists filled the air. The mists parted to reveal five large starships, and smaller vessels spilling from them.

"Hapes's fleet, and my mother's legacy," Tenel Ka said curtly. "Colonel Jag Fel, I place these ships under your command."

TWENTY-EIGHT

The council chamber of the Hapan court filled with frantically shouting figures. They fell silent, out of mingled fear and habit, as a slender, red-robed woman rose to speak.

"Someone must take command until a new queen mother is enthroned," Ta'a Chume said. Slowly, deliberately, she lifted a delicate jeweled crown and placed it on her own head.

"The Witch of Dathomir is dead!" someone shouted. "No more Jedi queens."

Murmurs of agreement swirled through the room, for it was widely known that the former queen despised her daughter-in-law. But Ta'a Chume sent a slow, glacial stare toward her would-be supporter. A profound silence fell over the hall. She let it reign for several moments before speaking.

"Yes, Queen Mother Teneniel Djo is dead," Ta'a Chume agreed, "and the Ni'Korish are responsible. Whatever failings Teneniel Djo might have had, Hapan law demands death to any who raise a hand against the royal family. The Ni'Korish have gone too far. Even now, guards are gathering these traitors. Before nightfall, they will be no more."

She lifted one hand, and guards stepped forward to take the man who'd shouted. For several moments the only sounds in the hall were his muffled protests, and the sound of his boots scraping across the polished floor as they dragged him away.

"What of the refugees?" someone asked in more subdued tones.

"Expendable," Ta'a Chume stated flatly. "They may purchase us needed time." She glanced pointedly toward Isolder. "A new queen will be named very soon."

Another faint murmur rippled through the hall, rising in volume as two young women strode forward. The crowd fell back to let them pass.

Jaina noticed that Ta'a Chume's eyes flickered from her to Tenel Ka, lingering on neither. The queen removed the crown she'd just donned and handed it to the prince. Through the Force, Jaina felt the woman's faint, feline satisfaction.

Suddenly she understood. If Isolder offered Jaina the crown now, at a time of crisis and before a roomful of people, she could hardly refuse it. Ta'a Chume fully expected Jaina to eagerly seize the power. With stunning clarity, Jaina glimpsed herself through Ta'a Chume's eyes. When the queen looked upon the Jedi pilot, she saw a younger version of herself.

But for all of Ta'a Chume's machinations, it was not Jaina who ultimately would hold the throne. No doubt Jaina would soon have met the same fate as Teneniel Djo. Sooner or later, Tenel Ka would have had little choice but to assume the throne. She would not stand and see others die in her place.

They stopped at the front of the audience chamber. Tenel Ka turned to face Jaina. "There are times when personal inclinations must be put aside," she said softly. "I will take up my mother's crown, and I will defend it if I must. But for now, we have a common foe."

The Jedi women regarded each other for a long, silent moment.

"Let's go," Jaina said.

A faint smile touched Tenel Ka's lips. She strode over to her father and dropped to one knee. Without hesitation he placed the crown on her head.

Thunderous ovation swept through the room. The newly crowned queen rose and whirled toward the crowd, cutting off their applause with a swift, impatient gesture.

"I am a warrior, a daughter of warrior women. Teneniel Djo foresaw the Yuuzhan Vong threat and prepared. Shipyards hidden in the Transitory Mists have rebuilt much of the fleet lost at Fondor. These ships are on their way. Go, and fight, and know that Hapes is strong."

She strode back toward Jaina, her pace quickening as she went. Jaina fell into step, and together the two Jedi women ran toward battle. The applause began again, with a fervor that swept them along like a gathering storm.

Jaina noted a familiar group of pilots at the back of the room, a disparate group—Hapans, Chiss, Republic, and rogue—who all chose to fly under Jag Fel's command. She nodded to Jag and Kyp as she passed. "See you up there."

Jag gave her a formal bow and then glanced to Shawnkyr. The Chiss pilots set off for the docking bay at a run, and Kyp fell into pace beside them.

Impulse struck, and Kyp acted on it at once. "Jaina never intended to marry the prince."

Jag looked politely interested. "I see. He is not a Jedi."

"True, but that's not the issue," Kyp said. "I'm guessing that the only man Jaina would ever take seriously is one who can outfly her."

Jag ran along for several moments before answering. "There are not many who fit that description," he observed neutrally.

"Yeah, I've noticed that," Kyp responded in kind.

They skidded to a stop beside their docked ships. Jag extended his hand to Kyp. They clasped hands briefly.

"Watch her back," the Chiss commander said softly, and then he swung up into his clawcraft.

Kyp took his promise very seriously. He stormed over to the Yuuzhan Vong frigate and raced up the deck.

"Whatever you're planning, forget it," he said bluntly.

Jaina pulled off the cognition hood and stared at him.

"I get the feeling you're about to toss your life away, sacrificing it as Anakin did. Not long ago, you told me that Anakin might have had the answers. We can't let them just disappear into mist along with you."

"Don't put that on me," Jaina said slowly. "You really think that I'm on a journey to discover what the Jedi should be?"

"It makes sense," Kyp said. "You've got the talent, the heritage. Maybe there's something to all this talk of destiny."

Jaina picked up the hood again. "Get out."

"Not until you tell me what you've got in mind."

She rose suddenly, in a fluid blur, one hand thrown toward the older Jedi. Dark lightning crackled from her fingers and surrounded him in a shining nimbus. He flew back and struck the wall hard. His eyes narrowed, and the deadly aura disappeared. Jaina's eyes widened in surprise.

"If I can summon it, I can dispel it," he told her. "You're not the only one who took that path."

Jaina drew her lightsaber. "Outside," she snarled.

Kyp gave her a mockingly courtly bow and motioned for her to go first. She shook her head. He shrugged and walked down the ramp, Jaina close behind him. As his feet touched the dock, she leapt into a backward flip and landed in the doorway. She shut off her lightsaber and took a step back. The living portal slammed shut behind her.

"Stang," Kyp muttered as he watched the alien ship rise swiftly into the air.

Jaina reached up to touch the cognition hood. Information flowed from every part of the ship, as it had from the first time she donned the hood. Before, she had always listened to the ship with detachment and distaste, as she might endure the necessary but loathsome companionship of a Hutt informer. Before, she'd had other Jedi aboard helping her interact with the ship. Without Tahiri's hard-won connection to the Yuuzhan Vong, without Lowbacca's skill with the organic navicomputer, Jaina could not afford the luxury of detachment. For the first time she opened herself fully to the living ship.

A strangely familiar sensation swept through her as the link between ship and pilot deepened. She'd experienced something like this twice before—once when she'd built her lightsaber and learned to use it as an extension of herself and her powers, and once again when she attuned the young villips Lowbacca had found in the ship's hydroponic vats. Now that Jaina considered it, the two experiences had more in common than she would have thought possible.

She glanced at the two villips resting on the *Trickster*'s console. She reached for the villip that she had painstakingly attuned and stroked it to life. After a moment, the scarred face of Warmaster Tsavong Lah appeared. He recoiled in astonishment at the face his villip revealed.

"Greetings, Warmaster," Jaina said in mocking tones. "Remember me? Jacen Solo's twin sister?"

"You will be sacrificed to the gods," the warmaster gritted out, "and then I will tear out your heart with my own hands."

"If you still have your own hands, you're probably not as far up the ladder as you wanted us to think. Put someone else on—someone with real authority and a few more replacement parts."

Tsavong Lah growled in fury. "With those words, you have earned yourself much pain."

"I take it the Vong don't get promoted for their conversational skills," she said. "Let's see if the priest's commander can do better."

She awakened the second villip, that which formed a link between this ship and the priest's villip. When a second scarred face came into view, Jaina brushed back her bangs to reveal the mark she'd drawn there—the symbol of Yun-Harla.

Two voices lifted in outraged howls. "I will bring you in, human," the younger warrior said, snarling. "This I swear, by all the gods, by my domain and my sacred honor."

Jaina passed a hand over the villips. Both inverted at once.

A Yuuzhan Vong fighter streamed toward her, and all others moved aside to let it pass.

Jaina reached for the energy that she had found within, that which hurled the dark lightning. She allowed it to flood her and direct her battle.

She sank deeper into the consciousness of the alien ship, losing herself in flight as she had always done. For what seemed like hours she and her challenger darted and spun, trading bolts of plasma, dodging and blocking like swordmasters. Jaina did not think—she acted.

For a while this seemed to be an effective strategy, but her identification with the living ship was too powerful. A plasma bolt slipped back the dovin basal shields and scorched along the side of the ship. Jaina jolted, screaming, as an unexpected searing pain raced down her left arm. She was surprised to see no physical damage there.

Barely conscious, she began to slide completely into

the darkness. Again she fell back in time, into the terrifying duel at the Shadow Academy. Again she fought Darth Vader, but this time she could not prevail.

Her opponent stepped back and ripped off the black helmet, revealing Kyp Durron's face. Light seemed to fill him as they continued to fight, pushing aside the remnants of his dark disguise and then tentatively reaching out to her.

Jaina felt the mingled joy and pain of Kyp's long, slow redemption, the isolation of his long years of restitution. She felt his regret for selfishly endangering the one person who could become all that he himself would never achieve.

And with absolute certainty, she knew that Kyp was wrong—she was not the one. The path to a different understanding of the Force was not her journey to take.

Another truth came to her, and she could no longer deny the nature of the path she had taken. It seemed strange, ironic, that Kyp Durron would be the one to try to save her.

An answer came to her, along with the image of Kyp's wry smile. *Did you ever think that you might be the one who's saving me? Come on back. We'll figure this out together.*

Slowly, she began to battle her way back toward the light. Kyp faded away, and her opponent took on Khalee Lah's face and form. Jaina fought fiercely, but every blow she landed took a toll on her own body.

Gradually she became aware of an array of lights taking focus before her. An insistent voice droned through her comm, dragging her into awareness. The ship's console blinked frantically as luminous creatures warned of massive system failure.

"Jaina, fall back. I've got you. I've got you."

The voice, and the power it held, jolted her back to consciousness. Jaina's hands were still on the controls, still firing the weapons—her connection with the ship remained. After a startled moment, she realized that Kyp had been talking to her through the comm system Lowbacca had installed.

Or perhaps he had been speaking through her vision.

Jaina glanced at the warrior's ship, which was circling around for another attack. The *Trickster* jolted as her opponent's dovin basal got a lock on her ship.

An X-wing streaked between them, sending a steady barrage at the Yuuzhan Vong fighter—and heading directly into the gravitic pull.

Suddenly freed, Jaina swept around to back up her rescuer. But the X-wing had taken a hit. It spiraled off, a comet followed by a tail of burning fuel. The ship exploded in a sharp white flare.

She reached out and felt the familiar presence—Kyp had gone EV in time. She wheeled around, leaving her vengeance unfinished, her questions unanswered.

She set course for her Jedi Master, and the shared path before them.

EPILOGUE

The night skies over Hapes's royal city still bled and strobed as Jaina set the *Trickster* down on the docks. She looked up, feeling no regret at being forced out of the battle before its conclusion.

This was not her fight, her path. Teneniel Djo's legacy had arrived, and under the command of Jag Fel it was swiftly pushing back the Yuuzhan Vong. Jaina had seen that much as she maneuvered the wounded Jedi Master aboard her ship.

She saw Kyp safely off the ship and arranged for medical treatment. Then she turned to face what she had become.

Ta'a Chume was in the palace, under house arrest pending investigation into Teneniel Djo's death. She rose quickly as Jaina entered the room, and her eyes swept the girl's flight suit.

"The battle?"

"We're winning."

"You should be commanding it."

Jaina shrugged. "Colonel Fel is doing just fine. Queen Mother Tenel Ka knows how to pick people."

Ta'a Chume received this news in silence. "With my help, you could have been a great queen."

Jaina sniffed and folded her arms. "I can't tell you how much that means to me."

"What about your vows of vengeance?"

"I'm not adding you to the list, if that's your concern. It's over," she stated. "All of it. I know what I am—a fighter, the sister and the daughter of heroes."

Something changed in the former queen's face. "I am seldom mistaken, but now I see that you are a fool, like your mother before you."

She continued in this vein, and was ranting still when Jaina left the palace.

Tenel Ka awaited her outside the secured rooms. "They say that anger is of the dark side," she said somberly. " 'They,' of course, have never met Ta'a Chume."

Jaina smiled faintly, and then noticed the tentative humor in her friend's eyes. On impulse, she folded her friend in an embrace. Tenel Ka's strong arm came up to encircle her.

"It won't be easy," the new queen said. "Not for me, not for you. I suspect that your road may be more difficult than mine. At least you will not be alone."

Jaina pulled away. "Neither will you."

Tenel Ka's only response was a faint smile. She lifted her hand, a somber, regal gesture, and then walked away. Her bearing was proud and her step quick. Her determination came through the Force, and with it, a sense of desolation so intense that it brought tears to Jaina's eyes.

Jaina swiftly pulled her emotions back under control. It was this very thing—her empathy for her friends and brothers—that had gotten her into trouble in the first place. The way she saw it, she had a long road back from what she'd become, and she couldn't afford any detours.

And as she strode back to her ship, she considered the road ahead. She'd have to face all the friends who had warned her, the family who had worried. At every turn, people would question her. She would have to make people believe that the dark side had no part in her actions, her decisions. The most difficult person to convince, she suspected, would be herself.

Kyp Durron was already at the docks, loading supplies into a Hapan light freighter. A bacta patch covered his forehead.

"Never thought you'd get here," he said. "It's almost time to go."

"Go?" Jaina echoed.

"We're taking some supplies to the Jedi base. Your mother asked me to bring you."

A pang touched Jaina's heart as she thought of what news of her slide would do to Leia. "Mom already lost two of her kids."

"I'll get you back."

She turned her eyes to Kyp's somber green gaze. With great effort, she lowered the shields that had kept her locked away. Perhaps there was one person who could understand, one person she wouldn't have to lock out.

After a moment, he tossed her a box of rations. She tucked it into the hold and turned for another. They worked together, falling into an easy rhythm. Soon the ship was loaded, and the Jedi Master and his apprentice strapped into their seats.

"So what's next?" she asked as they settled down.

"What do you want to do?"

Jaina considered this. She had always been confident—impulsive, even cocky. That was tempered now by deep humility in the power of the Force. "I'll keep flying, of course, but I'm not sure the Rogues will have me."

"Then why not continue the path you've started? There's a place for a trickster in the resistance. You're quick with a plan, you have a knack for strategy."

She tried the idea on, and the fit felt about right. "Not bad," she admitted. "And you?"

Kyp gave her a slightly sheepish smile. "I'm going to work toward the establishment of a Jedi Council, to building consensus instead of discord."

She burst out laughing. "I've seen my mother struggle

with such things. Trust me, this might prove to be your biggest challenge yet!"

He shrugged. "Neither of us need things to be easy. And on that note, I hear that Jag Fel has arranged a meeting with your uncle Luke. If there's a Jedi offensive on the horizon, I wouldn't be at all surprised if he's at the heart of it."

A quick, glad surge lifted Jaina's heart. Wistfully, she wondered if someday she could merit the friendship of someone like Jag, someone whose gaze, like Leia's, never seemed to swerve from a hero's path.

If Kyp picked up on Jaina's thoughts, he was tactful enough not to let on. "You ready?"

She responded with a firm nod, and then turned her eyes to the challenges ahead.

Khalee Lah strode into Harrar's chamber and dropped to one knee.

"The battle was a failure," he said bluntly. "The *Jeedai* escaped. It would seem that I was infected with the heresy, or the gods would have allowed me to die in glorious battle. My failure can only serve to tarnish my domain. The name of the warmaster, whom you name friend."

The priest absorbed this in silence. This request went far past hinting. In response, he reached for the mechanical abomination and handed it to the warrior.

"I will report to Tsavong Lah that his kinsman died in battle, through the trickery of the *Jeedai*, sacrificed by his own men. Put this upon your ship, and it will be so."

Khalee Lah bowed his head and accepted the device. He rose and strode from the room.

Left alone, Harrar took his villip and reported to Tsavong Lah what he had promised to say. "Jaina Solo proved to be a far more worthy foe than anticipated," he concluded, "and it may be some time before the twin sacrifice can go forward."

"The gods willed it so," Tsavong Lah said. "Continue pursuit, and we will speak of this matter again."

The villip inverted abruptly, leaving Harrar deep in speculation. His failure was not dealt with as harshly as he expected, and the priest of deception wondered if perhaps he was not the only one who had failed.

Was it possible, he wondered, that Jacen Solo might not have survived, after all?

ONE

"It seems to me that mine is becoming a very important planet, Honorable Shu Mai."

The president of the Commerce Guild smiled thinly. "Small keys can unlock very big doors, Senator Mousul."

As they conversed, the dignified quartet strode slowly through the galaxy. Not the actual galaxy, of course, but an immense, intricately delineated, fully three-dimensional representation. It filled the entire private chamber. Stars glowed all around them, enveloping the strollers in a haze of soft, multi-hued refulgence. By reaching out and touching a planetary system, a visitor could summon forth a detailed, encyclopedic description of that system and its individual worlds: everything from species and population to minute characteristics of flora and fauna, economic statistics, and future prospects.

One of the strollers was a blue-skinned Twi'lek female who was quiet and contemplative of aspect. Her companion was a very important and readily recognizable Corellian industrialist. The president of the Commerce Guild was short and slender, greenish of skin, with the typical coiffure for females of the Gossam species: a rising, upswept tailing. The fourth member of the group, trailing elaborate robes woven from the most exotic materials to be found on his homeworld, was the Senator from the world called Ansion. Despite his high standing, he looked nervous, like someone afraid of being watched. As for the Twi'lek and the Corellian, they were clearly master and supplicant—though the second was a very powerful supplicant indeed.

The president of the Commerce Guild halted. With a single, expansive gesture she encompassed shimmering pinpoints of light representing a thousand worlds and more. Amazing, she thought, how trillions of sentient beings and entire civilizations could be reduced to mere specks hovering in a single room. If only the reality were as easy to organize and manage as was this efficient, luminous depiction.

Given time and the assistance of carefully nurtured alliances, she reflected confidently, it would be.

"Your forgiveness, noble lady," the Corellian murmured, "but my associates and I also do not configure the importance of this world called Ansion."

Shu Mai clapped her hands softly. "Excellent!"

Among her three companions, confusion readily crossed species lines. "You find it satisfying that we do not see this place's significance?" the female Twi'lek asked.

"Absolutely." A tolerant grin creased the Gossam's face. "If you do not see it, then neither will our enemies. Pay attention, and I will do more than make it evident—I will make it visible."

Turning, she reached into the pulsing panoply of worlds and suns to pass the tips of the fingers of her right hand through a small but centrally located star. With words and gestures, she proceeded to manipulate the system she had singled out.

In response to her actions, a trio of laser-bright blue lines appeared, linking the first system to three others. "The Malarian Alliance. On the face of it, one of hundreds of such casual alliances." Her slim, deft fingers moved again. Yellow lines appeared, tying the first star to six additional systems. "Keitumite Mutual Military Treaty. Never invoked, but still in force." Her smile widened. She was enjoying herself. "Now, observe this." Her hands proceeded to play with the surrounding galographics like a musician strumming an expensive quintolium.

When at last Shu Mai finished, her three companions eyed her triumphant handiwork in silence. The four visitors were enclosed by a web of lines, straight and uncompromising: blue, yellow, gold, crimson—all the colors of the spectrum. Perhaps even, some dared to think, the colors of an empire.

And at the nexus of this web of intensely bright, unwavering lines that represented outstanding treaties and alliances, pacts and planetary partnerships, lay a single, suddenly far less insignificant world.

Ansion.

With a wave of one hand and a dismissive word from Shu Mai's lips, the elaborate network faded. It would not do to have someone not privy to the machinations of the group walk in unannounced and see what was being discussed. Awkward questions might ensue.

"Who would have suspected that a world such as this could lie at the center of so many interlocking treaties?" The blue-skinned female was suitably impressed.

"Precisely the point." Shu Mai inclined her head slightly in the female's direction. "There are other worlds that occupy comparable positions of strategic importance; worlds more heavily populated, thoroughly industrialized, and frequently mentioned as important players when the current unsettled state of affairs within the Republic is being discussed. In contrast, no one thinks to bring up Ansion. That is the beauty of it." Steepling her fingers, she glanced significantly at Senator Mousul.

"If we can get the Ansionians to commit to pulling out of the Republic, no one will really care. But because of their alliances, their withdrawal should be enough to sway their already vacillating partners in both the Malarian Alliance and the Keitumite Treaty to follow. You saw how many other systems are tied, in turn, to both of those pacts. The effect will be as of an avalanche; starting small, growing fast, and accelerating of its own accord. By the time the Senate knows what has hit it, forty systems or more will have withdrawn from the Republic, and we will be well on our way to solidifying the kind of changes we wish to see come about."

Mousul's fingers clenched tighter and tighter until whiteness showed beneath the skin. "That will be the spark that we need to propose the passage of extraordinary measures to cope with the emergency."

The Corellian industrialist was all but dancing with excitement. "It's wonderfully cunning, this plan you've devised! I know that the interests I represent will agree to send a force to Ansion immediately, to compel the inhabitants to withdraw from the Republic." For an instant, Senator Mousul looked alarmed.

"Which is exactly what we do not want them to do," Shu Mai countered sternly. "As I seem to recall, the Trade Federation already tried something similar elsewhere. The results were, shall we say, somewhat less than triumphant."

"Yes, well." The Corellian coughed uncomfortably into one hand. "There were unforeseen complications."

"That continue to resonate to this day." Shu Mai was unrelenting in her tone. "Don't you see? The beauty of this plan is the seeming insignificance of its linchpin. Send a fleet, or even a few ships, to Ansion, and you will immediately attract the attention of those forces that continue to frustrate us. Obviously, that is the last thing we wish. We want the Ansionian withdrawal to appear wholly natural, the result of internal decisions reached in the absence of external influences." She smiled benignly at Mousul.

"Will it be?" the Twi'lek asked pointedly.

Shu Mai eyed her approvingly. She would be useful, she knew. As would the others she had involved—if they could keep their wits about them.

It was Senator Mousul's turn to respond. "Like so many peoples, the Ansionians are divided as to whether they should remain within the Republic or step outside the corruption and sleaze that permeate it. Rest assured that there are among its citizens those who are sympathetic to our cause. I have taken care and expended considerable political capital to ensure that these elements are appropriately encouraged."

"How long?" the deceptively soft-voiced Twi'lek wanted to know.

"Before Ansion decides?" The Senator looked thoughtful. "Assuming the internal divisions continue to widen, I would expect a formal vote on whether to withdraw from the Republic within half a standard year."

The president of the Commerce Guild nodded approvingly. "At which point we can look on with satisfaction as those who have been traditionally allied to Ansion follow suit, and those allied to the allies fall in turn. Surely, as children all of you played with blocks? There is invariably one key block near the bottom that, if removed, will cause the entire structure to collapse.

"Ansion is that key. Remove that one block, and the rest of these systems will crumble." Her thoughts, as well as her gaze, seemed to focus on something outside the range of vision of her associates. "On the ruins of the old, decrepit Republic those of us with foresight will build a new political structure, perfect and gleaming. One without any weak links, free of the moralistic waste that encumbers and slows the appropriate development of a truly advanced society."

"And who will lead this new society?" The female Twi'lek's voice was tinged with just a touch of cynicism. "You?"

Shu Mai shrugged modestly. "My interests lie with the Commerce Guild. Who can say? That is something yet to be determined, is it not? The cause must succeed before leaders can be chosen. While I admit I would not turn down such a nomination, I believe there are others who are more qualified. Let us begin with small things."

"Like this Ansion." Having recovered from the previous mild reproach, the Corellian's enthusiasm had returned full strength. "What a pleasure it would be, what a wonderment, to at last be able to conduct business unencumbered by mountains of superfluous rules, regulations, and restrictions! Those I represent would be forever grateful."

"Yes, you would at last have the chance to secure the restrictive monopolies you so devoutly seek," Shu Mai observed dryly. "Don't worry. In return for your political and financial support, you and those you represent will receive everything they deserve."

The industrialist was not intimidated. "And of course," he added shrewdly, "this new political arrangement will open all manner of opportunities to the Commerce Guild."

Shu Mai gestured modestly. "We are always eager to take advantage of shifting political realities."

In the midst of mutual congratulations and expectations, she noticed that Senator Mousul was saying little.

"Something burrows in your thoughts like a worm with indigestion, Mousul. What is it?"

The Ansionian glanced back at his associate, a look of mild concern on his face. His large, slightly bulbous eyes stared evenly back at the president of the Commerce Guild. "You're sure no one else could winnow out the true nature of these plans for Ansion, Shu Mai?"

"None has thus far," the other replied pointedly.

Mousul straightened to his full height. "I flatter myself that I am intelligent enough to realize there are those who are smarter than me. They are the ones who concern me."

Stepping forward, Shu Mai put a reassuring hand on the Senator's shoulder. "You worry overmuch, Mousul." With her free hand and without regard for tact, Shu Mai gestured, and the point of light that was Ansion reappeared. "Ansion! Look at it. Small, backward, unimportant. If queried, I wager not one politician or merchant in a hundred could tell you anything much about it. No one except those of us in this room are aware of its potential significance."

Stymied by and angry at the casual venality and suffocating bureaucracy that had come to rule the Republic—and to complicate his business dealings—the Corellian industrialist could purchase entire companies and whole territories with a mere touch of his imprinting finger. But for all his wealth, he could not buy a glimpse into the future. At that moment, he would have gladly signed over a few billion for the answers to one or two questions.

"I hope you are right, Shu Mai. I hope you are right."

"Of course she is." Having agreed to this meeting somewhat reluctantly, the Twi'lek was feeling far more confident of the future following their host's detailed explanation. "I am both impressed and moved by the full scope and subtlety of President

Shu Mai and Senator Mousul's strategy. As they have so eloquently pointed out, this world is far too unimportant to attract anything in the way of significant outside attention . . ."

TWO

"Haja, sweet scent—what're you hiding under that big ol' robe?"

Luminara Unduli did not look up at the large, unshaven, rough-hewn, and unpleasantly fragrant man or his equally coarse and malodorous companions. She treated their knowing grins, the eager forward tilt of their bodies, and their leering eyes with equal indifference—though their collective body odor was somewhat harder to ignore. Patiently, she raised the spoonful of hot stew to her lips, the lower of which was stained a permanent purplish black. A series of interlocking black diamonds tattooed her chin, while more intricate markings decorated the joints of her fingers. The olive color of her skin contrasted strikingly with the deep blue of her eyes.

These rose to regard the younger woman who was seated on the other side of the table. Barriss Offee's attention shifted between her teacher and the men crowding uncomfortably close around the two of them. Luminara smiled to herself. A good person, was Barriss. Observant and thoughtful, if occasionally impulsive. For now, the young woman held her peace, kept eating, and said nothing. A judicious reaction, the older woman knew. *She's letting me take the lead, as she should.*

The man who had voiced the impropriety whispered something to one of his friends. There was a ripple of crude, unpleasant laughter. Leaning closer, he put a hand on Luminara's cloth-draped shoulder. "I asked you a question, darlin'. Now, are you gonna show us what's under this lovely soft robe of yours, or d'you want us to take a peek ourselves?" An air of pheromone-charged expectation had gripped his companions. Huddled over their food, a few of the establishment's other diners turned to look, but none moved to voice outrage at what was happening or to interfere.

Spoon pausing before her lips, Luminara seemed to devote greater contemplation to its contents than to the insistent query. With a sigh, she finally downed the spoonful of stew and reached down with her free right hand. "I suppose if you really want to see . . ."

One of the men grinned broadly and nudged his hulking companion in the ribs. A couple of others crowded closer still, so that they were all but leaning over the table. Luminara pulled a portion of her outer robe aside, the intricate designs on the copper- and bronze-colored metal bands that covered her upper forearms glinting in the diffuse light of the tavern.

Beneath the robe was a metal and leather belt. Attached to the belt were several small and unexpectedly sophisticated examples of precision engineering. One of these was cylindrical, highly polished, and designed to fit comfortably in a closed hand. The aggressive spokesman for the group squinted at it, his expression slightly confused. Behind him, a couple of his heretofore hopeful cronies abandoned their leering expressions faster than a smuggler's ship making an emergency jump to hyperspace.

"Mathos preserve us! That's a Jedi lightsaber!"

Expressions falling like hard rain, the band of would-be aggressors began to back off, split up, and drift hurriedly away. Unexpectedly deserted, their erstwhile leader was unwilling to admit defeat so quickly. He stared at the gleaming metal cylinder.

"Not a chance, no. A 'Jedi' lightsaber, is it?" He glared belligerently at the suddenly enigmatic object of his attentions. "I suppose that would make you a 'Jedi Knight,' sweet splash? A lovely, lithe Jedi at that!" He snorted derisively. "Sure and that's no Jedi lightsaber, is it? Is it?" he growled insistently when she failed to respond.

Finishing another spoonful of her meal, Luminara Unduli carefully set the utensil down on her nearly empty plate, delicately patted both her decorated and her untouched lip with the supplied linen napkin, wiped her hands, and turned to face him. Blue eyes peered upward out of her fine-featured face, and she smiled coldly.

"You know how to find out," she informed him softly.

The big man started to say something, hesitated, reconsidered. The attractive woman's hands rested, palm downward, on her thighs. The lightsaber—it certainly *looked* like a Jedi lightsaber, he found himself thinking apprehensively—remained attached to her belt. Across the table, the younger woman continued to eat her meal as though nothing out of the ordinary was taking place.

Abruptly, the gruff intruder became aware of several things simultaneously. First, he was now completely alone. His formerly enthusiastic companions had slipped away, one by one. Second, by this time the woman seated before him was supposed to be anxious and afraid. Instead, she only looked bored and resigned. Third, he suddenly remembered that he had important business elsewhere.

"Uh, sorry," he found himself mumbling. "Didn't mean to bother you. Case of mistaken identity. Was looking for someone else." Turning, he hurried away from the table and toward the tavern's entrance, nearly tripping over a scraps bowl on the floor next to an unoccupied serving counter. Several of the other patrons watched him go. Others eyed the two women fixedly before finding reason to return to their own food and conversation.

Exhaling softly, Luminara turned back to the remnants of her meal. Making a face, she pushed the bowl and what remained of the meal away from her. The boorish intrusion had spoiled her appetite.

"You handled that well, Master Luminara." Barriss was finishing up her own food. The Padawan's perception might occasionally be lacking, but never her readiness to eat. "No noise, no fuss."

"As you grow older, you'll find that you occasionally have to deal with an excess of testosterone. Often on minor worlds like Ansion." She shook her head slowly. "I dislike such distractions."

Barriss smiled gaily. "Don't be so somber, Master. You can't do anything about physical attractiveness. Anyway, you've given them a story to tell, as well as a lesson."

Luminara shrugged. "If only those in charge of the local government, this so-called Unity of Community, were as easy to persuade to see reason."

"It will happen." Barriss rose swiftly. "I'm finished." Together, the two women paid for the meal and exited the establishment. Whispers, mutterings, and not a few awed words of admiration trailed in their wake.

"The populace has heard we're here to try to cement a permanent peace between the city folk of the Unity and the Alwari nomads. They're unaware of the far greater issues at stake. And we can't reveal the real reason for our presence here without alerting those who would oppose us to the fact that we know of their deeper intentions." Luminara drew her robe tighter around her. It was important to present as subdued yet impressive an appearance as possible. "Because we can't be completely honest, the locals don't trust us."

Barriss nodded. "The city people think we favor the

nomads, and the nomads fear we're on the side of the city folk. I hate politics, Master Luminara." One hand fell to her side. "I prefer settling differences with a lightsaber. Much more straightforward." Her pretty face radiated a zest for life. She had not yet lived long enough to become inured to the new.

"It's difficult to persuade opposing sides of the rightness of your reasoning when they're both dead." Turning up one of Cuipernam's side streets, chaotic with traders and city folk of many different galactic species, Luminara spoke while scanning not only the avenue but also the flanking walls of commercial and residential buildings. "Anyone can handle a weapon. Reason is much more difficult to wield. Remember that the next time you're tempted to settle an argument with a lightsaber."

"I bet it's all the fault of the Trade Federation." Barriss eyed a stall dripping with jewelry: necklaces and earrings, rings and diadems, bracelets and hand-sculpted flash corneas. Such conventional personal ornamentation was forbidden to a Jedi. As one of her teachers had once explained to Barriss and her fellow Padawans, "A Jedi's glow comes from within, not from the artificial augmentation of baubles and beads."

Still, that necklace of Searous hair and interwoven pikach stones was just *gorgeous*.

"What did you say, Barriss?"

"Nothing, Master. I was just expressing my dissatisfaction at the continuing scheming of the Trade Federation."

"Yes," Luminara agreed. "And the Commerce Guilds. They grow more powerful by the month, always sticking their money-hungry fingers in where they're not wanted, even if their immediate interests are not directly involved. Here on Ansion, they openly support the towns and cities that are loosely grouped together as the Unity of Community even though the law of the Republic guarantees the rights of nomadic groups like the Alwari to remain independent of such external influences. Their activities here only complicate an already difficult situation." They turned another corner. "As they do elsewhere."

Barriss nodded knowingly. "Everyone still remembers the Naboo incident. Why doesn't the Senate simply vote to reduce their trade concessions? *That* would settle them down a bit!"

Luminara had to fight to keep from smiling. Ah, the innocence of youth! Barriss was well meaning and a fine Padawan, but she was unsophisticated in the ways of governance.

"It's all very well to invoke ethics and morals, Barriss, but these days it's commerce that seems to rule the Republic. Sometimes the Commerce Guilds and the Trade Federation act like they're separate governments. They're very clever about it, though." Her expression twisted. "Fawning and bowing before emissaries of the Senate, issuing a steady stream of protestations of innocence: that Nute Gunray in particular is as slippery as a Notonian mudworm. Money equals power, and power buys votes. Yes, even in the Republic Senate. And they have powerful allies." Her thoughts turned inward. "It's not just money anymore. The Republic is a soiled sea roiled by dangerous currents. The Jedi Council fears that general dissatisfaction with the present state of governance is giving way to outright secession on many worlds."

Barriss stood a little taller as she strode along beside her Master. "At least everyone knows that the Jedi are above such matters, and aren't for sale."

"Not for sale, no." Luminara sank farther into preoccupation.

Barriss noted the change. "Something else troubles you, Master Luminara?"

The other woman mustered a smile. "Oh, sometimes one hears things. Odd stories, unaccredited rumors. These days such tales seem to run rampant. This political philosophy of a certain Count Dooku, for example."

Though always eager to display her knowledge, Barriss hesitated before responding. "I think I recognize the name, but not in connection with that title. Wasn't he the Jedi who—"

Stopping sharply, Luminara threw out a hand to halt her companion. Her eyes flicked rapidly from side to side and she was suddenly no longer introspective. Her every nerve was alert, every sense on edge. Before Barriss could question the reason for the action, the Jedi had her lightsaber out, activated, and fully extended before her. Without moving her head, she raised it to a challenge position. Having drawn and activated her own weapon in response to her Master's reaction, Barriss searched anxiously for the source of unease. Seeing nothing out of the ordinary, she glanced questioningly at her teacher.

Which was when the Hoguss plunged from above—to spit itself neatly on Luminara's upraised lightsaber. There was a brief stink of burning flesh, the Jedi extracted the beam, and the startled Hoguss, its now useless killing ax locked in a powerful but lifeless grip, keeled over onto its side. The heavy body made a dull thump as it struck the ground.

"Back!" Luminara started to retreat, the now anxious and alerted Barriss guarding her Master's rear and flanks.

The attackers swarmed down from rooftops and out of second-story windows, came bursting through doorways and up out of otherwise empty crates; a veritable flash flood of seedy infamy. Someone, Luminara mused grimly as she retreated, had gone to considerable trouble and expense to arrange this ambush. In the midst of genuine concern for herself and her Padawan, she had to admire the plotter's thoroughness. Whoever it was clearly knew they were dealing with more than a couple of female tourists out for a morning's sightseeing.

The question was, how much did they know?

There are only two ways for non-Jedi to defeat Jedi in battle: lull them into a false sense of security, or overwhelm them with sheer force of numbers. Subtlety obviously being a notion foreign to their present assailants, a diverse rabble of bloodthirsty but untrained individuals, their employer had opted for the latter approach. In the crowded, active streets, the large number of attackers had gone undetected by Luminara, their inimical feelings submerged among those of the greater crowd.

Now that the attack had begun, the Force throbbed with an enmity that was out in the open as dozens of well-armed hired assassins fought to get close enough to their rapidly withdrawing targets to deliver a few final, fatal blows. While the narrowness of the street and the aimless fleeing of panicked bystanders eliminated a clear line of retreat and kept the two women from sprinting to safety, it also prevented those of their attackers who were wielding firearms from setting up a clear shot at their intended targets. Had they been tacticians, those in front swinging blades and other less advanced devices would have stepped aside to give their more heavily armed comrades room in which to take aim. But a reward had been promised to the ones who made the actual kill. While this served to inspire the truculent rabble, it also made them reluctant to cooperate with one another in achieving their ultimate objective, lest it be a colleague who claimed the substantial bonus.

So it was that Luminara and Barriss were able to deflect bursts from blasters as well as blows struck by less technical weaponry such as long swords and knives. With high walls shielding them on either side and merchants and vendors continuing to run for cover, they had room in which to work. Bodies began to pile up in front of them, some intact, others missing significant portions of their anatomy, these having been neatly excised by whirling shafts of intensely colored energy.

Barriss's exuberance and occasional shouted challenge were complemented by Luminara's steady, silently ferocious work. Together, the two women not only kept their attackers at bay, but began to force them back. There is something in the hushed, frighteningly efficient aspect of a fighting Jedi that takes the heart out of an ordinary opponent. A would-be murderer has only to see a few blaster shots deflected by the anticipatory hum of a lightsaber to realize that there might be other less potentially lethal ways to make a living.

Then, just when the two women were on the verge of pushing the remaining attackers around a corner and back out into an open square where they could be more effectively scattered, a roar of anticipation rose above the fray as another two dozen assassins arrived. This mélange of humans and aliens was better dressed, better armed, and tended to fight more as a unit than those who had preceded them. A tiring Luminara realized suddenly that the previous hard fighting had never been intended to kill them, but only to wear them out. Steeling herself and shouting encouragement to a visibly downcast Barriss, she once more found herself retreating back down the narrow street they had nearly succeeded in escaping.

Drawing new courage from the arrival of fresh reinforcements, their surviving assailants redoubled their own attack. Jedi and Padawan were forced steadily backward.

Then there was no more backward. The side street deadended against a featureless courtyard wall. To anyone else it would have appeared unscalable. But a Jedi could find hand- and footholds where others would see only a smooth surface.

"Barriss!" Lightsaber whirling, Luminara indicated the reddish-colored barrier behind them. "Go up! I'll follow." Dropping to his knees, a man clad in tough leathers took careful aim with a blaster. Luminara blocked both his shots before taking one hand briefly off the lightsaber to gesture in his direction. Like a living thing, the dangerous weapon flew out of his hands, startling him so badly he fell backward onto his butt. Protected by his fellow assassins, he did not panic like a common killer but instead scrambled to recover the blaster. They couldn't keep this up forever, she knew.

"Up, I said!" Luminara did not have to turn to sense the unyielding wall behind her.

Barriss hesitated. "Master, you can cover me if I climb, but I can't do the same for you from the top of the wall." Lunging, she disarmed a serpentine Wetakk who was trying to slip in under her guard. Letting out a yelp of pain, it stepped back and switched the hooked blade it was holding to another hand, of which it still had five remaining. Without missing a breath, the Padawan added, "You can't climb and use your weapon, too!"

"I'll be all right," Luminara assured her, even as she wondered how she was going to make the ascent without being cut down from behind. But her first concern was for her Padawan, and not for herself. "That's an order, Barriss! Get up there. We have to get out of this confined space."

Reluctantly, Barriss took a last sweeping swing to clear the ground in front of her. Then she shut down her lightsaber, slipped it back onto her belt, pivoted, took a few steps, and leapt. The jump carried her partway up the wall, to which she clung like a spider. Finding seemingly invisible fingerholds, she began to ascend. Below and behind her, Luminara singlehandedly held back the entire surging throng of eager killers.

Nearly at the top, Barriss looked back and down. Luminara was not only holding off her own assailants, but had moved forward to ensure that none of those in the back would have time to take aim at the climbing Padawan. Barriss hesitated.

"Master Luminara, there are too many! I can't protect you from up here."

The Jedi turned to respond. As she did so, she failed to see or sense a small Throbe standing behind a much larger human. The Throbe's blaster was small, its aim wild, but the undeflected shot still managed to graze the woman in the umber robes. Luminara staggered.

"Master!" Frantic, Barriss debated whether to ascend the remaining distance to the top of the wall or disobey her Master and drop back down to aid her. In the midst of her confusion, a subtle tremor ran through her mind. It was a disturbance in the Force, but one very different from anything they had experienced this dreadful morning. It was also surprisingly strong.

Yelling encouragement, the two men plunged past on either side of Luminara. Neither was physically imposing, though one had a build suggestive of considerable future development. Lightsabers flashing, they fell in among the bewildered band of assassins, their weapons dealing out havoc in bantha-sized doses.

To their credit, the attackers held their ground for another couple of moments. Then, their associates falling all around them, the survivors broke and fled. In less than a minute, the street was clear and the way back to the central square unobstructed. Letting go of the wall, Barriss dropped the considerable distance to the ground, to find herself facing an attractive young man who wore confidence like a handmade suit. Smiling cockily, he deactivated his lightsaber and regarded her appraisingly.

"I've been told that morning exercise is good for the soul as well as the body. Hello, Barriss Offee."

"Anakin Skywalker. Yes, I remember you from training." Automatically nodding her thanks, she hurried to her Master's side. The other newcomer was already examining Luminara's blaster wound.

"It's not serious."

Luminara pulled her garments closed rather more sharply than was necessary. "You're early, Obi-Wan," she told her colleague. "We weren't expecting you until the day after tomorrow."

"Our ship made good time." As the four emerged onto the square, Obi-Wan's gaze swept the open space. Presently, it was as void of inimical disturbance, as was the Force. He allowed himself to relax slightly. "Since we arrived early, we suspected there would be no one to meet us at the spaceport. So we decided to come looking for you. When you weren't at your stated residence, we decided to take a stroll to acquaint ourselves with the city. That's when I sensed the trouble. It drew us to you."

"Well, I certainly can't fault your timing." She smiled gratefully. It was the same intriguing smile that Obi-Wan remembered from working with her previously, framed as it was by its differently toned lips. "The situation was becoming awkward."

"Awkward!" Anakin declared. "Why, if Master Obi-Wan and I hadn't—" The look of disapproval the Jedi shot him was enough to destroy the observation in midsentence.

"Something I've been curious about ever since we were given this assignment." Barriss moved a little farther away from her counterpart and closer to the two senior Jedi. "Why are *four* of us needed here, to deal with what seems to me to be nothing more than a minor dispute among the native sentients?" Her impatience was palpable. "Earlier, you spoke of greater issues."

"You remember our discussions," Luminara explained patiently. "Well, the Alwari nomads think the Senate favors the city dwellers. The city folk are certain the galactic government will side with the nomads. Such perceptions of favoritism on the part of the Senate are dangerously close to persuading both groups that Ansion would be better off outside the Republic, where internal disputes could be settled without outside interference. Their representative in the Senate appears to be leaning in that direction. There is also evidence to support the contention that offworld elements are stirring the pot, hoping to induce Ansion to secede."

"It's only one world, and not a particularly important one at that," Barriss ventured.

Luminara nodded slowly. "True. But it's not Ansion itself that is so critical. Through a multiplicity of pacts and alliances, it could pull other systems out of the Republic as well. More systems than I, or the Jedi Council, likes to think about. Therefore, a way must be found to keep Ansion within the Republic. The best way to do that is to remove the suspicions that exist between the city dwellers and the nomads, and thereby solidify planetary representation. As outsiders representing the will of the Senate, we will find respect on Ansion, but no friends. While we are here, suspicion will be our constant companion. Given the fluid complexity of the situation, the matter of shifting alliances, the possible presence of outside agitators, and the seriousness of the potential ramifications, it was felt that two pairs of negotiators would make a greater and more immediate impression on the situation than one."

"I see now." There was much more at stake here, Barriss found herself thinking, than a disagreement between city folk and nomads. Had Luminara been instructed to conceal the real reason for their journey from her Padawan until now, or had Barriss simply been too preoccupied with her own training to see the larger issues? Like it or not, it appeared that she was going to have to pay more attention to galactic politics.

For example, why would forces beyond Ansion want to see it secede from the Republic badly enough to interfere in the planet's internal affairs? What could such unknown entities possibly have to gain by its withdrawal? There were thousands upon thousands of civilized worlds in the Republic. The departure of one, or even several, would mean little in the overall scheme of galactic governance. Or would it?

She felt sure she was missing some vital point, and the fact that she knew she was doing so was exceedingly frustrating. But she couldn't question Luminara further about it, because Obi-Wan was speaking.

"Someone or several someones beyond Ansion doesn't want these negotiations to succeed. They *want* Ansion to secede from the Republic, with all the problematic consequences that would ensue." Obi-Wan squinted at the sky, which had begun to threaten rain. "It would be useful to know who. We should have detained one of your attackers."

"They could have been common bandits," Anakin pointed out.

Luminara considered. "It's possible. Anyway, if Obi-Wan is right and that rabble was hired to prevent us from continuing with our mission, their employer would have kept those who attacked us in the dark as to his or her identity and purpose. Even if we had been successful in capturing one of them, an interrogation might well have been useless."

"Yes, that's so," the Padawan had to admit.

"So you were on Naboo, too?" Feeling left out of the conversation between the two older Jedi, Barriss turned curiously to her counterpart.

"I was." The pride in the younger man's voice was unapologetic. *He's a strange one,* she mused. Strange, but not unlikable. As stuffed full of internal conflicts as a momus bush was with seeds. But there was no denying that the Force was strong within him.

"How long have you been Master Luminara's Padawan?" he asked.

"Long enough to know that those who have their mouths open all the time generally have their ears shut."

"Oh great," Anakin muttered. "You're not going to spend all our time together speaking in aphorisms, are you?"

"At least I can talk about something besides myself," she shot back. "Somehow I don't think you scored well in modesty."

To her surprise, he was immediately contrite. "Was I just talking about myself? I'm sorry." He indicated the two figures preceding them up the busy street. "Master Obi-Wan says that I suffer from a surfeit of impatience. I want to know, to do, *everything* right now. Yesterday. And I'm not very good at disguising the fact that I'd rather be elsewhere. This isn't a very exciting assignment."

She gestured back in the direction of the side street they had left piled high with bodies. "You're here less than a day and already you've been forced into life-or-death hand-to-hand combat. Your definition of *excitement* must be particularly eclectic."

He almost laughed. "And you have a really dry sense of humor. I'm sure we'll get along fine."

Reaching the commercial district on the other side of the square and plunging back into the surging crowds of humans and aliens, Barriss wasn't so certain. He was very sure of himself, this tall, blue-eyed Padawan. Maybe it was true what he said about wanting to know everything. His attitude was that he already did. Or was she mistaking confidence for arrogance?

Abruptly, he broke away from her. She watched as he stopped before a stall selling dried fruits and vegetables from the Kander region to the north of Cuipernam. When he returned without buying anything, she eyed him uncertainly.

"What was that all about? Did you see something that looked tasty but on closer inspection turned out not to be?"

"What?" He seemed suddenly preoccupied. "No. No, it wasn't the food at all." He glanced back at the simple food stand as they hurried to catch up with their teachers. "Didn't you see? That boy over there, the one in the vest and long pants, was arguing with his mother. Yelling at her." He shook his head dolefully. "Someday when he's older he'll regret having done that. I didn't tell him so directly, but I think I got the point across." He sank into deep contemplation. "People are so busy getting on with their lives they frequently forget what's really important."

What a strange Padawan, she mused, and what an even stranger young man. They were more or less the same age, yet in some ways he struck her as childlike, while in others he seemed much older than her. She wondered if she would have time enough to get to know him better. She wondered if anyone would have time enough to get to know him. She certainly hadn't, during their brief encounters at the Jedi Temple. Just then thunder boomed overhead, and for some reason she could not quite put a finger on she was afraid it signified the approach of more than just rain.